MAN DOWN

NATHAN BURROWS

Dedicated to those who serve, and to those who support them.

AUTHOR'S NOTE

This book contains a lot of terminology that is specific to the British military, and also to the medical professions.

For readers without a military or medical background, at the back of the book is a glossary for further information on terms used which may be unfamiliar.

Bonus Content - also at the end of the book, just before the glossary, there's another *Author's Note* with a link to an exclusive novella just for readers of *Man Down*. It's not available anywhere else.

Enjoy!

PART I

1

The bullet was travelling at over seven hundred metres a second when it hit Private Robert Thomas from the Third Battalion of the Parachute Regiment. It weighed about the same as a fifty pence piece and was tumbling through the air when it smashed through the shrapnel-proof part of his body armour. Impacting just underneath his right collar bone, it missed the toughened Kevlar plate covering his sternum by inches. If it had hit the plate, Private Thomas would have ended up on the floor with a hell of a fright and a bruise across his entire chest. But it hadn't, so the bullet tore through the body armour and kept on going.

As it penetrated the body armour, the bullet flattened, producing a small mushroom shaped fragment which increased the surface area of the projectile. It also increased the damage to Thomas's soft tissues, ripping through his skin and pectoral muscle and pushing everything out of its way. Shattered fragments of his body armour, uniform, and scraps of mud and dust floating in the air rushed into the large vacuum in his chest that the bullet created as it tore through him. The mushroom missed his subclavian artery by a couple of millimetres, tearing a tiny nick in the lining of his right lung before transferring all its force into a massive punch to his shoulder as it impacted his scapula.

The punch was the first thing Private Thomas registered as he flew backwards through the air before slamming into the ground. A second after he hit the dirt, he heard a gunshot echoing through the poppy field his patrol had just entered. He lay still, trying to catch his breath while around him the other members of his patrol started moving, seemingly in slow motion. The next thing he felt was an excruciating pain in his right shoulder which was followed by shouting from other members of his patrol. The edges of his vision turned grey as darkness closed in, and the only thing on his mind was one word.

'Fuck.'

'Contact!' Staff Sergeant Martin Partridge screamed at the top of his voice, diving to the ground as soon as he heard the shot echo around the field and saw Private Thomas go down. Wriggling into the dirt as fast as he could, he slipped off the safety catch of his SA-80 combat rifle and brought the light enhancing SUSAT sight up to his right eye. Partridge scanned the low single storey buildings two hundred metres in front of the patrol, and while he could see people running around in reaction to the gunshot, he couldn't see any of them looking over a gun back at him. He shouted 'Contact' again just in case any of the fuckwits in his patrol hadn't heard him the first time around or missed the sound of the gunshot and the sight of one of their own going down at the same time. They might be fuckwits, but they were his fuckwits and someone shooting at them was a personal insult to his way of thinking.

Partridge watched the other members of the patrol crawling through the dirt trying to find cover in the dusty ground, which was not easy in the middle of a poppy field. There was a natural dip in the ground about twenty-five metres to his left where two of his patrol had found a spot out of any line of sight. To his right, the platoon medic, Corporal Alfie Rowley, and machine gunner Lance Corporal Craig Winters were trying to make themselves as small as possible behind a low mud wall. After a quick look back down the sights towards the buildings, Partridge scrambled through the dirt to the mud wall and rapped his knuckles twice — hard and without sympathy — on the top of Winter's helmet.

'Get your fucking machine gun out and train it on that fucking village!' he shouted. 'And do it fucking sharpish. If you see anyone with anything that looks like a gun, put some rounds down. Yes?' Winters looked at him blankly as if he hadn't heard him. Partridge knocked hard again on top of the helmet before leaning into Winter's face and shouting, 'Winters? Yes?'

The young soldier blinked as if realising that he should be doing something more productive than hiding behind a wall and got to his knees, his trembling hands trying to set down the legs of the bipod. Partridge looked at him sympathetically, knowing that being under fire was a new experience for Winters. There'd be time for a hug later. Much later.

Winters got the legs of the light machine gun locked into position and started to shuffle towards the edge of the wall to get a good line of sight on the buildings without exposing himself to any further fire from the village. Partridge would never tell him, but Winters was already doing much better than Partridge had the first time he came under fire in Iraq in 2003. Partridge had spent a good ten minutes hiding behind a large metal storage container as Chinese 107mm rockets rained down on them before he managed to sort himself out.

As he turned to the medic, Partridge grabbed Rowley's shoulder and squeezed. He nodded towards the supine figure of Private Thomas, a good twenty metres beyond their cover.

'Right, Doc. As soon as Winters has got his shit in a sock with that LMG we're going to run over there, grab an armpit each, and drag Thomas back here pronto. Then we'll see how good a medic you really are.' Glancing towards the dip where the rest of his platoon were taking cover, he could see one of them lying flat on the lip looking down the sights of his SA80 rifle towards the village. The whip antenna of the aerial from the radio that one of the other soldiers carried was swinging from side to side. With any luck, he'd be calling in some air support. The chances of getting any were remote when only one shot had been fired, but if there was anything in the area, they might get lucky. Partridge brought his rifle up to his eye and into the aim to have another look at the village, making sure that Winters had indeed got his shit in a sock and was covering the village with his light machine gun. He patted Rowley on the shoulder. 'Right sunshine, let's do one.'

Rowley got to his feet and took a deep breath. Seeing that Partridge had already started off across the field towards the lifeless looking body of Private Thomas, Rowley ignored the shaking in his thighs and went after the Staff Sergeant. Trying to keep as low as possible to the ground, he got to within ten feet of Private Thomas when he sensed, rather than saw, a puff of dust in the ground between him and Partridge followed by a loud 'zing'. A second later, the sound of another shot boomed around the poppy field.

'Fuck, fuck, fuck,' he muttered as he reached Partridge, who was already trying to drag Thomas back to the small wall which was their only chance of proper cover. Grabbing a handful of Thomas's uniform, Rowley was only vaguely aware of the other members of the patrol returning fire. Lots of it. The need for single aimed shots which had been drilled into them throughout their training had gone right out of the window. The deep bark of the Minimi machine gun was deafening as it spat rounds towards the village, and the rapid staccato of an SA80 rifle on full automatic accompanied the sound of the machine gun.

'Fucking move, Doc!' Partridge shouted over the barrage. Between them, they manhandled Thomas back behind the wall and dropped him onto the ground. Suddenly, everything fell silent.

Rowley knelt by Private Thomas and looked at him. *Right*, he thought. *Time to get cracking.* At least now the medic knew what he was supposed to be doing as he'd done this before. In a classroom. With a mannequin. A mannequin that no matter how much he fucked up wouldn't die. He shook Thomas roughly by the shoulders.

'Mate,' he said, a bit too quietly. 'Mate, can you hear me?'

There was no response from Thomas other than a gurgling moan, so Rowley grabbed Thomas's chin with his thumb and forefinger and pulled upwards, tilting Thomas's head back a few degrees. The gurgling stopped, but the moaning didn't. *So far so good*, Rowley thought. *That's the airway sorted for the time being.* As far as he remembered, breathing was next, so he had a quick squint at Thomas's chest to see if it was moving properly, but the body armour and combat vest the casualty was wearing made it impossible to see anything. He started fumbling with the clips on the front of Thomas's combat vest when he felt Partridge thump down in the dirt next to them.

'Right Doc, what's the score?' Partridge barked. 'Is he dead or what?'

'Give me a fucking chance, Staff,' Rowley snapped back. 'For fuck's sake, just give me a chance.'

Partridge reached across Rowley's hands and undid the remaining clips on Thomas's combat vest.

'Alright Doc, calm down. You're doing okay son. We've called it in, so we should get some help soon.' With the combat vest undone, Rowley was able to push it aside and have a closer look. The body armour was still in the way, so Rowley grabbed the edge of it and pulled the Velcro apart, exposing Thomas's chest. Rowley still couldn't see a great deal — a blackened hole in the top right side of Thomas's chest and a bit of blood leaking around the edge — but there wasn't as much blood as he'd expected. Rowley tried to see if Thomas's chest was going up and down like the mannequin in the classroom, but he still couldn't see what was going on. He looked closely at Thomas's face to check whether his lips looked blue, but it was difficult to tell when he was covered in dust and mud, so he grabbed Thomas's wrist to feel his pulse. The skin was warm, which Rowley thought was a good sign, and when he slipped his fingers to the inside of Thomas's wrist he felt a good pulse, but it wasn't so fast that it meant he might be bleeding out somewhere else. Rowley realised Partridge wasn't next to them anymore but was talking with the radio operator, which gave Rowley a chance to take a deep breath and think.

'Airway, ok. Breathing, probably ok. Circulation, ok for the moment,' Rowley muttered. 'Fuck, what's next?' His training didn't go much beyond what he'd already done. At least if Thomas had an arm hanging off or was leaking blood all over the sand, he'd have something to do — something to concentrate on. As it was, Rowley couldn't think of much else given the circumstances, so he grabbed Thomas's hand and squeezed. 'Hang on mate, you'll be okay.'

'Right Doc, we good to move?' Partridge was back. 'We've called it in and there's a trauma team on the way from Bastion. We just need to get to a decent spot so they can bring in the medics and then we can get him out of here. There's ground back-up on the way from the Forward Operating Base as well, but they might be a while if they fucking turn up at all.'

Rowley watched as Partridge shuffled off to give the same message to the other members of the platoon. The medic looked down at the face of his wounded friend, knowing full well that the only reason it was Thomas lying there instead of him was luck.

2

Just before the red phone rang in the Trauma Response Team tent at Camp Bastion, Paul Adams was trying to wash hair off his back. He had just had a buzz cut in exchange for four cans of Coke, and the tiny bits of blonde hair stuck to his skin were driving him mad. Adams looked at himself in the mirror, trying to see the hair so he could reach it with the flannel, and failing on both counts. What made it even more difficult was the thin sheen of sweat on his skin that was a constant companion in the oppressive heat in any part of the hospital without air conditioning. Like this part of the TRT tent. Adams was just about to give up with the flannel and accept that he did, in fact, need a shower when the shrill ring from the phone made him jump.

The phone — which was actually brown but had a sticker on top of the handset with the words 'Red Phone' scribbled in marker pen — was linked directly to the Operations Room in the hospital at Camp Bastion, the large, sprawling, and unfinished military camp in the middle of nowhere. It only ever rang when there was a casualty somewhere in Helmand Province. This meant the TRT had to stop whatever they were doing and get themselves down to the flight line where a Chinook helicopter would hopefully be sitting with its rotors turning, waiting to take them somewhere that everyone else was trying to get away from.

Adams glanced at his watch, knowing that they had a few minutes to get the information, their kit, and the Land Rover on the road. It took at least ten minutes to get the Chinook wound up and running, so although this was an emergency, they didn't have to start panicking just yet.

He dropped his flannel into the sink and briskly walked between the dusty camp cots, pausing only to slap his colleague's foot as he passed the cot where the paramedic was softly snoring. Sergeant Lizzie Jarman woke with a start and sat up, pulling the iPod earphones out as she scowled at Adams.

'What?' she grumbled. 'I was bloody well asleep, in case you hadn't noticed.' Her hand went to her face and Adams laughed at her irritated expression as she wiped her chin with the back of her hand. Adams remembered the unfortunate picture that had appeared on Facebook of her fast asleep and dribbling saliva down her face. The picture had disappeared within a few days, courtesy of a favour or two being called in from one of her more muscular friends on the base, but she was obviously still wary about waking up in public. 'What did you wake me up for?'

'Er, phone?' Adams said, pointing at the red phone that was ringing on the table.

He thought that it should really have a flashing light on top, or at least be a bit more red, as he picked up the handset. Adams reached for the clipboard next to it, with its attendant biro firmly attached to it with some string and far too much bodge tape and balanced it on his knee. Also on the clipboard were some poorly duplicated copies of the '9-Line', a military standard template for reporting casualties.

'Hello, TRT?' Adams said, and then listened as the details of their job started to come through. He looked at his watch again before swearing about the fact that the biro was attached to the right-hand side of the clipboard. He kept moving the tape to the middle so that they could all use it — Adams was hopelessly left-handed — but someone kept moving it back to the right-hand side.

Lizzie joined him, the laces trailing from the desert boots which she'd crammed on her feet. Standing behind him, she raised herself up on tip-toes to look over his shoulder and playfully prodded him in the ribs to try to get him to jump, with no effect. It probably wasn't the best time to be playful.

Adams was on the third line of the 9-Line, which was the first important line as far as they were concerned. The first two lines were the location of the incident and the call sign of the unit requesting assistance — neither of which the TRT cared about. The third line was the number of casualties and how urgent they were, which they cared about a lot.

He circled the scribbled letters '1 x Cat C' on the form to make sure Lizzie had seen them and carried on filling out the rest of the form, pausing occasionally to repeat back to the Ops Room what he'd heard to make sure that he'd got it down properly. This didn't stop mistakes from happening, though — they'd been called out the previous week for a Category A patient with abdominal pain which turned out to be constipation from the rations he'd been eating — but it was the best way that they had of getting the information as close to the truth as possible. Adams finished the form and hung up the phone.

'Looks like it might be interesting anyway,' he said, pointing to the letter 'E' that he'd scribbled in linc six. Wherever they were going, there was a good chance the enemy would still be there.

'What's your girlfriend's name again?' Lizzie asked him. 'Is it Sandra?'

'Sophie,' Adams replied. 'But where did that come from?'

'I was just thinking what a lucky woman she is, that's all.'

'Sorry, Lizzie,' he replied with a frown. 'You've lost me.'

'Put a shirt on would you, Adams,' Lizzie said, laughing. 'You're not exactly in the right sort of shape to be wandering around without one, despite what Sophie thinks of your physique.'

Adams patted his stomach. He didn't have a six pack, but the last few weeks in the desert had seen him lose a few pounds. 'I'm not in bad shape, thanks very much,' he replied. 'You've got more wobbly bits than me, and we're the same age.'

'Bugger off,' Lizzie said. 'We're not the same age and I've not got any wobbly bits. I've not turned thirty yet, and I know for a fact that you did last year.' She pointed at line eight, the 'A' indicating that it was a British soldier that needed picking up. 'One of ours. Best we get a shift on, matey,' she said. 'Where's the new Doc anyway? He's obviously not close enough to hear the bloody phone.'

Adams looked at Lizzie and considered making a crack about the fact that although Lizzie was in the same room as the bloody phone she hadn't heard it either, but on seeing her tense expression, he decided against it.

'I'm sure he'll hear the shout when the Ops Room puts

it out over the speakers,' he replied. 'If he doesn't, we'll just go without him.'

He sat in the relative peace of the toilets with his trousers gathered around his ankles. Laid out on his bare thighs was all the equipment he would need, which he'd gathered together over the previous couple of days. Often, he had picked it up in plain sight of other people working in the hospital complex and no-one had questioned him in the slightest. Why would they?

He rearranged the needles, syringes, and ampoules carefully on his legs. He didn't want any of them to fall to the floor and start rolling around the toilet. Picking up the small plastic ampoule of normal saline, which was essentially just sterile water, he checked the expiry date of the ampoule. This was one of the checks that was always done before anyone used ampoules like this one, and while it was done by two people, the checks were often perfunctory. Particularly in the busy Emergency Room which is where he wanted this one to be used. Even so, if the ampoule was out of date and someone noticed, all the work he'd done so far would have been a waste of time as it would be thrown away. The worst case was that the arsehole Quartermaster would be informed and go off on one, smug little prick that he was.

Satisfied that the ampoule was in date, he grabbed two sterile needles and carefully unpeeled the paper wrappers. Taking the hard plastic sheath off one the needles, he pushed them both through the bottom of the plastic ampoule before unwrapping a syringe and attaching it to one of the needles. He held the syringe in front of him and pulled back on the plunger, noting with satisfaction the contents of the ampoule emptying into it. At the same time, he could see bubbles entering the ampoule via the other needle which was letting air in to replace the fluid. He'd found this out by trial and error. The first time he tried the substitution he'd only used one needle, but when he with-

drew the saline from the ampoule, the plastic container just collapsed in on itself.

When the syringe was full and the ampoule empty, he twisted the syringe off the needle and squirted the contents between his knees and into the toilet with a satisfying splash just as the door to the toilet block opened. He quickly checked to make sure that there was nothing on the floor that could be seen through the gap under the cubicle door apart from his dusty boots and trousers around his ankles. After listening to the other occupant use the urinal, he grimaced when he heard them leave without washing their hands.

'Dirty bastard,' he muttered. People like that were the first to complain when the whole camp went down with norovirus. Turning back to the task at hand, he picked up the box which had been an absolute stroke of luck to get hold of. He'd been down at the pan, the area where aircraft were loaded and unloaded, a couple of days ago to collect a parcel when he noticed a box in the disposal area with a red cross on it, and a large label with the text 'Out of Temperature Range. For Destruction' written in marker pen.

After making sure that he couldn't be seen by the Quartermaster who he could hear doing something in the next tent, he had sliced open the box using his Gerber pocket knife to see what was inside — correctly figuring that it must be drugs of some sort or another — and rummaged through it. When he had seen the contents of the small white boxes, one of which he now had with him in the toilet, he'd quickly gathered them together and put as many as he could fit into the large side pockets on his combat trousers. Resealing the box with some gaffer tape, he had walked back through the store tents and back onto the pan, nodding a greeting at the Quartermaster as he went past him.

He shifted his weight slightly on the toilet and tried to ignore the sweat dripping down his back — the toilet block wasn't a priority for one of the limited air conditioning units on camp despite the God-awful smell — he opened the small white box and took one of the glass vials out. I don't need to check the date on this one, *he thought as he snapped off the glass top and put the tip of the syringe into the vial to empty it. After repeating this procedure with the rest of the vials in the box, he used the full syringe to refill the plastic ampoule.*

Once the syringe was empty and the ampoule full of what was now something much more harmful than normal saline, he gathered all the empty packaging and ampoules together and put them away in his trouser pocket. He held the plastic ampoule in front of him and dabbed the bottom of it with the nozzle of the superglue he'd bought earlier in the NAFFI shop, sealing the holes from the needles and making sure that none of the precious contents would leak out. After a final check to make sure there was no rubbish on the floor, he carefully put the ampoule into a side pocket and pulled up his trousers.

He flushed the toilet just in case and washed his hands. Better safe than sorry.

Lizzie Jarman ran her fingers through her short brown hair, the ends tinged with blonde from the desert sun, as she and Adams sat in the Land Rover outside the TRT tent with the engine idling. Her hair wasn't anywhere near as short as his, but it was still a lot shorter than it would be back home in the United Kingdom. She reached behind her head and tied what she could up into a crude ponytail, knowing that in a few minutes' time she'd be wearing a Kevlar helmet.

'Where the hell is he?' Lizzie said, glancing across at Adams in the driving seat. 'It's his first bloody shout — you think he'd be a bit more enthusiastic about it.' She twisted around in the passenger seat and looked back at the entrance to the tent. 'Any minute now he's going to run out of there like sodding Mr. Ben coming out of his closet.'

'You're showing your age there, mate,' Adams replied.

'No, hang on. I'm showing my age. There's no way you're old enough to remember Mr. Ben.'

'You're right, old timer. My dad used to tell me about Mr. Ben and all his adventures in the cupboard. When I was at school,' Lizzie replied. 'Primary school,' she added, for effect.

'Well, if Mr. Ben doesn't pop out of his cupboard within the next thirty seconds we're going without him. Even he is a Colonel.'

'Lieutenant Colonel,' Lizzie replied, with only a hint of irony.

It was fair to say that Lieutenant Colonel Nicholas 'Call me Colonel Nick' Hickman hadn't exactly endeared himself to either Adams or Lizzie when he'd arrived at Camp Bastion a little over two weeks ago. It wasn't about Colonel Nick being in the Army — neither Adams nor Lizzie cared about that — it was more about the way that the Colonel arrived as if he wanted to be noticed. He'd been sent out to replace another Army medical officer who'd been sent back as a compassionate case due to the man's wife choosing the exact moment that he'd been deployed to have a complete and utter meltdown. Lizzie had told Adams that she was convinced that he'd planned the whole thing with the wife so that he'd get the medal and a bar for being in theatre during the fun times even though he wasn't, but Adams was less sceptical. He wasn't married, although he hoped he might be before too long, but he'd seen the effect that deployments had on the people who were left at home.

'Call me Colonel Nick' as an opening line marked the original medical officer's replacement out as a bit of a cock in Lizzie's mind, not helped by the new arrival's public school accent and slight resemblance to Hugh Grant. As she explained to Adams, he wasn't even a proper Colonel.

'He's a Lieutenant Colonel. Not a bloody Colonel,' Lizzie had said. 'There's a difference. A whole rank's difference. A Colonel is a Group Captain, a Lieutenant Colonel is a Wing Commander. So why does he want to be called "Colonel Nick" when he's not a Colonel? You don't go around saying "Hi — I'm Flight Lieutenant Adams. Call me Squadron Leader Adams." Do you?'

'It's not the same, Lizzie,' Adams replied. 'That's just the way that they do things. The Army's got the history, don't forget — apparently, the RAF hasn't.'

'Well I'm not going to call him Colonel Nick,' she replied. 'He's Lieutenant Colonel Hickman as far as I'm concerned. And a little birdie told me that he's only got acting rank for the deployment.'

'You'll just piss him off, Lizzie,' Adams sighed.

'I know,' Lizzie replied with a wry smile. 'I know.'

The passenger door of the Land Rover flew open, making Lizzie spill the Coke which she'd finally managed to blag off Adams after five minutes of trying. She'd tried being nice, then she'd tried being flirty, which was difficult given the circumstances and was probably never going to work anyway. Then she'd tried 'give me a can of Coke, or I'll make your life shit for the rest of your tour' which, to her surprise, appeared to work. He had given her a strange look as he handed over the lukewarm can, dusted as it was with hair clippings, but she figured that she was the one with the can of Coke, so she'd won that small battle. Ignoring the wet feeling in her lap, she turned to Colonel Nick and fixed him with a look.

'About bloody time, sir.'

'Uh, okay. Sorry, bit late,' Colonel Nick replied, raising his eyebrows and tilting his head towards the back of the Land Rover. Lizzie stifled a laugh, thinking for a minute about making a Hugh Grant joke before deciding against it. The head tilt was obviously a practised move, but she had to admit to herself, it worked a tiny bit.

'If you'd been here earlier, you could have had the front seat,' she replied, tilting her own head at the back of the vehicle before adding a less than deferential, 'sir.' Lizzie watched him as he went around to the back of the Land Rover. She heard him swearing as he struggled with the latches on the rear flap before throwing his medical bag in and climbing up after it. The Land Rover dipped at the additional weight in the back.

'All aboard the happy bus,' Lizzie muttered, more to herself than to anyone else.

Adams glanced across at Lizzie, smiling when he saw the frown on her face. Unfortunately for him, she caught him smiling and fixed him with a glare that he'd seen before. He looked away and put the Land Rover in gear, aware that she was still glaring at him which just made him want to smile again. *Discretion is the better part of valour*, he thought as he decided against it.

The Land Rover lurched forward, wheels spinning for a moment in the soft gravel of the rough roadway outside the tent. Adams accelerated towards the Main Drag, the rough road which led from the hospital down to the flight line some two kilometres away. He crunched through the gears, the Land Rover complaining with each change, until they reached its terminal velocity of around sixty miles an hour. It was fast enough over the rough ground, and Adams could hear Colonel Nick in the back cursing as the vehicle bounced over every bump. Adams glanced in the rear-view mirror, smiling at the Colonel's predicament. As

Lizzie had said, if he wanted the front seat, he should have got there earlier.

When the Land Rover sped past Camp Bastion's headquarters building, Adams and Lizzie noticed the portly Garrison Sergeant Major striding from the front door toward the road, waving frantically at them to slow down. Adams and Lizzie both waved back as they sped past him, and then started laughing as he and his oversized moustache disappeared in a cloud of dust and sand.

'He did that last time,' Lizzie said. 'I thought you'd had a word to let them know why we're in a hurry.'

'I did,' Adams replied. 'I spoke to the Commanding Officer of the base after the formal complaint last week, and he just told me to crack on. He said he'd have a word with the GSM and then muttered something about how getting a bloody blue light and siren would be useful.'

'Well, if Brigadier Foster's going to pay for it, great. I can't see the CO of the hospital stumping up for that,' Lizzie said. 'Besides, even though we haven't got a blue light, you still couldn't drive it. It's an emergency vehicle.'

'Yes, I can. We'll play paper, scissors, rank — and I'll win.'

'No, you won't,' Lizzie said. 'You're not blue light qualified, so you're not allowed to. You might cause an accident,' she said, smiling at Adams.

'Yeah, right,' Adams replied, looking at the empty road ahead of them as they sped across the crushed gravel. 'The traffic's shit.'

As the Land Rover pulled up towards the edge of the helicopter landing site, they could see the Chinook with its rotors already turning. Parking up, Adams and Lizzie went to the back of the Land Rover to get their personal kit. Colonel Nick had jumped out of the vehicle the minute it had stopped, and Adams had to reach in to retrieve his and

Lizzie's grab bags. He mentally cursed the Colonel for not passing them out as he struggled to reach the equipment. Half running to catch up with the others, he noticed the fourth member of his team, Corporal 'Ronald' MacDonald standing on the ramp at the back of the Chinook. Ronald was making a circular motion in the air with an extended index finger — the signal for 'we're going now'. Adams broke into a run at the same time as Lizzie did, and when the Colonel realised that they were both running towards the helicopter, he got the message and did the same.

When Adams got to the ramp with Lizzie, Ronald leaned towards them both and shouted to make himself heard over the noise of the large rotor blades whirling a few feet above their heads.

'We've got to go,' Ronald said. 'The casualty's been upgraded to a Cat A. We need to get moving sharpish.'

Adams looked across at Lizzie and saw her biting her bottom lip. Category A was the most urgent category there was. As they walked into the bowels of the Chinook helicopter to take their seats, Adams wondered what they would find when they got to wherever it was in the badlands they were going.

3

S taff Sergeant Partridge and his platoon had managed
to drag Thomas, who had come around enough to
swear profusely, about eight hundred metres away from the
spot where he was hit. Partridge figured that they were far
enough away from the building where the shot had come
in from to be out of range of most small arms, and if
Thomas had been hit with a sniper rifle then he wouldn't
be swearing as much as he was. He'd be dead.

There was still no sign of any backup from the Forward
Operating Base, so Partridge made sure that the radio
operator had called back in with the updated coordinates
for the pick-up. Fingering the smoke grenade he was going
to put down the minute he heard the distinctive sound of
the Chinook approaching, Partridge glanced around the
area with a practiced eye. He wasn't bothered about the
smoke grenade giving their position away as the insurgents
knew damn well where they were, and a sodding great big,
loud, slow-moving helicopter would certainly give the
game away. The advantage of the Chinook was two-fold as
far as he was concerned; the first advantage were the two

machine guns mounted on it, one on the back and one on the side. The second advantage was the fact that the minute it touched down and the rear ramp went down, there would be a significantly larger amount of firepower available as the Force Protection team on board the helicopter hopped off.

A few yards away, Partridge could see that Rowley was becoming increasingly concerned about Thomas. A few minutes ago, Thomas had been effing and blinding like the squaddie that he was, although Partridge figured that he was probably allowed to swear a bit as he had taken a round not too long ago. He'd now gone quiet again, very quiet, and was almost unresponsive. Partridge watched as Rowley went back through his immediate action drills with a concerned frown on his face. If Rowley — who was a medic — was worried, then so was Partridge.

What Rowley, or indeed Thomas, didn't know was that when the bullet had smashed through the body armour, it had nicked the lining of Thomas's lung as it travelled through his shoulder. It was only a tiny nick, but every time Thomas took a breath in, a small amount of air entered the space between the two linings of the lung. Every time he breathed out, this hole closed like a one-way valve, and the air in the middle of the linings stayed where it was. As the air built up between the two linings, the amount of space that the lung had to expand got less and less. The effect of this was quite simple, brutal, and completely silent. Thomas's lung was being squeezed hard, drastically reducing the amount of oxygen getting into his bloodstream, and each breath he took increased the pressure.

'Staff, I'm not happy at all with this,' Rowley said to Partridge. 'There's something wrong — he was swearing his head off ten minutes ago, now he's not saying anything at all.'

'Of course there's something wrong with him,' Partridge replied. 'He's been fucking shot.'

'How long is the helicopter going to be, do you think?' Rowley said. 'He needs a proper medic to have a look at him, not me.'

'Don't be too hard on yourself, son. You're doing okay. I'll get on the net and ask them to hurry the fuck up.' Partridge half-ran back to the radio operator to get him to give the Ops Room the good news.

Corporal Colin MacDonald — known universally as 'Ronald' for obvious reasons which was just as well as he hated the name Colin — unclipped his flying helmet from the cord attached to the side of the Chinook. It cut off his ability to talk to the helicopter crew but from what he'd just heard on the radio, they were about five minutes out from the landing site. Catching Adams's eye, Ronald pointed to the floor with one index finger and then held up his hand with his fingers and thumb splayed to indicate they were five minutes away from landing. He then looked across at Lizzie, and she gave him a thumbs up indicating that she'd seen the message. Colonel Nick, who was sitting next to Lizzie, also gave him a thumbs up, mouthing 'five minutes' to confirm that he understood.

Around them, Ronald watched the soldiers who formed the Force Protection team getting themselves ready, picking up their SA80 rifles and checking each other's kit, buddy-buddy style. When they landed, they would be the first ones off the ramp to form a protective cordon facing outwards in a wide semicircle around the helicopter, closely followed by Lizzie and Adams. Not for the first time, Ronald thought how reassuring it was that if the shit hit the fan, there were quite a few well-armed people in between the medics running off the back of the helicopter and whatever or whoever it was that was making the shit hit the fan.

Ronald glanced out of the small rectangular window towards the ground; they were losing height fast. He knew what would happen next — the Chinook would lazily circle around the proposed landing site in a clockwise direction. This aimed the machine gun on the side window towards the ground, meaning that if there was a threat on the ground it could be dealt with. The only problem was that if Ronald knew how the helicopter was going to approach the landing site, then so did the insurgents on the ground.

A few thousand feet below them, Staff Sergeant Partridge heard the familiar sound of the Chinook in the distance. Slapping Rowley on the shoulder, he shouted to the rest of the platoon.

'Right boys, the TRT's incoming. Unless you want to tab back to the FOB, best we all climb on.' Partridge wasn't one hundred per cent sure that this was the best decision, as technically they should go back to the Forward Operating Base, but in the absence of any backup from them, they could fuck off as far as he was concerned. He could get his team back to Bastion and then get them back on one of the regular supply drops that went out pretty much every day to the FOBs. With any luck, there'd be a bit of a delay getting a lift back, and they could all have a spot of downtime and some relatively decent scoff. He waited until the black speck in the sky became the recognisable silhouette of a Chinook and pulled the pin on the smoke grenade before lobbing it into the middle of the field.

Ronald plugged his comms cable back into the side of the helicopter just as the pilot finished talking.

'Say again,' Ronald said, thumbing the switch so that he could be heard by the rest of the aircrew.

'Two minutes out,' the pilot repeated his message. 'Smoke seen. We're coming in hard over the top of the trees. No obvious threat, but get him in as soon as. No point hanging around.'

'Rodger dodge,' Ronald said before flicking the switch back again. He looked in the general direction of the rest of the TRT and held up two fingers in the air. No one acknowledged him this time; there was no need. A few of the Force Protection team shuffled their buttocks forwards on their canvas seats, getting ready to get up and go the minute they touched down. Ronald could see Lizzie struggling to get her latex gloves on. She finally managed to get the second glove on and was trying to pull the ends of the gloves down onto her fingers when Ronald tapped her on the shoulder.

'You okay?' Ronald mouthed at her as she looked up at him. She gave him a wan smile, looking grateful but annoyed at the same time. They'd talked through the first few jobs they'd been on many times, both agreeing that this was the worst bit of the whole shout. At least when they had a casualty or two in front of them they could focus on the wounded, but this part — before they had a casualty — was the worst. It was the unknown that was the difficult part — not knowing what was wrong with whoever they were going to pick up, not knowing if there was someone in the trees with a rocket-propelled grenade waiting to have a pop, and not knowing what was going to happen in the next few minutes. Ronald watched Adams as he moved across the back of the Chinook towards Colonel Nick. He gave a quick thumbs up to Ronald on the way. On the other side of the helicopter, Ronald saw Lizzie close her eyes and take a deep breath.

Lizzie watched from her seat in the back of the Chinook as the loadmaster lowered the ramp when the helicopter started to settle on the ground. Over the top of the noise in the back of the helicopter, she heard someone screaming, 'FP! Go! Go! Go!' Without any further prompting, the Force Protection team swarmed past the crewman, jumping from the ramp.

Fanning out into a perfect semicircle around the rear of the helicopter, they all went to ground and brought their weapons up into the aim, scanning both the immediate vicinity and the horizon for anything that looked as if it was remotely threatening. It was a well-practiced and effective manoeuvre, designed to show anybody in the area with less than honourable intentions that there was a whole bunch of well-armed, well-trained people ready to neutralise any threats quickly and without prejudice.

Lizzie coughed as debris, dust, and God only knew what rushed into the back of the Chinook, partially blinding the medical team despite the protective goggles over their eyes. With Adams right behind her, Lizzie moved down towards the ramp clutching a canvas stretcher with wooden handles that was good enough for the Cold War, so considered by senior officers — who'd never carried one in their lives — more than good enough for Afghanistan.

With Adams right behind her, Lizzie paused at the base of the ramp, waiting until some of the dust had died down and the FP team had got themselves into position. She turned around and looked back into the rear of the Chinook to see what the other two members of the TRT were doing. Colonel Nick was on his knees, getting an intravenous line ready, and Ronald was flicking at a syringe, probably a flush for a cannula, to get any bubbles out of it. As she watched, he put the plastic ampoule back onto the end of the syringe so that anyone who picked it up could look at the ampoule and instantly tell what was in it. If it was an Emergency Room back in the United Kingdom, before it was used the ampoule would be checked by at least two people, who would check the contents, the expiry date, and then sign and countersign when it was used with the exact details; but they weren't in an Emergency Room, so it would just be used and binned.

Colonel Nick shuffled on his knees, and Lizzie noticed that he didn't have any knee pads on, which was a fail on his part. Maybe no-one had told him how useful they were, though. She was currently on her fourth set in as many weeks, and her Mum was sending out a box with a bunch of knee pads from a local DIY store so that she had a decent supply. They didn't last for long, especially when they got soaked in blood.

Lizzie felt a tap on her arm and looked around at Adams, who was nodding in the direction of the ramp at the loadmaster pointing away from the Chinook. As the dust started to clear, they stepped off the ramp and started moving in the direction that the crewman was pointing. Lizzie looked up to see a small group of soldiers dragging a casualty towards them. Holding on tightly to the stretcher, she crouched down and ran as fast as she could underneath the fast-moving rotors with Adams a couple of feet behind her. Fifty feet away from the helicopter, they reached clear air. Lizzie shouted at Adams above the noise of the helicopter as the searing air from the rotors and exhaust buffeted her arms and legs.

'Must be a ground patrol caught in the open. They've not even got a stretcher between them.'

'Medic's front left!' Adams shouted back. 'I'll talk to him; you have a quick look at the casualty.'

Lizzie nodded as they set off towards the slow-moving group through the dry earth, their feet kicking up clouds of fine brown dust with every step. Even though she knew there was a bunch of lads behind her who were all very well-armed, this didn't make her any less scared. Even though it probably wasn't, it felt safe back in the Chinook. It was a thick metal shell around her, and the power in the engines was reassuring. Lizzie glanced back over her shoulder at the helicopter, sitting with its rotors spinning. Every step she took through the dust was a step further away from safety.

4

Adams and Lizzie were both exhausted by the time they reached the small group of soldiers, and Adams cursed under his breath at how hard he was blowing. Throwing the stretcher onto the ground, they helped the two soldiers who were trying to drag the casualty towards the helicopter manhandle their wounded colleague onto the stretcher. Kneeling down, Lizzie started quickly assessing their casualty, but Adams knew that she was only interested if he was still alive or not. A proper look would have to wait.

'What have we got?' Adams asked the soldier with a red cross on his arm.

'Gunshot wound right shoulder,' the young medic replied, glancing down at Adams's rank slides before raising his eyebrows and adding, 'sir.' It wasn't the first time that a soldier on the ground had been surprised by an officer turning up, but at least this medic recognised the rank slides for what they were. He watched as the medic looked at Lizzie, hiking his eyebrows even higher as he realised she was female. 'It was about forty-five minutes ago. He was okay at first, but he's gone off on me. I don't know why,' the medic summarised. If they'd been in an Emergency Room doing a handover, the medic would be dressed down for such a glib handover, but given the circumstances, this was more than enough for Adams.

'Okay, thanks,' Adams replied. 'Nice one. Lizzie? How's he looking?'

'Well, he's breathing,' Lizzie said, the strain obvious in her voice. 'Apart from that, difficult to say.' She slipped a pair of protective goggles onto the casualty to protect his eyes from the helicopter downdraft.

'Good enough for government work,' Adams said. 'Right then, everyone got a corner?' He paused to give Lizzie and the soldiers time to move to the handles of the stretcher and grab one each. 'Okay, three, two, one, lift.' As they lifted the casualty, he heard Lizzie moan and could feel the strain in his own shoulder. The stretcher was bloody heavy. He looked towards the helicopter which was only about a hundred yards away but could have been a mile. The team moved as quickly as they could towards the rear ramp, all of them anxious not to hang about for a minute longer than was necessary.

When they reached the rear of the Chinook, Ronald and the loadmaster both grabbed the front handles of the stretcher, freeing Adams and Lizzie up to get into the back of the helicopter and go up towards Colonel Nick who was waiting at the front with an oxygen mask in his hands. Adams leaned in towards the Colonel to shout in his ear.

'GSW right shoulder. Forty-five minutes ago. Medic says he's gone off.' Colonel Nick nodded, unfurling the stethoscope from one of the pockets of his combat vest. The stretcher was unceremoniously dumped on the floor of the Chinook, and Colonel Nick knelt down next to it.

Adams pointed towards the rest of the casualty's

platoon, who had followed them into the back of the
Chinook, and then pointed towards the webbed seats along
the side of the helicopter to indicate where they should sit.
As they shuffled onto their seats, Adams reached for the
casualty's dog tags to see what his name was. According to
the sweat and blood covered silver discs, this was Private
Thomas. He would be nineteen in a couple of months'
time.

In his peripheral vision, Adams saw the loadmaster
grabbing the platoon radio operator's rifle and turning it
round so that the muzzle was pointing at the ground. If
there was a negligent discharge for any reason, then at least
the round wouldn't go through the roof and into the
engine of the helicopter. That was a lesson that had been
learnt the hard way on more than one occasion. As the FP
team got back on board the helicopter, Adams felt the helicopter start to shudder as the pilot pulled back on the
collective. Adams steadied himself and grabbed onto the
seat as the helicopter started to rise into the air.

Watched by Adams and the rest of the TRT, Colonel
Nick slipped off the casualty's helmet to make sure that his
airway was clear and that he didn't need any of the toys in
the medical kit to stop him suffocating on his own tongue.
Beside him, Ronald had the cuff of the automatic blood
pressure machine ready and had already attached the
clothes peg type clip that measured blood oxygen concentration to one of Thomas's fingers. On the other side of
the stretcher, Lizzie was cutting the sleeve of Thomas's
uniform from the wrist up to past the elbow, getting ready
to put a cannula into one of his veins. The team worked
methodically, each of them knowing what to do and what
the others were doing, even though it was Colonel Nick's
first shout. It was no different to a trauma resuscitation in
an Emergency Room back in the United Kingdom, apart

from the fact they were in the back of a slow-moving heli-copter that was almost certainly being shot at from the ground.

Adams felt a tap on his knee. Looking up, he saw Ronald pointing towards the screen of the medical moni-tor, where a small flashing digital display read 'SaO2 82%'. An alarm on the monitor would be sounding, but none of them could hear it over the noise of the rotor blades above their heads. The reading wasn't good — the casualty's oxygen saturation was way too low. It should have read over 95%. Adams tapped Colonel Nick on the knee to make sure that he'd seen the reading, but as the Colonel was already fiddling with an oxygen mask, Adams figured he probably had. Ronald started squirting saline from a plastic ampoule onto some gauze to clean one of Thomas's other fingers, just to make sure that the reading was accu-rate, but the wave on the screen which showed the pulse looked clear, so it probably was. The wave on the screen started to wobble as the helicopter gained power, and the aircraft's nose tilted downwards as the helicopter headed back towards Camp Bastion.

Adams looked up at the platoon to see them all staring at their wounded colleague on the stretcher. He could tell from the look in their eyes that they were all thinking the same thing — *that could have been me*. Adams's eyes locked for a few seconds with the oldest member of the platoon, a man who looked as if he'd seen it all before. They nodded at each other briefly before Adams turned his attention back to Thomas.

Major Robert Clarke hung up the red phone that connected the Emergency Room at Camp Bastion to the main base Operations Room. Unlike the phone in the TRT tent, this phone was red, and gave them a direct line to the Ops Officer who had been talking with the inbound helicopter. There was a similar, smaller, Ops Room in the hospital, but if there was a casualty on the way, then the hospital stood back and let the communication take place directly between the medical team and the main base Ops Room. There had been more than one argument about this in the past, but as the senior nurse running the Emergency Room, Clarke had managed to argue his case that information going from the main base Ops Room, through the hospital Ops Room, to him was one link too many. Especially when the Ops Officers themselves were junior officers with only a first aid course between them.

'Listen in!' Clarke shouted to the rest of his medical team milling about the Emergency Room. 'We've got one Category A casualty inbound, ETA ten minutes. GSW to the chest, doesn't sound too well.' Pointing at one of the nurses in the room, he said, 'Corporal. Can you start getting a chest drain kit ready, please?' The nurse nodded and moved towards the back of the Emergency Room to get the necessary equipment together.

Located right at the front of the hospital, the Emergency Room was in fact nothing more than a large tent, branching off the central corridor that formed the spine of the main hospital. Other branches included the radiology department which housed the x-ray machine, a small four bed intensive care unit, an operating theatre, and a couple of wards which could hold up to twenty patients each. Other smaller tents linked to the same complex included a pharmacy, medical stores, and the hospital Ops Room which was nominally running the facility. The biggest problems that they had in the hospital, apart from the egos of one or two of the more senior medical staff, were dust and heat. Both of which were unrelenting.

Clarke swept his hands over his thinning brown hair and took a deep breath. Looking towards the door to the Emergency Room, he could see lots of people standing around, waiting. There had been an air of tension in the whole complex since TRT had deployed. Everyone in the hospital had heard the Tannoy — the 'giant voice' public address system that annoyed the entire hospital when it was used — requesting that Lieutenant Colonel Hickman return to the TRT tent, and the second much terser Tannoy a few moments later with the same message.

When word got out that this was a combat casualty, as opposed to a soldier with gut rot, the excitement started to grow. It was a bizarre paradox — the more seriously injured a casualty was the greater the anticipation among the medical staff. Clarke checked off in his head the people he wanted to see standing around. The radiographer was there, and he'd seen the Charge Nurse from the ITU a few minutes ago. She had since disappeared, no doubt back to the ITU to get her team sorted. A passing nurse had told him a few minutes ago that the surgeon had been woken up and was in the shower, no doubt singing while he scrubbed his nails — according to the nurse at least. Looking back towards his team in the ER, he was about as happy as he could be that they were all ready.

The reality was that Major Rob Clarke himself was not happy at all. This wasn't an unusual state of mind for him though, so nobody else in the ER took too much notice as he well knew. In his late forties, a couple of stone overweight, and with a rapidly expanding area of bare skin on his head, he walked towards the back doors of the ER where one of the doctors, Squadron Leader Andrew Webb, was standing looking through the plastic window.

When Webb had arrived in the hospital a few weeks ago, Clarke had taken an instant dislike to him, more so than he usually did with new doctors. Clarke had been working in Emergency Rooms since the Squadron Leader was still doing his GCSEs let alone going to medical school, and the nurse had seen people like him come and go. Rise and in many cases, fall when life — or the loss of it — took them down a peg or two.

Clarke used an off-white handkerchief to wipe the sweat from his brow. As he approached the doctor, the Major reflected that he was getting too old for all this nonsense. It wasn't so much working in the ER — this was effectively what he did for a living back in the United Kingdom after all — it was more about the heat and the stress of working with a new team almost every week. At least back in Derby Infirmary the air conditioning worked, and he knew all the people who worked in his department, having worked with many of them for years. The teams might change over time, but the core of senior doctors and nurses remained essentially the same which meant that they worked together well. Clarke knew very well that this wasn't the case here, and that tensions between some of the staff were barely below the surface, ready to erupt seemingly over nothing.

Clarke nodded at Webb, who nodded back with a grunt. Clarke saw this as progress of sorts, thinking that this was the most interaction the two of them had had since coming on shift a couple of hours ago. If they were back home, the chances were that the two of them would go for a pint after a shift one evening, talk about football or rugby or something, and just get on with it. Then, over time, they'd build up a good working relationship, and maybe one day in the future even pass for friends. There'd been no time for that, though. They were in it together whether they liked it or not.

Clarke left the doctor where he was and walked across the room to stand next to the nurse who had been assigned the role of scribe for the incoming casualty. This was the best place to put more junior personnel, as they didn't have to do anything other than write on the large A2 sized resuscitation chart on the dais in front of them. If they kept their eyes open and their wits about them, they couldn't go wrong, and it got them used to the whole dance of a trauma resuscitation before they had to put their shoes on and go dancing for real. He knew that this particular nurse, Corporal Emma Wardle, was one of the most nervous nurses he'd worked with in the twenty or so years he'd been working in hospitals. She was also stunning, with fine blonde hair cut into a bob and the most kissable lips that Clarke had seen in years.

'Are you okay?' Clarke asked Wardle in a whisper, leaning in towards her so that he wouldn't be overheard. 'You look a bit nervous.' He was being a bit too informal with her for two reasons; one was to try to relax her and not stress her out even more than she was already, and the second was the fact that she even looked good in combats. In Clarke's opinion, that took some doing, although he knew from experience that the bar got lower the longer he was away from home.

'Oh hello, sir,' she replied. 'I'm doing okay.' Wardle looked at Clarke, and he could see that she was trying to smile. She wiped her hands on her scrubs and Clarke wondered if her palms were sticky from the heat, or nervousness. 'I think,' she added.

'Listen, Corporal Wardle,' Clarke said. 'There's plenty of time before the casualty gets here, so why don't you go and get a cold drink, hydrate yourself a bit. Just take a minute or so.'

'Are you sure, sir?' Wardle said. 'I mean, I'm scribe so I need to be here, don't I?'

'Who's in charge?' Clarke smiled. 'Go on mate, go and take a minute to relax, or gather, or whatever it is you need to do. You'll hear the helicopter landing anyway, and if you're not here, then I'll get started on the chart for you.'

'Oh, thanks sir. I'll just, er, nip to the bathroom then.' She smiled at Clarke, letting out a deep breath. 'I'll only be a sec.'

Clarke watched Corporal Wardle walk across the ER to the main corridor, as did Webb who was still standing by the door. With a resigned sigh, Clarke mumbled to himself under his breath.

'If only.' He knew he could be a lecherous old bugger at times, but at least he was one with realistic expectations.

A few short moments later, everyone in the ER fell silent as they heard the thudding of rotor blades in the distance, getting louder and louder with every second.

5

In the back of the helicopter, Thomas wasn't doing very well. The air that had been slowly building up in his thoracic cavity had virtually collapsed his right lung, and it was starting to compress his heart. Inside Thomas's chest, things were starting to get very serious indeed.

Adams didn't know this just yet, but he had noticed Colonel Nick giving up on trying to listen to any breath sounds with his stethoscope. Every one of Adams's instincts was telling him that something was wrong, very wrong, but he couldn't work out what. Being thrown around in the back of a helicopter as the pilot flew low and fast to avoid any ground fire wasn't conducive to concentrating anyway.

Glancing at the screen of the monitor, Adams ran through Thomas's vital signs in his head. The airway was okay, and there was a Guedel airway that Adams had put in just to be on the safe side. There was plenty of oxygen in the rebreather bag on Thomas's face, but the oxygen saturations on the monitor were still only sitting in the low eighties and falling. According to the blue blood pressure cuff, his blood pressure was way too low, and Thomas's pulse was racing at over one hundred and twenty beats per minute. Staring at the screen again, Adams ran through Thomas's vital signs another time, trying to work out what was going on.

Adams didn't need to count Thomas's breaths to see that his respiration rate was very high, but that wasn't the only thing that wasn't right. He grabbed the wounded man's shoulders, causing Colonel Nick to look up sharply, but all Adams was doing was making sure that Thomas was flat on the stretcher and that he wasn't leaning to one side. If Thomas was flat on the stretcher — and he was now — then one side of his chest wasn't moving in the same way as the other one. If anything, Adams wasn't sure the right side of his casualty's chest was moving at all, but the vibration from the helicopter made it difficult to see. Adams put his hand on Thomas's neck, noting as he did so that the veins in the soldier's neck were pumped up and rigid. As he started trying to find Thomas's windpipe with his fingers, the penny finally dropped.

'Bollocks,' Adams muttered. Thomas's windpipe was not in the middle where it was supposed to be, but was pushed across to the left. Adams scrabbled in his medical bag and grabbed a grey cannula and a handful of alcohol wipes.

'Tension pneumothorax!' Adams leaned forwards and shouted in the Colonel Nick's ear, pointing a gloved finger at the screen where Thomas's oxygen saturations had dropped to eighty percent. From the look of surprise on the doctor's face, Adams wasn't sure whether he'd noticed or not.

Giving the cannula to Colonel Nick, Adams felt for the top of Thomas's sternum and moved his index finger into the rib space on the right-hand side until he was lined up with the middle of Thomas's collar bone. Counting in his head, he moved down three more rib spaces which put his index finger directly over the gap between Thomas's fifth and sixth ribs. He pushed down hard, hoping to leave a red mark on Thomas's skin for the Colonel to aim at with the cannula, and ripped the packaging open of a couple of swabs so that he could do his best to clean the area on the casualty's chest.

Colonel Nick ran his fingers over Thomas's neck, confirming what Adams had just told him. How had he not noticed that? It was an almost textbook presentation. The doctor hid his irritation that he was pretty much being told what to do by a more junior member of the team and peeled the paper off the plastic wrapper of the cannula. Adams had scrubbed around the point where the cannula was going to have to go through Thomas's chest wall. The Colonel repeated the same procedure of counting the rib spaces, reaching exactly the same location as Adams had. Holding the cannula like a dart, Colonel Nick pushed the needle straight through the gap in between Thomas's ribs and into what was hopefully the collection of air under-neath. It was far too noisy in the back of the Chinook to hear the hiss of escaping air that would tell him he was in the right place, but he could see a blood-stained bubble expand and then burst over the end of the cannula. That was, he thought, good enough for government work.

The doctor glanced at the oxygen saturation trace on the monitor, noting with satisfaction that they were starting to creep up slowly. Out of habit, he checked the flow rate on the oxygen cylinder, and the amount of oxygen left in the cylinder, before reaching for the button on the monitor to check Thomas's blood pressure. While the blue cuff was inflating on Thomas's arm, he looked up to see Ronald looking at him. Colonel Nick tapped his watch and raised his eyebrows.

'What's our ETA?' he saw Ronald mouth after pressing the microphone toggle switch. A few seconds later, Ronald held up both hands, fingers and thumbs all extended. Ten minutes. Then he swooped his hand, miming a rapid landing.

'Get me a chest drain kit ready!' Colonel Nick shouted in Adams's ear. 'Pronto.'

'There's no time!' Adams shouted back. 'We're only ten minutes out.'

'He needs a chest drain,' Colonel Nick replied.

'They'll have one prepped in the hospital!' Adams shouted. 'There's no time. We need to get ready for the transfer.' He held the Colonel's gaze for a few seconds, and then glanced up at Lizzie who was retrieving an observation chart from the floor under the stretcher. Colonel Nick wasn't sure if Lizzie had seen the exchange and chosen not to join in, or just not seen anything. Adams was avoiding his eyes as he started to pack up the equipment onto the stretcher ready for the transfer to the land ambulance when they landed.

Ten minutes later, Colonel Nick sat on the hard bench in the back of the battlefield ambulance, holding onto the edge of the seat as it bounced its way across the uneven ground between the helicopter landing site and the hospital. Even though it was only a few hundred yards, there was still no proper road between the two locations. Over the noise of the engine, he could hear the engines of the

Chinook behind them start to wind up as it prepared for the short hop back to the main helicopter pan at the other end of the camp. Only the military would locate the helicopters about as far away as possible from the hospital that they were supposed to be serving.

He stared across the ambulance at Adams and wondered for a second what the nurse's game was. Nick couldn't believe that he'd refused to set up a chest drain. It only would have taken a couple of minutes to put in, and could have made a big difference to the casualty. Although, he thought as he looked at the screen of the monitor, he didn't seem to be doing too badly with the needle decompression. Oxygen saturations were about where they should be. That wasn't the point though, the point was that he — the doctor — had asked for something and then not got what he had asked for.

Adams looked up and their eyes met for a second. Colonel Nick raised his eyebrows slightly, seeing if he could get a reaction from him, but there was nothing. Adams really was a difficult man to read.

'He looks stable anyway.' Adams nodded at the monitor. 'For the moment at least.' He looked back at Colonel Nick before continuing. 'Colonel, I know that you're pissed off with me about the chest drain, but the risks of putting one in mid-flight are really high. It's not just the environment, it's everything. The vibration can throw you anywhere, and you have to work entirely by feel because you can't hear sod all.'

'Put many chest drains in then, have you?' Colonel Nick snapped back.

'That's not the point,' Adams sighed. 'It doesn't matter how many I have or haven't put in. I just don't want to see you fuck up. Not on your first shout anyway.' There was the hint of a smile playing on Adams's face, which at first irritated the hell out of Colonel Nick, but the more he thought about it, the more he realised that Adams might have a point. 'He responded well to the needle decompression and was holding his oxygen sats well. Where would you rather put a chest drain in? The back of a Chinook that's flying tactically, or a stable, well-lit Emergency Room?'

'We can talk about it later,' the Colonel said, determined to put a stop to the conversation for the time being. 'Let's get him in first, then we can argue the toss.'

'It's up to you,' Adams replied. 'But at the moment, it's just the two of us chatting. If we go over it later, then it'll be in front of the others as part of the hot wash-up. Your call.'

Colonel Nick stared at Adams for a few seconds. The problem was, Adams was right. That didn't mean he had to like it, but the nurse was offering him an olive branch of sorts.

'Fine,' Colonel Nick said after a brief pause.

When he had completed his handover to the hospital personnel, Colonel Nick took a step back to let the Emergency Room personnel get to Thomas and start their dance. The sound level in the ER went up as the staff went to work, each performing a well-rehearsed role. Looking around, he spotted Adams over by the fridge in the corner and walked across to join him, undoing the clips on the front of his combat vest. When Colonel Nick got to the fridge, he grabbed the bottle of water that Adams was holding out for him.

'Thanks,' Colonel Nick muttered, still annoyed about the earlier conversation. He took the bottle anyway. Adams had already got rid of his combat vest and body armour and was just in the process of undoing his combat jacket to try to cool down. They were both soaked in sweat and red-faced.

'Job done,' Adams said, looking back at the ER staff swarming around their casualty. 'He should be okay, I would have thought. Lucky chap though — if that round had been an inch or so lower, he'd be freight.'

Adams bent over to retrieve his kit, and the two of them left the ER to go back to the TRT tent where, hopefully, someone would have put the kettle on despite the heat. As they walked back down the main hospital corridor Nick noticed that Adams was carrying his Kevlar helmet.

'Oh crap,' Nick said, stopping. 'I've left my bloody helmet back in the helicopter.'

'Don't worry Colonel,' Adams replied as he continued walking. 'I'm sure that Lizzie or Ronald will have picked it up and shoved it in the back of the wagon for you.'

'Oh, okay,' Nick said before cursing to himself under his breath, annoyed that he'd forgotten something so simple as that. He hadn't thought before blurting out that he'd forgotten it, and if he'd been a bit more switched on then he could have kept quiet and gone down to the pan later to get it back. If one of the others had picked it up though, then it was too late by now anyway.

'I mean, it could be worse,' Adams continued. 'You could have left your gun behind. That'd be a lot more difficult to explain. And besides, it's not as if anyone's going to take the piss out you for the next four months or anything like that.' Nick grimaced. That was exactly what he was afraid of. He glanced across at Adams, who was looking at him with a wry smile.

They reached the TRT tent, and Adams held the canvas flaps that served as a door open for Nick. He mumbled a 'thank you' and walked through, throwing his kit down on the floor. He pulled a handkerchief out of his trouser pocket and was wiping the sweat from his forehead when he heard Adams say:

'Before you get too comfortable Colonel, the first one back makes the tea.' Nick looked up at Adams.

'Really?' he asked.

'Yep. TRT rules. I'll have a NATO standard. Lizzie's a Whoopie Goldberg, and Ronald's a Julie Andrews if I remember right. Makings are over there.' Adams pointed towards a small fridge with a kettle on top of it and a piece of paper which described who drank what. A 'NATO standard' was white tea with two sugars, 'Whoopie Goldberg' was no milk or sugar (or black, none), and a 'Julie Andrews' was milk but no sugar (white, none).

'Very good,' Nick said as he read the paper and got the nun references. 'Very good.'

At the other end of the camp, the Chinook was winding down its engines, having landed on the pan after the short hop back from the HLS outside the hospital. Lizzie waited until the whine of the rotor blades had decreased to a reasonable level and took her green plastic military issue ear defenders off with relief. They might do the job in terms of keeping the noise out, she thought, but why on earth did they make them of plastic?

Using the top of her left arm, she wiped the sweat from the side of her head and then did the same for the other side. Looking across at Ronald, she smiled as she saw that he was doing the same thing.

'Bugger me, it's hot,' she said. 'And we're dressed for the bloody Arctic.' She started to unclip her combat vest so that she could get to the Velcro which held her body armour together. Heavy and inflexible, this was the main culprit in terms of being uncomfortable when it was this hot. Her breasts were aching from being compressed by the heavy armour, and she could feel the sweat rolling down her cleavage. 'Ronald?' she asked.

'You ok, mate?' he replied.

'Do your tits get squashed by the body armour like mine do?' Ronald muffled a laugh and looked across at Lizzie with what looked to her like an expression of anger on his face.

'Lizzie?' he responded.

'What?'

'Fuck off.'

They both laughed at the same time. Ronald was quite a well-built man, courtesy of what Lizzie considered to be far too much time in the gym. It had been a running joke between them for some time about which of them had the larger chest. Lizzie shrugged herself out of her combat vest and undid the Velcro on her body armour, sighing with relief as the pressure of the armour was relieved. They both walked to the ramp at the back of the heli-copter, and she shrugged the body armour off her shoul-ders, placing it on the rear ramp. It was closely followed by her combat vest and helmet. Ronald, who'd made an iden-tical but much neater pile with his own kit, looked across the HLS towards the Land Rover.

'You got the keys?' he asked Lizzie. 'I'll go and get the wagon.' Lizzie pulled the keys out of her pocket and threw them to Ronald.

'There you go, mate,' she replied.

'Cheers. Back in a sec.' He stepped down off the ramp and walked across to where the Land Rover was parked.

Lizzie turned and walked back into the body of the

helicopter to start gathering the medical kit together for loading on the vehicle. She thought about last week, when Adams had forgotten to hand over the keys when he went off in the ambulance with a patient to the hospital, and she'd only realised that he'd still got them after the helicopter had made the short hop back to the main pan.

Lizzie and Ronald had waited for nearly an hour until Adams had worked out where they were and come back to get them, full of apologies. Lizzie could have walked over to the engineers' workshop and phoned the hospital from their tent, but she'd wanted to make a point. Besides, there were worse ways to spend an hour than hanging around with Ronald. Lizzie grunted as she picked up Colonel Nick's medical bag, and she carried it towards the back of the helicopter to start making another pile of equipment.

Ronald reversed the Land Rover so that it was end to end with the helicopter, and he jumped out to help Lizzie load the kit. She looked across at him, laughing.

'Look what I found,' she said, holding up a helmet.

6

Almost sixty kilometres due north of Camp Bastion, Lance Corporal Michael Perry was lying on his back in the blistering heat, watching a bird of some description soaring in lazy circles through the blue sky high above him. He wasn't too sure why he was lying on his back, but one thing he did notice was that it was quiet. Not just quiet, but silent. He couldn't hear anything at all.

The sun was blocked out for an instant, and he recognised the silhouetted face of the radio operator and patrol medic, Corporal Danny Mulumbu, above him. Perry could see that Mulumbu was shouting something at him, but although he could see his lips moving, he still couldn't hear anything.

Mulumbu roughly shook Perry by the shoulders, and then put two fingers to Perry's neck which he tried to swat away, annoyed. He heard a high-pitched whistling noise somewhere in the distance, and the sound of Mulumbu's voice started to filter through. Perry tried to sit up, but something wasn't working properly. He managed to get his elbows underneath him and raised his upper body just enough so that he could look at something other than the sky. He could see Mulumbu kneeling next to him, trying to get something from his trouser pocket. Perry glanced down towards his legs.

'No, no, no!' he screamed when he saw what was left of them. His left leg had been torn off at the knee, and his right leg was at such an odd angle that it had to be broken somewhere high up near his hip. Perry couldn't feel any pain though — the only thing that he could feel was rising panic. He threw his head back, jolting the helmet down over his brow. 'No!' he screamed again before taking several deep breaths. Perry looked back down at what was left of his legs and saw that Mulumbu had managed to get a combat tourniquet out of Perry's trouser pocket. The radio operator was trying to undo the black fabric straps, his hands shaking as he struggled with them. Perry's hearing was returning bit by bit, and he could hear Mulumbu panting. To Perry's right, the other members of his patrol were fanning out with their guns pointing outwards in a classic defensive posture.

A sharp white-hot pain shot up Perry's left leg. Screaming, he looked down to see that Mulumbu had grabbed Perry's trousers and was trying to lift his thigh up to work the tourniquet onto the shattered stump. Perry grabbed Mulumbu's arm in a tight grip.

'Stop, stop for fuck's sake Danny!' he shouted. 'Fucking let go.'

'Sorry mate,' Mulumbu replied. 'I've got to put this on. You're bleeding really bad.' He tightened his grip on Perry's trouser leg and lifted the stump into the air.

Perry screamed, letting go of Mulumbu's arm and hitting the ground with a closed fist. He panted, blowing his breath out through his cheeks like a woman in labour. He'd never known pain like it in his life. Perry watched

Mulumbu work the loop of the tourniquet over the shattered remains of his left leg and then shut his eyes tightly as
if he was trying to anaesthetise the pain by blocking out
the image.

'It's on, Perry. Okay mate? It's on now.' Perry looked
back up and saw that Mulumbu had put his left leg back
on the sand. 'You're doing alright fella, doing good. Yeah?'
Mulumbu started to twist the rod on the tourniquet that
would tighten it up and squeeze Perry's femoral artery
until it was closed, stopping the bleeding. With each twist
of the rod, a new sharp pain shot up Perry's thigh.

'Morphine mate. Where's the fucking morphine?
Come on Danny, morphine mate. Please. For fuck's sake,
please.' Perry felt Mulumbu's hand go back into his
trousers, looking for the small green box with the
morphine auto-injector that they all carried. He shut his
eyes again, trying to ignore the pain, and heard Mulumbu
open the plastic box and snap the top of the syringe.

'Right shoulder, Perry. Okay?' Mulumbu said, tapping
Perry's right upper arm.

'Yes mate, come on,' Perry replied. Mulumbu pressed
the syringe hard against Perry's deltoid muscle and pressed
the button. Perry heard the click of the injection, but any
pain from it was lost. He saw Mulumbu pull the needle out
and bend it against the ground, snapping the needle off
completely before putting the used syringe back into
the box.

A small bead of sweat ran slowly down the side of
Perry's forehead before another wave of agony struck
when Mulumbu moved his left leg to straighten it up. Perry
screamed, even though he tried hard not to. 'Jesus Christ,'
he said through clenched teeth. He tried to remember
what advice his girlfriend had been given when their first
and so far only child had been born. Shutting his eyes

tightly, he huffed and puffed, trying to breathe the pain away. The only problem was that he wasn't having a baby in a warm, comfortable, and clean hospital in the United Kingdom. He was bleeding to death in the middle of Afghanistan.

A sharp slap to the injection site on his shoulder made Perry open his eyes.

'Mate, I need to put a bandage on that.' Mulumbu pointed at what was left of Perry's left leg, a large combat bandage in his hands. 'It's gonna hurt, sorry. Got to be done though.' Bracing himself for the pain, Perry nodded at Mulumbu. He understood what Mulumbu had to do. He didn't like it, but he understood. Perry shut his eyes again, screwing them up to try to distract himself. He thought about his family, about how bloody angry his girlfriend would be when she found out that he'd lost a leg like he left it on the bus or something. He tried to picture his son's face. Charlie was eighteen months old, and when Perry had left for the desert he'd just started to say a few words. In her last letter, Perry's girlfriend had described how Charlie had finally taken his first steps less than a week after he'd left.

Perry had cried when he read that he'd missed it by only a few days, and he cried again now as he lay on the sand with his legs in bits and realised that he couldn't even remember what his son's face looked like. White hot pain brought him back into reality, and he realised that Mulumbu was wrapping the bloodied stump of his left leg in a bandage.

Perry opened his eyes as he sensed rather than saw a shadow across the sun. He couldn't see who it was who'd blocked out the sun, but he soon recognised the harsh Northern Irish accent of his platoon commander.

'Fuck me, Perry. What've you done to yourself, mate?'

Perry closed his eyes again. All he wanted to do was to shut the whole thing out. Maybe it was the morphine finally starting to kick in, but he felt really, really tired.

Corporal Danny Mulumbu looked down at his friend lying in the sand in front of him. Looking around, Mulumbu could see the crater in the ground where the mine or improvised explosive device had gone off, taking Perry's left leg with it and bending his other leg in completely the wrong direction. The crater was on the edge of a wadi, or dried river bed, so the chances were that it was one of the thousands — if not millions — of mines left behind during one of the many wars in the area over the last few years. His patrol was completely off the beaten track, trying to find a vantage point to set up a forward observation post which would look over a road where the Taliban were rumoured to have set up unofficial checkpoints over the last few weeks.

Mulumbu figured that as this wasn't an area where insurgents or the military operated in frequently if at all, the location of the explosion in a wadi probably meant that the mine had been swept there during the winter by a flash flood. The insurgents wouldn't have taken the time and effort to set up an improvised explosive device here on the off chance that a patrol might stumble across it.

Whether it was a mine or an IED was completely irrelevant, he thought, as it had completely done the job on Perry. What it did mean was that the chances of them being close to an unofficial minefield were fairly high, although they were all on firm ground. Even Perry had been blown back out of the wadi onto the firmer ground by the blast. Mulumbu looked up towards the slightly higher ground where the rest of his patrol were setting up an emergency helicopter landing site for the medical team that should be on their way from Camp Bastion.

'How you doing there, big man?' he said to Perry, using his unofficial nickname for the smallest bloke in the patrol. Perry didn't reply, so Danny knelt by his side. It could be that the morphine finally kicked in, he thought, and he didn't want to wake Perry up if that was the case. He'd be in enough pain during the transfer to come as it was. Perry didn't look too bad, given the circumstances. His breathing was regular, not too quick, and he was a healthy enough colour. Mulumbu had a quick look to make sure that the tourniquet was still doing its job of keeping Perry's blood where it should be — inside him — and couldn't see any leaks. He remembered back from his Common Core first aid training that you could bleed to death without anyone seeing a single drop of blood if you had internal injuries, but that was more from stuff like being run over by a bus or something like that. Mulumbu sat down next to his friend, and with a quick glance to make sure none of the other members of the patrol were watching, touched the side of Perry's face. 'Not long now mate.' he said. 'Hang in there. Not long now.'

7

L izzie dried her hands on the rough paper towels from the dispenser in the female toilets. Dropping the paper into the bin, she sighed. That was a straightforward enough job. One casualty, and fairly simple. It had got a bit sticky at one point, but they'd done what they'd set out do, which was to deliver the casualty to the hospital in a better state than he'd been in when they'd picked him up. From that point of view, job done.

But, and this was a big but, there was the small issue of the new doctor, Colonel Nick. Her first impression of him wasn't good, that was fair to say, but she had to admit to herself that there was something about him that she quite liked. She figured that Ronald had probably picked up on this, but then again he would, but she thought to herself that she didn't need this. Lizzie looked at herself in the mirror on the wall. She wasn't in bad shape, she thought, although the crow's feet that had started to appear around her eyes over the last few months were irritating. Even more irritating was that Adams had called them 'laughter lines' when she'd first mentioned them to him, and seeing how annoyed she was by this phrase, had kept using it since. She used a finger to pull at the skin next to her eyes to smooth them out but the minute she let go, there they were again. The worse thing was that the more tanned she got, the more obvious they got, or at least that's how it seemed. Lizzie was running her fingers through her hair, trying to tame it, when the door to the toilets opened behind her and one of her room-mates, Corporal Emma Wardle, walked in.

'Hi, mate,' Lizzie said to Emma's reflection in the mirror. 'How did it go?'

'Not too bad in the end, Lizzie,' Emma replied. 'Major Clarke put me in as scribe.'

'Oh, okay,' Lizzie said. 'So, it all went well, then? You were shitting yourself the other night.'

'No, it was fine. Went really smoothly, I thought. Not that different to back at home, but then again we never got many gunshot wounds in Barnet General.'

'Mate, I've been a Paramedic for nearly five years now and that's the first proper one I've seen,' Lizzie said. 'He should be okay, shouldn't he?'

'He's in theatre already. The ITU's getting all excited waiting for him to come out, but the transfer team are hovering like vultures.'

One of Lizzie's closest friends was an intensive care nurse on the RAF critical care transfer team, or CCTT, so she knew a little bit about how they worked. The quicker they could get a patient in the air and on the way back to a decent hospital the better. She knew as well that there was a real element of pride attached to being able to move patients who were badly injured so quickly.

'He might not even make it as far as the ITU if the CCTT have their way,' Lizzie said. 'He'll just be loaded straight into the back of a Hercules before he's even come round from his anaesthetic.'

'They're certainly keen, that's for sure,' Emma laughed as she went into one of the cubicles, closing the door behind her.

'So, Major Clarke was really supportive, was he?' Lizzie asked through the door.

'Yeah, he was. I was quite surprised seeing as he's normally so grumpy with everyone.'

'Yeah, well. You know why, don't you?' Lizzie said, smiling.

'Enough Lizzie,' Emma laughed.

'What Major Clarke really wants…' Lizzie continued.

'I said, enough!'

Lizzie walked out of the toilets into the main hospital corridor and turned down towards the TRT tent. Nodding at a radiographer who was pushing a large x-ray machine down the corridor towards the operating theatre, she ran her fingers through her hair again. Having her head squashed inside a Kevlar helmet for so long didn't do it any favours.

Adams wouldn't notice what state her hair was in, or even what colour it was. Ronald wouldn't care because, well, because he was Ronald. But the new doctor might. She caught herself thinking this, and swore quietly under her breath.

Reaching the end of the long corridor, Lizzie turned and entered the TRT tent, pushing the heavy canvas flaps of the tent door aside as she did so. Walking straight to the table with the kettle on, she picked up the tea that Colonel Nick had made her and sat down next to Adams on one of the green canvas chairs next to the main desk. She took a large sip of her drink.

'My God,' she exclaimed, looking into the cup with disgust. 'Is that tea?'

'Yep,' Adams replied. 'The Colonel made it especially for you.'

'Well, that's the subject of the next training session sorted out then,' Lizzie said. 'How to make a decent bloody cup of tea.' Adams looked at her, grinning. 'He's behind me, isn't he?' Lizzie asked, already knowing the answer from the look on Adams's face.

'Yes, I am,' Colonel Nick said, walking through from the small stores section. 'And what's wrong with your tea anyway? It's got milk and two sugars as briefed.'

Lizzie felt herself going red and hated herself for it. The Colonel might be a bit of a cock, but he wasn't a bad looking one.

'It's not that there's anything wrong with it, as such,' she said. 'It's just not quite how I drink it, that's all.'

'I think the damage is probably done, Lizzie,' Adams laughed. 'But you'll have to lead the next training session now.'

'Where's Ronald?' she asked, glaring at him and trying to change the subject. The look from Adams told her that he'd picked up on the change.

'He's in main stores, finishing off restocking the bags.'

'What, all of them?' Lizzie replied, annoyed. She felt very protective towards Ronald, suspecting that he'd just been told to do it by Colonel Nick and hadn't had the bottle to tell him to do his own bag. 'We normally do our own bags unless someone specifically offers to do them for you,' she said, with a pointed look towards Colonel Nick. The Colonel raised his hands in a mock gesture of surrender. 'Sir,' Lizzie added as she caught the sharp look on Adams's face.

'He offered to do mine with his, Sergeant Jarman,' Colonel Nick said. 'Said it would be quicker as he knew where everything was. Besides, I was making the tea.'

'Right,' Lizzie replied, momentarily caught out. 'But at some point, you'll need to get yourself familiar with where all the kit is.'

'Fair point, Sergeant Jarman,' Colonel Nick replied with a half-smile that irritated Lizzie no end. 'I'll be sure to do that.'

They looked at each other for a couple of seconds before she said, 'I'll go and help him. It'll be even quicker then.'

Lizzie walked back to the rear of the tent and emptied her cup into the sink, making sure that the Colonel saw what she thought of his tea in case he hadn't got the message earlier, before walking through the back of the tent and out into the main base. As she walked across the dusty gravel to the main store building a couple of hundred yards away, she wished that she hadn't been so quick to get irritated with the Colonel. Ronald was a big lad, she thought, and was quite capable of looking after himself without her acting as his bloody mother. Just as she got to the door of the stores, Ronald came out with a medical bag in each hand.

'Give me one of those, mate,' she said. 'I'll give you a hand.'

As soon as Lizzie had left the TRT tent, Adams heard Colonel Nick clearing his throat.

'Sergeant Jarman's a bit of a live wire, isn't she?' the doctor asked.

'Lizzie's okay,' Adams replied, looking up from the paperwork he was filling out. 'Just a bit hot-tempered at times, that's all.'

'Even so,' Colonel Nick said. 'That's not how I'd talk to a senior officer, no matter how hot-tempered I am.'

Adams thought before replying. Several options ran through his head, all discounted fairly quickly. He could tell the Colonel that he wasn't really a senior officer, he was only a Lieutenant Colonel, but he wasn't sure how he'd take that. He could apologise on Lizzie's behalf, but he figured that she'd be really annoyed if she found out. In the end, Adams chose the path of least resistance and just stayed silent.

'Don't you think, Adams?' Colonel Nick pressed him.

'Er, well, sir,' Adams replied after thinking for a couple of seconds on the best approach. 'Thing is, we do normally all do our own bags. It's kind of an unwritten rule and I know that Ronald offered to do yours, but that's just him.' Colonel Nick looked at Adams with a surprised expression. 'I don't think that he was expecting you to say yes,' Adams added.

'Well he shouldn't have fucking asked then, should he?' Colonel Nick retorted. Figuring that there was no best way to answer that question, Adams again stayed silent. 'And what's with the "Lizzie this", "Ronald that"? What's all that about, Adams? You're an officer. They aren't. You're the senior RAF one here, and it doesn't look like they know that to me. And if they don't respect you, they're not going to respect me. Are they?' Adams looked at the Colonel, trying to keep his expression neutral.

'Sir,' he said, looking the Colonel directly in the eye. 'You're right. I'm the senior RAF officer here, and they're not officers. But as far as respect goes, I'd prefer it to be earned. If you get to the point where you have to demand it, you're probably buggered,' he said, before adding, 'sir,' just to be on the safe side.

The two men sat in silence for several minutes, Adams completing his paperwork and Colonel Nick leafing through a dog-eared paperback book that Ronald was reading. Adams wondered if he should say something else — an apology of sorts by way of a peace offering — but when he looked over at Colonel Nick, he thought better of it. From the expression on the doctor's face, he didn't look as if he was in the mood for any further conversation.

'Right then,' Adams said, putting the clipboard he was balancing on his knees on the side. 'Paperwork's all done. I'm going for a shower. Do you want anything from the accommodation block, Nick?' The Colonel glanced up sharply.

'Nick?' he said through gritted teeth. 'Did you mean Colonel Nick?' Adams took a deep breath and was about to reply when the flap at the end of the tent was pushed aside. Lizzie and Ronald walked through, carrying a medical bag in each hand. They looked uncertainly at each other as if they sensed the tension in the air. At exactly the same time, the red phone on the desk rang. Adams looked away from Lizzie and Ronald's concerned faces and muttered under his breath.

'You have got to be fucking joking.'

8

Brigadier James Foster, despite being the most senior officer in Camp Bastion, knew when he had to listen rather than talk. He sat back in his rickety canvas chair and held the receiver of the telephone a couple of inches away from his ear until the Garrison Sergeant Major had finished talking.

'Yes, Mr Irvine,' the Brigadier said when he could finally get a word in edgeways. 'I will speak to them about their driving, but at the same time it's important to remember why they're driving so fast down the main drag.' This prompted another outburst from the GSM. Foster sighed and moved the receiver back away from his ear as there was a knock on his door. A few seconds later, one of the Ops Officers — a young Lieutenant whose name Foster had forgotten — stuck his head around it.

When he saw that the Brigadier was on the phone, he raised a hand in apology, but Foster waved him in. The young officer would have waited for a reply if it wasn't urgent.

'Right, Mr Irvine, let me stop you there,' Foster said into the phone. When the GSM's voice had tailed off, he continued. 'You've made your point, several times. I've said I'll speak to the team, and I will do. Now something has cropped up and I need to go, so thank you.' Without waiting for a reply, Foster replaced the receiver on the handset and turned his attention to the Ops Officer.

'Sorry to interrupt, sir,' the young man said. Foster looked at him, realising that he was about the same age as his youngest son. 'We've just deployed the TRT again. There's a Cat A up near Sangin. IED, we think. Serious leg injuries.'

'Bloody hell,' Foster replied. 'How's the other one doing?'

'He's in Intensive Care.'

'Are the aeromedical evacuation lot involved?'

'They're already arguing with Intensive Care, apparently,' the Ops Officer said. Brigadier Foster allowed himself a wry smile. He'd already had a one-way conversation with the team leaders of both groups about playing nicely, but perhaps another one would be needed when things had settled down.

'Okay, thanks,' he said to the young Lieutenant. 'I'll pop down to the ER, make sure they don't need anything from me.'

'Did you want me to ask the TRT to come and speak to you when they get back, sir?' the Ops Officer asked. He nodded at the phone on the Brigadier's desk. 'I take it that was the GSM about their driving again?'

'I think that's probably the last thing they'll want to do when they get in, don't you?' Brigadier Foster replied with a smile.

≈

'Listen in!' Corporal Emma Wardle jumped as Squadron Leader Andrew Webb, the doctor in charge of the Emergency Room, shouted just as she walked into the ER. *My God*, she thought. *Does he ever love the sound of his own voice?* 'I've just heard from the Ops Room that the TRT's on its way back out to another Cat A casualty. We need to make sure that everything's re-stocked and ready to go.'

Emma had already stocked up after her role in the previous resuscitation. As scribe, this was pretty straightforward as it only involved replacing the trauma chart on the scribe's table and making sure that the pen was working for the next one. It wasn't as simple as that though, as the doctors rarely helped to restock the rest of the department.

She moved across to the head of the trauma bay and started to check through the emergency intubation equipment even though she didn't think it had been touched.

'Corporal Wardle?' she heard Major Rob Clarke say behind her.

'Sir?' she replied, turning to look at him. He was just wiping his face with a dirty looking handkerchief. Even though the tent was air-conditioned, he still had a red face and looked as if he was suffering more than anyone else in the room from the heat. It was still stifling, despite the air conditioning.

'Corporal Salah has gone to Intensive Care to follow that last casualty through. That means that we're a nurse down. Can you step up please and assist the anaesthetist? I'll get one of the kids to do scribe and keep an eye on them.' He nodded towards a couple of Combat Medical Technicians who were standing in a corner of the Emergency Room, looking lost.

'Er, I can do, sir,' she replied. 'I've not done that before though. I mean, I've seen plenty, but not had the chance to—'

'You'll be fine,' he cut her off. 'The gas man will be at the head, doing his thing if it's needed. Keep an eye on him and make sure he's okay, but your main job is to get an initial set of observations and make sure that the casualty's got a decent line in. Put one in if he hasn't got one already on your side.'

Emma swallowed and nodded at the Major.

'Okay, sir,' she said. 'I can do that.' As Major Clarke walked off to talk to the Combat Medical Technicians, she ran through the job ahead in her mind. Help the gas man, get some observations, check the intravenous line or put one in. She mentally rehearsed the procedure for cannulation, which she'd done loads of time in the Emergency Room she worked at back in the UK, but she'd never inserted one in the middle of a trauma call.

Feeling the familiar butterflies start to build up in her chest just at the thought of it, she took a few deep breaths and moved to check the trolley with some of the other emergency equipment on it, paying particular attention to the cannula tray. There were a few bits and pieces that needed to be restocked, as there normally were after a trauma call, so she started a list of things that she'd have to go and get from the main hospital store. Cannulas, saline flushes, alcohol wipes, they all went onto the list.

She paused for a moment, looking up just in time to catch Major Clarke looking away from her from the opposite side of the tent. What Lizzie Jarman had said in the toilets suddenly came back to her. She knew that Lizzie had only been joking, but now she began to wonder if there was something behind what she'd said. She made a mental note to have a proper chat with Lizzie when they were back in the accommodation that evening to see if she was being serious or just taking the mick. Emma jumped as Squadron Leader Webb started shouting again.

'Right people!' he bellowed to the four or five people who were still in the room. 'TRT's just left, so we've probably got about thirty minutes before we need to pick up the pieces.'

9

The Chinook turned in lazy circles just over three thousand feet above the Sangin district of Helmand Province. Adams was sitting next to Ronald, the only member of the medical team who was able to talk to the pilot via a microphone attached to his flying helmet. When he saw Ronald stop talking, Adams tapped him on the shoulder.

'What's going on, mate?' Adams shouted as Ronald pushed the headset off one ear. 'Why aren't we getting in there?'

'Insurgent activity in the area!' Ronald yelled back. 'The Captain's not happy. No news on the casualty though.'

'For Christ's sake,' Adams said, although he knew that the Captain was spot on. He stood and walked back down the aircraft to pass the message on to the rest of the medical team. Lizzie was sitting further back towards the rear ramp with her eyes closed. She looked as if she was asleep, but as Adams touched her on the shoulder she jumped and opened her eyes, looking at him with a startled expression.

'Lizzie,' Adams leaned in and put his mouth next to her ear. 'We're circling until we get confirmation that the area's safe for us to go in.' He saw her eyes widen at the news, but a couple of seconds later she shuffled down the seats to pass the message on to the Force Protection team leader. Adams moved across to Colonel Nick who, on hearing about the delay, just nodded at him.

Happy that the team knew what was going on, Adams sat back down on the seat and retrieved the paperback book that he'd been pretending to read, but his mind was buzzing. Just as he did before every landing, he ran through his own internal checklist about what if the worst happened, and he didn't come back. Before he'd left the United Kingdom, Adams had taken ages to make sure that everything was in place, and that there was nothing that was going to embarrass anyone if he didn't come home. He was sure that his computer was clean, and that both his browsing history and 'private' folder had been deleted. Even though he was sure that no-one would be that upset about finding a bit of porn on his computer, it was one less thing to worry about.

He'd written letters to all his family, which were in his desk drawer back in the UK and would only be read by the intended recipients if he didn't get back to shred them. The life insurance policy he'd taken out paid double if he died on operations. Even though his parents didn't really need the money, it wouldn't hurt. Adams's final mental check was to double check that the photo of his girlfriend Sophie was safely tucked behind the Kevlar plate in the front of his body armour.

Adams tried to push these thoughts to the back of his mind as he felt the helicopter bank and start to descend.

Out of the corner of his eye, he saw the loadmaster point to the floor of the helicopter and hold up his hand to indicate five minutes, a signal which Ronald immediately repeated. Adams earmarked the corner of the book and tucked it behind his seat. He checked his personal kit, and picked up his rifle to sling it across his back, muzzle downwards.

Around him, all the other members of both the medical and Force Protection teams were all doing their own checks. Adams moved across to Lizzie and gave her a quick buddy-buddy check before she did the same thing for him, reaching out and pushing Adams's toughened scissors behind his rank slide on the front of his uniform. He was very attached to those scissors, but only because he'd had to order them in from Amazon specifically. Being left-handed, he'd not been able to use the scissors they were issued to cut through a piece of paper, let alone the tough material of a combat uniform. Lizzie gave him a weak smile and he used his knuckles to knock a couple of times on the top of her helmet, grinning at her as he did so.

Turning around, Adams gave a thumbs up to both Ronald and Colonel Nick, who returned the gesture. Colonel Nick was sporting a new-looking pair of kneepads. Remembering that he didn't have any on their last job, Adams wondered where he'd got them from. There certainly hadn't been enough time to get all the way to the camp's main stores when they'd been back at Camp Bastion, and the medical stores refused to keep any stock at the hospital because they weren't medical kit. He wondered if Lizzie had given him a pair, despite her apparent ambivalence towards the doctor.

Seeing the back of the ramp start to descend and the loadmaster holding up a single finger, Adams reached up and pulled down his protective goggles over his eyes.

Around him, everyone else did the same thing. He felt the
nose of the Chinook lifting as they came in to land, and as
the back end of the helicopter touched down, the interior
became so full of dust, vegetation, and God knew what
from the desert floor that he could barely see Lizzie on the
other side of the helicopter. While he was waiting for the
thumbs up from the loadmaster, Adams noticed that the
plant materials that had been sucked into the back of the
helicopter were the dried-out heads of poppy flowers.
They'd touched down in the middle of a poppy field.

As soon as he got the signal from the loadmaster,
Adams picked up the stretcher and moved down the ramp.
At the end, he looked in the direction that the loadmaster
was pointing with a flat hand to see a solitary figure
standing and waving at them through the dust a couple of
hundred yards away. He knew that Lizzie would be right
behind him, so he jumped down off the ramp and started
running across to the soldier. On his right-hand side, he
saw Lizzie running alongside him, her rifle swaying on her
back with every step. She was gradually moving in front
him, which annoyed him, but then again he was older and
was also carrying a stretcher. His lungs started to burn with
every deep breath of the hot air. If he ever went for a run
in a sauna, he thought, this is probably what it would be
like. The only difference would be that if he was running
in a sauna, he wouldn't be wearing so many layers of
clothing and body armour.

When they reached the soldier who was waving at
them, Adams was only a few yards behind Lizzie. He
stopped, pushed his goggles back up on to his helmet, and
used the back of his hand to wipe his forehead. The casualty was about twenty yards away, down a slight slope
leading to a wadi. Even from this distance, Adams could
see that this was a bad one; the soldier's left leg was missing

below the knee, and he thought that the femur on the right was probably snapped.

'Hey, I'm Adams,' he said, shaking the soldier's hand. 'What've you got?' The soldier glanced at the rank tab on the front of Adams's combat vest.

'Hi, er, sir. I'm Mulumbu. Patrol medic,' he replied, pointing at the casualty. 'He went down into the wadi and then that was it. Must have stepped on a mine, I reckon. Blew him back onto the hard standing, such as it is. His leg's gone. The other one looks fucked. I put a tourniquet on, and gave him his morphine, but apart from that…'

'Mulumbu. Cracking job, mate.' Adams looked across at Lizzie and then down at the stretcher with a nod. Getting the message, Lizzie moved the stretcher so that it was laid down next to the casualty and pulled the arms apart to make it into a proper stretcher. 'Best not fuck about, lad.' Adams pointed at the stretcher that Lizzie was now kicking to secure the struts in place and said to Mulumbu, 'Let's get him on that so that we can get the hell out of here.'

Mulumbu raised his eyebrows and looked at Adams, a look of surprise on his face. Adams knew full well what he was thinking. Officers weren't supposed to talk like that. At the end of the day, Adams didn't give a monkey's what Mulumbu or any other soldier thought of his officer qualities — all Adams wanted was to get the casualty back on the helicopter and up in the air. Where it was safe.

'Ok, sir,' Mulumbu replied. 'Got it.'

Adams knelt on the opposite side of the casualty from Lizzie, who gave him a quick thumbs up. This didn't mean anything other than the casualty was still alive. Knowing full well that what he was about to do would hurt the soldier lying on the floor in front of him, Adams reached out and grabbed two handfuls of uniform, one by his shoulder and one just above his shredded thigh, and pulled the soldier onto his side. Lizzie jammed the stretcher into the sand at an angle, and eased the stretcher back towards the horizontal as Adams rolled the casualty onto it. Together, they moved him into the middle of the stretcher, both ignoring the groans that the movement caused. If anything, a groaning casualty was a good thing as it proved that they could maintain their airway. It was the quiet ones that concerned them more.

Adams stood, readjusting the rifle slung across his back as he did so. Looking at Mulumbu, Adams barked, 'Right then. Off we fuck. Get on the back of the stretcher, would you? You're about the same size as the two of us put together. On your count, Lizzie.' Adams knelt by the head end of the stretcher and waited while Lizzie fiddled with the extra pair of safety goggles that she'd pulled out of one of the pockets in her combat vest. She finished putting them over the casualty's eyes and grabbed the handle of the stretcher with her right hand.

'Okay!' she shouted, after a quick glance to make sure that Mulumbu was where Adams had told him to be. '1 — 2 — 3 — Lift.' All three of them stood up as one, and started shuffling towards the helicopter.

10

I n the captain's seat of the Chinook, Flight Lieutenant Davies took one hand off the collective thrust and flexed his fingers a couple of times. He flicked the switch to get himself onto the comms channel with the team in the back.

'How're they doing?' he asked.

'They've just picked him up now,' Kinkers replied, his lazy Australian drawl obvious even over the crackling radio. 'Moving back towards us slowly. There's only one on the back of the stretcher. He's a big lad, so they're a bit slow.'

Davies's attention was drawn by some movement on the right-hand side of the helicopter in his peripheral vision. The Force Protection team was reorganising itself from the normal semi-circle around the ramp of the helicopter into a loose semi-circle on the right side of the Chinook. He saw the Team Leader shouting and pointing towards a small copse about two hundred yards away from them.

'Kinkers!' he shouted down the radio to the loadmaster. 'Get on the right-hand gun. There's something going on by those trees.'

'Roger,' the pilot heard after a brief second. 'I'm on it.'

Davies flicked the comms switch back to the main channel and spoke to his co-pilot.

'Taff,' he said. 'Get ready to lift sharpish, mate. FP are getting excited about something in the trees.'

'Seen,' Taff replied. One of the things Davies liked most about his dour Welsh co-pilot was that he was a man of few words. The pilot craned his head around over his shoulder to try to see what was going on through the Plexiglass window. He wasn't sure, but he thought he could see some movement in the copse, which would explain why the FP team was getting excited. Although the trees were at least two hundred yards away, that was well within the range of any of the rifles that the insurgents were using. But that also put them all within range of the FP team, and Davies knew who he would put his money on. That didn't change the fact that the biggest threat to the aircraft was a rocket-propelled grenade, though. Davies knew full well that other than evasive manoeuvres in the air, there wasn't anything that he would able to do to avoid the unguided missiles. Added to that was the fact that he wasn't in the air at the moment, but sitting on the ground with rotors turning, like a large, fat, noisy duck. The insurgents had been using rocket-propelled grenades — RPGs — for years, and there were many wrecked Russian helicopters in Afghanistan that proved how effective they could be.

Looking over his other shoulder, the pilot could see the two remaining medics in the back, kneeling on the ramp and waiting for the stretcher with the casualty.

'How far away are they, Kinkers?' Davies said into his

microphone to the loadmaster, trying to keep the fear out of his voice.

'About fifty yards,' Kinkers replied. 'I think there's some people over in those trees, but I can't see much. Might just be locals interested in what's going on, I can't tell.'

'Ok mate,' Davies said. 'Just make sure that they can see that there's someone on the gun. When we lift, I'm going to go hard left and nose down for a couple of hundred metres, and then sharp right and up as quick as she'll go.'

'Got it,' Kinkers barked back. Davies flexed his fingers again, glanced across at his co-pilot, Taff, and tried not to look as anxious as he felt.

Lizzie's arms were burning from the weight of the stretcher as she stumbled as quickly as she could towards the back of the helicopter. They'd all seen the FP team reorganise themselves, which could only mean that there was some kind of threat over to the right-hand side of them, perhaps in the trees that she could see in the distance. They were already going as fast as they could, and as she looked across at Adams, she could see that he was struggling just as much as she was. Her rifle had originally been slung across her back when they'd picked up the stretcher, but it had since slid around and was now bouncing against her side with every step, rubbing painfully against her hip.

Hearing Adams shout 'Stop', she lowered the stretcher to the ground, the ache in her arms instantly starting to fade. She pulled her goggles down over her eyes as they were just about to go straight into the hot downdraft of the two huge exhausts on the back of the Chinook, and she checked that the safety goggles were still in place on the casualty. Pushing the rifle back to where it was supposed to be across her back, she got ready for the command to lift from Adams.

When it came, she stood up again and grimaced as the pain came back into both arms straight away. Every inch of her body was sweating, and a river of perspiration was running down her back and front. The body armour she was wearing wasn't designed with women in mind, and she couldn't differentiate between the pain in her chest from the body armour or the exertion. After a couple of steps, her rifle readjusted itself and swung back down to her hip, banging against the raw skin where it had been rubbing before. 'Oh, for fuck's sake,' she winced under her breath. There had to be an easier way of doing this.

At last, they reached the rear ramp of the helicopter and she handed over her corner of the stretcher to Ronald, who was standing a few yards from the helicopter. He must have seen how much she'd been struggling. She was relieved to give him the stretcher but irritated with herself at the fact that he'd obviously seen that she needed help. Lizzie stepped onto the ramp and followed the others to the front of the helicopter where Colonel Nick was kneeling next to the medical kit, his stethoscope draped around his neck. *That'll be in case anyone doesn't realise that he's a doctor*, she thought. She sat in one of the canvas seats to the side of the casualty and reached into an ice box which had some water in it, grabbing a bottle for herself and throwing one at Adams who had sat down on the other side. He looked at her, mouthing 'thank you', and then they both turned to watch as the IP team started streaming back onto the helicopter.

The second the last man scrambled onto the back of

the helicopter, Lizzie saw the loadmaster shouting frantically into his headset. Above her head, she heard the pitch
of the massive motors changing and the body of the
Chinook shook from side to side as the rotors clawed at the
air. With a lurch, the enormous helicopter leapt into the air
as Lizzie breathed a sigh of relief. Within a few minutes,
they would be high up in the blue sky, well beyond the
reach of anything the insurgents on the ground could
throw at them. All they had to do now was get there.

11

C olonel Nick grabbed the seat next to him as the aircraft lifted and banked hard over to one side. Around him, he saw the soldiers in the FP team grabbing what they could to hold on to, a couple of them exchanging nervous grins.

For fuck's sake, Colonel Nick thought. *What was the bloody pilot trying to do?* He was going to have a word when they got back, if they got back at all the way the idiot in the front was flying. As the aircraft levelled out and started climbing hard, the doctor turned his attention to the casualty on the stretcher in front of him. The soldier was, Colonel Nick thought, in a bit of a mess.

Ronald had already put the oxygen mask on the casualty's face, and Colonel Nick could see from the mist inside the plastic mask that he was breathing okay. The small monitor on the floor hadn't yet picked up the oxygen saturation from the probe on the casualty's finger, but he was still a nice pink colour. Colonel Nick reached down and found the soldier's metal dog tags, reading the surname imprinted on them.

'Perry? Corporal Perry?' Colonel Nick shouted over the noise of the rotor blades. 'Can you hear me?' There was no response from the casualty, and Colonel Nick couldn't really do much more until Perry's chest was exposed. Ronald was busy unclipping Perry's combat vest so that he could get to the body armour underneath, and Adams was making short work of the lad's uniform with a large pair of toughened scissors. Colonel Nick had over-heard some banter between Adams and Lizzie about the scissors earlier, something to do with them being 'special'. It was only now that he realised that Adams was left-handed, and so wouldn't be able to use the scissors he'd been issued with.

Colonel Nick looked up at Lizzie, who was busy preparing an intravenous line ready for when someone had managed to get a cannula in. Her face was bright red and didn't look happy at all. Adams had got a cannulation kit ready next to him, so no doubt he was going to do the honours as soon as he'd finished with his special scissors. Both Lizzie and Adams were dripping with perspiration. Colonel Nick looked down the helicopter at the FP team, several of whom looked away from him as their eyes met. Colonel Nick didn't think it was a rank thing. They were all soldiers, but the FP team's job was to kill people and his was to save lives.

As he looked back down at the casualty, he could see the other members of the medical team were all hard at work. Adams had shoved his scissors back behind his rank tabs on the front of his uniform and was putting an elastic tourniquet around Perry's upper arm, ready to put a cannula in. Lizzie was kneeling next to him, still looking hot and uncomfortable.

Ronald had finally managed to get access to Perry's chest, ripping the Velcro of the body armour apart and undoing the front of his combats. Finally, Colonel Nick thought, he could get to work. He looked at Perry's neck first, running his hands over it to feel for any distended neck veins or a non-central trachea. This was supposed to be part of the standard drills anyway, but after missing it off on the last job with the tension pneumothorax, he wanted to be especially careful.

Finding nothing untoward, he continued to run his hands over Perry's chest, making sure to get them as far around towards his back as he could, checking for blood as he went. There were no obvious injuries, the chest had equal air entry on both sides. Colonel Nick remembered the looks he got from the team on the previous job when he'd used his stethoscope in flight, so he didn't bother this time. They were right anyway, although none of them had said a word. He hadn't been able to hear a thing over the noise in the back of the helicopter. He didn't bother percussing the chest for the same reason.

Moving his hands down to Perry's abdomen, he noted with satisfaction that it was soft, so nothing nasty going on there. He put his palms on Perry's hip bones and pressed down sharply, noting with satisfaction that the pelvis seemed to be intact. *So far, so good*, he thought.

By this time Perry was almost naked on the stretcher. Ronald had finished cutting off the clothing that he'd been able to get to, leaving Perry lying on a bed of his own ruined uniform. Colonel Nick turned his attention to Perry's legs. The damage to the left leg was obvious. The entire lower limb was missing, with the stump raw and ragged, and he could see the casualty's patella hanging on by a thread of skin. The tourniquet wrapped above where the knee had been was doing its job and stopping any major haemorrhage. Looking at the right leg, the femur was obviously broken. Colonel Nick turned to Ronald.

'We need a Kendrick splint, McDonald!' he shouted in Ronald's ear. 'Femur's gone.'

Looking surprised, Ronald pointed at the already prepared splint that was lying next to the stretcher. He picked it up and started to manoeuvre the various straps and splints into place so that it could be put on to straighten the broken limb. As he tentatively moved Perry's badly deformed leg, Colonel Nick kept a close eye on the casualty's face. If there was any sign of pain then he would stop and give the man some morphine, but there was no response at all. Not a good sign. Unless a person with such a badly fractured femur was deeply unconscious, the slightest movement of the broken leg would be agonising.

Corporal Emma Wardle cupped her hands around the mug of tea as if her hands were cold. She was far from cold though. Quite the opposite, in fact. She was only doing so in case her hands started shaking again.

She was sitting on a chair at the main desk in the Emergency Room with a couple of the other staff, waiting for the next casualty to arrive. She'd heard along the grapevine that this was a bad one — an amputated leg, they'd heard. Although if it turned out to be completely different, it wouldn't be the first time it had happened. She just wished that she wasn't so bloody nervous.

Emma thought back to when she first started out as a student nurse, almost four years ago. Her parents had been thrilled when she'd originally said that she wanted to become a nurse.

'That's fantastic,' her dad had said at the time. 'You'll make a fantastic nurse,' he'd said, and her mum had agreed. She made a mental note to write to her at some point over the next few days to see how she was getting on without him. Even though he'd been dead for two years now, Emma always felt sad when she thought about how he would have liked to have seen her graduate from the university. She still spoke to him sometimes like he was still alive. At least the dreams she had where he was still alive were getting less and less as time went on, as was the pain that she felt when she woke after one of them and he died all over again.

The familiar noise of the rotor blades of a Chinook brought her back to reality. Shaking her head to clear away the memories, she put her tea down on the desk and walked across to the trauma bay, checking that her blonde hair was still tucked up into a bun as she did so. Around her, the other members of the team all began to move to their positions. The whole thing was theatre, she thought, and not for the first time. Everyone had a part to play, a scene to be in, and a character to act out. This was a first night for her though — the first time that she was centre stage and doing something as opposed to watching from the wings. While she waited for the casualty to arrive, she checked the drawer of equipment again, although she'd checked it at least three times already.

A moment later, Emma heard the Chinook's engines winding down, which meant it had landed and the casualty was about to be unloaded. Knowing she only had a few minutes to go before the ambulance arrived, she took a few deep breaths.

Emma looked around the Emergency Room. She could see Squadron Leader Webb over by the main desk where her tea still sat. Major Rob Clarke was standing next to him, looking as miserable as usual. When he saw her looking at him, his face lightened and he smiled, so she gave him a brief smile in return, hoping that she didn't look too nervous. Over by the desk with the trauma chart, one of the Combat Medical Technicians was chewing the pen that was attached to the chart holder with a piece of string. Emma could almost taste the tension in the room.

Adams snagged his fingernail on the handle of the ambulance door as he tried to open it when the ambulance pulled up outside the hospital. Ignoring the pain, he waited until the driver opened the door from the outside. As the casualty was being pulled out of the ambulance, Adams saw the Colonel getting his kit together. At least he had his helmet with him this time. He knew that Lizzie and Ronald would be sorting out the helicopter while Perry was being processed and that any kit that they'd left behind would be swept up by them, but it was still good to see that the Colonel had at least learned from his earlier mistake. Adams followed the group with the stretcher towards the doors of the Emergency Room and stopped outside the door to unload his rifle. He waited for Colonel Nick to catch up with him.

'If you want to go in and do the handover, sir,' Adams said, 'I'll mind the weapons. Just come back out after so that we can clear them.' Colonel Nick handed over his rifle to Adams and followed the stretcher into the Emergency Room without a word. Adams undid the clasps on the front of his combat vest and shrugged his way out of it so that he could get out of his body armour. *I bet he won't bring back any water,* he thought. Sitting down next to his equipment, Adams dug into his pocket for a packet of cigarettes. He didn't smoke much, but he figured that he was probably entitled to one now. As long as Lizzie didn't catch him.

A few minutes later, Colonel Nick came back outside.

'Here you go, Adams,' he said, surprising him by handing him a bottle of cold water. 'Andrew Webb's in there, conducting the orchestra.'

'Cheers, sir. Nice one.'

'Have you been smoking?' Colonel Nick asked.

'Er, yes,' Adams replied. 'Sorry.'

'What are you sorry for? I don't care. I smoked like a chimney all through medical school. It was the only thing that got me through sometimes,' Colonel Nick said.

'Could you do me a favour though, sir?' Adams said.

'What? Don't tell Sergeant Jarman?' Colonel Nick looked across at Adams and laughed. 'You're secret's safe with me, Adams. For the time being, at least.' As Adams stood up and picked up the weapons, he thought that maybe the Colonel was beginning to grow on him.

Adams unlatched the magazine from the bottom of his rifle and put it into one of the pouches on his combat vest. He pointed the weapon towards the small sand-filled bunker outside the door of the tent, drew the bolt back and secured it in place so that he could look inside the chamber to make sure that there wasn't a round still in there. The last thing he wanted to do was have a negligent discharge inside the hospital. Colonel Nick looked over his shoulder into the chamber and said, 'Clear.' As Adams released the bolt and fired off the action, Colonel Nick went through the same drills so that Adams could check his weapon as well.

'All set then, sir?' Adams said as he picked up his kit. 'Let's go and watch the show.'

Adams felt the cool blast of air from the air conditioning unit as he walked into the tent with relief. He noticed that Colonel Nick was as soaked through with sweat as he was. They both put their kit in neat piles in the corner of the room, and Adams went to the fridge to get them both some more water — the first bottle had barely touched the sides. He dodged the medical team who were just transferring the patient from the stretcher onto the trolley in the trauma bay and walked back to stand next to Colonel Nick.

'You think he'll be okay?' Adams asked the doctor.

'Who knows?' Colonel Nick replied with a shrug of his shoulders. 'We've done our bit,' he said, nodding at the medical team who were swarming around Perry. 'Now it's their turn.'

12

He watched, invisible, as the medical team got the patient ready for the slide over to the trolley. They would all be concentrating on their task for the next few seconds, so this was his moment of opportunity. He fingered the ampoule in his pocket, getting ready to swap it over for one of the ampoules that had been laid out ready for the resuscitation. Glancing at the medics to make sure that they were all concentrating on their patient, he turned his back on them to shield the cardboard tray with a saline ampoule and syringe laid out on it.

In one swift movement, he picked up the ampoule in the tray and substituted it with the one that had been in his pocket. The only difference between the two ampoules was that the one in his pocket was warm, but he was sure that no one would notice. Right then, he thought. Let's go fishing and see if we catch anything. His heart raced as he walked towards the back of the tent to join the staff who were watching the medical team working. He couldn't wait to see what happened next.

13

All Lizzie wanted to do was get to the TRT tent and have a shower, but she had to get the Land Rover unloaded first. She knew that all of them felt just as uncomfortable, but she was feeling particularly sorry for herself. Her shoulder still ached from carrying the stretcher earlier, but there was no way that she would admit that to any of the others. Lizzie knew full well that if she did then Ronald would get all protective and masculine, and Adams would just take the piss. But as the only woman working on the TRT, she wasn't going to give any of them the opportunity to treat her any differently. She stepped up onto the ramp and walked back into the helicopter to join Ronald who was just doing a final sweep.

'There's a bit of blood on the floor just here,' Ronald said, pointing at a dark red stain near to where the patient had been lying. 'Nothing drastic though. I'll come back down later with a spill kit and sort it out.'

'Okay, mate,' Lizzie replied. 'Let me know if you want me to come with you.'

'What, so you can sit there and watch me work? That's

what you did last time.'

'Yeah, whatever,' Lizzie laughed. 'Come on, let's do one. They should have made the tea by now. But if the bloody Colonel's made it like he did last time, I swear, I won't be happy.'

'He's just using the cooking trick,' Ronald said.

'What do you mean?'

'Like when you cook something so badly that you never get asked to do it again.'

Lizzie rolled her eyes at Ronald and walked back down the helicopter into the heat. She stepped off the helicopter and saw the pilot and the loadmaster having an intense discussion by the side of the helicopter. As he saw Lizzie step down from the ramp, the pilot beckoned her over to them.

'You okay, sir?' Lizzie said as she walked up to them. A few seconds later, Ronald joined them.

'Hi chaps,' the pilot said. 'You know Kinkers, don't you?' He gestured at the loadmaster standing next to him, and for the first time, Lizzie realised that he wasn't wearing a British uniform. The pattern on his camouflage uniform was slightly different to theirs, and on the top of his shoulder was a small Australian flag. 'Kinkers, this is Lizzie and Ronald.'

'G'day,' the loadmaster said, his eyes fixed firmly on Lizzie, before starting to laugh. 'Sorry, I know it's a cliché, but I can't help it.'

'Blimey, you're a long way from home,' Lizzie replied, admiring his blonde hair and triangular shoulders. He would look very good on the beach, she suspected.

'Yeah, well,' the loadmaster said, leaning back on the side of the helicopter, winking at Ronald before giving Lizzie a lazy grin. 'I heard the women in the British military were way better looking than in ours.'

'Jesus, Kinkers,' Davies said, shoving Kinkers in the side. 'You're so full of shit, you know that? If your wife heard you say that, she'd beat you senseless.'

'Bloody right there, mate,' Kinkers replied, his blue eyes twinkling at Lizzie.

'Well, I'm pleased to meet you, anyway,' Lizzie said, returning his smile as she wished more British men had teeth like the Australian's. 'It's normally a bit noisy when we're working together, so it's nice to have a proper conversation.'

'I don't think he knows what a proper conversation is,' Davies laughed.

'Hey Lizzie,' Kinkers replied. 'Just ignore the taxi driver in the baby-grow and look at this.' He pointed to a small hole in the fuselage of the helicopter. 'See that hole?'

'Er, yes,' Lizzie replied. Ronald leaned in for a closer look at the area that the loadmaster was pointing at.

'Well, that's not supposed to be there. And it wasn't there when we took off. Nor was this one, or this one, or this one.' Kinkers pointed out a line of similar holes. He knelt and looked under the helicopter. 'There's more here. These are the entry holes here, and the ones on the side are the exit ones. You can tell by the way the metal edges go.'

'Fuck,' Ronald whispered. 'Sorry, I mean—'

'No, no. You're right.' Davies cut Ronald off with a wave of his hand. 'That's what I said when I saw them. There must have been someone in those trees after all, and they've had a pop as we took off and banked. That would fit. It's not like we could have heard them, and there was no-one left on the ground.' The pilot patted the side of the helicopter. 'We'll have to ground her. And I'll get the engineers to take a look and patch her up. I don't think there's much in this area to get damaged though, so she should be okay. In the meantime, if we get another shout, we'll have to take Thunderbird 2.' Davies pointed in the direction of another Chinook sitting on the pan a few hundred yards away. He turned to Ronald and Lizzie. 'Have you got any idea how much paperwork this means?'

Ronald and Lizzie said goodbye to the aircrew and climbed into the Land Rover. Lizzie sat in the driver's seat, looking across at Davies and Kinkers who were still looking at the underside of the Chinook. She jumped as Ronald slapped her thigh.

'Jesus wept, Lizzie,' he said. 'Would you stop staring at the Australian bloke. Did you see those bloody holes?'

'Er, yes,' she replied, turning to look at him. 'I did. I was standing next to you.'

'For fuck's sake. Those rounds could have gone anywhere.'

'I know,' Lizzie said. 'I know.'

'Ok, everyone ready? One, two, three.' Corporal Emma Wardle looked at Squadron Leader Webb as he counted down to coordinate moving the casualty from the canvas stretcher to the trolley in the emergency department.

On 'three', the medical team smoothly dragged Perry from the stretcher and onto the trolley. Emma had one hand grabbing his left shoulder, and the other clutching his belt. She tried not to look at the shattered stump of his left leg as he was moved across to the trolley. Emma looked up at the anaesthetist next to her to see if there was anything that he needed her to do. He looked up at her and gave her a quick thumbs up to let her know that all was good.

Emma reached across Perry and picked up the intravenous bag that had been put in between his legs during the transfer from the helicopter. Hanging it up on the stand attached to the trolley, she opened the valve on the line to get the fluid flowing. She frowned as she realised that there were no drips in the plastic chamber just below the bag. Looking down at the cannula in Perry's arm, she squeezed the rubber plug to try to clear whatever was blocking the line. Emma looked back up at the drip chamber, but there was still no sign of any movement.

She turned to her left and saw Major Clarke standing next to her. Without a word, he pulled a pen out his pocket and started to wind the tubing of the intravenous drip around the pen.

'Bit of an old trick this one,' he said. 'It pushes fluid down towards the cannula, sometimes clears it without the need for a flush.' He unwound the tubing from the pen and they both looked up at the chamber. Nothing. 'Just flush it would you, Corporal?' Squadron Leader Webb barked, making Emma jump.

Fingers trembling, she picked up the plastic ampoule from the pulpwood tray on the work table next to her, along with a syringe. She squinted slightly to read the minute text written on the side.

'Could you check this for me, sir?' she said to Major Clarke. Holding the ampoule so that they could both read the text, she continued, 'Normal saline, still in date.'

'Yep, got that,' he replied, before continuing in a quiet whisper. 'Just ignore Webb. You're doing fine.'

Emma twisted the top off the ampoule and transferred the clear liquid inside to a syringe. She flipped the small cap on top of the cannula and inserted the top of the syringe into it before pushing down on the plunger, watching the area around the cannula carefully for any signs that the small plastic tube inside Perry's vein had become dislodged while he was being transferred. There was no swelling around the cannula, so she emptied the syringe and disconnected it from the cannula. A quick glance at the chamber underneath the intravenous fluid bag showed the liquid dripping as it was supposed to.

Major Clarke walked back to his vantage point in the corner of the Emergency Room. As he passed the combat medical technician who was acting as scribe for the day, he paused.

'Did you get that? 10ml saline flush, left antecubital fossa,' Emma heard him say to the medic, who dutifully wrote it down on the chart.

Adams and Colonel Nick stood in the corner of the Emergency Room, both sipping water from plastic bottles as Major Clarke walked back across to join them.

'She's a bit green, that one.' he said, nodding towards Emma. 'But she's doing okay.' Adams looked across at Emma. He'd never say anything, but the young nurse was very attractive. Adams's thoughts were interrupted as the casualty on the trolley sat bolt upright and started shouting. He saw Emma jump back as Perry sat up before recovering and grabbing his hand with one of hers as she gently started to push him back towards the trolley. On the other side of the trolley, one of the other nurses was doing the same thing.

Adams couldn't make out what Perry was saying, but he was becoming increasingly agitated and thrashing around.

'For fuck's sake,' Major Clarke said, setting off toward the trolley. 'Come on, let's give them a hand.'

'What's going on?' Colonel Nick said, to no one in particular as they spread out around the trolley. 'My God, he's white as a sheet,' he continued. Adams was standing next to Emma, whose hands were shaking as she tried to hold onto Perry's arm.

'Here,' Adams said to her. 'Let me help.' He took Perry's arm to keep it steady. Adams nodded towards the monitor, saying to Emma, 'Get some up to date vitals. He's going off by the looks of it.' Emma reached up to the monitor and pressed the button that would measure Perry's blood pressure.

'Pulse, one seventy-five,' she said, loudly enough for the scribe and the rest of the team to hear. 'Sats, er, not sure.' Emma scrabbled around the trolley to find the oxygen saturation probe which had detached itself as Perry thrashed around.

'They were in the high nineties,' Adams heard the anaesthetist say as they both looked at the oxygen flow meter to make sure that there was still plenty of gas. The monitor bleeped to signify that it had finished taking Perry's blood pressure.

'Fucking hell,' Major Clarke said. 'Two forty over one ninety-five. That can't be right.' Adams saw Major Clarke look at Squadron Leader Webb and Colonel Nick in quick succession before turning back to Emma. 'Take it again.' She pressed the button again on the monitor, and the team all looked towards it, waiting to see what the new reading would be.

While they waited, Adams moved across to the resuscitation trolley and opened a drawer marked 'Blood Gases'. He picked the plastic ampoule and syringe that Emma had used to flush the cannula and put them both into the sharps bin that was attached to the trolley, replacing them instead with the arterial blood gas syringe he knew was about to be asked for. Adams tapped Emma on the elbow and nodded toward the syringe on the trolley.

'Oh, thanks sir,' she said with a very brief smile.

The new reading was just as high. Knowing that this meant it was unlikely to have been caused by the patient thrashing around on the trolley, Adams started to run through a mental checklist. Perry's symptoms just didn't make sense. The quick heart rate could be a loss in blood volume, but then the blood pressure wouldn't be through the roof. It would be going in the other direction. He glanced up towards the screen, just in time to see an unusually large heartbeat register on the electrocardiograph screen.

'He's throwing off ectopics,' Colonel Nick said, pointing at the screen. Webb looked at the screen, concern creasing his brow. 'There's another one,' Colonel Nick continued as the line on the screen lurched again.

'Shit, shit, shit,' Webb muttered. 'Right, get me a blood gas set,' he said, looking at Emma who already had the tray in her hands.

'There you go, sir,' she said, offering him the tray, her hands still shaking. Adams caught Emma's eye. She might look terrified, he thought, but as Major Clarke had said, she was doing okay. While Webb put the needle onto the end of the syringe for the blood gases, Adams whispered in Emma's ear.

'Hold his hand still, palm up so that the Squadron Leader can do the gases.' Emma nodded in agreement and, by the time Webb turned back with the fully assembled syringe, she had Perry's arm in exactly the right position for the blood gases.

Webb pushed the needle into Perry's wrist, trying to find the radial artery.

'Come on, come on,' he whispered. Adams looked at the screen above their heads.

'He's firing off salvos of ectopics now,' Colonel Nick

said. 'Major Clarke, can you grab the crash trolley, please? I think he's going to arrest.' Clarke hurried away to get the emergency trolley with the defibrillator and the drugs that would be needed for a cardiac arrest.

'Yes,' Webb said with relief a second later as the needle punctured the radial artery and the syringe attached to it filled with bright red, frothy blood. When the syringe was full, he pulled it out and pushed a gauze pad onto the puncture site. 'Press here,' he snapped at Emma. 'Hard.'

'Yes sir,' Emma replied. Clutching the syringe, Webb rushed across to the blood gas machine in the corner of the tent.

As Major Clarke arrived with the crash trolley, Adams could see longer runs of ventricular tachycardia on the monitor.

'What is going on?' Adams said to both Colonel Nick and the anaesthetist as they all watched the irregular jagged beats continue across the small screen. Adams heard a gurgle and looked down at Perry at the same time as the anaesthetist. There was pink, frothy sputum at the corners of Perry's mouth.

'Shit,' the anaesthetist said. 'Pulmonary oedema. I'm going to have to tube him.' He turned to Major Clarke. 'Can you get the kit ready for a rapid sequence....'

'Nope, he's in VF,' Colonel Nick said, eyes fixed on the flat line on the screen. 'Webb?' he called across the room to the other doctor who was standing by the blood gas machine, waiting for the results. 'He's arrested.'

'Bollocks,' Webb said, running back across to join them. 'Get those results when they come out,' he ordered one of the medical technicians standing near the machine. Webb stared for a second at the wavy line on the monitor.

'Fuck,' Webb repeated. 'Oh fuck.'

14

Lizzie put the Land Rover into gear and set off towards the hospital at the other end of the camp. She turned to Ronald in the passenger seat.

'That's really shaken me, mate, to be honest.'

'Me too, Lizzie,' Ronald replied. 'Like you said, those rounds could have gone anywhere.'

'I didn't hear anything though. Did you?'

'Nope, not a thing. Must have been when we were landing or taking off, do you think? I know the FP boys were getting a bit excited about some movement in the trees near the HLS. The captain was talking about it over the radio.'

'That explains the cheeky take off then,' Lizzie said. 'I thought the Colonel was going to fall over when we banked around.' Lizzie looked at Ronald and smiled. 'Now, that would have been funny,' she said, laughing.

They drove on in silence. Lizzie thought about whether to put what had happened today into her diary. She'd been keeping one religiously since she'd arrived in Afghanistan but was careful what she wrote in it, knowing full well that if anything did happen to her, her family would be reading it at some point. She could always have a chat with Adams and see what he thought. As they drove past the main camp headquarters, Ronald turned to her.

'Nice and slowly here, Lizzie. Best not upset the grown-ups.' She laughed at his comment and slowed right down as they went past the HQ of the main base. They both stared dead ahead as the Land Rover crept past. Lizzie tried to see out of the corner of her eye whether the Garrison Sergeant Major was looking out of one of the windows of the HQ building, but she couldn't see anything. *Just as well*, she thought. She'd probably burst out laughing, which he probably wouldn't find funny in the slightest.

'Is he watching?' Ronald asked.

'Can't see him,' Lizzie said, trying to keep a straight face just in case the GSM was hiding somewhere, waiting to catch them. As they passed the HQ, she sped back up again.

They arrived at the parking bay at the back of the TRT tent, and Lizzie reversed the Land Rover into its allocated space. She would have preferred just to drive straight in — reversing wasn't her strongest skill as Adams never failed to point out — but the camp rules were that all vehicles were to be reversed into their spaces.

'Very good, mate,' Ronald said as they both hopped out of the Land Rover. 'You're getting better every day.'

'Oh piss off, Ronald,' Lizzie replied with a smile. 'Now move. Ladies first.' She pushed in front of Ronald and into the tent, sighing with relief as the cold air-conditioned air washed over her.

'Oh for God's sake, they've not even made the bloody tea!' Lizzie exclaimed. 'Mind you, after last time, it's probably just as well.'

'Their kit's not here either,' Ronald said. 'They must still be down in the Emergency Room. Shall we go down there and give them grief?'

'Sounds like a plan to me,' Lizzie replied, flicking the switch on the kettle as she walked past it.

As they walked down the dark corridor in the central spine of the hospital, Lizzie was almost pushed into the wall by a nurse running out of the intensive care unit and down towards the Emergency Room. Lizzie was about to shout something at his back when she heard raised voices coming from the flaps that led to the Emergency Room. Followed by Ronald, she pushed past the same flaps that the nurse had just burst through.

Inside the normally quiet and controlled department was a scene of hurried activity as the medical team worked on the casualty on the trolley. A medic was astride the patient, administering cardiac compressions, while other members of the team rushed around the equipment. To her horror, Lizzie realised that the casualty on the trolley was the one that they had just delivered to the hospital.

Adams looked down at the lifeless body of Perry on the trolley, whose arms were jerking with each cardiac compression.

'You okay?' he asked Corporal Wardle who was standing right next to him. Almost too close. 'They're about to call it anyway. I'm just going over there to talk to my oppos.' Corporal Wardle nodded, her eyes teary, and Adams walked across the room to join Lizzie and Ronald.

'He went off a couple of minutes after we got him in here,' Adams said to them both. 'Sat bolt upright, started shouting, then bang. He was in VF. We must have been working on him for fifteen or twenty minutes, and he's not responded to anything. He's been in asystole for a while now, so I reckon that they're about to call it.' Adams nodded towards Squadron Leader Webb, Major Clarke, and the anaesthetist, who were huddled deep in conversation a few feet away from the trolley.

Squadron Leader Webb turned away from the group and spoke to everyone in the room.

'Right, Ladies and Gents. He's been in asystole for nearly fifteen minutes, not responded to anything. Unless anyone disagrees, we're calling it.' Adams watched as the Squadron Leader looked around the room. No one said a word. Webb looked at his watch. 'Time of death, 14.21.'

Adams tapped Lizzie on the forearm.

'Lizzie,' he said. She didn't respond but was just staring at the casualty. He tapped her arm again. 'Lizzie?'

'Sorry, yep?' she replied.

'Can you keep a close eye on Corporal Wardle, mate. She's really shaky.' They both looked across at Emma, who looked as if she was just about to burst into tears.

'Of course,' Lizzie said. 'Of course I will.' Adams walked back across the room and collected his equipment, returning to where Lizzie and Ronald were standing. Colonel Nick was a few feet behind him, with his equipment already in his hands. Adams walked through the doors of the Emergency Room, followed by the rest of the team.

As they walked into the TRT tent, Adams put his kit on the floor and sat down in one of the green canvas chairs with a thud. Colonel Nick put his kit down next to Adams's and went to the kettle to make the tea.

Adams waited until everyone was sitting down and the Colonel had done the business with the kettle and watched as Lizzie took a tentative sip of her tea. On any other day, the grimace on her face as she tasted it would have been funny. 'We were always going to lose one sooner or later,' he said to the group in general. 'And we did get him to the Emergency Room. He was alive when we got him in.'

'That doesn't make a blind bit of fucking difference!' Ronald exclaimed.

'Ronald,' Adams said, noticing Lizzie flinch at Ronald's words.

'Sorry, sir, but he's still fucking dead.'

'Got that, Corporal MacDonald,' Adams said, sharply. 'Thank you.' Adams didn't use rank that often for his subordinates, and when he did, it was a clear message that one of them was talking out of turn. Adams fixed Ronald with a stare before turning to Colonel Nick.

'What do you think happened then? He just went off in the space of a couple of seconds.'

'Young, fit bloke. No co-morbidity,' Colonel Nick replied. 'People like him can compensate for quite a lot longer than you think. Then the body just gets to a point and gives up.'

'I guess,' Adams replied. 'But I thought he was doing okay.'

'He was stable in the helicopter,' Lizzie chipped in. 'I mean, yeah, horrendous injuries. But that is a shock.' She reached across and squeezed Ronald's knee. Adams caught the sympathetic expression on Lizzie's face as she looked at Ronald, and he loved her for it.

'I don't get the hypertension, though,' Adams said.

'What, when?' Ronald asked.

'Just before he arrested, his blood pressure went through the roof. I thought it was the cuff at first, he was wriggling around a fair bit, but it wasn't that,' Adams said. 'Then a few seconds later he went into VF after a run of ectopics. One of them must have hit the T wave.' Seeing the surprised expression on Colonel Nick's face as he said this, he added, 'I've seen it before. We had a motorcyclist back in Birmingham who'd come second in a fight with a lorry. Smashed himself right up, internal bleeding, the works. He had a run of ectopics, and then went straight into VF. I was talking to Professor Middlebrook about it afterwards and he was explaining it.'

'Oh, right,' Colonel Nick said. 'Middlebrook's a good bloke. He was my mentor when I was doing my emergency medicine rotation.'

'Mind you,' Adams continued, not wanting the Colonel to go off down a rabbit hole, 'we shocked the motorcyclist straight back out of it, and he went to theatre. I can't remember what they found, but they patched him up okay in the end.'

'Our chap had the full protocol,' Colonel Nick said. 'There was nothing else that could be done.'

Adams stood up, stretched, and walked across to the sink to wash up his cup. As he emptied the rancid tea down the sink, he tried to do it quietly so that Colonel Nick wouldn't notice. It probably wasn't the time to take the piss out of him about his poor skills in the tea making department. Adams turned to the others.

'Right, Ronald?' Ronald turned and looked at Adams. 'Can you throw the kit into the back of the wagon? I'll come down to stores with you to do the re-stock.' Without a word, Ronald picked up the bags and walked out of the rear doors of the TRT tent.

'Is he okay, do you think?' Lizzie asked Adams.

'He'll be fine,' Adams replied. He'd been surprised by Ronald's outburst as he was normally by far the most placid member of the team and he didn't think he'd ever heard him swear before. Adams wanted to have a quiet chat with him, and during the re-stock would be a good opportunity.

'I'm going to grab a quick shower,' Colonel Nick said, getting to his feet and heading towards the door. Adams knew he needed one as well, but figured he could have one later.

'Sir?' Adams called out to the Colonel. 'Shall we all meet back here in half an hour? We can go down to the coffee shop and do the formal debrief there.'

'Sounds like a plan to me,' the Colonel replied as he left the tent. 'I'll see you both then.'

When it was just the two of them in the TRT tent, Adams crossed to where Lizzie was sitting.

'Well, that was all a bit shit,' he said, looking at her. Lizzie glanced up at him and he could see tears pricking the corners of her eyes.

'Don't say anything else,' she replied in a quiet voice. 'Not about what happened back there.' She nodded in the direction of the ER and a fat tear escaped, rolling its way down her cheek.

'It's okay to be upset, Lizzie,' Adams said. 'It's what makes you human.'

Lizzie put her hands over her face, and her shoulders heaved.

'It's not fair, Adams,' she replied through the sobs. He leaned over and pulled her into a tight hug. They sat in silence for a few moments, perched awkwardly on the canvas chairs.

'I stink,' Lizzie said, pulling her hands away from her face and wiping her nose with a crumpled tissue.

'I know,' Adams replied. 'You smell like a male changing room after football.'

'Oh, thanks,' she said with a wry grin. 'You're not any better yourself.'

'Maybe you should go and find Emma and make sure that she's okay. I know Major Clarke is around somewhere, but he'll probably be too busy trying to catch a sneaky look down her scrubs to be that sympathetic. She might need a shoulder to cry on?'

'Don't we all,' Lizzie replied with a grateful smile at Adams. 'Don't we all.'

15

W ell, that had gone a lot better than he was expecting. He was sitting in the toilets, which was the only place in the entire hospital where he could get some proper privacy. It was fitting, he thought, to be sitting here in the same place as he had prepared his tools for the job. The job that was now finished. It had gone perfectly as far as he was concerned. The switch of the ampoule had been seamless, the timing had been just right when everyone was focused on moving the casualty. And now all the evidence was safely hidden in a clinical sharps bin which would be incinerated within a couple of days. No one would be looking in there, even if they knew that a crime had taken place. One of the few advantages of being in this God forsaken place was that the last thing anyone wanted was bags of clinical waste hanging around in the heat. They got incinerated in a far corner of the compound where the stench from the smoke wouldn't drift back over the base, and as far as he knew, the bags were burnt every night. Grinning in the cubicle, he allowed himself a few moments to reflect on his achievement. There had been some talk a few days ago about installing video cameras in the Emergency Room bays so that they could replay trauma calls, supposedly to learn from them. That would be one video he would watch over and over again if he had the chance. It was a shame that nothing had come of the conversation. When the military could barely afford bullets, the last thing they were going to spend any money on was video cameras for a hospital.

He thought back to the nurse who'd killed the soldier on his behalf. Corporal Emma Wardle. Blonde hair, an innocent looking face like butter wouldn't melt. A tiny nose with a dusting of freckles and full lips made for a lot more than just talking. She was beautiful, and she'd killed for him. He felt himself growing harder as he thought about her. He wondered what her sex face looked like. Would she be noisy, or would she moan softly? He shifted on the toilet seat to relieve the discomfort in his trousers, thinking about and dismissing straight away the idea of relieving himself properly in the toilet. He'd go to his usual spot later, he thought. There were a couple of Portaloos around the back of the hospital that were rarely used and were in an area where no-one went, especially at night as it was pitch black. He'd go there this evening and relieve that particular pressure. But he knew who he'd be thinking about.

When the soldier sat up and started shouting, he'd jumped along with most of the other people in the Emergency Room. He'd not been expecting that, nor had he expected the soldier to arrest so quickly. He'd done plenty of homework into the effects of adrenaline overdose and knew that it would be quick to take effect, but he'd not expected it to be almost immediate. He didn't even know if it would actually kill the casualty or not, although he thought it probably would. Well, he knew the answer to that one now.

There would be a post-mortem of course. The dead soldier would be boxed up and shipped home before being paraded through the streets wrapped in a red, white, and blue union flag. But he wasn't worried about a post-mortem. He was sure that the fact the soldier's leg had been hanging off would be enough for the coroner. That was why he didn't use the ampoule on the earlier casualty. He was badly injured, but it was only a chest wound. Very survivable. If he'd killed him, it might be more obvious that he'd been murdered. But even then, it would take an eagle-eyed pathologist to notice. He got to his feet and flushed the toilet, grinning again as he opened the cubicle door before walking to the sink to wash his hands even though he'd not actually used the toilet. Just in case anyone came in.

He wasn't even worried about a toxicology screen. What was the first drug that was used in a cardiac arrest? Adrenaline. The soldier would be full of it.

16

Emma Wardle was trying really hard not to start crying in the Emergency Room. She was working with Major Clarke to get Perry's body ready to be taken to the morgue and struggling to keep her emotions in check.

'Emma,' Major Clarke said in a soft voice. 'I can get someone else to give me a hand with this if you want?'

'No, thanks, sir,' Emma replied. 'I'll be fine. I want to do it.' She didn't want to be treated with kid gloves. Even though she knew that the Major was doing what he thought was the right thing to do, Emma didn't want to be treated any differently just because she was a woman. She was fairly sure that he wouldn't talk to a male nurse that way.

'Okay, only if you're sure though. I'll go and get the body bag, and a couple of med techs to help us roll him.' Major Clarke wandered out into the store at the back of the Emergency Room, leaving Emma to her thoughts.

Alone with Perry, Emma looked down at his face and stroked his cheek with her gloved hand.

'You poor bastard,' she murmured. *He was so young*, she

thought. She'd never met him before, but she felt a strong connection with the dead soldier. She'd noticed a similar thing before, but with older people who'd died. Never with someone who was a similar age to herself. Emma wondered if he had any brothers or sisters, or a girlfriend. His family, his loved ones, were going to be devastated when they found out what had happened to him.

Clarke walked back into the room carrying a thick rubber black body bag, followed by a couple of sheepish-looking medical technicians. They clearly didn't want to be there, but Clarke was a Major and they were both junior ranks so that was that.

'Right,' Clarke said. 'Corporal Wardle, can you make sure that all the various medical bits and pieces are properly secured? They'll need to be in the same place when he gets back home.'

Pleased to have something to do, Emma picked up some surgical tape from the trolley next to her and started taping down the cannula in Perry's left arm. Clarke unrolled the body bag next to Perry's body and started to give instructions to the others how to roll him into the bag.

'On three, roll him onto his side towards you. I'll tuck half of the bag under him, then roll him back. Then he goes over the other way so you two come around this side for that bit. Right?' Both the medical technicians nodded. Emma was used to this manoeuvre as a nurse, but she figured that Clarke was just making sure that the med techs knew what to do. This probably wasn't something they'd ever done before.

'One, two, three,' Clarke counted. The team rolled Perry onto his side, and Clarke did exactly what he said he was going to do. After the second part of the roll, Perry was lying on top of the body bag. Clarke and Emma untucked the rolls of the bag and put Perry's arms across his chest, doing up the industrial zipper on the bag as far as Perry's neck.

'Hold on a second, sir,' Emma said. Clarke stopped what he was doing and let go of the zip. Emma looked across at Clarke and said, 'Thanks.' She looked down at Perry's eyes, now closed with a strip of surgical tape across them. Looking up at Clarke, she said 'Can I…?'

'Of course, you can,' he replied.

Emma reached out her hand and took the zip in her fingers. She gently closed the body bag over Perry's face.

Adams walked into the equipment store and dumped the medical bags onto a counter. He crossed his arms and turned to Ronald.

'Right, mate. We've got half an hour. Let's get these squared away as soon as we can. But we do need a little chat first, I think.'

'Yep, okay,' Ronald said, looking nervous. Adams knew that Ronald knew what was coming, but it wasn't going to make any difference to the conversation. 'Er Adams, about what I said back in the tent, I–'

'Just wait a second and listen in,' Adams cut him off, staring at Ronald until he nodded in agreement. 'What you said back there was bang out of order. I've just left Sergeant Jarman in tears over the whole sorry incident, and you bumping your gums like that doesn't help.'

'I know, but–'

'McDonald, zip it. I'm talking, you're listening.' Adams waited for a few seconds before continuing. 'Now we're a team, all four of us. That means we work together as a team, and sniping at each other isn't how we work. If you need to let off steam, then you wait until it's just you and me, or you and Lizzie if that works better for you. But when we're together, then you stay professional at all times. Do you understand?'

'Yes, sir,' Ronald replied with a baleful look. Adams pointed at a chair. 'Sit down, mate, and consider yourself bollocked. I've done my officer bit. Now, do you want to talk about what happened? As Adams and Ronald?'

'Not really, sir.' Adams gave Ronald a reproachful look.

'Ronald, I've told you before. If I'm not bollocking you and it's just us around, then it's Adams. Every time you call me sir it makes me feel old.'

'Okay, got it.'

'But if you do want to chat, as mates, then you know where I am.' Ronald nodded and picked up one of the medical bags.

'Er, Adams?' he said a couple of seconds later.

'Yep?'

'I'm sorry about what I said. I'll make sure I say the same thing to the others as well. It won't happen again.'

'We're all good, Ronald. That would be the right thing to do, though. You're allowed to be upset. Wouldn't be human if you weren't,' Adams replied. 'I just said exactly the same thing to Lizzie. Now come on, let's get these bags packed.'

The two men worked together in silence for a few moments, replenishing the medical bags with the equipment that had been used during the flight back to the hospital. Each bag had a contents list which they worked their way down. If something that was on the list wasn't in the bag, then they'd go and get it from the wooden shelves that were lined with box after box of medical equipment.

'Did Lizzie tell you about the helicopter?' Ronald asked Adams. 'I forgot to mention it.'

'No,' Adams replied. 'What? Has Flight Lieutenant Davies broken it or something?'

'No, it's not that. There's a load of bloody bullet holes in it, though.' Adams stopped what he was doing and looked at Ronald.

'Seriously?' he asked.

'Yep, there's a line of them along the bottom. Davies was saying it was probably when he took off and banked around. No one heard anything, and he didn't realise until we got back.'

'Jesus,' Adams said. 'That could have been nasty.' It wasn't just the thought of people on board the helicopter being hurt that got to Adams. He was only too aware that a single round in the wrong place could bring an aircraft down. It had happened before the previous year in Iraq with a Hercules transport plane that had been brought down by small arms fire.

They both fell silent, lost in their own thoughts as they repacked the bags for the next shout. About twenty minutes later, they swapped bags and quickly started going through them again. Nothing could be left to chance. Adams looked across at Ronald when they had finished.

'Right then. Let's get these back into the tent and go for some coffee.'

Lizzie wrapped the towel around herself as she stepped out of the shower. *What a day*, she thought. She couldn't wait to get into bed and go to sleep. Although the camp cots that they were given weren't exactly beds as such, they were comfortable enough. Lizzie couldn't work out why they'd all been issued with mosquito nets, though. She'd not seen a single mosquito since she'd arrived, and talking to one of the environmental health techies in the hospital, there probably wasn't one within about a hundred miles. Still, she reflected, they gave them a bit of privacy.

Lizzie walked back into the accommodation tent where Emma was just getting undressed. There were normally four of them in the room, but one of their roommates was back in the United Kingdom on her 'Rest and Recupera-tion' week — one of their favourite topics of discussion in the evenings was what they had planned for their R&R — and the other one was working nights.

'Shower's free, mate,' Lizzie said. They only had one female shower in the block. The hospital had more women working in it than most military units, but they were still far outnumbered by the men. There'd been at least one embarrassing incident in the showers despite the signs on the door.

'Cheers, Lizzie,' Emma replied. 'Is the shampoo still in there?'

'Yeah, fill your boots.'

'Thanks, mate. I should be getting a parcel in the next few days off my mum with some more,' Emma said. 'I'll pay you back.'

'No worries.' Lizzie waved her hand and sat down on her camp cot. 'How's she doing?' Just before Emma had left for Afghanistan, her mother had been called back to the local hospital to be told that she had a suspicious looking shadow on her mammogram. As far as Lizzie knew, she was the only person who Emma had told.

'It's difficult to tell when you only get twenty minutes a week on the phone,' Emma replied, 'and according to her letters, everything's fine. Which I know it's not.' Lizzie paused for a second, not quite sure what to say. She looked at her room-mate's face and decided not to say anything. If Emma wanted to talk about it, she would.

Once Emma had left for the shower, Lizzie took the towel off and put her pyjamas on. She reached into the plastic box under her cot with most of her possessions and retrieved her diary before starting to write.

A few minutes later, Emma came back dressed as Lizzie had been earlier with only a towel. Lizzie carried on writing as Emma put her pyjamas on, thinking about how Emma didn't care about being naked in front of any of the other women in the tent. Mind you, Lizzie thought, if she had a figure like Emma's she probably wouldn't care either. Lizzie paused, wondering again how best to write about the bullet holes to the helicopter in her diary. In the end, she decided to go with a vague reference to 'damage to the underneath'. When she was reading it back in the future, that would be enough to remind her what had happened. But if someone else was reading it, they wouldn't know what the damage was from. The only problem with this plan is that it didn't give her the opportunity to write about how the damage had frightened the shit out of her.

The two women chatted about nothing in particular for the rest of the evening. It wasn't as if they could chill out in front of a television and have a couple of glasses of wine, after all. Lizzie was waiting for Emma to bring up the subject of the soldier who'd died earlier that day, but she didn't. Lizzie thought that perhaps, like with her mother being unwell, Emma didn't want to talk about it now. She would when she was ready, so Lizzie didn't press it.

'You ready for lights out, mate?' she asked Emma a while later.

'Go for it,' Emma replied. 'I'm knackered.' Lizzie crossed to the door of the tent and turned out the lights. A soft glow from some floodlights outside gave her just enough light to get back to her cot without stumbling into anything. She climbed into her sleeping bag and zipped up the mosquito net.

'Night then. Chat tomorrow,' Lizzie said. Emma mumbled something in reply, but Lizzie couldn't make it out. She lay back, made herself as comfortable as she could, and went straight to sleep.

At some point during the night, Lizzie woke up. *Crap*, she thought. One thing she didn't need was bloody insomnia on top of everything else. She turned over in bed and saw Emma sitting on the edge of her own cot, her hands covering her face.

'You okay, Emma?' Lizzie whispered.

'Nope,' Emma said. She took her hands away from her face and Lizzie could see through the faint light that her face was streaked with tears. 'I'm not okay.'

Lizzie unzipped her sleeping bag and mosquito net and went over to sit next to Emma, putting an arm around her shoulders as she did so. Emma started crying properly, the sobs wracking her body.

'It's not fair, Lizzie,' Emma sobbed. 'It's not fucking fair. He was only a kid. He was younger than me.'

'I know,' Lizzie said, remembering her earlier conversation with Adams. 'It's shit. It's not fair, you're right.' Lizzie stroked Emma's hair as if she was a small child, and said nothing else. Emma would just have to cry it out. A moment later, Emma continued.

'Do you know what the worst thing is?'

'What's that?'

'I don't even know his bloody first name. I was there when he died, and I don't even know his first name.' Emma started sobbing again as Lizzie held her tightly. 'I looked at his dog tag before I zipped up the body bag to get his proper name, and all it had was an initial on it.'

The two women sat there for a while in the near dark, until Emma started to calm down.

'I'm sorry, mate,' she said to Lizzie. 'Bit stupid, really.'

'Not at all, Emma,' Lizzie replied. 'For fuck's sake, not at all.' Emma reached out to grab some tissues from the cardboard box that served as a bedside table and blew her nose.

'God, I must look a mess,' Emma said.

'Now come on, you look lovely.' They looked at each other. Lizzie continued, 'Do you know what the really funny thing is?'

'What?'

'If we were lesbians, this is the bit where we'd fall into bed and have amazing sex.' Emma looked at Lizzie, with a mock horrified expression which soon gave way to laughter. Composing herself, Emma looked down at her lap, and then back up at Lizzie.

'Lizzie?'

'Yes?'

'Kiss me,' Emma said. Lizzie laughed and slapped Emma on the leg as she got up and walked back to her cot.

'Go back to bed, you silly cow.' As they lay there in the darkness, Lizzie carried on, 'Do you know what Adams said to me a couple of days ago?'

'Er, Lizzie? He's spoken for. And your boss. That's wrong on both counts.'

'No, nothing like that. He said something about seeing Squadron Leader Webb trying to look down the front of your scrubs without you noticing.'

'Oh, piss off, Lizzie,' Emma laughed.

'Well, it proves that it's not just me that's noticed

Webb's got a thing for you. And Adams would know, being a bloke.'

'Whatever.'

'He's probably playing with it now.'

'Adams, or Webb?'

'Maybe both of them? Maybe they're having a competition in their accommodation to see which one–'

'Lizzie. Just shut up and go to sleep,' Emma said. 'You've got a filthy mind. If the single men of Cyprus knew where you're going for your R&R, they'd be quaking in their boots.' Lizzie smiled in the darkness and rolled onto her side.

'I hope so. Night, Emma.'

'Night, mate.'

17

The next day dawned in exactly the same way that every day dawned in Afghanistan in the summer. Hot. Colonel Nick looked down at his watch with disgust. He was slow today.

He'd started running around the perimeter of the base a couple of days after he'd arrived at Camp Bastion. It was almost exactly ten kilometres along a hardened track that had been topped with gravel to make it easier for the Force Protection patrols in their Land Rovers to stay on track. Although there weren't any mines within Camp Bastion, or at least there were none that had been found, it was still reassuring to know that the ground was safe.

Colonel Nick had spent a week or so up at Kandahar before being able to get on a helicopter flight down to Camp Bastion, and there were areas there that were still active minefields. And inside the wire. They were all clearly marked, but he couldn't help but wonder who had marked them and whether or not they really knew what they were doing.

He wiped the sweat from his forehead, which was a

fairly futile thing to do. His lungs hurt, his legs hurt, his head hurt, and he was about five minutes slower than his best time over the ten kilometre track. This was not a good start to the day. Looking at his watch again, he decided that he should just accept the crap time and slow up a bit for the last couple of kilometres. No point getting too hot this early on.

As he jogged, he thought over the events of yesterday. They'd all sat in the coffee shop after the kit had been put together and had what Adams had called a 'cold debrief'. It wasn't exactly much of a coffee shop though, more of a portacabin with a fat, sweaty civilian serving instant crap in polystyrene cups. Lizzie had tried to lighten the mood by asking for a flat white and three cappuccinos, but the miserable bastard behind the counter hadn't even cracked a smile. Mind you, Colonel Nick had thought, the poor bugger probably heard a different version of the same joke a fair few times a day.

The cold debrief was apparently a run through of the day's events, looking at what had worked well, and what hadn't worked well. Adams had explained the debrief process to Colonel Nick not long after he'd arrived, trying to sell it as the latest crew resource management technique. Aircrew used it all the time, apparently. Any incident at all got torn apart in a cold debrief, not to apportion blame as Adams explained it to him as if he was a stupid child, but so that the team could learn and improve.

Well, that was a load of bollocks as far as Nick was concerned. He couldn't see a bunch of aircrew using it after they'd made a smoking hole in the ground. He'd sat there, thinking that it was a complete and utter waste of time, but played along anyway. At least they were only going over the most recent job, as opposed to the earlier one where he and Adams had words. Nick needed to get on with the others, at least on the surface.

The Colonel tried to wipe the sweat off his brow again, but only really succeeded in moving the sweat around his face. He squinted to see how much further he had to run and figured it was probably about a kilometre and a half. *Christ, this is tough going*, he muttered to himself.

He thought about Adams and Lizzie as he carried on pounding the gravel, spurts of dust puffing up behind each step. They were a strange pair, he thought. More like an old bloody married couple than proper professionals. Adams was always 'mate' this, and 'mate' that, even with the juniors. They rarely called him sir, and there was no real respect on either side as far as he could see. Adams would have been weeded out pretty quick at Sandhurst, Nick thought with satisfaction. He probably wouldn't even have made it as far as the front gate. And what the fuck was all that 'must have landed on the T wave' bollocks about? He was a nurse for God's sake. Nick was just waiting for the first time Adams called him 'mate'. He had his response ready and waiting.

Nick wondered if there was any history between Adams and Lizzie. He didn't think there was, but you never knew. Maybe a drunken fumble one night after Exchange Drinks in one of the Messes. He couldn't see anything more than that, if at all. Lizzie didn't strike Nick as the sort of woman who would go for that type of encounter, though. And as far as that idiot 'Ronald' MacDonald went, Nick had tagged him as gay within about ten minutes of meeting him. At least he wasn't one of the ones who flounced about. They had a few of them in the Army, and they couldn't bloody touch them anymore. Nick was sure it was the same in the Air Force as it was in the Navy.

He glanced at his watch again, sighed, and tried his best to pick the pace up.

Adams was sitting in the TRT tent, trying to complete a crossword in one of Lizzie's magazines, when he was disturbed by the flaps to the tent bursting open. He looked up to see Colonel Nick walking in, sweating profusely.

'Hey, Colonel,' he said. 'Good run?' Nick looked at Adams with an incredulous expression.

'No, it wasn't,' he replied. 'Too bloody hot.' Nick walked over to the fridge in the corner of the tent and opened it to grab a bottle of water. 'Want one?' he asked Adams.

'No, ta,' Adams said. 'I've just put one out. Hey, I've got a question for you.'

'What?'

'Six letters, "Cuts up in the office", starts with an "S",'Adams said. Nick took a long drink from the bottle of water and wiped his mouth with the back of his hand.

'Shreds,' Nick replied.

'Bugger, of course it is.'

'Why are you doing Lizzie's crosswords for her, anyway?'

'Just to piss her off, really,' Adams said.

'Aren't the answers in the back though?'

'Well, they are. But that would be cheating.' When Nick walked off towards the main door of the tent grabbing a towel as he went past the laundry pile, Adams was sure he'd heard the Colonel swear under his breath.

A few minutes later, Adams jumped as Lizzie burst in.

'Oi, you bugger. So, it is you. Stop doing my bloody crosswords.' She swatted her hand at Adams's head, who put the magazine down on one of the camp cots and threw the pen on top of it. He raised his hands in mock surrender.

'Alright, alright. Calm down. I'm only trying to help.'

'Well don't, you twat,' she said. Adams laughed in return.

'Oh, you're such a lady,' he replied. 'Make yourself useful and put the kettle on.'

Lizzie walked over to the kettle and flicked the switch before looking curiously in the cups on the sideboard.

'Are these clean?' she asked.

'Relatively speaking, I suppose they are,' Adams replied. Lizzie carried the cups to the sink at the back of the tent and started to rinse them under the tap.

'Where's the Colonel?' she asked him. 'Ronald said he saw him going for a run earlier.'

'Yeah, he's back,' Adams said. 'He came through a while ago, looking like a beetroot, and went for a shower I think.'

'Bloody mad if you ask me,' Lizzie said. 'Running in this heat. It might be early, but it's still sodding hot.'

'Well, he is Army. Tough guy and all that.'

'Whatever.'

'When he gets back, we need to go down to the line. The helicopter's been fixed apparently. And there's a new FP team taking over, so we need to go and try to make friends with them. Can you get Ronald from wherever he's hiding?'

'He's farting about in the Emergency Room. They've got some sort of training session on down there that Major Clarke's running.' Lizzie finished making the tea and walked across to where Adams was sitting. She put the tea down next to him. 'I'll go and get him, then,' she said, grinning, 'while you load the kit into the back of the wagon in case we get a shout.'

As Lizzie walked out of the door of the TRT tent, Adams sighed. He should have seen that coming really. He picked up the magazine and reopened it to the page with the crossword that he'd been doing. The Colonel would be back soon. He could help with the kit.

Lizzie tried not to be too annoyed with Adams as she walked down the central corridor of the hospital towards the Emergency Room. She'd been trying to find out who was doing her crosswords for the last couple of weeks and had narrowed it down to either Adams or Ronald. Her money had been on Ronald though, as half the answers were wrong anyway, and she figured that Ronald wouldn't think to look in the back of the magazine for the answers. She'd given Adams a bit more credit, but she was wrong.

She walked into the Emergency Room tent and stopped as she realised that Major Clarke was still in the middle of the teaching session. Lizzie stood by the door until she managed to catch Ronald's eye. He was sitting next to Emma, who looked as if she was hanging off every word that the Major was saying. Poor thing, Lizzie thought. She'd got no idea about the effect that she had on men. Lizzie had tried to have that chat with her several times, but Emma just wasn't getting it.

Ronald looked up towards Lizzie and, when she managed to catch his eye, she tapped her watch. Ronald nodded and then shrugged his shoulders ever so slightly, telling Lizzie that he was stuck where he was for the time being. Emma looked up at Lizzie as well and gave her a small wave.

Lizzie walked slowly back into the main corridor of the hospital, wondering how she could kill some time before they went down to the helicopter. She didn't want to go back to the TRT tent, as she was still annoyed with Adams and would also have to help load up the Land Rover if she went back there too soon. She ambled down the corridor before deciding to go down to the Ops Room at the far end of the hospital. The main reason for going there, she told herself, was to let the Ops Officer know that they were going down to the pan. It wasn't as if there was a particularly good mobile phone signal where they were, so they had to let the Ops Room know if the TRT was leaving the hospital for any reason, and exactly where they would be. The second reason was that the young Lieutenant in the Ops Room was particularly cute.

Reaching the Ops Room, she knocked on the wooden door. This was about the only secure area in the entire hospital and had a proper door instead of canvas flaps. As she waited for someone to answer the door, she wondered what the point of having a wooden door on a canvas tent was. If anyone wanted to get in, they could just use a Stanley knife on one of the walls and walk straight in. The door was swung open, and a stern face looked out. It wasn't the Lieutenant that she was hoping to see, but the Garrison Sergeant Major.

'What?' he barked.

'Er, hello GSM. Sergeant Jarman from the TRT.'

'Yes, I know who you are,' the GSM replied. 'What do you want? We're busy.'

'Oh, sorry, sir. I just wanted to let the Ops Room know that the TRT's heading down to the pan to do some training with the new FP team. We'll probably be down there until lunchtime, and I'll check back in when—'

'Right, well don't go too far,' the GSM interrupted. 'There're some troops in contact up near Kajaki, so you lot might be needed if it goes tits up.'

'Ok, sir,' Lizzie said. 'Will do.' She turned to walk back to the TRT tent, disappointed that she'd not had the chance to see — let alone talk to — the Lieutenant.

'And don't drive too bloody fast, Jarman,' the GSM added as he closed the door to the Ops Room.

Lizzie wandered back to the TRT tent. When she walked in, Adams was sitting where she'd left him a few minutes ago, still engrossed in her crossword magazine. She glanced to her left and saw all the medical kit still stacked up in the corner. Lizzie put her hands on her hips and pursed her lips.

'For God's sake, Adams,' she said. 'You've not even put the bloody med kit in the wagon.' Marching across to where he was sitting, she grabbed the magazine out of his hands. 'Lazy bastard.'

'For God's sake — sir — is what I think you meant to say,' Adams said, laughing. 'I'm an officer. You're supposed to at least call me sir when you insult me.'

Lizzie rolled the magazine up in her hands and started hitting Adams with it.

'Sir, you are a lazy bastard,' she punctuated each word with a swipe at him.

Adams reached his hands out and grabbed the magazine with one hand, pinching her side with the other. Lizzie laughed and tried to wrestle the magazine from him while also trying to stop him tickling her. She pushed against him as he pulled the magazine away from her until, suddenly off balance, Lizzie stumbled and ended up sitting on the same chair as Adams. She grabbed his tickling hand and was trying to bend his fingers back to make him stop when they both heard a discrete cough from the direction of the door. They looked up together and saw Ronald and Colonel Nick standing at the door to the TRT tent looking at them.

Lizzie felt her face start to colour instantly. She pushed herself to her feet, taking the opportunity to grab the magazine as she did so. Avoiding the incredulous stare of Colonel Nick, she said to Ronald.

'He was doing my crossword.'

18

Ronald picked up the medical bag from the TRT tent and carried it out to the Land Rover. *Well, that was awkward*, he thought. But well worth Lizzie and the Boss's embarrassment just to see the look on Colonel Nick's face.

'Fucking priceless,' he said to himself as he heaved the heavy bag into the back of the Land Rover. Turning around, he found himself face to face with Lizzie. Unable to help himself, he started laughing.

'The fuck are you laughing at, McDonald?' Lizzie asked. Ronald carried on laughing.

'Sorry, Lizzie,' he said, 'but that was bloody priceless. Why were you sitting in Adams's lap?'

'I wasn't,' she replied. 'I was trying to get my magazine back.'

'Bollocks. If there was nothing in it, then you wouldn't have gone like a tomato.'

'Oh, come on, Ronald. You know me. It doesn't take much to make me blush, you know that.'

'Yeah, well. I guess getting caught giving a private dance to your boss would do that,' Ronald replied. Lizzie looked at him and started laughing. Ronald continued, 'Did you see the look on the Colonel's face?'

'Yep.'

'I don't think he likes us much, Lizzie.'

'I don't think he does,' Lizzie said. 'Maybe he's jealous.' Ronald laughed again and turned to Lizzie.

'Well, he's not made of wood, is he?' Lizzie looked at Ronald and started to go red again.

'Shut up, Ronald,' she said, nodding in the direction of the TRT tent. 'They're coming.'

Ronald climbed up into the front seat of the Land Rover and watched the two officers throw their medical bags into the back. Lizzie opened the passenger door and got in, ignoring Ronald who was looking across at her.

'Piss off,' she whispered to him, finally smiling. Ronald looked into the rear-view mirror to make sure that the other two had got on board and put the Land Rover into gear.

'Right then, Sergeant Jarman,' he said. 'Let's go and have a look at this helicopter.'

'Oh, I forgot to say, I spoke to the GSM in the Ops Room. There's a contact going on upcountry somewhere.'

'You'd better let them know in the back.' Ronald nodded towards the rear of the Land Rover. Lizzie turned around and opened up the small window that separated the front cabin and shouted through it.

'Sirs, I was just in the Ops Room at the hospital. Just so you know, there's a contact going on somewhere.' She turned back to face the front, closing the window. 'Well, they look like they're having a right laugh in the back there.'

The window opened up again a few seconds later, and Ronald saw Adams lean his head through as far as he could.

'Question for you, Jarman,' he asked.

'Yes, sir?' Lizzie replied.

'Why's he driving?

'Sorry, sir?'

'Why is Corporal McDonald Driving, Sergeant Jarman?' Ronald looked up in his mirror and caught the mock-serious expression on Adams's face. 'He's not got a blue light license, has he?' Adams continued. 'Even if we don't actually have a blue light?'

'Er.' Lizzie paused for a second. 'On the job training, sir. I'm prepping him for the exam for when he gets back to the UK.' Ronald kept his eyes firmly to the front, knowing that if he looked at either Lizzie or Adams he would start laughing. He heard the window close behind him.

'Slow down, Ronald, for fuck's sake,' Lizzie barked, pointing at a tented complex to the side of the road. 'There's the HQ.'

'I thought you said that the GSM was back in the Ops Room?' Ronald said.

'Doesn't matter, mate,' Lizzie replied. 'He'll still know.'

A few minutes later, the Land Rover pulled up at the side of the helicopter landing site. Colonel Nick opened the door to the back and jumped down. He was irritated that he'd ended up in the bloody back of the Land Rover again, and even more irritated that the two juniors were in the front. He'd thought about raising it with Adams on the way down, but it was too hot and noisy in the back, and being bounced around made it difficult to say anything, let alone have a conversation. Adams didn't look in the slightest bit fussed anyway. One thing he did need to speak to the RAF officer about though was his over-familiarity with the troops. That had to be stopped.

Colonel Nick walked to the front of the Land Rover where Lizzie and Ronald were standing. As Adams walked around to join them, he waved at the pilot who was over by the side of the helicopter. They left their medical kit in the vehicle and walked the couple of hundred yards to where the pilot was standing.

'Hello, sirs,' Davies said as the group of medics reached him. 'Lizzie, Ronald. How're tricks? Are you–'

'We've come to have a look at the damage to the helicopter,' Colonel Nick said, cutting the pilot off. 'Seeing as we were actually in the back when it was damaged, we thought maybe we should have a look, assess the battle damage.' Davies looked at the Colonel blankly in response. 'Is it this one?' Nick asked, nodding at the helicopter they were standing next to.

'Yep, this is her,' the pilot said. 'I've just taken over, so need to finish off my handover checks. Then I'll tell you what the score is, and show you the damage so that you can assess it.' Davies turned his back on Colonel Nick and walked past the FM aerials on the side of the helicopter, flicking them as he walked past.

Colonel Nick knew full well that the pilot was fucking him about. He watched as the Flight Lieutenant knelt down by the huge tyres, checking them with his hands. After running his hands over them, Davies looked at his palms in much the same way that medics did when looking for bleeding.

'Tosser,' Colonel Nick mumbled under his breath. Davies got back to his feet and walked back past them to get to the side door of the helicopter.

'Wheels look good,' he said as he walked past. 'No hydraulic fluid leaking from the brakes.' Colonel Nick was certain that as the pilot walked past to the stairs, he smirked at Adams.

'Where're the toilets, Adams?' Nick asked.

'Over there if it's number one,' Adams replied, nodding at a length of drainpipe a few hundred yards beyond the helicopter pan. The pipe was set into the ground at a forty-five-degree angle with the open end at waist height. 'The indomitable desert rose. It's a bit further if you need a sh–'

'Thank you, Adams,' Nick interrupted, looking at the makeshift urinal and wondering for a moment if he could wait until he got back to the hospital. Even though the drainpipe was buried in the sand and was supposed to drain urine away straight into the ground, desert roses stank at the best of times. In the middle of the day, this one would be eye-watering. So pungent that he would be able to taste it for the rest of the day, no matter how many times he cleaned his teeth.

'Great,' he mumbled as he wandered off, deciding that he couldn't wait.

When Nick got back to the medical team, they were sitting in the shade under the helicopter. Davies was just making his way down the ramp at the back. He nodded at the Colonel, who ignored him on general principle.

'Okay, I give up, Ronald,' Colonel Nick heard Lizzie say. 'What is it that begins with "S"?'

'Sand!' Ronald replied, looking pleased with himself. Nick looked at them incredulously. The idiots were playing 'I-Spy'.

'Ready when you are, sir,' Davies said.

'Finally,' Nick said. 'All your handover checks okay, were they?'

'Peachy creamy, Colonel,' Davies replied with a smile. He patted the side of the helicopter with the flat of his hand. 'She's good to go.'

'This one? I thought it was battle damaged?'

'The engineers are pretty good, sir,' Davies said. 'They worked most of last night to assess the damage, and it was just superficial. No major arteries hit, as it were.' Davies walked towards the rear of the helicopter and pointed at a black square patch on the side. 'That was one of the holes,' he pointed at another similar patch a few inches away. 'That was another.'

Colonel Nick peered closely at the patches on the fuselage.

'Are you having a laugh?' he said to the pilot.

'Er, no sir,' Davies replied.

'But that's bodge tape,' the Colonel said. 'Your engineers have fixed a bunch of bullet holes with bodge tape?'

Staff Sergeant Partridge parked his Land Rover next to the one with the red cross on the side and hopped out. After telling the other soldiers in the Land Rover to stay put, he wandered over to join the small group he could standing by one of the helicopters on the pan.

As he approached, he could see the pilot talking to a Lieutenant Colonel with a red cross on his arm. Partridge coughed to get their attention. As the Colonel turned around, the Staff Sergeant braced up with his arms rigid by his side.

'Sir, Staff Sergeant Partridge from Three Para,' he said.

'At ease, Staff,' Colonel Nick replied. 'What can we do for you?'

'I'm the temporary Force Protection Team, Sir,' Partridge said. 'Well, there's six of us altogether. The rest of them are back in the Land Rover, but I thought I should come down and introduce myself before they all turn up and start scaring people.'

'Good job, Staff. I'm Colonel Hickman. The senior officer on the TRT. Welcome aboard.' He pointed at the other members of the medical team. 'These are the rest of the medics. Flight Lieutenant Adams, Sergeant Jarman, and Corporal McDonald.' Partridge nodded at them in turn.

'Morning, sir. Chaps.' Adams looked at the Staff Sergeant closely.

'Didn't we pick you up with one of your lads the other day?' he asked. 'GSW to the chest?' Partridge nodded.

'Yes sir, that's kind of how I ended up being reassigned to the FP team,' he said. 'Turns out I shouldn't have come back to the hospital with him, according to the CO anyway.' Lizzie started laughing.

'Let me guess,' she said. 'He thinks that as you obviously like helicopters so much, you can fly about on them for a bit?' Partridge nodded, smiling.

'Yes, something like that anyway,' he said. 'His language was a bit more colourful though, to be honest. It'll only be for a day or so, just until we can get a lift back to the forward operating base.'

Partridge looked across at the Flight Lieutenant in the flying suit, who was standing just behind the rest of the group.

'I'm guessing you must be the pilot, sir,' he said.

'Yep, I'm the driver. Davies,' he replied, extending his

hand for a handshake. 'Good to have you aboard. Partridge, was it?'

'Yes, sir, that's me.'

'Anyone call you Alan?' Davies asked.

'Not for long, sir,' Partridge replied with a smile. 'Not for long.'

'Ah, I see,' Davies laughed. 'Okay, so are you and your chaps happy with stage one drills, or do you want me to get the loadmaster to go through them with you?' He was referring to the basic training that all troops had to go through to work in and around helicopters.

'Well, I think we're good sir, but a refresh might be worthwhile. The lads should be down in a minute. I was hoping to do a spot of training with them anyway, bus and de-bus, that sort of thing.

Two loud rings sounded from the direction of the crew tent next to the pan, cutting off any further conversation. Davies turned and started running back towards the tent, while Adams, Lizzie, and Ronald all started running back towards the Land Rover.

'Come on, sir,' Partridge heard Adams shouting back across his shoulder at the Colonel. 'We've got a shout.'

The Staff Sergeant watched them all running in different directions, before starting to run in the direction of his own Land Rover.

Exactly eight minutes later, Davies climbed into the right-hand seat of the Chinook and shouted 'helmets' to the rest of the crew to let them know that any further communication would be via their headsets. On his left, Flight Lieutenant Taff, his co-pilot, was shrugging himself into his harness. Once he was settled, the co-pilot flicked his comms switch.

'Just waiting on authorisation, Kinkers,' Taff said. 'You good to go in the back?'

'Yep, we've got six FP and four TRT on board,' the disembodied Australian voice of the loadmaster came back.

'What's the score, then?' Davies asked. 'Any news from the scene?'

'Three footballs apparently,' Taff replied, using the generic terms for casualties among the aircrew. 'I had to double check the location though — it's in the arse end of nowhere. Nothing at prayers this morning about action in that area, so I reckon it's the North Face gang.' The North Face gang was a nickname for anyone in any of the various British special forces units that were operating in the area and was based on the fact that all they seemed to wear was clothing branded with the distinctive North Face logo. Taff held up his hand to silence Davies for a second. 'Auth's come through,' he said, his Welsh accent elongating the words. 'We're good.'

'Good in the back?' Davies asked.

'Clear above and behind,' Kinkers replied.

'Lifting.' Davies pulled back on the cyclic to lift the helicopter into the air.

19

C olonel Nick closed his eyes as the helicopter touched down in the freshly ploughed field almost twenty minutes after taking off from the relative safety of Camp Bastion. He reached up and pulled his goggles down, blinking furiously to clear the dust that had rushed in during the final descent. Trying to ignore the grit behind his eyelids, he fumbled around for his weapon which had fallen to the floor as they had landed.

When he'd managed to retrieve the rifle from under the seat, he looked towards the back of the helicopter just in time to see the last of the FP team jumping off the ramp and into the dust cloud outside. Adams was standing near the back of the ramp, clutching a folded stretcher in his hand and looking back towards the inside of the helicopter. As Nick struggled to his feet, he saw Adams disappear into the cloud as well.

Bollocks, he thought as he broke into a run through the cabin. *The bastard's got a head start on me.* Nick passed the loadmaster and jumped off the ramp onto the soft ground before running through the cloud of dust that the helicopter had thrown up. It was ridiculously difficult to run through the earth, which was talcum-powder soft on the surface but damp and heavy just underneath.

Nick broke through the edge of the dust cloud and saw the FP team in a semi-circle just outside its reach, all facing outwards and looking down the sights of their rifles. Looking around, he could see Adams about fifty yards away, running towards a WMIK — a lightly armoured Land Rover named after its weapons mount installation kit and known as a 'wimmick' — that was parked at the edge of a compound. As he ran after him, Colonel Nick realised that either Adams was busting a gut to get there first and make a point, or he was in a lot better shape than he'd given him credit for.

Colonel Nick arrived at the vehicle only a minute or so later. Adams was deep in conversation with a soldier with a small red cross on his arm — the patrol medic — but as he watched, they wound up the conversation. Nick had missed the handover. Two soldiers were sitting by the WMIK, one with a bandage around his upper arm and another with an oversized, filthy bandage swathing his head. Both walking-wounded. Trying to get his breath, the Colonel gasped at the medic.

'Right, what's the story?' Neither the medic nor Adams appeared to hear him. The next thing Nick knew, Adams was shouting at the two walking-wounded casualties.

'See that helicopter?' Adams yelled at them, pointing in the direction of the Chinook with a trembling hand. The two soldiers nodded in reply. 'Well, fucking go over there and get on it sharpish. Straight line, here to there, watch the downdraft.' The two wounded soldiers started to get to their feet.

'No, wait. I need to triage them,' Colonel Nick said, now more in control of his breathing.

'No time, sir,' Adams replied. 'If they can get to the helo, then they're good. If they can't then we'll pick them up as we go by. There's a Cat A in the wagon. He's the priority.' Adams started to assemble the stretcher, kicking the struts that locked the canvas in place.

'I said, wait!' Colonel Nick barked. The wounded soldiers both looked at his rank slides, and then back at him. The Colonel knelt down and started to examine them. He could see out of the corner of his eye that Adams and the medic were struggling to get the casualty out of the back of the WMIK. Another couple of soldiers were rushing over to help them, so he returned his attention to the task at hand.

Colonel Nick finished his examination of the walking-wounded casualties a couple of minutes later. It was a fairly rudimentary examination, but it would have to do under the circumstances. The one with the huge bandage on his head was hiding a painful looking but superficial crease in his scalp and the other had a fairly deep wound to his arm, either from shrapnel or possibly a round. Neither of them was bleeding badly, so weren't in any immediate danger from their wounds.

He replaced the bandage over the second casualty's arm, noting with satisfaction that his humerus seemed intact, and checked for a radial pulse while he looked around to see where the next casualty was.

With a surge of anger, Nick realised that the stretcher was halfway back to the helicopter already. He could see Adams and the ground team struggling through the soft earth, kicking up dust clouds behind them. He'd not even had the chance to examine the most seriously wounded casualty in the relative quiet of the area that they were in. Too late, Nick realised that he should have looked at him first.

'Come on, let's go,' Nick said to his two walking-wounded colleagues. They got to their feet and started making their way towards the Chinook.

As they walked towards the waiting helicopter, Colonel Nick became more and more angry with every step. He was the senior officer on the ground, he was the senior clinician, and he'd effectively been disobeyed in the field. By a fucking nurse as well. He could see in the distance the stretcher being loaded onto the helicopter, with a couple of the FP team helping to manoeuvre it over the top of the machine gun in the middle of the ramp, and one of the FP team running from the helicopter towards his group. As the soldier got closer, the Colonel realised that it was the new Staff Sergeant.

'Sir!' Partridge shouted as he got to within a few feet of the casualty party.

'Staff,' Nick replied, putting as much authority into his voice as he could so that he could be heard over the noise of the rotor blades a hundred feet away.

'Get a fucking move on, sir!'

'What did you say?'

'I said, get a fucking move on, sir.' Partridge looked at the two casualties before yelling at them, 'Double fucking time, boys. Now!' The two wounded soldiers broke into a run towards the helicopter, closely followed by Partridge. Colonel Nick stood for a second, not quite believing what had just happened before he started running after them.

As Colonel Nick climbed onto the ramp after the others, he felt a hand on the back of his body armour drag him further on to the ramp as the helicopter started lifting before he'd even got both feet off the earth.

Ronald McDonald looked down the length of the cabin just in time to see Colonel Nick being unceremoniously dragged onto the rear ramp by Kinkers. The loadmaster had one hand on the scruff of the Colonel's neck, and the other on the strap that now attached them both to the main body of the helicopter. Ronald felt the helicopter lift and turned his attention to the stretcher that Adams and a couple of soldiers had dragged towards the front of the cabin.

Ronald knelt down by the head of the stretcher and looked at the casualty lying in front of him with a bloody bandage wrapped around his head. *Right then*, he thought. *Best crack on.* Lizzie was opposite him, busy with an oxygen mask. Further towards the rear ramp, Adams was sitting on the canvas seat, trying to undo his helmet. He was drenched with sweat and had a face like a proverbial beet-root. Next to him were the other two casualties that had climbed onto the helicopter by themselves. Ronald barely glanced at them. Walking-wounded, and as long as they were walking, they weren't that badly hurt. If they stopped walking though, that was when Ronald would be more interested in them.

As Lizzie slipped the oxygen mask over the casualty's face, Ronald pressed the power switch on the monitor to turn it on and clipped the oxygen probe to the stretcher casualty's finger. Turning his attention to the soldier, Ronald had a quick look at his chest to see how well he was breathing. Satisfied that the casualty's airway was doing what it was supposed to be doing, Ronald lifted up the edge of the bandage while he waited for the oxygen probe to take a reading.

It took him a couple of seconds to process what he could see below the bandage. There was what looked like jelly mixed with blood underneath, oozing out in between fragments of bone. Ronald had only seen brain tissue before in medical textbooks, but he'd never seen it in a real casualty. He looked up at Lizzie and could see by the horrified look on her face that she'd seen the same thing that he had.

Ronald got to his feet and stumbled over the tightly packed FP team to reach Adams, who had finally managed to get his helmet off and was taking a long drink from a plastic bottle of water. He looked fucked. Ronald tapped him on the shoulder to get his attention and leaned in close to shout in his ear.

'Adams!' Ronald shouted. 'His fucking brains are coming out.'

'I know,' Adams replied. 'Get him.' He pointed towards Colonel Nick, who had managed to get to his feet and was making his way down the cabin. Ronald caught the Colonel's eye, raised his eyebrows, and pointed at the casualty, hoping that the doctor would pick up on the urgency.

The Colonel shrugged his medical bag off his shoulders and threw it onto a seat before picking his way through the feet of the FP team towards the stretcher. Ronald joined him after a few seconds, leaving Adams where he was. Leaning in close to Colonel Nick's ear, Ronald shouted, 'Sir, there's exposed brain tissue under the bandage!' He watched as the Colonel looked towards the monitor on the floor and processed the information.

'Tell Jarman to get a tube ready,' Nick said. 'His sats are going off.' Ronald looked at the monitor and saw that the oxygen saturation was reading as eighty per cent. He could see that Lizzie was already getting the intubation kit out of the bag, so Ronald walked past her back toward the front of the helicopter.

Clipping the cord dangling from his helmet into the

communications cable, Ronald flicked the switch to talk to the rest of the crew.

'This boy's not well at all. Can we get a message to the hospital, get them to prep for a bad one?'

'Roger that,' he heard the pilot reply. 'Will do. We'll get a shift on.'

Ronald felt the helicopter tilt forwards by a couple of degrees and sensed the increase in power as the pilot put his foot down, or whatever it was that they did in the front to make the thing go faster.

Squadron Leader Andrew Webb was not a happy man. As he sat outside the back entrance to the Emergency Room in a cheap canvas chair, he re-read the latest bluey — a pre-stamped letter for military personnel and their families — from his wife while he sipped a cup of tea. Normally, the early evening was his favourite time of day as the temperature was far more comfortable and he could sit outside without sweating too much, but this evening he didn't get the normal sense of peace from the easing temperature.

According to the letter from Leanne, his wife, their youngest was being what she called 'a little shit' at school. He was only eight, and every time that Webb went away he played up one way or another. Apparently, this time he'd got into a fight at school over whose turn it was to take a penalty at an after-school football club. Being eight, it was probably not much of a fight, but it had still led to his youngest being banned from the club. And the bathroom tap was leaking and Leanne wanted to know what to do about it.

'Call a fucking plumber,' Webb said to himself as he

got up to get rid of his cup, folding the bluey and putting it into his back pocket as he did so. The TRT had been out for about an hour and should be back soon unless they'd diverted to the other field hospital that the Canadians were running up at Kandahar. They should have heard if this was the case, though. He walked back into the Emergency Room, and over to the desk at the back putting his cup on the side as he did so. Picking up the phone, he dialled the hospital Ops Room.

'Squadron Leader Webb here,' he said. 'In the ER. Any news on the TRT?'

'No sir,' the Ops Officer replied. 'Nothing heard as yet. We'll give you an ETA and update as soon as we have one from them. There's some crap weather between us and them at the moment, so it could be affecting the comms.'

'Right,' Webb said. 'Make sure you do.' He put the phone down without another word and turned to survey the Emergency Room. Apart from an army medic fiddling with something in the corner of the room, it was empty. He knew that all the people he would need when the TRT got back were all within a couple of minutes, so he wasn't too bothered. It wasn't as if they could go anywhere, anyway. He sat back down in a chair and retrieved the letter from his pocket to read it through again.

'What the fuck am I supposed to do about a leaky tap from three thousand miles away anyway?' he mumbled to himself. All the personnel in the hospital got the same welfare package as everyone else in Bastion, which was a paltry twenty minutes on the phone and thirty minutes on the internet. And that was if the bloody connection was working. Webb certainly didn't want to waste any of the valuable time on crap like household repairs, but that seemed to be all Leanne wanted to talk about, anyway. She'd probably got a list of things for him to do pinned to the fridge for him to work his way through when he finally got his R&R in a month or so. What he wanted was to go home, relax, have a drink or three, and lots of sex. With his wife. He read the letter again, knowing that he was being unreasonable, but he was still pissed off.

Webb was reaching for a blank paper bluey from a pile on top of the desk, thinking that he might as well pass the time writing back to Leanne over another cup of tea, when the phone on the desk rang. He picked up the receiver.

'ER,' he said. 'Squadron Leader Webb.'

'Sir, it's the Ops Officer down the corridor. Just got word that they're about fifteen minutes out.'

'Any update on casualties?'

'No, sir. Nothing as yet. Three on board, that's all we know. The original call came in as a Cat A and a couple of Cat C's, but there's been no update from the medical team.'

'Okay, thanks. Is there a Tannoy going out?' Webb asked.

'Yes, sir. Any second now.'

A few seconds after Webb had put the phone down, he heard the loudspeakers spring into life with a clipped request from the voice he'd just heard on the telephone for the trauma team to return to the ER. Knowing that the peace was only going to last for a few more seconds before the room was full of people, most of whom were supposed to be there, and a fair few who weren't, he opened the fridge and took out a large bottle of cold water.

He wrote 'WEBB' in large angry letters on the label with a red marker pen and put the bottle down onto the desk, knowing that the fridge would be empty within a few minutes of everyone else arriving. He'd tried a note saying 'ER Personnel Only' on the front of the fridge, but it hadn't seemed to make a blind bit of difference.

Webb stood with his hands on his hips as the Emergency Room started to fill up within seconds of the announcement over the hospital public address system. He watched as a few of them wandered over to the fridge and took out bottles of water, but no one touched his bottle on the desk. He nodded at Major Rob Clarke as he walked in, and watched him start to organise his nurses. Clarke might be a miserable old bastard, Webb thought, but he knew his stuff and was good with the juniors so he'd give him that at least. When Webb was sure that all of the required team members had arrived, he took a deep breath and shouted.

'Ladies and Gentlemen. Listen in!'

20

C olonel Nick stood on his own in the corner of the Emergency Room, trying to keep his expression as neutral as possible while he watched the medical staff bustling around the Cat A casualty. Within a few minutes of arriving at the hospital, the soldier with the head injury had been anaesthetised — although that was fairly pointless as far as Nick was concerned. He was fucked. Even if he survived long enough to get back to the United Kingdom, the chances were he would either die later down the line of an infection picked up along the way, or just spend the rest of his life drooling in a wheelchair and shitting into an adult-sized nappy. Not much of a life, really. If the soldier was a horse, it would be a quick bolt gun to the back of the head and job done.

The casualty's likely prognosis wasn't what was bothering Nick, though. It was Adams. Or more specifically, Adams's absolute failure to appreciate the chain of command in the field. *Look at him*, Nick thought as he watched Adams talking to the pretty little blonde nurse from the Emergency Room. *What a fucking hero he thinks he is.* Nick had been considering 'having a chat' with Adams for a while, and what had just happened in that field had convinced him that he couldn't wait. He walked over to the two nurses and when they didn't acknowledge him, he cleared his throat.

'Oh, hello sir,' the female nurse replied. 'Sorry, didn't see you there.'

'Adams, let's go,' Nick said, fixing him with a hard stare. 'Leave this lot to it.'

'Yep, okay. I'll see you later, Emma. We'll talk then.'

'Cool.' Nick saw the look the two nurses exchanged, and his anger grew. Was Adams having a sniff, or was he just mates with the woman? It didn't matter either way to Nick, but it irritated him, anyway.

The two men left the Emergency Room and started walking in silence down the long central corridor towards the TRT tent. As they passed the doors to the observation ward, Nick turned and pushed Adams towards the doors.

'In here, Adams,' he said as he gave the nurse a shove in the small of his back to get him through the canvas flaps leading to the empty ward. To Nick's surprise, Adams didn't complain, but just pushed the doors aside and walked through them.

Inside the observation ward were two neat rows of empty beds, unmade, each with a bedding pack on the mattress. If this ward was full of casualties then something, somewhere, had gone badly wrong. But for the time being, it was just the two of them in there, which was just how Nick wanted it. Adams took a few steps further forwards and then turned to face Nick.

'So,' Nick barked, making Adams jump. The nurse flinched and took a step backwards, giving Nick the impression that Adams thought he was about to take a swing at him. 'So, Adams. What part of the chain of command don't you understand?' Adams didn't reply but glared at Nick. 'I asked you a question, soldier,' Nick continued, making sure that his anger came through.

'I'm not a soldier, Colonel,' Adams replied. 'I'm an airman.'

'What's that got to do with anything?' Nick replied. 'I could still charge you for disobeying an order.' To Nick's surprise, Adams started laughing.

'Sorry, Colonel,' Adams said. 'I thought we were in here to talk about how you fucked up out there, so we wouldn't have to do it in front of the others.' His anger building, Nick took a step forward.

'What did you just say?' he asked Adams in a much quieter voice. Maybe Adams wasn't that far off the mark if he thought Nick was about to hit him.

'You fucked up,' Adams replied, no longer laughing. 'I don't know if you've realised, but there's a whole bunch of people out there who are trying their best to kill us. When we're on the ground, we're there for as short a time as possible. This isn't an exercise.'

'Oh, thank you for reminding me,' Nick said. 'I don't know if you've realised, but I gave you an order out there, which was to wait and triage the casualties properly. I'm the senior clinical lead here. You're only a nurse.' Adams didn't reply but folded his arms over his chest. 'Maybe I will charge you after all,' Nick continued.

'You go for it, Colonel,' Adams replied, walking past Nick and back towards the door of the observation ward. 'I think we're done here. You need to have a word with yourself.'

'Wait!' Nick shouted. 'We're not fucking done.' Adams

spun round on his heel and took a step back towards Nick. Now it was Nick who was wondering if a punch was coming his way.

'You fucked up, Colonel Hickman. You triaged the walking-wounded, ignoring the bloke with his fucking brains hanging out of his head. And while you were taking your time doing that, you were putting the helicopter, all the crew, and the soldiers on the ground at risk.'

'Adams, shut up and list–'

'So go for it,' Adams interrupted. 'Charge me, and let's get all that out in the open. I'm sure the General Medical Council would have a view.'

Nick stood, thinking hard about how to recover the situation. He needed to say something to re-establish control, but by the time he realised this, Adams had already walked out of the observation ward.

He rolled the ampoule over and over in his pocket as he looked in through the windows to the intensive care unit. The medics on the other side of the flaps were bustling around their casualty, whose head was heavily wrapped in bandages. He recognised most of the medical team, but there were a few there who he didn't. They must be the critical care retrieval team, there to take the casualty back to the United Kingdom.

Pulling the ampoule out of his pocket, he looked at it closely, although the light in the corridor wasn't very good. Even though he couldn't see any puncture marks in the plastic, for a moment he wasn't even sure if he'd got the right ampoule. This was the only ampoule that he'd had in his pocket though, so it must be the right one. He got a handkerchief from his other pocket and wrapped the ampoule in the material. Returning his hand to his pocket, he rolled the ampoule over and over inside the handkerchief to make sure that there wouldn't be any fingerprints left on it. Although this was overkill — the chances of anyone even figuring out what he was doing were so remote that it was laughable — you could never be too careful.

The last recipient of one of his 'special' ampoules had done very well, dying the way that he did. When he'd thought about it later, though, the next ampoule would be better used on an unconscious casualty who wasn't going to suddenly leap up and start shouting like the previous one had. The casualty inside the intensive care unit would be absolutely perfect. He knew that this soldier wasn't going to be waking up any time soon. Looking at the medical equipment that the retrieval team were organising, he could see that the amount of sedation the casualty was getting was virtually none. The soldier was, in a word, fucked. He knew he didn't have much time though; this one would be on the road — or more accurately in the air — before too long. He pushed the canvas flap of the ICU tent aside and walked into the unit.

As he stood just behind the retrieval team, who were all focused on preparing the casualty for the long journey ahead, he had a sudden thought. If he could get the ampoule into the ones that the retrieval team would be using, then it would be used at some point during the journey. He wouldn't get to see the results, which would be a shame, but at the same time, he'd be nowhere near the casualty when the ampoule was used. That would be perfect, and well worth the risk of letting the ampoule out of his sight. He'd just checked it after all, and it was perfect. No signs of any tampering at all, and now it was nice and clean as well.

He sidled closer to the team, eyeing the medical grab bag that was on a table next to the casualty. Peering inside, he could see a wooden pulp tray containing some ampoules that were identical to the one in his pocket, along with some syringes. He knew that this was a pre-prepared tray for administering intravenous drugs. Putting all the equipment together that was needed to flush the line after giving medication directly into the cannula was something that he'd done many times himself when moving patients. It saved messing about trying to find things in bags.

'Right then, chaps. Are we all set?' he heard the officer in charge of the retrieval team say to the others. They all looked up at him, a few of them responding. While they were paying more attention to their boss than anything else, he pulled the ampoule out of his pocket and dropped it into the wooden pulp tray inside the bag, grabbing a couple of the ampoules that were in the tray as he did so and putting them back in his pocket. That would increase the chances of his ampoule being used.

The team started pushing the trolley towards the door of the ICU. He knew that there would be an ambulance outside to take the casualty and the team down to the landing strip where they would be loaded onto a Hercules C130 transport plane. From there they would go to Kandahar, where a huge C17 would be waiting for the long trip back to the United Kingdom. The team with the casualty would be with him all the way, and with a patient as sick as theirs was, the ampoule would certainly be used at some point. He was sure of that.

With a start, he realised that the team hadn't picked up the grab bag. Bollocks, he thought. It's not theirs. Now he had to get that ampoule back again, which could be tricky. It was difficult to explain why you were rummaging around in someone else's medical bag. But it must be theirs. He picked the bag up and followed the team who were negotiating the canvas doors of the tent. He tapped the medic closest to him on the shoulder. She turned around to face him, letting go of the trolley and stopping.

'Excuse me,' he said. 'Is this yours?'

'Oh shit,' she replied before glancing down at the rank tab on his chest. 'Nice one, sir. Christ, I'd be shot if I let the boss leave this behind.' The medic smiled at him, showing a set of slightly crooked front teeth. He'd be thinking about that smile for a while, that was for certain. 'Thank you. I'll bring you back a present from the UK next time I'm over.'

'I'll hold you to that,' he said, returning the smile. *'A bottle of Jack Daniels would be good.'*

Lizzie Jarman looked up as Adams pushed his way through the flaps into the TRT tent. From the look on his face, she could tell that he wasn't happy. Without a word, he walked over to the brew table and put the kettle on. He threw a teabag into his mug and spooned a couple of sugars into it, before sitting down in a chair next to the table. Lizzie looked at Ronald, who was still fiddling with the medical equipment bags by the opposite door of the tent. Catching his eye, she looked at the door, and then back again at him. When he just shrugged his shoulders, she did it again. *My God*, she thought, *he could be really thick at times*. He looked back at her with a questioning expression, so she slowly mouthed the words 'go away' at him.

Ronald got to his feet.

'I'm just going to pop down to the NAAFI,' he said. 'Does anyone want anything?'

'No, ta,' Lizzie replied.

'Boss?' Ronald said, after a few seconds. Adams just looked at Ronald and shook his head.

'Okay.' Ronald looked pointedly at Lizzie. 'I'll be back in a bit.'

Lizzie watched as Ronald walked to the far end of the tent. As he reached the door, he looked back at Lizzie and stuck two fingers up at her. She couldn't help grinning as the flap closed behind him. Walking over to where Adams was sitting, Lizzie grabbed one of the chairs next to him and sat down.

'You okay?' she asked.

'Yep, all good.'

'Doesn't look like it to me.' Adams didn't reply. 'Good stuff,' Lizzie continued after a few seconds. 'I'll just make myself a cup of tea then. Seeing as no-one's offered to make me one.' Adams stayed silent, staring at the kettle instead of replying. An uncomfortable silence descended between them, which was unusual.

She waited for a minute until the kettle had boiled, and then watched Adams make two cups of tea, taking forever to squeeze the teabags. He handed one to her and sipped at the other one.

'So,' Lizzie said eventually.

'So, what?' Adams replied.

'So, what's up?'

'Nothing.'

'Bollocks.'

'That's no language for a lady to be using. I said it's nothing.'

'Adams, you know I'm no lady,' Lizzie said. 'All woman me, but definitely not a lady,' she continued, trying to lighten the mood. Adams said nothing but just stared into his tea. After a few minutes of silence, Lizzie had had enough.

'Oh, for God's sake, Adams. What is it?'

'I said it's nothing, Lizzie. Just leave it.'

'No, Adams. I won't leave it. You mope in here, make a jack brew, and just sit there with a face on. Come on, don't be a dick.' She paused, waiting for a reaction from him. Nothing.

She reached across and rubbed the back of his neck with her hand.

'You've got hair like a hedgehog,' she said, softly. After a few seconds, Adams replied.

'How many hedgehogs have you stroked?'

'Er, none.' She paused. 'Is there a joke in there about

pricks somewhere?' Adams snorted in response. *Finally*, Lizzie thought.

'In fact, you're right. Hedgehogs don't technically have hair,' he said. Lizzie squeezed the back of his neck before giving him a playful slap on the back of the head.

'So, I take it you and the Colonel have had words, then?' Adams looked up at Lizzie when she said this.

'How'd you know that?'

'Woman's intuition, lucky guess, I don't know. I'm right, then.'

'You could say that,' Adams replied. 'He wasn't happy about the last job. He wants to charge me for disobeying an order.' Adams slammed his mug down on the table, spilling the tea. Lizzie fought the urge to mop it up, and let Adams carry on. 'I told him to bring it on. Let the world know about him wanting to triage the other casualties first, ignoring the most seriously injured one. But what would I know? I'm only a nurse, apparently.'

Lizzie looked at Adams and her heart went out to him. She leaned across and gripped his hand.

'Where's the Colonel now?'

'No idea, I just walked off. I mean, for fuck's sake,' Adams continued, 'I could see his brains coming out of the fucking bandage, and the other two were walking-wounded. Triage, my hairy arse.'

'I saw him still farting about in the back of the helo after we landed at the scene. Did he catch up with you before you got to the casualties?'

'No, I beat him there,' Adams replied with a grim smile. 'Nearly bloody killed me, though. I was blowing out of my arse when I got to them, but I didn't want to give him the satisfaction of catching up. Mr "Oh I've just been for a run, look how sweaty I am." I mean, seriously?'

'Yep, I'm with you there,' Lizzie said. 'So, what was his problem?'

'He was saying that he's the senior clinical lead, and that I should have waited until he'd finished the triage,' Adams replied. 'Meanwhile, every Terry Taliban within earshot of the helicopter is getting suited and booted. Get them on and get the fuck out of there. That's triage out there, but he wouldn't listen.'

21

A couple of hours later, Adams was lying on one of the camp cots in the TRT tent reading the latest Peter James book *Looking Good Dead* that his girlfriend had sent out to him. When he heard the flaps at the far end of the tent open, he looked up to see the pilot, Davies, and the Australian loadie walking in.

'We would have knocked,' Davies said with a smile, glancing at the canvas flap, 'but you don't seem to have a door.'

'Hello, chaps.' Adams put his book down and sat up on the cot. 'You're a bit far from home. What brings you into this neck of the woods?'

'Well, it's either good news or bad news, depending on which way you look at it,' Davies replied. 'The Chinooks are all grounded. Technical fault with the low-level altitude sensor, apparently.' He nodded towards the engineer. 'Kinkers knows a bit more about it than me, though.' Adams got to his feet to shake the loadie's hand.

'G'day mate,' Kinkers said with an easy grin. 'So, this is where the magic happens, is it?'

'Not really, no,' Adams replied. 'This bit's just a crew tent, but I can ask Ronald to show you around the rest of the hospital when he gets back if you want? You'll get a better tour off him than you would off me. He seems to know everyone in the whole bloody place.'

'That'd be awesome, mate,' Kinkers said, his Australian twang more pronounced than usual.

'Kinkers is keen to meet some of the nurses, apparently,' Davies said as the exchange officer's grin broadened.

'What a surprise,' Adams replied. He thought that a couple of the nurses would probably quite like to meet Kinkers, but didn't say anything.

'You must be like a pig in shit working here, don't you think?' Kinkers said. 'This is probably the only place in the whole country that blokes actually want to work in.'

'I'm a married man, Kinkers,' Adams said. 'Well, as good as anyway. That's if she says yes.'

'Seriously?' Davies laughed. 'When's the poor girl going to get hit with the big question?'

'Week or so,' Adams replied. 'When I'm on R&R. I'm planning a weekend away at a posh hotel, romantic dinner, plenty of wine.'

'You're bloody mad, mate.' Davies was still laughing.

'Is she fit?' Kinkers asked, his eyes twinkling.

'Well, I wouldn't be asking her to marry me if she wasn't,' Adams retorted.

'You got a pic? Me and Davies here will give you a professional opinion.' Adams thought about the photograph of Sophie tucked behind his Kevlar plate in his body armour. They had been staying at a hotel in Brighton, and the photograph was of Sophie standing by the large window of their bedroom looking out over the seafront, a sly smile on her face testament to what they'd been doing not long before he'd taken it. It was his favourite photograph of her by some distance, not because of the memories it generated, but because she looked absolutely beautiful. 'Adams?' Kinkers broke Adams's concentration, and he looked at the Australian loadie. 'Over here, mate. Get back in the room and show us a pic of the lovely lady.'

'I can't, Kinkers,' Adams replied.

'Why not?'

'Because if I did, then I'd die. It happens all the time in films.' Davies started giggling, but Adams was only half-joking. He didn't believe in superstition, but at the same time, he wasn't going to tempt fate. 'Would you two gents like a cup of our finest tea while we're waiting for Ronald?' Adams asked them, keen to steer the two men away from Sophie. 'We've got both Tetley and PG Tips. I'm afraid we're out of Darjeeling and Earl Grey, though.'

Davies and Kinkers looked at each other and nodded in agreement. Adams went to the table to put the kettle on and looked inside a couple of mugs to see if anything was growing inside them. He picked up two of the cleaner looking ones and walked to the back of the tent to rinse them in the sink.

'So, what's the deal with the Chinooks then? How come they're grounded?' he called over his shoulder.

'There was a hard landing up at Kandahar by all accounts,' Davies replied. 'One of the crews on C Squadron pancaked in a complete brownout with a bunch of VIPs in the back. The loadie couldn't see shit, so they were going on instruments. The low-level altimeter said they were at thirty feet, but they weren't.'

'Yeah, that's right,' Kinkers chipped in with a laugh. 'Typical pilot, blaming the loadie.'

'They banged it down with a proper thud,' Davies continued. 'In fairness, and I know the pilot pretty well, if he thought he was at thirty feet then he would have been coming in pretty quick. It's a pride thing — come in hard, flare at the last minute, and then kiss the wheels to the dirt. If you think that you're at thirty feet, then you're still descending hard.'

'Still pilot error though,' Kinkers said. 'Can't blame the loadie for that one.'

Adams listened to the aircrew banter as he finished making the tea. There was a sense of comfortable nonsense about the whole conversation, despite how serious the subject actually was.

'So, what does that actually mean?' Adams asked.

'Well, the post-crash investigation — which was my mate Rich going around with a head torch — found out that the filter for the low-level altimeter was clogged up with sand. He fed it back to the UK as a big fucking problem, and the response back was to ground the fleet until we can get some new filters flown out,' Davies explained.

'Ouch,' Adams said. 'I can't see that going down well with the big cheeses.'

'Damn right,' Davies replied. 'Pretty much everything's stopped. All offensive ops have been paused; no support means no operations. It should only be a few days though, just until they manage to get some replacements sent out.'

'There you go, gents.' Adams finished making the tea, and handed them both a mug. 'Does either of you want sugar? It's on the table if you do, and there are some sweeteners somewhere if you've got no sense of taste.'

The flaps to the TRT tent opened again and Lizzie walked through, closely followed by Ronald. Not for the first time, Adams thought that Ronald was like a puppy the way he was always following Lizzie around

'Hello sirs, Kinkers,' Lizzie said with a smile. 'I take it you've told the boss about the dodgy filters then, Kinkers?' Adams hadn't realised that Lizzie knew the loadmaster, and he thought he caught them exchange a discreet smile. He could be wrong and if he was, it wouldn't be the first time. She continued, 'I heard that it was actually the pilot who — to avoid everyone finding out that he's actually a bit shit — filled the sensor thing with sand!'

'Yeah, not sure about that,' Davies laughed. 'It's a good dit though. I'll have to remember it for the next squadron Dining-In night. That should get him fined at least one bottle of port, if not more.'

'What the hell's a dit?' Kinkers asked.

'It's slang for a story, and you should never let the truth get in the way of a good one,' Lizzie said, raising smiles from them all. 'So, what's the plan then? We can't go flying for a couple of days, so we should go out on the lash. What d'you all think?'

'I can't go out tonight, Lizzie,' Adams replied, running his hand over his crew cut. 'I'm washing my hair. Sorry.'

'Have you lot had the guided tour of the hospital yet?' Ronald asked Davies and Kinkers. They both shook their heads. 'If you want to have a bimble round, I'll give you the tour if you like?'

'Great idea, mate,' Kinkers said. They got to their feet and followed Ronald to the main door of the TRT tent. As they were walking through the flaps to the tent, Adams heard one of them talking in a theatrical whisper, 'Is there anywhere to get a decent cup of tea in this place?'

'Very funny,' Adams said under his breath. He turned to Lizzie, who had sat down in one of the green canvas chairs. She had a serious expression on her face which hadn't been there a few minutes before. 'You okay, mate?' he asked.

'That casualty died on the way back to the UK,' she said in a low voice.

'What, the head injury?'

'Yep. Me and Ronald have just been to the paradigm terminals to check emails and what have you. I had an email from my mate on the critical care retrieval team. She's in Ramstein.'

'Why Ramstein?' Adams asked.

'They diverted there after the patient arrested mid-flight. They worked on him for ages, but couldn't get him back,' Lizzie replied. 'To be honest, I don't think they knew what to do once they'd realised that he wasn't responding. It's not happened before, losing a patient in the air, so they diverted to Ramstein to sort stuff out.'

'Oh, shit,' Adams said. 'Is your mate okay?'

'Yeah, she's fine. They're holding there waiting for a flight back out here. I didn't want to say anything in front of the helicopter crew because I know they bust a gut to get him back here. I guess they'll find out anyway at some point.'

Lizzie looked at Adams, and he saw she was on the verge of tears. 'I just didn't want to be the one to tell them that he didn't make it.'

'He was in a bad way though, Lizzie,' Adams said. 'You saw how badly injured he was. I've worked in Accident and Emergency for nearly ten years, and I'd never seen anything like that. If anything, he shouldn't have survived as long as he did.'

'That's not the bloody point, Adams,' Lizzie snapped. 'He did survive. We got him here, alive. We got him here and into the operating theatre, alive. So, what the hell happened?'

Adams knew that there was no answer to that question. People died, he knew that. So did Lizzie, but he figured that this probably wasn't the time for that conversation. He wondered what the best thing to do was. His instinct was to give her a hug, but he didn't want to tip her over the edge and make everything worse by trying to make it better.

'Do you want a cup of tea, mate?' he said, not being able to think of anything better to say.

'No, I don't want a sodding cup of tea,' Lizzie replied, looking up at him with tears now streaming down her cheeks.

Adams crossed the room and knelt in front of her, putting his arms around her and drawing her towards him. She started crying hard, so he tightened his grip on her.

'This is so shit, Adams,' Lizzie sobbed. 'Absolutely shit. They're kids, and they're dying.'

Adams held her, saying nothing. He looked towards the doors of the TRT tent and caught a glimpse of Colonel Nick looking in through the windows at them both before the doctor turned and disappeared from sight.

22

Private Bill Mitchell, who was driving, and his passenger Lance Corporal Steve Ruffles were in the middle of what their Platoon Commander called a 'reassurance patrol'. They were based in the Forward Operating Base in the district centre of Sangin, which was about five kilometres away from their current location. The whole base had been on lock-down for the last twenty-four hours since all the Chinooks had been grounded. They had to preserve everything — rations, water, ammunition — until the supply lines opened up. But, as their Commanding Officer had been quick to point out, there was still a need to make their presence felt in the area. If the insurgents knew that they didn't have any re-supply, that would be a problem. They could just chip away at the FOB bit by bit until the troops inside eventually ran out of stuff. Sergeant Hawkins, the platoon commander, had been quite explicit when he'd said that it would be just like the fucking film *Zulu* all over again. Hence the patrol.

The WMIK Private Mitchell was driving was one of a convoy of three vehicles picking their way around the outskirts of the village. It was a route that they'd done many times before, which concerned Lance Corporal Ruffles a lot. Although the vehicles were relatively well equipped with a fifty-calibre machine gun on the back, and a general-purpose machine gun on the front, predictability was not something that turned out well — generally speaking. Ruffles had tried to voice this at morning prayers, but Sergeant Hawkins was not as convinced as he was about the issue.

The area was a maze of rough tracks, like the one that they were driving down now. Low slung mud walls and basic houses. It was crisscrossed with irrigation ditches which connected the poppy fields and provided an ideal way for the Taliban to move around undetected from the ground.

'I don't like this at all, Ruffles,' Private Mitchell said in a thick Scottish accent. 'Where the fuck is everyone? Last time we came down here we got stuck in a traffic jam of bloody goats.' They were creeping their way down a lane with a mud wall on one side, and an irrigation ditch on the other. Beyond the irrigation ditch was a field full of discarded poppy heads, a sign that the opium growing season had finished for the year. The only life that they could see was a farmer standing at the door of his small hut on the other side of the field, who was just standing there watching them.

'Alright Mitch, let's stop here,' Ruffles said. 'I need a piss, anyway.' He turned to the back of the Land Rover, where the remaining two soldiers of his four-man fire team were sitting on the thin rubber mattresses in the back of the vehicle. 'Getting out in a minute, boys. Look lively.' He held his hand out of the passenger window, palm up so that the vehicles behind him would realise that they were coming to a halt.

Private Mitchell pushed down on the clutch and put the Land Rover in neutral, coasting forward for a few feet. He was relieved that they were stopping, although he probably wouldn't admit that to the rest of the patrol, but he had a real sense of something not being right. They'd been down this track only a couple of days ago, and it had been packed. Goats had been the main issue, but there'd been children running towards them waving, no doubt hoping for sweets from the soldiers, the odd adult looking at them with suspicion. And more goats. Now, there was nothing apart from a single farmer watching them from a hut across the poppy field.

'Signs of life, Ruffles,' he whispered.

'How'd you mean, Mitch?'

'There aren't any.'

The wheels of the Land Rover inched forwards until eventually — unseen by the occupants — the weight of the front wheel on the driver's side forced two parts of a hidden pressure plate together. Once the plates touched, it completed an electrical circuit. The sort of circuit that in the shitty comprehensive school that Private Mitchell had gone to back in Glasgow would have lit up a small bulb.

In this case the completion of the circuit didn't provide current to a bulb. The wires led to a large anti-tank mine that the Soviets had left behind on their way out of Afghanistan after they'd finally realised that they couldn't actually defeat the Mujahedeen. A mine that had been doctored with pressure plates made from aluminium cut from the sides of a can of Coca-Cola, soldered with some wires from a torch that didn't work anymore, and powered by a battery from a smoke alarm that was 'cheeping' every couple of minutes. All scavenged from the bins of the FOB that the patrol was from. Apart from the mine. It was the Russians who had thrown that away.

The last thing that Private Mitchell remembered was taking his foot off the accelerator of the Land Rover and moving it across towards the brake pedal. When the circuit completed, the chain reaction that it caused was far more than a bulb lighting up. The detonator in the mine triggered, causing a much larger explosion in the main body of the mine. The whole explosive component of the mine was aimed upwards, and a large molten mass of metal erupted towards the sky. It was designed to penetrate inside a tank, and rattle around until it was spent, but it hit the right-hand wheel and the right side of the main engine block of the Land Rover, both of which were propelled upward with horrendous and unstoppable force.

Inside the WMIK, the blast ripped Private Mitchell's feet off at the ankles, sending his boots high into the air with his now amputated feet still in them. At the same time, white-hot molten metal ricocheted off components of the engine, diverting back into the main cabin of the Land Rover. The jagged fragments peppered both occupants of the front seats, with devastating effects.

Several shards of debris ripped into Private Mitchell's thighs, some of them tunnelling through the flesh from his knees to his hips. Another fragment shredded his right testicle before bouncing off his pelvis and embedding itself in his rectum, while others drove themselves deep into his lower abdomen. The energy in the shards that hit his body armour was dissipated, but the few that hit his face ripped their way through the soft tissues.

To Private Mitchell's right, Lance Corporal Ruffles was not so lucky, if what had just happened to his friend could be considered lucky. He'd not done his body armour up when the convoy had left the FOB, figuring that he could just shove the Velcro together if they ran into a problem. The shrapnel flying through the air was utterly indiscriminate and gave him no warning before finding the gaps between the body armour, ripping into the soft tissue behind them.

Fifty feet behind the lead WMIK, Sergeant Hawkins's chest tightened as he saw the vehicle with Private Mitchell and the rest of his fire team erupt into flames.

'Fuck, contact, contact!' he shouted just in case any of the rest of the patrol hadn't heard or felt the explosion. Hands shaking, he struggled with the passenger door. They'd stopped wearing seatbelts a while ago, once they realised that getting out of a vehicle quickly was more likely to keep them alive than wearing a seatbelt. Flinging the door open, Hawkins looked back and could see the rest of the patrol moving their vehicles into a semblance of an all-round defensive posture, which was about all they could do on the narrow road. Soldiers scrambled to man the guns on the back and the front of the WMIKs. All the vehicles were hampered by a mud wall on one side and a ditch on the other which meant that they could only go forwards or backward.

Hawkins was sure that the explosion had been caused by an improvised explosive device and not a legacy mine. They'd been down this road many times in the last few weeks without any problems. The locals used it as well which was normally a good indicator of whether it was still mined. The main question that he wanted an answer to was whether it was a pressure plate IED or a command wire IED triggered by someone watching them. The first one was bad enough but the second one almost certainly meant that they'd driven straight into an ambush.

As his feet hit the floor, he slid his right hand down the

SA80 rifle he was carrying, and with his thumb, snapped the safety catch off. The first thing they'd all done as they left the base was make ready, so he knew that the weapon had one in the chamber and was ready to go. Hawkins ran towards the burning Land Rover and could see two soldiers struggling to escape from the back. When he got to the vehicle, he slammed the palm of his hand against the catch on the door, ignoring the sharp pain as the metal dug into the meat of his hand. Grabbing the tailgate, he yanked it towards him and opened up the back of the Land Rover. The soldiers inside half climbed and half fell out of the back and onto the dusty ground. There was no time to see if they were wounded or not, although one of them had blood streaming down his face.

Hawkins ran to the driver's side of the Land Rover, his hand shielding his face from the fierce flames that were now pouring out of the front. His question about whether this was an ambush was answered by the sharp crack of gunfire coming from a line of small trees behind the farmer's hut. Rounds zinged past him, punching into the mud wall behind with small dust explosions marking where they had landed, while the occasional round ricocheted off a vehicle with a metallic scream.

Seconds later, he heard the returning fire from his own patrol and the guns on the WMIKs opened up. Hawkins also heard the 'whump' of a grenade launcher from over his shoulder and knew that at least he had decent covering fire. Out of the corner of his eye, he saw the simple hut explode into a million pieces, and a small part of his mind wondered if the local who'd been in it a few minutes earlier had survived, whether he was the one who had pressed the button on the command wire, or whether he was just the world's unluckiest poppy farmer.

Sergeant Hawkins grabbed the handle of the driver's

door and flung it open. He reached inside and grabbed the soldier inside — Mitchell he thought his name was — and pulled him out of the vehicle. As Mitchell fell out, Hawkins saw that where his feet should be were two shredded blackened stumps and that he was bleeding badly from several wounds to his lower abdomen and face. Ignoring the bloody triangular flap hanging off Mitchell's cheek, he hoisted the wounded soldier over his shoulder as best as he could and started to stumble back towards the rest of the patrol.

On his way back, two of Hawkins's platoon ran past him towards the lead WMIK which was now burning furiously, thick black smoke pouring from the wounds in the front of the vehicle. Hawkins reached the nearest vehicle and heaved Private Mitchell into the front before turning to run back to the burning vehicle. He stopped as he saw the two soldiers that had gone past him were moving as fast as they could, dragging an unconscious casualty between them. It was the passenger — Ruffles — one of the most liked soldiers in the whole FOB.

Hawkins dropped to his knee, exhausted, and tried to take stock of the situation. He could hear crackling in his headset as the platoon radio operator fed a sit rep back to the FOB. The enemy fire had dissipated, with the Taliban no doubt melting away through the irrigation canals. About the only positive that he could take from this whole sorry mess was that the platoon's response had been swift and brutal. If it wasn't for the casualties, he'd be tempted to 'close and prosecute' — army terminology for follow and kill the fuckers.

He got to his feet, and after slipping the safety catch on his rifle back on, whirled the index finger of his left hand in the air to let the rest of the patrol know that it was time to go. He hadn't even managed to get a single shot off, he reflected as he climbed into what was now the lead WMIK. Hawkins pressed the PTT button on his radio.

'Right boys,' he said, 'Let's get the fuck out of here. And keep an eye in case the fuckers have doubled around on us.'

23

Lizzie lay back on the canvas cot and sighed deeply. She looked across at Adams on the cot next to her, his nose still stuck in the book that he was reading. On the other side of the tent, Ronald was curled up in one of the canvas chairs, fast asleep. Lizzie waited for a minute and then sighed again, more theatrically this time.

'What?' Adams said, not even looking up from his book.

'What d'you mean, what?' she replied. 'I didn't say anything.' Adams turned down the corner of the page that he was reading and turned to face her.

'What are you sighing about, Lizzie?' he asked with a smile.

'Oh, I was just wondering,' Lizzie replied. 'Do you think he's single?'

'Who?'

'Who'd you think?' she said. 'The bloody cleaner?'

'Jesus Christ,' Adams replied. 'You're such a lady. I can't believe that you've not been snapped up. I really can't.'

'Oh, sod off Adams,' Lizzie said. 'Don't be such a twat.' She rolled onto her front and looked at him with a mischievous expression. 'The pilot. Daniels.'

'I think he's called Davies, Lizzie,' Adams said. 'You might want to get his name right before you claw him into bed.'

'But he flies a helicopter,' she laughed. 'He must be good with his hands.' She rolled onto her back and put her hands behind her head. 'I like the idea of clawing him into bed, though,' she laughed. 'That would be fun.'

'Lizzie,' Adams said. 'I love you like a sister, but please don't involve me in your sexual fantasies.' He picked up his book and unfurled the page that he'd marked.

'Too late for that, Adams,' Lizzie said under her breath, still smiling. 'Way too late for that. So, do you think he's single then or not? Come on, help me out here.'

With a frustrated sigh, Adams put his book down on the table between them.

'Do you want me to find out for you?' he said.

'Oh, go on then. But be subtle, for God's sake,' she answered.

'Jesus,' Adams said. 'It's like being back at school, this is. What's in it for me?'

'I'll make the tea until we go on R&R,' Lizzie laughed. Adams threw his book at her, missing her head by inches as she dodged away from it. She leapt up from the cot, giggling as she did so. 'I think that's a fair trade. Don't you?'

'Apart from the fact that's in a couple of days' time, how about you don't make the tea until we go on R&R?' Adams said. 'That would be a much better deal.'

They both turned as they heard the flaps to the TRT tent open. Colonel Nick was standing in the doorway, holding one door open with his hand.

'Sorry to disturb you both when you're busy, but can you come to the Ops Room. There's a situation developing.'

Adams and Lizzie looked at the Colonel, and then back at each other.

'Yeah, no worries, sir,' Adams said.

They both got to their feet and walked towards the door to the tent. Adams, who was just behind Lizzie, jabbed her just under the ribs with his index fingers. Colonel Nick turned around and gave her an odd look as she jumped in response, but he missed her elbowing Adams in the stomach in retaliation.

Colonel Nick walked down the main corridor of the hospital with purpose — or at least that was the impression that he wanted to convey. He didn't understand how, when soldiers were out there on the ground fighting, those two idiots behind him were arseing about like nothing was happening.

They reached the door of the Ops Room at the far end of the hospital, and Colonel Nick banged on the door with his fist.

'Easy, Colonel,' he heard Lizzie say behind him. 'It's only plywood.' He turned and fixed her with a hard stare. The door opened behind him as an army Lieutenant opened it, and Colonel Nick pushed past him and into the cramped tent.

'What's going on, then?' Colonel Nick said. 'I need an update.'

The Lieutenant, who was quite obviously not happy with the situation, swallowed.

'Well, sir,' he said. 'There're troops in contact up near Sangin,' He pointed towards the small screen with the mIRC, a military internet relay client which was an instant messenger service for troops in the field. 'We've got multiple reports coming in from the same contact, but it looks bad.

'Where?' Colonel Nick asked.

'Outside Sangin somewhere,' the Lieutenant replied. He pointed towards the mIRC screen on the desk. 'They're still trying to get their heads around what's going on.'

'So how are we going to get them out if the bloody cabs are all grounded?' Colonel Nick asked nobody in particular. He turned to Adams. 'Is Captain Flash Heart still about?' He saw Adams suppress a smile at the Black-adder reference.

'No sir, he's gone back to the line,' he replied.

'Can we listen in to the radio chatter here?' Colonel Nick asked the Lieutenant.

'No, sir,' the young officer replied. 'It's just the mIRC. You'd need to go to the main Ops Room down by the heli-copters to listen in directly.'

'We could always head down there anyway, sir,' Lizzie said. 'Grab Ronald and the medical kit from the tent just in case.' Colonel Nick looked at her, thinking that she had a point.

'I didn't think that we were allowed in there,' Colonel Nick said.

'As long as you're with us, sir,' Lizzie replied with a grin, 'you'll be fine.'

'Right then,' Colonel Nick said. 'Let's go. Thank you, Lieutenant.'

Colonel Nick walked out of the ops room and into the TRT tent directly across the main corridor. He was closely followed by Lizzie and Adams who had finally managed to stop messing about. Nick picked up his body armour from the corner of the room and threw it on.

'Corporal McDonald,' Colonel Nick said. Ronald, who was still dozing in one of the canvas chairs, opened his eyes and looked around. 'Get your arse into gear, we're going down to the line.' Ronald jumped to his feet and the remaining three members of the team struggled to get their kit together.

Colonel Nick half-ran towards the rear door. He called over his shoulder as he did so. 'I'm driving,' he said. Lizzie looked up at him with a surprised expression. Colonel Nick paused for a second to see if she would say anything. Instead, she grabbed her body armour and medical bag and started towards him.

'I'm calling shotgun, then,' Lizzie said. Colonel Nick couldn't help himself. Against all his better judgement, he smiled as he saw the downcast look on both Adams's and Ronald's faces. All their bloody childishness was wearing off on him.

Sergeant Hawkins could see frantic activity as they approached the Forward Operating Base in the district centre of Sangin. There'd been a definite air of tension as they'd driven back through the town itself, with excited locals running around everywhere. The message that the Taliban had scored a direct hit on the Brits had obviously got around. He started to relax as their convoy, one vehicle less than it had been when they'd left earlier in the day, got within the range of the guns at the FOB. The whole patrol had been on high alert since leaving the scene of the ambush, knowing full well that they were extremely vulnerable.

He stared at a young man standing by the side of the road who was staring at them while talking into a mobile phone. Hawkins wanted to pull out his sidearm and shoot him in the head in case he was telling his Taliban mates that the convoy was approaching the base, but he could just be telling his Mum that he was on his way home for tea. Hawkins had no way of knowing, and despite what had happened to them, he wasn't the sort of soldier who would shoot an unarmed civilian anyway. No matter how much he would like to.

As the lead WMIK reached the main gates of the FOB, the heavy doors opened outwards to let the convoy inside. Hawkins breathed a sigh of relief as they passed through the entrance. When the vehicles stopped just inside the gates, he jumped down from his Land Rover and ran towards the casualty he'd dragged from the damaged vehicle. A couple of medics had beaten him to it though, and he was gently but firmly pushed back by one of them. He turned and looked back towards the vehicle with the other casualties and saw a lifeless body being laid down on the ground next to it. The lack of activity around the soldier told him everything he needed to know. Lance Corporal Ruffles was dead.

Hawkins dropped to his knees, tears unexpectedly springing to his eyes. He rubbed them away, angry with himself when he felt a hand on his shoulder. Looking up, he saw the second in command of the FOB crouching next to him. The two soldiers looked at each other without a word. Hawkins couldn't think of a single thing to say and, he figured, neither could the officer. He looked at the young Captain who must have been half his age, and the look that

Hawkins saw on the young man's face was one of shared pain. Despite the fact that the officer had been nowhere near the action, Hawkins instinctively knew that they both felt Ruffles's death just as keenly. The tears returned, and this time Hawkins made no move to wipe them away.

Adams was grumbling. He knew he was grumbling, and he really didn't care. He sat on the thin rubber cushion in the back of the Land Rover which Colonel Nick was driving about as fast as the thing could go towards the line. Opposite him, Ronald sat on the other seat.

'She won't let me bloody drive,' Adams said, 'but she'll let him.' He pointed towards the driver's seat. 'How does that work, mate?' Ronald just looked back at him, a half-smile on his face. Adams continued, 'And calling fucking shotgun? Seriously? That's just taking the piss.' Ronald's smile broadened.

The Land Rover sped past the main headquarters building for Camp Bastion, a cloud of dust billowing out behind it. Adams looked out of the back window just in time to see the Garrison Sergeant Major running out of the main building.

'Did you see that, Ronald?' Adams asked. 'Fucking priceless, mate.' The smile on his face now matched Ronald's. 'There'll be hell to pay for that.'

A few minutes later, the Land Rover pulled up with a skid outside the main Ops Room next to the pan. Adams heard the front doors slam as Colonel Nick and Lizzie got out and he struggled with the catch to the tailgate until it finally loosened so that he could clamber down. With Ronald a couple of steps behind him, he walked towards the the Ops Room where Colonel Nick was discussing something with whoever it was who had opened the door.

Adams walked up behind them just in time to hear Colonel Nick arguing about 'restricted access'. An angry-looking Flight Sergeant was standing by the door with his arms crossed over his ample belly, blocking any access to the Ops Room.

'Hi, Flight,' Adams said. 'You mind if we come in?' The Flight Sergeant's demeanour changed the minute he saw Adams.

'Hey, sir,' he replied. 'How're you doing?' Adams ignored the fierce look on Colonel Nick's face.

'Not too bad at all,' Adams said. 'Got something going on up at one of the FOBs, apparently. We thought we'd come down and listen in if that's okay? Is Davies in there?' Adams pointed at the door.

'Yeah, he's in there. Go on in, sir.' The Flight Sergeant opened the door and held it open. Adams walked past Colonel Nick and into the Ops Room, smirking at Lizzie as he did so, knowing that Colonel Nick wouldn't be able to see his face. Lizzie, who was facing Colonel Nick, was struggling to keep a straight face. *Single Service rivalry was great fun*, Adams thought as he walked through the door.

Inside the tent, there was a lot of activity. Adams shuffled to the side of the tent so that he would be out of the way, and to his relief, Colonel Nick and the others followed him. Adams looked across at Lizzie, catching her eye. When he saw her eyebrows go up in the universal 'what?' gesture, he looked across at the table in the far corner with a kettle and mugs on and nodded at it. Her response was exactly what he expected, which was Lizzie slowly mouthing 'sod off' at him. Adams grinned back as she shook her head in a dismissive gesture and held the grin until he saw her smile back.

The Ops Room had a silent air of urgency to it. One of the Ops Officers was glued to a mIRC screen in one corner, while another was deep in conversation with Davies across the room from the medical team. The pilot acknowledged Adams with a brief wave.

'Casualties — here,' an officer wearing headphones said, pointing at a small brown patch on one of the maps. Everyone in the room turned to look at him. 'One KIA, one Cat A, and a couple of Cat Bs so far.'

Davies said something to the Ops Officer, who nodded in agreement before walking over to the medics.

'I need to talk to the rest of the crew, but I think we should go,' Davies said to them. 'There's no other way of getting them out of there. No chance of a road move and the Americans don't have anything in the area.' He was referring to the Pave Hawk helicopters that the Americans operated, known as 'Pedros' after their call sign. They carried the American equivalent of a paramedic — give or take a few qualifications — in the back. Adams had worked with them before in Iraq a couple of years ago and knew that although they were good, they couldn't be as good as a four-man TRT.

Adams remembered that Colonel Nick was standing next to him, so he continued, 'What do you think, sir? Do you agree?'

'It doesn't look like we've got any choice,' Colonel Nick said. 'But what about the aircraft? I thought we were grounded?'

'We'll get everyone together at the cab, and I'll brief then,' Davies said before raising his voice and calling across the room to the Ops Officer he'd been talking to earlier. 'Jimmy, can you get the FP lads down to the cab for a brief, and we'll make a final decision then.' Adams saw the Ops

Officer raise a thumb in confirmation, and he turned to follow Davies out of the Ops Room.

As far as he remembered, Adams thought that all operations on the ground had been paused until the helicopters were cleared for flight. If that was the case, why were there injured soldiers on the ground? And who was going to go and get them?

24

A t the Forward Operating Base in Sangin the Commanding Officer — Major John Fletcher — was trying to assimilate information from a wide variety of sources and work out what the fuck he was supposed to do about the situation that had developed on his watch. He had one dead soldier, one soldier with horrendous injuries, and another couple who were hurt. As well as this, he had an entire platoon house of soldiers who were scared and angry in equal measure. Every few seconds, there was the sound of gunfire from the village. Fletcher didn't think it was much of a threat — just the locals letting them know that they were still there — but he still jumped with every sharp crack.

When he'd heard that he was going to be the company commander of a field unit, he'd been delighted, telling his wife in a bluey that this was his chance at promotion, without any doubt. The elation that he'd been feeling since they took over the district centre had all disappeared over the last hour or so, and the only thing that he felt now was overwhelmed and terrified. He was looking around the small room that he'd made into his command post in the lower floor of a half-finished two-storey building when his second in command came in through the curtain that served as a door.

'Update?' Major Fletcher barked, trying to hide the nervousness in his voice. His 2IC, a young Captain with a cut-glass British accent that wouldn't have sounded out of place in Buckingham Palace, swallowed before replying.

'One dead, three wounded.' He swallowed again. 'One of them seriously.'

'Who's dead?'

'Lance Corporal Ruffles, sir.'

'Fuck.' Major Fletcher slammed his fist down on the thin wooden desk, knocking over a cup of cold tea. 'Fuck. I know his bloody girlfriend.' He looked around for some tissues to mop up the tea before it ruined all the papers on his desk, not that it really mattered anymore. 'She was at the regiment barbecue before we left. What was her name?'

'I'm not sure, sir,' his second in command replied after a few awkward seconds' silence. 'I've not met her.'

'Fuck,' Major Fletcher muttered under his breath. 'I can't bloody remember.' There was another awkward silence. 'What about the others?'

'One lad's lost both his legs and looks in a bad way. Private Mitchell. The other two — they were in the back when the WMIK went woof — they look okay, but the medics are with them now. Sergeant Hawkins is in a bit of a state as well. Hardly surprising.' Fletcher clenched his fists and put them on the table in the middle of the spreading tea stain. He closed his eyes and took a few deep breaths as he saw his chances of promotion any time within the next ten years slipping away. It was his decision to mount the reassurance patrol. 'Sir?' the

Captain asked. When Fletcher didn't reply, he asked again. 'Sir?'

'What?'

'What are we going to do?'

Fletcher thought for a few seconds before replying.

'We need a plan,' he said, returning to familiar territory. He was an Army officer. That's what officers did. Plan. 'Let's put together a plan for extraction. Even though the helos are grounded, that's not going to last forever.'

'It's only the Chinooks that are grounded, sir,' the Captain said. 'The Ops Room at Bastion has been on the radio, and there's an Ugly on the way up to deny the locals any access to the damaged WMIK.' The young officer was referring to an Apache gunship — black, nasty, and very dangerous if you were on the other side.

'Oh, thank fuck for that,' Major Fletcher replied. The gunship would calm the locals down a bit, and perhaps the sporadic gunfire he could hear from the village would settle down. 'Right then,' he continued, spurred into action with something to actually act on. 'Let's work on a plan to get the casualties out to the secondary LZ for when they can get something else in.'

There were two landing zones that had been identified as potential sites for helicopters to land that were both within easy reach of the district centre. The primary LZ was out in the open, not far from where the WMIK had been hit and the troops ambushed. That one was out of the window for the moment at least. The secondary LZ wasn't the best, as there were too many places for the Taliban to hide in the vicinity for anyone's liking, but it was the best they had.

'Let's go to the radio room to work this out,' Fletcher said. 'And get Hawkins. I want him in on this plan for his own sake. If he knows that he helped get them out, then he might not top himself.' The Captain nodded and pushed his way back through the curtain into the blistering heat outside.

Fletcher took a deep breath and followed him. The bright sunshine was dazzling, but as his eyes adjusted, he could see his soldiers looking at him as he strode across the courtyard in the middle of the compound towards the radio room on the opposite side. He felt his heart fluttering in his chest as he realised that they were looking at him for guidance. It had been his decision to mount the patrol and he was supposed to be in charge. Which meant that he had blood on his hands. British blood.

Flight Lieutenant Davies stood on a plastic icebox full of water in the back of the grounded Chinook and looked at the medical and Force Protection teams. Some of them were sitting on the floor, the others on the canvas seats down either side of the cabin.

'Right chaps,' he said, running his palms down the legs of his flight suit. 'This is the situation. There's at least one Cat A up at Sangin and a couple of Cat Bs. One KIA as well, so they're getting hit pretty hard. But we're technically grounded as the altimeter isn't working properly. We,' he pointed at Taff and Kinkers, 'are happy to go in and see if we can put down without it to get the casualty, but we're not going unless everyone is happy. You've all got the right of veto, so either we all go, or we don't go.'

Staff Sergeant Partridge was furthest away from the pilot, standing towards the rear ramp of the helicopter. He raised his hand.

'Sir,' he said. 'We've already talked about this. Everyone's happy in my team.' Davies looked at the Staff

Sergeant, and then around at the Force Protection team. A few of them nodded in agreement, reassuring Davies that Partridge hadn't just made an arbitrary decision on their behalf. Davies looked towards Adams and the medics and saw a thumbs up from the Lieutenant Colonel. Next to the doctor were the rest of the medical team, all nodding.

'Okay then,' Davies said, clapping his hands together. 'Let's Foxtrot Oscar.' He jumped down off the icebox and made his way into the front of the cab. Behind him, the two teams both scrambled off to get their equipment.

Davies settled into the right front seat, clipping himself into the various bits of equipment. He shoved the helmet onto his head and pressed the radio toggle to speak to the Ops Room.

'Ops, this is Sandman 34,' Davies said as Taff sorted his stuff out in the left-hand co-pilot's seat.

'Sandman 34, this is Ops. Send,' he heard the Ops Room reply.

'Ops, Sandman 34 requesting clearance to depart on medevac.' There was a pause on the other end. Davies figured that there was now a frantic conversation going on between the Ops Officers. After thirty seconds or so, a reply came back.

'Negative, Sandman 34. Wind up and wait out,' the disembodied voice in his head said. Davies turned to Taff.

'Let's start up and wait for clearance, Taff,' he said. Davies looked over his left shoulder and could see the teams in the back were getting back on, loaded down with equipment. Kinkers was standing at the ramp supervising them as they climbed on board. As Davies said 'helmets' into the intercom, he saw Kinkers look up towards the cockpit and wave.

Davies started his pre-flight checks. He checked the inverter, made sure that he had the correct numbers set on the caution advisory panel. He heard the intercom click, and the words 'Clear power unit' from Kinkers in the back.

'Roger that,' Davies replied. He flipped the switch to release fuel into the engines, counting to five under his breath, and hit the button that was helpfully marked 'start'. Above and behind him, he heard the clicking of the auxiliary power unit closely followed by a reassuring tone in his ears that told him all was well. Davies ran through the rest of the checks as quickly as he could, until within a few minutes both engines were started and they were good to go.

'Ops, this is Sandman 34,' Davies said into his radio. 'Permission to go please.'

'Sandman 34, this is Ops. Negative, negative. Wait out.'

'Oh for fuck's sake,' Davies said. 'Come on.'

'Sandman 34, say again,' the Ops Room asked.

'Ops, this is Sandman 34, Thanks for clearance. Bad line though, will do a comms check when we're in the air.' Davies flexed his fingers on the cyclic between his legs.

To his left, Taff started laughing before reaching across Davies's lap and flipping the toggle of the external radio to the 'OFF' position.

'I'll get on the blower and let the chaps on the ground know we're coming in, will I?' Taff asked.

'Sounds like a plan to me,' Davies replied with a grim smile. He settled his hands into their familiar position and pulled the stick back. '3-2-1, lifting.'

Sergeant Hawkins sat in the lead WMIK of the hastily organised convoy that was sitting behind the heavy metal doors at the front of the compound and drummed his fingers on the dashboard. He looked up and watched the Apache gunship lazily circling a few hundred feet above them like a large, very angry wasp.

A few minutes ago, he'd heard a muffled 'crump' as the Apache put a missile into the WMIK that they'd had to leave behind. Just before this, he'd heard a short burst from its machine gun, probably to get the local kids and scallys away from the vehicle before it was 'denied' permanently. There was no point in giving the Taliban more weapons.

'What the fuck's going on, mate?' Hawkins asked the driver next to him who just shrugged his shoulders in reply. Their mission was fairly straightforward as far as Hawkins was concerned. Get to the LZ, secure it with the help of the Apache, and get the casualties onto the TRT Chinook that was inbound. 'They are coming, aren't they?'

Hawkins jumped as the doors in front of them started to open, and the Land Rover jolted forwards. He grabbed the general-purpose machine gun that was mounted on the front of the vehicle, and from the shadows moving across his peripheral vision he could tell that the soldier manning the fifty-calibre machine gun behind him had done the same thing.

'Come on, then,' Hawkins muttered. 'Come and have a fucking go.'

The convoy moved slowly out of the gates of the compound, quickly picking up speed as they got onto the road outside. The Apache had dropped right down to about a hundred feet above them to protect the four vehicles as they made their way to the secondary LZ a few minutes' drive away. Around him, Hawkins could see young men on mobiles, almost certainly 'dicking' them as they left the base. The local Taliban would know that they were on the move.

The gunship above them moved in front of the convoy

to circle above the LZ as the vehicles approached. Hawkins was fairly sure that the Taliban wouldn't have a pop while the helicopter was overhead. The insurgents weren't afraid of a scrap, as the casualties in the vehicles behind him knew only too well, but the locals weren't stupid. Taking on an Apache gunship with a few AK-47s and RPGs was like taking a banana to a gunfight, let alone a knife.

Hawkins could see the secondary LZ a few hundred metres in front of them, already protected by a Gurkha patrol. With an Apache overhead and a bunch of Gurkhas on the ground, the LZ was about as safe as it could be. His vehicle moved into position, taking up one of the flanks, and Hawkins climbed out of the WMIK to watch as the other vehicles in the convoy took up similar positions to defend the area.

As they approached the landing site, Davies listened as the Apache pilot spoke with the ground troops — call sign 'Widow' — over the secure radio.

'Widow 23, this is Ugly 16,' the pilot said.

'Ugly 16, this is Widow 23. Send, over,' was the reply from the ground.

'Widow 23, I'm nearly bingo on fuel. Ugly 19 is en route to take over. I have visual on Sandman 34 to the east. Confirm that the landing site is secure and cold?'

'Ugly 16, I can confirm that the landing site is cold.' There was a brief pause over the airwaves.

'Sandman 34, did you get that?' the Apache pilot asked. Davies reached for the switch of his radio and flicked it twice in quick succession to let them know that he had got the message, before toggling back to the internal intercom.

'Right then chaps, we're a couple of minutes out. We have an Apache overhead, but he's almost out of juice. There's another Ugly on the way to replace him, though.' Davies flicked his eyes left and right, up and down, making sure that his helicopter was where he thought it was in relation to the ground before continuing. 'The LZ is secure, but we're not hanging about when we get there. I'm going to have to come in slowly as we're only on visuals.' Davies hauled the helicopter in a wide left-hand arc to line them up for the approach. As he did so, the departing Apache flew past on their right-hand side, the pilot raising a hand as he went past. Davies didn't return the greeting but concentrated instead on getting ready for the landing. Below him, he could see several WMIKs surrounding the landing site and a fair few soldiers on the ground.

'There's a lot of guys on the ground already. I can't see the point in getting FP out and down, so if everyone's happy we'll just send the medics out to get the casualties. Kinkers, could you confirm with them and let me know?'

Davies pulled on the collective and cyclic controls, flaring the aircraft to bring the speed down. He levelled the nose so that the helicopter was ready for the landing. 'In the gate,' he said.

'Seventy-five feet, twenty-five knots in the gate,' Taff said from the co-pilot's seat.

'Medics only, good to go,' Kinkers barked over the intercom from the rear of the helicopter.

'Fifty feet,' Taff said. Davies' hand automatically went to the RADALT to silence the alarm, before he remembered that it wasn't working.

'Clear below, forty,' Kinkers said over the intercom. 'Dust cloud building, thirty, twenty, at the ramp.' Sweat was pouring down Davies' forehead, but the last thing he wanted to do was not have both hands on the controls. He stared at the instrument panels in front of him, even though the most important one wasn't working as Kinkers's voice droned in his ears. 'Front door, four, three, two, one, wheels on.'

Davies glanced out of the front window to try to get an idea of whether or not he was too high to touch down, but he couldn't see anything beyond the dust swirling around the Plexiglass screen. With a silent prayer that Kinkers was correct, he touched the helicopter to the ground.

'Ramp down,' Kinkers said a second later. 'Nicely done, boss.'

Sergeant Hawkins watched as the large Chinook landed a few hundred yards in front of him. Two figures leapt from the ramp at the back, one of them with a stretcher, and looked frantically around through the dust cloud. He stood up in the front of the WMIK and waved his arms at them, noticing at the same time that the soldier in the driver's seat was flashing the headlights. Both medics started running towards them, hampered by the large rucksacks they had on their backs.

Hawkins climbed out of the WMIK and went to the back of the vehicle where Private Mitchell was lying on a stretcher, his wounds hastily patched up by the platoon house medic. Hawkins reached into the Land Rover and squeezed Mitchell's shoulder.

'TRT's here, mate,' he said. 'Time to go.' Private Mitchell opened his eyes and looked at Hawkins with bloodshot eyes. The large 'M' on his forehead told Hawkins that the medic had dosed him up with some morphine, and although he was no expert, Hawkins thought that from the state of Mitchell's eyes the medic had been quite generous with it. Fair play to the medic, Hawkins thought as he looked at the other two casualties sitting in the back of the Land Rover. They both looked back at him with looks of relief on their faces. Hawkins gave them both a brief smile before he turned away and walked back to the front of the vehicle. He didn't bother going to the WMIK behind them. The only person in it was Lance Corporal Ruffles and he didn't need any reassurance inside his body bag.

Reaching into the passenger seat footwell, Hawkins grabbed his rifle and started towards the helicopter. There was an irrigation ditch in front of them which was the main reason why the vehicle couldn't take the casualties any closer to the landing site — it was the secondary landing site for many reasons, and the ditches surrounding it were one of them. Looking over at the medics, who were still running despite the heat, he saw with horror a spiralling column of smoke emerge from some trees behind the Chinook and head straight towards it.

25

In the front of the helicopter, Davies saw the same column of smoke as Hawkins. It was preceded by a flash to the right, which is what had caught Davies's attention in the first place.

'RPG right, RPG, fuck!' he shouted as he snatched at the collective and pulled it towards his groin as hard as he could. The engines screamed in complaint but did their job as the aircraft jolted upwards and into the air. The second that they were off the ground he shoved the collective hard over to his right with his left hand, sending the helicopter into a hard bank. At the same time, he pushed the throttles forward with his other hand to give the absolute maximum amount of power to both engines. The helicopter jarred itself over to the right-hand side, almost reaching ninety degrees while both rotor blades spun only feet from the ground before he corrected the bank and adjusted the cyclic to push them upwards into the sky.

'Smoke trail below,' Davies heard Kinkers on the inter-com. 'Fuck me, that was close,' the loadie continued.

'Fucking hell!' Davies breathed deeply a couple of

times before looking across at his co-pilot, Taff. 'Fucking hell. Bastards. Fucking bastards.' Davies took another deep breath before blowing it through his cheeks.

'Well, it's a good job I'm not offended by bad language, Davies,' Taff replied in a laconic voice as the helicopter climbed rapidly to the safety of the sky.

Lizzie was running across the landing site to the vehicle with the casualties, closely followed by Adams, when they were enveloped by a dust cloud. She turned and looked over her shoulder as the helicopter lifted off and banked sharply. For a second, she thought it was going to carry on banking until gravity took over and it all went horribly wrong, but at the last minute, the Chinook corrected and started climbing.

'Where the hell are they going?' Lizzie shouted over the noise of the helicopter, slowing down to a walk. She looked at Adams, who had a face like a beetroot from trying to run over the rough ground in the heat. He slowed down as he reached her, breathing hard.

'Keep. Fucking. Going,' Adams gasped, pushing Lizzie in the chest. 'RPG. Trees.' Any reticence that Lizzie had soon disappeared as she heard sharp cracks of gunfire from somewhere close by. She broke into a run and started sprinting towards the vehicles at the edge of the landing site.

'Ditch!' she heard Adams shout behind her. 'Get in the fucking ditch.' Looking ahead, she could see a shallow ditch in front of the vehicle they were headed towards. There were soldiers in the Land Rover, one of them swinging the machine gun on the back around to face towards them.

As Lizzie got to within a couple of feet of the ditch, which was deeper than it had looked from a few feet away, she felt Adams shove her hard in the small of her back. Losing her footing, she stumbled, but just before she got to the edge of the ditch the rucksack on her back was violently jolted to one side. Adams must have grabbed it so that he could yank her into cover.

Lizzie landed face first in the tepid water at the bottom of the ditch and was then nearly crushed by Adams flying over the top of the lip, knocking the wind out of her. Just above them, she could hear the fifty-calibre machine gun on the back of the WMIK delivering the good news to someone, hopefully the bad guys. Lizzie and Adams untangled themselves from each other until they were sitting on either side of the ditch, spent casings from the machine gun above them raining down and fizzing as they hit the water in the bottom of the ditch.

She watched as Adams struggled with the straps of his rucksack and kicked out at the stretcher that had somehow followed them into the ditch. He racked back the slide on his rifle to push a round into the chamber, and with his thumb checked to make sure the safety catch was still on. The last thing he needed was a negligent discharge.

'Mate,' he said, breathing hard. 'I think we're in the shit here.'

'No kidding, you fat bastard,' she replied over the noise of the machine gun above them. 'They never bloody mentioned this in the Careers Office.'

As soon as Ronald heard Davies shouting 'RPG', the medic grabbed the metal back of the seat with both hands. The helicopter jolted upwards and started climbing, and he could feel the rotor blades thrashing at the air. Looking towards the back of the cabin, he could see over the open ramp that the horizon was tilting as the helicopter went into a hard bank. Seconds later, a spiralling smoke trail shot across the piece of sky that he could see through the open rear of the Chinook. The helicopter kept tilting over, further than he'd ever known it do before, and for one terrifying second, Ronald thought it was going to keep banking until it was upside down.

Sitting next to Ronald, Colonel Nick didn't have the advantage of a headset connected to the internal radio channel. Ronald watched as the Colonel was thrown out of his seat and catapulted onto the other side of the helicopter. Ronald had a split second where he could have grabbed the Colonel's uniform to try to stop him sliding across the floor, but if he had let go of the back of the seat, he didn't think he would be able to hold on himself.

Ronald's heart pounded in his chest as he tightened his grip on the stanchion at the back of the seat, his knuckles turning white with the effort. All around him, soldiers and equipment were sliding around inside the helicopter. He hung on — helpless — until the helicopter gradually started to right itself and he felt himself starting to be pressed back into his seat as it gained altitude.

'Jesus Christ,' Ronald said, releasing his grip on the stanchion and flexing his fingers a couple of times to get the blood back into them. The helicopter was pretty much level and climbing hard now, so he jumped out of his seat and went across to where Colonel Nick was folded underneath the seats on the opposite side.

'Are you okay, sir?' Ronald shouted over the noise of the rotor blades. Colonel Nick looked up at Ronald with a dazed expression on his face. 'Sir?' Ronald shouted again. 'Are you okay?'

'My leg,' Colonel Nick replied. 'I think my knee's fucked.' Ronald helped the doctor extricate himself from underneath the seats and watched him as he gingerly ran his hands over his left knee. A few seconds later, Colonel Nick had got to his feet. He was grimacing as he did so, but if he could stand then there was nothing broken.

Ronald could hear the frantic conversation between the pilots in the front and the Ops Room back at Camp Bastion through his headset. They were trying to get information back to Bastion about what had just happened, but at the same time, the troops from the FOB were calling in a contact on the ground. The confusion in the voices of the Ops Officers as they tried to process the information was obvious

Turning from Colonel Nick, Ronald surveyed the interior of the helicopter. Strewn across the floor were soldiers, equipment, weapons, and bottles of water. He unclipped the cable that linked him to the comms system and walked back down through the helicopter towards the ramp, examining the soldiers as he did so to see if there were any other injuries. As he got close to the ramp at the back of the helicopter, he saw Kinkers sitting in one of the canvas seats with a dazed expression on his face. A thin trickle of blood ran down the side of his forehead. Ronald reached out his hand and shook the loadie's shoulder. Kinkers looked up at him, seeming to be confused for a second before he grinned and shouted at Ronald.

'That was a bit sporty, mate!' Despite the situation, Ronald felt himself returning the Australian's infectious grin.

Ronald walked back up towards the front of the helicopter and grabbed the spiral communication cable to plug himself back into the intercom. He looked up towards the front of the helicopter and saw the co-pilot looking back at him over his shoulder, his eyebrows raised. Taff tapped his microphone twice in quick succession, so Ronald flicked the switch on his intercom so that the co-pilot could hear him.

'We've got some minor casualties back here, sir,' Ronald said. 'The Colonel's hurt his leg — but he's up and about — and Kinkers down the back looks like he's had a smack to the head.'

'Okay, cheers. Might knock some sense into him' the co-pilot replied. Ronald heard the intercom going mute as the two pilots discussed something between themselves. A second later, it burst back to life. 'Is Kinkers fit to fire a gun?' Taff asked.

'Er, I don't think so,' Ronald said. 'He's quite dazed, although I think it's only a minor head injury.'

'What triage category would you say they both were?'

'Both Cat B, I would say.'

'Nice one, cheers,' the co-pilot said.

Ronald heard the intercom go mute again as the pilots carried on their discussion. He looked back down the helicopter and saw the Force Protection team moving around the cabin, picking up their equipment. Colonel Nick was moving down the cabin, checking on the young soldiers, as was Staff Sergeant Partridge.

The medic returned to the back of the helicopter to check on Kinkers, who had taken his heavy flying helmet off and was dabbing at his forehead with a tissue. After pulling the loadie's hand away and examining the small wound above his eyebrow, Ronald tapped him on the knee and gave him a thumbs up.

Picking his way through the Force Protection team, Ronald walked towards the front of the helicopter and sat down next to Colonel Nick. He plugged his intercom cable back in and looked behind him out of the window. Far below him, he could see fields crisscrossed with irrigation ditches. The medic looked back down the interior of the helicopter. Something wasn't right. It took him a few seconds to work out what was wrong.

There was no sign of Lizzie or Adams.

26

F light Lieutenant Davies eased the helicopter into a lazy left-hand turn to keep them over the top of the area that the troops were in. They were flying at about two and a half thousand feet, well beyond the range of any RPGs or small arms fire.

'Ops, this is Sandman 34,' Davies said. After a few seconds, he heard the Ops Room reply.

'Sandman 34, this is Ops. Go ahead.'

'This is Sandman 34. We are currently circling at altitude above the contact, two Cat B casualties on board,' Davies said. 'Any news on the replacement Ugly?'

'Are the Cat Bs from the ground? What happened to the Cat A?'

'The Cat Bs are ours. We had to abort the pickup, and they got thrown about a bit.' The Ops Room didn't reply, and Davies imagined the frantic arguments that must have been going on.

'Ugly is a few minutes out. Call sign Wildman 19. Ground troops are reporting heavy fire on the ground, so hot hot hot.'

'Roger that, Sandman 34 out.'

Davies flicked the switch on the intercom to return to the internal channel. 'Like we don't know it's bloody hot down there. What do you think, Taff? Stay, or go?' he asked his co-pilot. Taff looked down at the fuel gauge on the console in front of them.

'Well, we've got about an hour of fuel left,' Taff said. 'As long as the casualties in the back are okay, we could hang around for a little bit and see what happens.'

'Sounds like a plan,' Davies replied. 'I might go down the back and see what's going on while we wait for the Apache if you're happy with that?'

'Sure, no problem,' Taff said.

'You have control.' Davies lifted his hand from the cyclic as Taff responded.

'I have control.'

Davies undid his harness and shrugged his shoulders to loosen the straps. He unclipped his helmet from the intercom system, climbed through the seats, and stepped into the main cabin. Davies walked across and sat on one of the empty seats next to Ronald, clipping himself back into the intercom as he did so.

'How's it going, mate?' Davies said to Ronald, who looked absolutely terrified.

'Not too bad, sir,' Ronald replied. 'What's the plan?'

'We're going to circle for a while,' Davies said. 'There's an Apache on its way which should be here in a few minutes. Should calm things down a bit down there.' Davies put his hand on Ronald's shoulder. 'Are you sure you're okay?' He watched as Ronald nodded, but Davies wasn't convinced in the slightest.

'I'm fine,' Ronald said. Davies squeezed Ronald's shoulder before getting to his feet and walking towards the back of the cabin. When he reached Kinkers, Davies did exactly the same thing and put his hand on the Australian's shoulder.

'You okay, mate?' he said. Kinkers grinned back at Davies before he replied.

'That was a bit cheeky.'

'Yeah, sorry,' Davies laughed, pleased that his crew-mate had at least got his sense of humour back after a bang to the head. He got to his feet and walked back down the cabin, stopping to talk to some of the soldiers as he did so. Patting Ronald on the back as he walked past him, Davies climbed back into the front of the helicopter and did up his harness.

'They all seem okay back there,' Davies said to Taff. 'Kinkers seems none the worse for a tap on the head.'

'Good stuff,' Taff replied. 'Maybe it did knock some sense into him?' They both heard Ronald's voice crackle through the intercom.

'Sorry, sir,' Ronald said. 'Small problem back here. What are we going to do about Adams and Lizzie?'

Davies turned and looked over his shoulder, searching in vain for the two medics. Of course, he remembered, the minute that he touched down they would have jumped off to go and get the casualties. He'd been so overwhelmed with trying to get the helicopter out of danger that he'd completely forgotten about them. Davies turned the intercom switch so that only Taff could hear him.

'Bollocks, Taff,' he said. 'There're two medics still down on the ground.' Switching the intercom back to its original position, he continued, 'Don't worry, mate. We'll go back in and get them as soon as we can.' He switched channels again to speak with the troops on the ground.

'Widow 23, this is Sandman 34,' he said. When there was no reply, he repeated himself a few seconds later.

'Sandman 34, send.' Both Davies and Taff could hear

the sharp crack of gunfire in the background of the brief message.

'Widow 23, be advised you have two of our medics with you at your location.' There was another delay before the next message came back.

'Sandman 34, Roger that,' Davies crinkled his brow as the rest of the message started to break up with static.

'Widow 23, say again,' Davies said. There was no reply. 'Widow 23, say again.' He repeated himself another couple of times before giving up. 'Widow 23, this is Sandman 34, nothing heard.' Flicking the switch on the intercom, he turned to Taff. 'When we loop back around and are directly overhead, I'll try to raise them again.'

'Who's down there?'

'Adams and Lizzie,' Davies replied with a grim smile. 'I don't care how much fuel we've got, we're not going back without them.'

'She shouldn't be down there, mate.'

'Nope. I think we're in the shit when we get back. I can feel a swift return to the UK coming up.'

'Got that right, Taff,' Davies said, his smile even grimmer. 'There's an interview without coffee on its way, that's for sure.'

'Stoppage!' the soldier who was manning the fifty-calibre machine gun shouted as the gun stopped firing. The sharp crack of gunfire still rang around the area, so it was obvious that somebody was still shooting. Adams, huddled just below the lip of the irrigation ditch, had absolutely no idea whether it was the soldiers shooting at the insurgents, the insurgents shooting at them, or both. 'Get some eyes on the tree line!' the soldier in the WMIK shouted down at

Adams. 'There's still some Terry over there.' With a look at Lizzie, Adams shuffled up onto the lip and raised his SA80 rifle to his shoulder.

'Stay down there,' Adams said to Lizzie as he got himself into position and looked down the sights of his rifle towards the trees. He looked left and right, but couldn't see anything at all. Everything had fallen silent in the last couple of seconds, and Adams could hear the soldier behind him swearing as he struggled to clear the stoppage in the heavy machine gun. Had all the insurgents disappeared?

'What's going on, then?' Lizzie said as she shuffled into position next to Adams and looked down the sights of her rifle.

'For fuck's sake, Lizzie,' Adams replied. 'I said stay there, didn't I?'

'Oh, did you? Didn't hear you.' She gave him a side-ways look before looking back towards the trees. 'So, where's Terry Taliban gone then?' A couple of shots rang out to their left-hand side, but now that Adams was on top of the ditch, he could place the firing as theirs. He returned to the sights of his rifle, making small movements to try to keep the whole area in sight.

He caught a flash of movement over by the tree line in his peripheral vision. There was still someone there for sure, but it had been too swift for him to see anything other than the movement of the branches. He eased the safety catch off his rifle and squinted down the sights, trying to see where the movement had come from, his side to side movements focused in on the area where he thought he'd seen movement.

Adams couldn't see anything at all, so he gradually increased the lateral movement until he found himself looking at an insurgent pointing an RPG back at them.

'Fuck', Adams said as he squeezed the trigger without thinking. The rifle butt pushed back into his shoulder as the shot rang out, and he watched as the insurgent fell backward in a puff of red mist. A second later, an RPG round spiralled up into the sky through the branches of the trees. Adams brought the rifle down out of the aim. 'Oh fuck,' he said under his breath, his heart hammering in his chest as he realised what he had just done.

'Nice shot, fella,' a voice behind him said. 'That's seventy-two virgins for him, but none for you.' Adams looked up to see the soldier on the WMIK looking down at him. The gunner's eyes flicked across to Lizzie, and Adams saw him frown. He'd obviously just realised that Lizzie was not just a medic, but a female one. 'Oh,' the soldier said looking at Lizzie. 'Sorry. No offence meant.'

Adams looked at Lizzie and could see the fear and excitement in her face. She looked pale, but had twin red spots in the centre of each cheek and was very animated.

'I can't believe you shot that bloke with the RPG,' she said, far more quickly than she usually spoke. Adams flicked his safety catch back on and slid down the bank of the ditch a couple of feet. He blew a deep breath out through his cheeks.

'Neither can I,' he replied. 'Neither can I.'

Lizzie slid down until she was next to him. Adams could hear radio chatter from the WMIK above him and looked up to see a soldier crouching at the top of the ditch, staring down at him.

'Are you two medics?' he asked. 'There's a Chinook up there that's missing a couple.' Adams pulled his sleeve around to show the soldier the embroidered red cross on his uniform.

'Yep, that'll be us,' he replied.

'Well, fuck me, aren't you two crabs in the wrong

place?' The soldier turned slightly and spoke back into his radio.

'We have them,' he said. 'And one of them's a bloody good shot.'

Three thousand feet above Adams and Lizzie, Davies turned to Taff.

'Mate, did you get the last bit of that message?'

'I got bits and pieces of it,' Taff replied. 'Did he say what I think he said?'

'What do you think he said?' Davies asked, hoping that his co-pilot had heard something different to what he thought he had heard.

'I thought he'd said that one of the medics had been shot.'

'Fuck,' Davies said. 'That's what I thought he'd said.' He flicked the switch on his radio to talk to the Ops Room. 'Ops, this is Sandman 34,' Davies said as he put the Chinook into a lazy turn.

'Sandman 34, this is Ops.'

'Ops, confirm ETA arrival of second Ugly call sign.'

'Sandman 34, he's about inbound now.'

'Roger that Ops, Sandman 34 out.' Davies switched channels with his thumb to talk to the rest of his crew. 'Gents, there's a second Apache on its way. When the Ugly's on target, that's when we'll drop in to pick up the casualties and the medics.'

'Sounds like a good plan to me,' Taff said in the left-hand seat. 'Although if we're coming in fast, not having a RADALT might make things interesting.'

Davies tilted the cyclic to put the helicopter into a slow descent. Looking over his shoulder, he could see Kinkers and Ronald talking in the back of the helicopter. Davies heard Kinkers' voice come through the radio.

'Boss, I'm going to put Ronald on one of the side guns so that's it's obvious that it's manned. What's our angle of approach? I don't want to put him on the wrong one.'

'Good stuff Kinkers, as long as he's happy with that. Don't forget he's a medic, though.'

'He's fine, boss. Don't worry.'

'Okay, wait one.'

Davies and Taff discussed the best approach for a few minutes as they slowly lost height and the terrain below them became clearer.

'I think if we spring around and approach the HLS over the top of the FOB, then we've got some ground cover from the troops inside and it's a completely different approach to the last time.' Taff pointed with his finger to show Davies the exact angle that he would need to line the helicopter up on.

'Yep,' Davies said. 'I like that idea. In which case Ronald would be better off on the starboard gun.'

'Roger that,' Kinkers said from the back of the Chinook before he was cut off by an unfamiliar voice bursting in on the radio.

'Sandman 34, this is Ugly 19.' Both Davies and Taff looked around them to try to locate the new arrival.

'Ugly 19, this is Sandman 34. We don't have you on visual,' Davies replied.

'Sandman 34, I'm above and behind you.' The pilot switched radio channels to speak to Kinkers.

'Kinkers, there is an Ugly on our six, high.' Davies glanced over his shoulder and saw the loadie moving to the back of the cabin towards the ramp. A few seconds later, Kinkers replied.

'Yep, I got him. He's gaining fast and coming down to our starboard side.'

'Just make sure Ronald doesn't shoot at him.' As Davies switched channels back again, he could hear Kinkers laughing.

A moment later, Davies looked out of his right-hand window and saw the black Apache helicopter come into view a couple of hundred feet away. He waved a hand in greeting and received a middle finger from the co-pilot in the back seat in reply.

'Ugly 19, I have you on visual, dick finger and all,' Davies said.

'Sandman 34, Roger that. Sorry about my back seat. They wouldn't let him join the RAF because his legs are too short.' Davies laughed and saw the co-pilot in the back seat of the Apache reach forward and slap the helmet of his colleague in front of him. The Apache shifted and went nose down into a rapid descent. 'See you at the party, Ugly 19 out.'

27

Adams and Lizzie both jumped as an Apache helicopter appeared from nowhere behind them, the rapidly spiralling chain gun on its nose ripping the tree line to shreds. As the echoes of the long burst of gunfire sounded around them, Adams could hear the whoops and cheers of soldiers that he couldn't see. He watched the helicopter bank around and could see the cannon on the front moving as it kept its aim on the trees. Adams assumed that there was a Forward Air Controller some-where in the area talking the helicopter in, but he didn't know for sure. He also didn't care.

'My God,' Lizzie said. 'I can see why they call them Uglies.' The two of them sat in the ditch for a few moments, listening to the helicopter circling above them. There were several more bursts of gunfire, but then all they could hear was the rotor blades of the Apache.

'You can get out of the ditch now, if you want?' Adams heard a deep voice from above his head a few minutes later. He looked up to see a tall, good looking soldier staring down at him and Lizzie. 'Any Terry left over will be

long gone by now.' He pointed up at the sky where the
Apache helicopter hovered like a very angry hornet,
constantly moving its position as the crew looked for
targets. 'They do tend to have that effect.'

Adams slid back down into the bottom of the irrigation
ditch, closely followed by Lizzie. He picked up the medical
bag that he had left in the water at the bottom of the ditch
when he'd climbed up to the top and slid his arms back
through the straps. Once his own bag was secure, he
picked up Lizzie's and helped her put it on. They both
climbed up to where the WMIK was parked.

Breathing hard from the exertion of climbing out of
the ditch, Adams walked to where the soldier was standing.

'Er, excuse me,' Adams said as the soldier looked up at
him. 'Me and my mate here are a bit lost. We are trying to
find Camp Bastion, do you know where it is?' The soldier
looked at Adams and laughed as he glanced down at
Adams's ranks slides.

'You are a bit lost, sir, aren't you?' He put his hand out
for Adams to shake. 'I'm Lance Corporal Jackson, known
as Jacko.' Adams shook Jackson's hand, taking in his
suntanned, sweat-covered face.

'I'm Adams,' he replied, still shaking Jackson's hand.
Adams turned and waved at Lizzie with his other hand.
'This is Lizzie.' Jackson let go of Adams and looked over at
Lizzie, fixing her with an intense stare. His eyes were so
green they were almost turquoise.

'Lizzie,' Jackson glanced down at her rank slides as
well. 'Sergeant Lizzie, in fact. I'm Jacko.' He held out his
hand, which Lizzie duly shook. Adams smiled as he saw
Jackson shaking Lizzie's hand for far longer than he had
shaken his, but she didn't seem the slightest bit bothered.

There was a crackle of static from the radio in the
WMIK. Jackson released Lizzie's hand.

'Would you excuse me for a moment?' he said. 'Duty calls.' Lizzie smiled at him and he gave her a broad grin in return. Adams noticed with irritation how perfect his teeth were.

'Sure,' she replied. Jackson turned and walked over to the radio, picking up the headset attached to it.

Lizzie leaned forward and whispered in Adams's ear.

'Don't take this the wrong way, Adams,' she said, 'but I think I'm going to apply for a transfer up here.' Adams laughed and whispered back.

'Lizzie, I hate to break it to you, but that is the look of a man who has not seen a woman for a very long time.' Adams smiled as she crossed her arms and frowned before he continued, 'The minute his plane touches down at Brize Norton,' Adams said, 'you'll be officially ugly again.'

'You're just jealous,' Lizzie replied. 'Because your arms aren't a patch on his.' Adams looked across at Jackson and grimaced when he realised that she was right.

'Fair one,' he said. 'I'll give you that. But I bet he can't do crosswords as well as I can.'

'I couldn't give a monkey's.' Lizzie said.

'Oh, bollocks.' Adams suddenly realised that they didn't have the stretcher with them. 'We've left the stretcher in the bottom of that sodding ditch.'

'Sorry, who was carrying it?' Lizzie said. 'I'm fairly sure it was you.' Adams looked at Lizzie, and then over at the ditch.

'Can you maybe nip down–' he said.

'No, I bloody well can't. You left it there, so you can go back and get it.' She nodded across towards Jackson. 'I'll monitor things up here.' Adams swore under his breath and loosened the straps on his rucksack before putting it on the ground at Lizzie's feet.

'Keep an eye on that then,' he said, 'if it's not too much trouble.'

Lizzie put her medical bag down next to Adams's and watched as he trudged back towards the irrigation ditch. What she really wanted to do was to take off her helmet and run her fingers through her hair. As she looked at the soldiers around her, she could see that although they had a variety of different uniforms, the two things they were all wearing were body armour and helmets. Besides, she thought, judging by the sweat dripping down the back of her neck, if she did take her helmet off it wouldn't be a pretty sight.

She heard Jackson calling out, and when she looked up, he was beckoning her towards him. Lizzie walked across to him, leaving the bags where they were in the sand. As she got closer to him, she could see the serious look on his face.

'Lizzie, you and your boss need to get cracking, mate,' he said. He really was attractive, Lizzie thought, but she reminded herself that there was a time and a place for everything. And now definitely wasn't the time or the place. 'The Chinook's on its way back in to get you guys and the casualties.'

'Okay, no worries,' Lizzie said, resisting the urge to wipe sweat from her face. 'Adams is just getting the stretcher he left in the ditch, then he'll be back and we'll get ourselves sorted.'

'Do me a favour though, would you?' Jackson said. 'Keep an eye on him over the next few days.' Lizzie looked at him, surprised at how serious he sounded after being so flirty a few minutes ago. 'I'm guessing that he's probably not slotted someone before.' Lizzie thought for a second.

'I'm pretty sure that he hasn't,' she replied.

'He won't have processed it yet,' Jackson said. 'But at some point, probably when he's back in his scratcher, he'll come down hard.'

'Okay, thanks. I'll make sure we look after him. Where're the casualties?' Jackson pointed towards one of the Land Rovers.

'They're in the back of that one,' he said. Lizzie started walking towards the vehicle. She looked over her shoulder and raised one of her hands.

'Cheers, Jacko, I'll see you later.'

As she walked the short distance to the Land Rover, her boots kicked up small clouds of fine dust. Lizzie looked down at her feet and could see dried out poppy heads on the surface of the soil. By the time she reached the Land Rover, Lizzie was sweating hard. She pulled her damp shirt away from her skin a couple of times to try to ventilate her chest, but it didn't make any difference. Lizzie reached the Land Rover, and another soldier got out as she approached the driver's door.

'Corporal Booker,' he said with a broad smile and a handshake. 'I'm the medic in the FOB.' As she shook his hand, Lizzie noticed the small red cross on his arm.

'Sergeant Jarman,' Lizzie said. 'I'm the paramedic from the TRT, and my boss is about somewhere as well.'

'Well, you certainly chose an interesting time to turn up,' Corporal Booker said. Lizzie gave him a dry smile.

'Yes, that's one way of putting things.'

'Your main man's in the back of the wagon,' he said. 'I think I may have given him a bit too much happy juice as he slept through everything. There's a couple of walking wounded in there as well.'

Lizzie saw Adams approaching the Land Rover, both their medical bags slung over his shoulders and the stretcher tucked under his other arm. He looked just as uncomfortable in the heat as Lizzie felt, and made a disparaging comment about her leaving the medical bags behind. Ignoring the barb, she introduced Adams to the medic, and as the two of them shook hands, she looked into the back of the Land Rover. Lizzie could tell the casualty was still alive, as he was snoring loudly. Acting from instinct, she put her fingers under his jaw to lift it forwards.

'There is no point, sergeant,' Corporal Booker said, laughing. 'He's not obstructed, he's just out for the count.' Lizzie's actions had no effect at all and she felt slightly foolish as she let go of his chin.

Lizzie and Adams listened as the medic ran through all the clinical details of the casualty.

'Private William Mitchell, age nineteen. He was the driver of a wagon that went over a mine. Took the whole front of the Landy off, and his feet with it. Traumatic amputations both mid-shin level and a lot of soft tissue damage further up, as well as burns from the fire. He'll need a urologist if he survives, I reckon.'

'Jesus Christ,' Adams mumbled. 'Poor fucker.'

'Not as unfortunate as his passenger,' Corporal Booker replied. 'He's in the Land Rover over there,' he nodded towards another vehicle, 'in a body bag.' Lizzie looked towards the second Land Rover and bit her lip. The medic continued with his handover. 'Mitchell's not got tourniquets on as there wasn't any bleeding — I think the fire after the blast cauterised any vessels — but he's used up most of my bandage supply with all the soft tissue injuries. He got peppered with shrapnel as well.'

Corporal Booker continued detailing the medical treatment that Mitchell had received since the explosion. Lizzie made a few notes, and realising that the intravenous bag with its line leading to the casualty's arm was empty, she opened one of the side pockets of her medical bag for a replacement. The inside of the pocket was soaking wet, and she pulled out an empty intravenous bag. The bottom of the pocket was completely shredded. Lizzie held the bag up in the air like a fisherman displaying his catch.

'Can I have some fluid from your bag please, Adams?' Lizzie said. 'I think this one burst when you jumped on top of me.' Ignoring the strange look he received from the medic, Adams opened his bag for a replacement. Corporal Booker knelt and examined the outside of Lizzie's bag. He put his hand into the pocket that Lizzie had taken the intravenous bag from and stuck his index finger back out through a small hole in the bottom of the pocket. Lizzie looked down at him with surprise.

'How come my bag's got a hole in it?' she asked him. Despite the heat, Lizzie felt the blood drain from her face when she heard his reply.

'It's not just a hole in the pocket. It goes all the way through,' Corporal Booker said, still wiggling his finger. He looked at Lizzie. 'I think you've had a very narrow escape. If that round had hit six inches further forwards, it would have gone straight through you.'

Adams saw Lizzie's face going white as she realised how close she had come to being shot. He took a step towards her and reached out his hand to rub her shoulder.

'Are you okay, Lizzie?' he said. 'You've gone a bit pale there, mate.' Lizzie looked back at him, her mouth slightly open.

'I thought it was you, grabbing my rucksack to get me in the ditch.' She stared at him with wide eyes.

'I never touched you at the top of the ditch, Lizzie,'

Adams said. 'I just gave you a shove a few feet away from it to get you moving.'

'Oh, my God,' Lizzie whispered, her face going even whiter than it had been despite the heat. 'My God, that was close.'

'Six inches lower down and that would have gone right through your arse cheeks.' Adams said, hoping for a smile as he grabbed some intravenous fluids from his rucksack.

'It's not funny, Adams,' she whispered. 'Not funny at all.'

Adams reached back into his bag and came out with a bottle of water. He cracked open the top and handed it to Lizzie.

'Have some water, Lizzie,' he said. 'You need to sit down or anything?' Lizzie took a long sip of the water.

'No, I'm fine,' she said. 'Just a bit shaken up, that's all.'

Adams looked up as he heard a short beep on a vehicle horn. He could see Jackson over by the WMIK holding his hand up with three fingers extended.

'Three minutes until your taxi's here,' Corporal Booker said. 'I'll go and get some bodies to help with the stretchers.'

'Okay, cheers,' Adams replied. 'We'll get the casualty sorted.' As the Corporal jogged away, Adams turned to Lizzie. 'Okay, mate,' he said. 'Let's get cracking. Our ride home is on its way.'

Lizzie climbed into the back of the Land Rover and started fussing around the casualty, who was snoring like a walrus. Adams watched as she put a pair of protective goggles over the soldier's eyes. She looked as if she was happy to have something to do, although he was still worried. He wondered what would have happened to Lizzie if he hadn't pushed her — whether or not the bullet would have hit her. That would have been an entirely different day altogether.

A few minutes later Corporal Booker returned, accompanied by Jackson.

'It's just him, I'm afraid,' the medic said. Lizzie poked her head out of the back of the Land Rover and Jackson smiled at her. Adams was relieved to see a weak smile appear on her face. 'I've had to send the others to get the one in the bag.' As Corporal Booker said this, Lizzie's smile faded away.

'Hey, it's my favourite nurse,' Jackson said. 'How's tricks?' Lizzie climbed down from the vehicle and brushed some dust from her knees.

'Not too bad, thanks, but I'm not a nurse. I'm a paramedic,' she said before nodding at Adams. 'He's the nurse. Now, Jacko, I hope you're feeling strong?' Lizzie tilted her head towards the casualty on the stretcher. 'He's a big lad.' Adams rolled his eyes at Lizzie as Jackson flexed his biceps in response. She arched an eyebrow back at Adams and her smile grew broader.

Between them, they manoeuvred the stretcher out of the Land Rover and put it on the sand in the shade next to the vehicle. Lizzie connected the casualty to a small monitor, wrapping the blood pressure cuff around his large arm and pressing a button on the front, while Adams struggled with a pair of latex gloves. When he retired, he thought, he was going to invent some gloves that could be put on no matter how sweaty someone's hands were and make a bloody fortune. As he fiddled with the latex to get his fingers into the gloves properly, he heard a beep from the monitor which Lizzie had placed on the bottom of the stretcher where Private Mitchell's feet should have been.

'Blood pressure's still a bit low,' Adams said before

reaching down to the monitor and pressing a button to silence the alarm.

Adams looked around in the sky when he heard the distinctive sound of the Chinook's rotors somewhere in the distance, but he couldn't see it anywhere.

'Are we good to go?' he asked Lizzie. She nodded, before adjusting the goggles on Private Mitchell's face. Lizzie got to her feet and stood next to Adams, pointing at a black speck in the sky. 'There we go,' she said. 'There's our ride.'

'Bloody hell,' Adams replied. 'You've got good eyesight.'

The small group on the ground watched as the black speck gradually became the unmistakable silhouette of a Chinook. The Apache helicopter was still circling tightly over the top of the nearby village, its machine gun moving back and forth in a show of force, as the other much larger helicopter approached.

At the last minute, just before the Chinook disappeared into a cloud of dust, it spun around on its own axis until the ramp of the helicopter was pointing in their direction. As it settled on the ground, a familiar brown cloud enveloped it until it was lost from their sight.

'Right then,' Adams said as he knelt next to the stretcher. 'Has everyone got a bit?' Once he was happy everyone was ready, Adams continued, 'One, two, three, lift.'

They shuffled slowly towards the helicopter. Adams felt his rifle smack against his hip with every step, and as he looked across at Lizzie, he could see that she was finding it as difficult as he was. The large medical rucksacks on their backs didn't exactly help either. As they got closer to the helicopter, Adams recognised Partridge kneeling on the ground about twenty yards from the ramp.

As they went past him, Adams saw Partridge stand and take the handle that Lizzie was carrying from her. Her look of annoyance was short-lived, and Adams nodded at Partridge as Lizzie peeled away from the stretcher and started running towards the ramp of the helicopter.

They stumbled forward with the stretcher as the Apache buzzed overhead, its chain gun jerking from side to side, and as the Force Protection team streamed out of the helicopter and ran towards them, Adams realised that although they weren't safe just yet, the odds had suddenly got a lot better.

28

Emma Wardle nibbled at a bit of loose skin on the nail of her index finger as she watched Squadron Leader Webb pacing up and down the Emergency Room. No-one seemed to be sure exactly what was going on, but there was a rumour going around the hospital that one of the medics on the TRT had been shot or injured somehow. She'd half overheard a whispered conversation between one of the Ops Officers and the Squadron Leader, and she was now worried sick about Lizzie and the others. Emma didn't particularly like the RAF doctor, but she knew that she'd have to ask him what was happening. She looked at the clock on the wall of the tent and realised that the TRT had been out for a long time, much longer than normal. Emma took a deep breath and waited until the Squadron Leader paced close to where she was standing.

'Sir?' Emma asked. Webb stopped in his tracks and stared at her.

'Yes, what?' he barked. Emma gripped her hands together when she heard the strain in his voice. *It was too late to back down now*, she thought.

'I was wondering if you knew anything about what's happening with the TRT?' She glanced back towards the clock. 'It's just that they've been gone ages, and...' Emma paused, not sure what to say.

'And, what?' Webb said, his face softening.

'Well, I'm worried about Lizzie. And the others, of course, but Lizzie's my room-mate.' Webb looked at her, and Emma thought for a second that he looked just as worried as she was. He sat on one of the chairs by the desk and ran his hands through his hair.

'I'll be honest, I don't know,' he said. 'I was talking to the Lieutenant from the Ops Room earlier. You probably overhead us talking, did you?' Emma nodded.

'Sorry, I did. I didn't mean to, though. It's just you were talking right when I was walking past.'

'It's okay, don't worry. I'm not having a pop at you,' Webb said. 'The Lieutenant was saying that they'd got some broken messages over the net that said one of the medics had been shot.'

Emma wrung her hands together, resisting the urge to bite her nails again. She looked at Webb, who was sitting in the chair, drumming his fingers against the armrest. They both turned as someone came into the Emergency Room.

'Have you got a second, sir?' the Lieutenant from the Ops Room said after a quick glance at Emma.

'It's okay, carry on,' Webb said. 'She knows what's going on. Or at least, she knows what I know.'

'The latest from the Chinook is that they've got one dead, one Cat A, and three Cat Bs.'

'Any idea who's who?'

'None at all.'

'What did they originally go out to collect?' Webb asked.

'The original 9-liner said one Cat A and a couple of Cat Bs.'

'So between the original call and them lifting off to come back, someone's died?'

'Looks that way, sir,' the lieutenant replied. 'But they don't always call in the KIAs because,' he shot a quick glance at Emma, 'well, because they're dead.'

'ETA?'

'About fifteen minutes.'

'Okay, put a Tannoy out for the team.'

'Will do, sir.' The Lieutenant turned on his heel and started walking back towards the door. 'If I hear anything else, I'll let you know.'

Emma got to her feet and followed the young officer out of the Emergency Room. He gave her a strange look as she walked through the door after him, but she ignored him and turned in the opposite direction towards the toilets at the far end of the hospital. All she wanted was some time to herself for a few minutes. Emma knew that the toilets opposite to the Emergency Room would be busy as personnel responding to the Tannoy would pop in there before all hell broke loose. She pushed the door to the toilets open, and when she saw that she was on her own, stood in front of one of the mirrors and put her hands on the sink.

'For Christ's sake, Lizzie,' Emma said to her reflection. 'You'd better be okay.' Emma rubbed the crucifix she wore around her neck. 'Please be okay.' They were so close to their R&R — only days to do before they could get some respite. For something to happen to Lizzie so close to the mid-tour break would be an absolute disaster.

Emma pressed the button on the tap and leaned forward, cupping her hands underneath the running water. As she splashed water over her face, she silently prayed, even though this had never worked in the past. Drying her hands on the paper towels, she took a deep breath and walked back out into the corridor.

'Trauma call, ten minutes,' Emma heard the Lieutenant's voice echo around the corridor as the Tannoy went out. Within seconds, people started filling the corridor and heading towards the Emergency Room. By the time she got back to the Emergency Room, it was a hive of activity. Three of the four trauma bays were being prepared for use as personnel checked equipment and machines. Emma walked across to where Squadron Leader Webb was standing by the desk at the far end of the room.

'Any news?' she asked him.

'No, nothing,' he replied with a sigh. 'We'll find out soon enough, though.' Emma watched as he looked around the room, making sure that everything was in place to receive the casualties. He walked across to a small group of personnel standing by the door, and after a few quiet words from him, they left the Emergency Room.

The medics in the Emergency Room all quietened down as they heard the distinctive sound of a Chinook helicopter overhead.

Emma stood outside the back door to the Emergency Room, biting her nails. She watched as the Chinook disappeared behind the accommodation tents where the hospital's helicopter landing site was located.

She turned to see Major Clarke standing next to her.

'Hello, sir,' Emma said.

'Corporal Wardle,' Major Clarke replied. 'You look a bit nervous,' he paused. 'I take it you've heard the rumours?' Emma nodded her head in reply.

'I'm really worried,' she said.

'I know, Squadron Leader Webb told me.'

'What if it is one of ours?' Emma felt her voice trembling. 'What if it's Lizzie that's hurt?'

'There's nothing we can do about it, Emma.'

'Yes, but if it is one of the medics who's been shot, I don't know if I could handle it.'

'I think you need to give yourself more credit,' Major Clarke said. 'If it is one of ours, it doesn't make any difference to what we do.'

She thought about what Major Clarke had said. He was right, but it didn't make her any less scared. They stood in silence for a few minutes, listening for the sound of the ambulances on the gravel. After what seemed to Emma like ages, two dark green battlefield ambulances came around the corner from behind the accommodation. Both of the ambulances had small blue lights on top, which were on but barely visible in the sunlight.

As they got closer to the hospital the rear ambulance veered off and drove towards the rear end of the facility, to where the mortuary was located. The remaining ambulance turned and started reversing towards the door of the Emergency Room. When it got to within a few feet of the tent, Major Clarke slapped his hand twice on the glass window in the back door. The ambulance came to an abrupt stop and the door was flung open from the inside.

Emma leaned around and tried to see inside the vehicle, but the difference between the bright sunlight outside and the dark interior meant that she couldn't see anything.

The other door to the ambulance opened, and Emma saw Adams jump down onto the gravel. Emma grabbed his arm hard.

'Where's Lizzie?' she said. Adams just looked at her, the sweat streaming down his face. 'Where is she? Is she okay?'

'She's fine,' Adams said with a curious look at her. 'She's back at the helicopter.'

'Oh, thank fuck for that,' Emma said under her breath.

As Emma and Major Clarke each grabbed a handle of the stretcher and prepared to slide it out of the ambulance, Major Clarke said, 'Corporal Wardle, I don't think I've ever heard you swear.' Emma looked at him, her face reddening.

'Sorry, sir,'

'Don't be,' he replied.

～

Lizzie sat in the back of the helicopter, listening as the rotors wound down. She undid the buckle of her helmet, took it off, and placed it on the seat next to her. Her scalp was itching like mad from the sweat and sand, and she felt absolutely disgusting. Opposite her, Ronald did the same thing with his helmet, and sat there looking at her. When the noise from the engine had died down, he said to her, 'Are you okay?'

Lizzie looked at him and around the empty helicopter. She was glad that the Force Protection Team and Kinkers had got off at the hospital, and that it was just the two of them left. The loadmaster hadn't wanted to get off, but Davies had been insistent as he'd had a bang to the head. Tears sprang to her eyes as she looked at Ronald.

'Apart from being shot at, pushed into a ditch, jumped on by Adams, and then watching him shoot someone, you mean?' Ronald stood and crossed the helicopter, sitting down next to her. 'So no,' she continued. 'I'm not okay, not by a long stretch.' Her voice broke as she finished the sentence, and when Ronald wrapped his arm around her, she started crying in earnest.

After a couple of minutes, Lizzie looked up to see Davies looking back at her from the front of the helicopter. He looked away when he saw her looking at him, and Lizzie reached into her pockets for a tissue. It was time for her to man the fuck up, she thought, otherwise they'd be here all day. She pulled a sodden mass of tissue from her pocket and examined it. It must have got soaked in the bottom of the ditch. Lizzie looked at Ronald, who was offering her a clean white handkerchief that looked as if it had been ironed. Knowing Ronald as she did, it probably had.

'If I use that, Ronald,' she said to him, 'it'll never be the same again.' Ronald smiled at her.

'If you use that,' he looked at the handkerchief, 'I never want it back anyway.' Lizzie smiled through her tears and took the handkerchief from him. She wiped it across her face, and when she had finished, she looked at the damp stains that the mud, sweat, tears, and snot had left on it.

'Sorry,' she said as Ronald laughed. 'I did warn you, though.'

Davies climbed through the gap between the front and the back of the helicopter, closely followed by Taff. Lizzie looked at the two officers and gave them what she hoped was a stoic smile.

'Did I hear that right?' Davies asked Lizzie. 'Did you say that Adams shot somebody?'

'Yes,' Lizzie nodded. 'There was a Taliban with an RPG pointed straight at us. Adams shot him.'

Davies arched his eyebrows and looked at his co-pilot.

'I wonder if that was the Terry who nearly hit us?' Davies said to Taff.

'Fair play to Adams if it was,' Taff replied.

∼

Thirty minutes later, the initial chaos caused by the arrival of the casualty had died down. Emma enjoyed the air of quiet urgency in the Emergency Room as everyone got ready to take the casualty to the operating theatre. People were busy, but everything was controlled. Many of the personnel who had been there for the initial treatment of the casualty had disappeared back to their own departments, some of them because they would be playing a part in the next stages of his treatment. Emma heard Major Clarke on the phone arguing with someone, probably from the operating theatre, as he was trying to find out if they were ready for the casualty.

She watched as the anaesthetist at the head of the trolley that Private Mitchell was laying on checked through all his equipment. He picked up the laryngoscope, opened it to make sure the light was working, and tightened the bulb in the device to make sure that it didn't fall out. Emma knew that the equipment was all good to go as she'd done exactly the same checks on the kit when she'd come onto shift but at the end of the day, it wouldn't be her actually using it. The anaesthetist looked up and saw Emma watching him.

'I'm going to tube him, are you happy to help?'

'Er, okay, thanks,' she said, surprised but pleased. It was normally one of the nurses from the Intensive Care Unit who helped out with intubation unless it had to be done in a real hurry. 'I'll just check with Major Clarke, though.' The anaesthetist smiled at her, the edges of his eyes crinkling in a way that Emma thought was really sweet. Lizzie would no doubt think something else completely, Emma thought as she walked across to the desk.

'Well when you find him, bloody well tell him that the rest of the hospital is waiting for him, would you?' she heard him say just before slamming down the phone. He turned and glared in her direction. 'Bloody doctors. The orthopaedic surgeon's just "nipped out" apparently. God knows where. It's not as if he can pop to Sainsbury's, is it? They've had to send someone to find him.' His face softened as he took a deep breath. 'Everything okay, Corporal Wardle?'

'Yes, sir,' Emma replied. She nodded her head towards the anaesthetist, who was checking the dials on the front of the ventilator. 'Are you happy for me to help him tube Private Mitchell? He's asked me to assist.'

'Are you happy?' he replied. 'You've assisted with one before, haven't you?'

'Er…' Emma paused. She'd seen plenty being done, but never assisted with an intubation. Major Clarke looked at her and smiled.

'Go for it, you'll be fine,' he said. 'Just give me a shout if you need a hand. You've obviously impressed the gas man,' he looked at the anaesthetist before continuing, 'if he's happy with you instead of one of the "special ones" from ICU.'

'Okay, great stuff.' Emma smiled. 'Can I have the keys, then?' Major Clarke reached into his pocket and pulled out the keys to the drug cabinet.

'Fill your boots,' he said.

Emma took the keys and walked over to the drug cupboard, holding them up for the anaesthetist to see as she did so. He walked across to join her as she opened the cupboard. Emma reached for the book while he got vials and ampoules out of the cupboard, lining them up on the counter.

'I just need some sux,' he said. Emma bent down and opened the fridge to get the ampoules of suxamethonium, a powerful muscle relaxant. She put them on the counter, and the anaesthetist lined them up with the other ampoules before laughing. 'Sorry, a touch of the obsessive compulsive.'

'I noticed,' Emma replied. 'But I bet your CD collection's in alphabetical order.' As soon as she'd said it, she realised how tacky it sounded, but it was too late.

'It might be,' he said, before pausing and looking at her. *Here we go*, she thought. *This is where he asks me if I want to see it at some point.* Why did she say that, for God's sake? 'But my wife keeps changing it around just to piss me off.'

Emma breathed a sigh of relief, and began to write down the names of the drugs that the anaesthetist had assembled.

'Can you get some saline flushes ready, please?' he asked Emma.

'Sure,' she replied. 'I'll just finish this first.' When she had finished writing in the drug book, Emma looked around for the tray of flushes that she had seen on the counter earlier on. Somebody had moved it down to the end of the counter, so she retrieved it and grabbed a handful of syringes on her way back to the anaesthetist. Working in silence, they both drew up the syringes and labelled them with the name of the contents.

Emma and the anaesthetist walked back across to Private Mitchell, who was still out for the count. Emma rubbed his shoulder so that she could let him know what was going on, but other than a grunt he was unresponsive. She pressed a button on the monitor to recheck his blood pressure, as the anaesthetist stood at the head of the trolley. When the monitor bleeped with the new figures, Emma wrote them down on the back of her hand.

'All set then?' the anaesthetist said. She nodded in reply as he laid the trolley flat. The anaesthetist flipped the small plastic on the cannula and injected the first of the anaesthetic drugs. 'Flush, please,' he said to Emma, who injected one of the saline ampoules into the cannula to flush the drug into Private Mitchell's system. When he had finished giving the casualty the anaesthetic cocktail, each drug followed by a saline flush, the anaesthetist picked up the endotracheal tube and laryngoscope. Tilting Private Mitchell's head back, he used the laryngoscope to push his tongue out of the way. 'Cricoid pressure on, please.'

Emma reached forward and pressed on the front of Private Mitchell's Adam's apple with her thumb and first two fingers to try to give the anaesthetist a better chance of seeing the vocal chords, and also to reduce the risk of any stomach contents getting into the patient's lungs.

'That's better,' the anaesthetist said, 'I can see the chords.' He slid the endotracheal tube into the correct position and used an empty syringe to fill the balloon at the end with air, securing the airway. Emma took her hand off the patient's throat and glanced across at the monitor.

'Shit,' she whispered when she saw the flat line on the screen. She quickly checked the leads connecting Private Mitchell to the monitor, but they were all where they should be. 'Shit,' she repeated. 'I think he's arrested.'

29

He leaned against the door of the Emergency Room with his arms folded, trying to keep a wry smile off his face. He'd been stood there, absolutely invisible to everyone, for the last few minutes watching the intubation and waiting for his magic bullet to hit home. The look of horror on the nurse's face when she realised that her patient had arrested was an absolute picture. She looked stunning when she was scared, and he wondered what her face would look like if she found out that she had administered the lethal concoction herself. Oh boy, would that be a picture worth taking.

He didn't care who it was who dealt the fatal blow, although he did admit to himself that he was disappointed that he'd not got to watch the last one die. He'd heard about it, though. It sounded like it went perfectly. From his perspective, at least.

'Can we have a hand over here?' he heard a female voice shout to the other medics in the room. The few personnel left in the room looked up and hurried over to help. He watched as the pretty little nurse ran to get a stool from the other side of the room so that she had something to stand on to do cardiac compressions. He knew that he should at least do something, as opposed to just stand and watch, so he made his way over to the trolley to see if any of his adapted ampoules were still *there. He could get rid of them while everyone else was concentrating on the casualty.*

As he walked past the nurse, who was by now on her stool with her hands clasped in front of her on the casualty's chest, he made sure that he brushed against her backside as he did so. He knew that she wouldn't notice, and he was right.

'One, two, three, four, five,' he heard her count out loud, each number punctuated with a compression. He wondered what she would look like if she was doing the compressions naked. He knew that her breasts would be pushed together by her arms as there was no other way to do the compressions, and he felt himself hardening as he imagined her astride him, with her arms pushed together in the same way.

He saw the tray with the ampoules sitting on top of the trolley. Some of them hadn't been used, so he definitely needed to get rid of them in one of the sharps bins. As he grabbed the tray, one of the medics turned around with a syringe full of blood, and barged into him, scattering the ampoules everywhere and covering him in blood from the syringe.

'For fuck's sake, be careful,' he said. The medic looked at him, horrified.

'Oh crap, sorry,' he muttered.

He looked at the front of his uniform, and then at the ampoules which were all over the floor. He couldn't exactly go scrabbling round to retrieve them all, and he wasn't even sure how many of them there were. Especially not now that he was covered in blood. He would have to go and get changed and leave the ampoules where they were. He gave the medic a withering look and turned on his heel to walk towards the door.

30

Adams swore as he burned his lip when he took a sip of the hot soup in his insulated mug. He was sitting next to Lizzie, both of them in green camping chairs a couple of hundred yards away from the bright lights of the hospital. Both chairs were tilted back so that they were pointed at the sky. The night was completely cloudless, and they could both see hundreds if not thousands of stars.

'You all packed for R&R, then?' Adams asked Lizzie.

'Bloody right I am,' she replied. 'Been packed for weeks. How about you? You all sorted?'

'I think so,' he said. Adams had spent about thirty minutes sorting out his stuff earlier that day before they'd gone out on the shout, but it wasn't as if he had a great deal to take home with him. 'What are your plans, then?'

'Well, first I'm going to get absolutely wasted,' Lizzie said.

'That'll be one glass of wine then.' She laughed at Adam's reply.

'Then I'm going to spend my time sunbathing, eating good food, and just relaxing.'

'Going on the prowl for some poor innocent Cypriot lad, more like.'

'Shut up, Adams,' Lizzie said. Adams glanced across at her and saw a sad expression on her face. 'Maybe if Emma was with me like we'd planned, we might go out of an evening, but I'm not doing that on my own. She can't not go home, though.'

'It's a shame she can't come with you,' Adams replied. 'Any news on her mother?'

'Don't think so,' Lizzie said. 'She's not said anything. Still waiting for test results, apparently.'

'That's a bit shit.'

'Wow, did you see that?' Lizzie pointed her finger at the sky where a shooting star had just shot past. 'That was impressive, wasn't it?'

'Yep, certainly was.'

'Did you see it?'

'Yes, I told you I did,' Adams replied. Lizzie paused for a few seconds before turning back to Adams.

'So, what did you wish for?' she asked him. Adams looked through the dark at Lizzie, barely able to see her.

'If I told you,' he said, 'it wouldn't come true, would it?'

'I guess,' Lizzie replied. 'But how about if I guessed? Would you tell me then? If I was right? Because I think it involves Sophia and a ring?'

'Her name's Sophie, and no I'm not saying. The same principle applies. That's just me telling you in a different way. So, it wouldn't come true either.'

'Oh, you're no fun,' Lizzie said. 'Seriously though, if you could wish for anything, what would it be?' Adams looked at Lizzie again, irritated that he couldn't see her very well.

'Now there's a question,' he said before lapsing into

silence. They sat in the dark for a few minutes, watching for shooting stars that never came. Finally, Adams replied, 'I can't tell you, Lizzie.'

'Oh, okay,' she replied.

'It's just that, well, there's just so many things. And they are all intertwined, each reliant on the others for success.'

'Wow, that's deep,' Lizzie said. 'Utter bollocks, but still quite deep.' Adams laughed and looked at Lizzie.

'That's what I like about you, mate,' he said. 'Your ability to just cut right to the heart of the matter.'

They sat there looking at the sky for a few more minutes, the shooting stars that they'd come to watch seemingly finished for the night. Adams noticed Lizzie getting fidgety in her chair, but ignored it. After a while, Lizzie took a deep breath and exhaled loudly.

'Jesus, what a bloody day it's been.'

'Yeah, you could say that,' Adams replied. 'It was all a bit, er, full-on I guess.' Lizzie laughed.

'Just a bit.'

Adams could feel Lizzie looking at him in the darkness. He turned to look at her and saw that he was right.

'Adams,' she said. 'Can I ask you about something?' Adams paused before replying.

'Course you can.'

'What was it like?' she said. 'When you shot that Terry. What was it actually like?'

'What do you mean?'

'What was it like?' she repeated.

'Do you mean how did I feel when it happened?'

'I think so.'

'I didn't really feel anything. And I'm not even sure that I did shoot him.' Adams remembered the puff of red mist he'd seen as his round had hit home and hoped that Lizzie couldn't see his face. He wasn't very good at lying. 'Besides, the Apache raked the area a few minutes later, so it doesn't make any difference, anyway.' He glanced across at Lizzie, who was staring at him. 'If I did hit him, it only brought things forward by a few minutes.'

'You must have felt something though,' she said. 'You can't shoot someone and not feel anything. And what if that RPG had come our way?'

'Yeah, but it didn't. So, it doesn't matter.' Adams desperately wanted to change the subject, but couldn't think of a way of doing it without seeming obvious. He wasn't lying to Lizzie. He really didn't feel anything, either at the time or now. What he didn't want to discuss with her was how much that fact terrified him. He'd almost certainly taken a man's life, and he was just numb inside.

A white line of light streaked across the sky. Adams pointed at it, grateful for the distraction.

'Yep, seen,' Lizzie said. 'But don't change the subject.' He sighed, knowing that he would have to take a more direct line with her.

'Lizzie,' he said. 'I don't want to talk about it. Please?'

'Okay,' she replied after a few seconds. 'But if you do….'

'I know where you are, yes.'

A few minutes later, Adams figured that enough time had passed for him not to be accused of changing the subject again.

'What about you, though?' he said. 'You nearly got shot in the arse out there. How do you feel about that?' Lizzie laughed, and Adams felt the mood lift between them.

'Sodding delighted,' she said. 'Can you imagine being medevaced home, having to lie face down on the stretcher all the way back because you'd taken a round in the cheeks?' Laughing, she carried on. 'I'd never bloody live that down, would I?'

'You'd be a legend, mate,' Adams replied. 'An absolute legend. Every dining-in night you ever went to for the rest of your career, there'd be a cushion on the chair.'

'Oh, piss off. The only advantage would be if I could persuade the surgeon to do a bit of liposuction while he was digging around back there.' Adams started laughing as well.

'That's a bit extreme, Lizzie,' he said. 'Taking a bullet in the backside just to get it thinned out a bit. There's got to be an easier way to lose some of the wobble.' He saw her look at him, her mouth open as if she was shocked.

'Are you saying I've got a big arse?'

'No, not at all,' he laughed.

'You so are!' She shoved the arm of his chair, spilling the soup out of his cup. 'Bastard,' she said, pushing at his chair again.

'Oi, mind my soup,' he retorted, scrabbling around and looking for the lid. He saw her cross her arms and pretend to look annoyed. 'It's not big at all.' Adams paused for effect and waited until he saw Lizzie look at him. 'Just probably not as firm as it used to be, that's all.'

Lizzie reached down and picked up the lid to Adams's cup from the sand between their chairs. She flung it at him, missing his head by a couple of inches.

'Idiot,' she crossed her arms again. 'Now bugger off and make me a cup of tea.'

Adams walked through the back door of the TRT tent. He tipped what was left of his soup into the sink, gave his mug a quick rinse, and picked up Lizzie's from the draining board. While he waited for the kettle to boil, he looked around the tent and wondered if it was his turn to sweep the floor.

'Penny for your thoughts, sir?' Adams heard Partridge say from the main entrance to the tent. He turned to see the Staff Sergeant leaning against one of the doors, smiling at him.

'If you really want to know,' Adams said, 'I was wondering whose turn it is to sweep up, and hoping that it's not mine.' Partridge walked into the tent and sat on one of the chairs near the kettle.

'Any chance of a brew?' he said to Adams.

'Sure, no problem,' Adams replied. 'Julie Andrews, isn't it?' Partridge laughed before replying.

'White, none. Very good, sir.'

The two men remained silent as the kettle boiled. Adams threw tea bags into the mugs and spooned sugar into both of them.

'Is Lizzie about?' Partridge asked.

'She's outside. We're, er, looking at the sky. There's no light, and loads of shooting stars.' Adams looked across at some folded camping chairs stacked up against the side of the tent. 'Grab a chair and join us. If you want?'

'You sure that's okay?' Partridge asked.

'Of course it is,' Adams replied. Partridge looked up at him from where he was sitting.

'I was hoping I might catch up with you at some point,' he said to Adams. 'I heard that you've had a bit of excitement on the ground while we were farting about up in the air, even though it's supposed to be the other way around.' Adams looked at Partridge, wondering exactly what he had heard. Earlier on, on their way back to the accommodation block, Lizzie and Adams had agreed to keep what had happened out on the ground as quiet as they could. Adams knew that Ronald and the aircrew knew what had gone on, but he couldn't see the point in making it public knowledge. They'd only have to repeat the story over and over again.

'So what have you heard, then?' Adams asked Partridge as they watched the kettle.

'Well,' Partridge said. 'I read the after-action report up at the ops room, so I've got a pretty good idea of what happened.' Adams looked at the soldier, his eyebrows raised.

'Right,' he replied. 'I wouldn't mind reading that myself. Seeing as I was actually there.'

'No reason why you can't,' Partridge said. 'It's on the secret side, so you'll have to go to the Ops Room to read it. But it's quite…' Partridge paused for a second, '…complimentary.' The kettle switch flicked itself off as it reached boiling point. Adams picked it up and poured the steaming liquid into the mugs.

'In what sense?' he said. Partridge looked at the ceiling as if he was trying to remember the exact words used.

'There's mention of a single aimed shot from one of the medical team taking out a Terry just before he let off an RPG at one of the patrols,' Partridge said. 'From about two hundred metres out. Hell of a shot by the sound of it, especially when you're under fire. Plus, and don't take this the wrong way, but you're not a soldier.'

Adams stirred the teabags before squeezing them against the side of the mugs and throwing them in the bin. He turned to Partridge and looked at him, wondering what his point was. Was he trying to make him feel better about killing someone? He didn't have to, Adams knew. He couldn't feel anything.

'Did this report mention Lizzie nearly getting hit?'

'Yes, it did,' Partridge said. 'But that's not what we're

talking about. You're a medic, right?' Adams looked at the red cross on his arm.

'Well, obviously.'

'So, I'm thinking that you probably haven't fired a shot in anger before. Let alone kill someone.' Adams nodded in reply, not quite sure what to say. 'And now I'm guessing that you're feeling one of two things. Either you're cut to shreds inside at the thought of killing another human being — despite the fact that he was trying to kill you — but you're hiding it well. Or you don't feel anything, and you're cut to shreds because you think you should.' Adams regarded the soldier closely. Partridge continued, 'Either way, you're cut to shreds.'

Adams returned to the safety of making tea, not trusting himself to say anything. What Partridge had said had hammered home in a way that he'd not thought possible. He felt Partridge's hand on his arm and turned to see the soldier standing next to him. 'Adams, I'm not a medic, I'm only a soldier, but I've been where you are. You can't go back to before, no matter how much you want to.' Partridge turned and walked over to the stack of folded chairs, picking one up before returning to Adams and picking up one of the mugs of tea. 'It's a small club, and most of us who're in it wish we weren't. But once you're in, you're in. If you want to chat, don't bother with some poncey tree-hugger with more letters after their name than in it. They won't get it. Only people in the same club will.' He fixed Adams with a piercing stare. 'I won't be here when you get back from R&R. I've been reassigned to the Quick Reaction Force up at Kandahar.'

'Right,' Adams said, wondering if the Staff Sergeant was done. He didn't envy the soldier being posted to the QRF, though — they were always running into places everyone else was trying to run away from.

'But Kandahar's not that far away. You can call me up there. If you need to.' Adams looked at him, wishing that the soldier would just fuck off with his cup of tea and leave him alone to think for a few minutes. As if he sensed what Adams was thinking, Partridge turned his back and walked towards the door of the tent.

∼

Lizzie sat in her chair, grateful for the peace and quiet. She watched as a flurry of shooting stars threw their way across the sky. 'Wish upon a star, my arse,' she mumbled under her breath. What had happened earlier was still fresh in her mind. She couldn't believe what had happened. They weren't supposed to be out and about on the ground, much less right in the middle of a firefight. Lizzie completely got why the helicopter had to disappear in such a hurry, but she hadn't been expecting to be left behind when it did.

She thought back to when she'd realised that a round had gone right through her bag. The hollow racing feeling in her chest that she'd felt when she realised how close she'd come to being a casualty — or even killed — started to come back, and she put a hand over her heart to try to slow it down. And Adams shooting that bloke? Really? *Jesus Christ*, she thought. *What a day*. She was looking forward to going to bed, although she knew that when she did, she wouldn't sleep but would just lie there and replay the whole day, over and over again in her head. Lizzie also knew that this was what she needed to do to process things.

A soft cough behind her made Lizzie jump. Turning in the chair, she looked over her shoulder and squinted at the figure standing behind her that was silhouetted against the lights of the hospital.

'Who's that?' she asked, realising the shadow was too big to be Adams.

'It's Partridge,' a disembodied voice came out of the darkness. 'Staff Sergeant Partridge.'

'Oh, hi,' Lizzie said with a smile. 'Can't see a bloody thing out here.' She watched as Partridge unfolded a chair and sat down in it with a thump. How he managed to do this without spilling the tea he had in his hand she would never know. She stared at the mug, trying to work out in the darkness whether it was hers or not.

'Adams is on his way with your tea,' Partridge said. Lizzie looked up at him, realising that she'd been staring.

'Sorry,' she said. 'I thought you had my mug.'

'No, don't worry,' Partridge replied. 'Your boss isn't that daft.' He glanced over his shoulder and looked back towards the hospital. 'Can you do me a favour?' he whispered.

'Depends on what it is,' Lizzie replied, as she looked in the same direction and saw a shadow walking slowly towards them.

'Just keep an eye on him, okay?' Partridge said. 'He might be a bit fragile in the next few days. I don't think it's hit him yet.' Lizzie nodded in reply, not wanting to say anything that Adams would hear. She wasn't going to be with him over the next few days. He would be back at home with his girlfriend, while she was sunning herself alone in Cyprus.

'Him and me both,' she whispered back at Partridge before Adams reached them.

'There you go, mate,' Adams said when he got to where they were sitting

'Cheers,' she replied. 'Partridge was just astounding me with his knowledge of astrology.'

'Don't you mean astronomy?' Adams replied.

'No, he definitely said that the moon was waning over Uranus,' she said, carefully pronouncing Uranus to rhyme with 'anus'.

'You're so funny, Lizzie,' he said. 'You're wasted in the military. You should be on the stage.'

'Whatever,' she said, smiling. Lizzie looked past Adams to Partridge. 'So, Staff, we were just talking about our R&R. A few more days to push and we'll be out of here. When's yours?'

'Been and gone,' Partridge replied, 'and it's Partridge by the way, not "Staff". That just makes me feel old when people say that.'

Lizzie bit her lip to stop the obvious comment about his age coming out. Looking at the Staff Sergeant, he must have been in his late forties which, to her at least, was old. But she didn't think she knew him well enough just yet to get away with telling him that.

'What did you do, then? Anything interesting?' she asked.

'Not really, no. Family stuff mostly, caught up with some friends, had far too much to drink. Standard time off really.'

'Have you got kids?' Adams asked.

'Just the one. She's eighteen now, just finishing her A-levels at college. She's already more qualified than me and the wife put together.' Adams and Lizzie laughed at his deadpan delivery. 'It is a bit weird though, going home where no-one knows what's happening out here. I don't know how to describe it. People getting upset over utter shite, like whose right of it is at a roundabout, while out here our lads are dying.' Lizzie saw him sit back in the chair and look up towards the sky. 'So where are all these shooting stars, then?' he asked. Lizzie looked again at Adams, relieved that Partridge had changed the subject.

They all turned when they heard hurried footsteps behind them. A figure was jogging through the sand towards them from the hospital.

'Here you are,' Ronald said, out of breath, when he reached the group. 'I've been looking for you everywhere.'

'Why?' Lizzie sat forwards in her chair. 'Is everything okay?'

'Not really,' Ronald said. 'That casualty we brought in,' he took a few deep breaths before continuing, 'he arrested in the Emergency Room. They worked on him for a while but called it a few minutes ago.'

Lizzie stared at Ronald, open-mouthed. Beside her, she heard Adams swearing under his breath.

'You're joking,' she said. 'You're bloody joking.' There was no reply from Ronald.

'Like I said,' Partridge muttered, 'our lads are dying.'

PART II

31

E mma Wardle looked out of the window of her mother's lounge in their small terrace house on the outskirts of Watford. The early morning sky was dark grey, and it hadn't stopped raining since she'd got up. Emma looked at the droplets running down the window pane, knowing that in a few short hours she would be back in the searing heat of Afghanistan. Outside the house, she heard a car horn beep. Her taxi had arrived.

'Mum?' she called out. 'My cab's here. I need to get going.'

Emma's mother walked into the lounge, her eyes red-rimmed. She clutched a sodden tissue in her hands as she looked at her daughter. Emma swallowed, determined not to start crying as well.

'Oh Mum,' she said. 'Don't cry. I'll be back before you know it, and for good next time.' Her mother didn't reply but held out her arms for a hug. As she stepped forward with her arms out in return, Emma could feel tears pricking at her eyes. She squeezed her mother tightly, breathing in her perfume, not trusting herself to say anything in case her voice broke. After what seemed like ages, her mother finally let go of her and pushed her back a step, keeping both hands on Emma's arms as she looked at her.

'You be careful, pet,' she said. 'And call me or e-mail when you get there so that I know you're okay.'

'Okay,' Emma replied. 'But you have to let me know the minute you hear anything from the hospital.'

'I will, pet. Promise.' Emma looked at her mother, trying to work out — as she had been doing for most of the week — whether the results had already come through and her mother wasn't saying anything so Emma wouldn't worry. That would be just like her. As if she could read Emma's thoughts, her mother continued, 'Don't give me that look, young lady,' she said with a weak smile. 'I promise you'll be the first to know when they come back.'

Emma just nodded in reply before picking up her bag and heading out of the lounge to the front door. Opening it, she walked down the small path to the taxi. When she reached the car, she turned and waved at her mother, who was standing in the doorway, still clutching her tissues in one hand and waving with the other. Emma opened the car door, threw her bag onto the back seat, and climbed in.

'Brize Norton is it, love?' the taxi driver asked from the front seat.

'Yes, please,' Emma replied, before bursting into tears as the taxi slowly moved away. A few yards down the road, the driver stopped the car and turned around, handing her a small packet of tissues.

'There you go, take these.' He smiled at her, the wrinkles at the corner of his eyes showing her that he didn't mind smiling. For a brief minute, he reminded Emma of her dad, even though the driver didn't look like him at all. Apart from the easy wrinkles when he smiled. 'You're not the first person to start crying in my cab, and I'm sure you won't be the last.'

'Thank you,' she sniffed as she took the tissues. 'I'm sorry.' The cab driver pulled away from the kerb.

'Don't be daft,' he replied, glancing at her in the rear-view mirror. Emma could see from his eyes that he was still smiling. 'You blub away, love. Let it all out.'

Despite herself, Emma smiled at his comment. She dabbed the tissue to her eyes and watched as the grey terraced houses of the council estate she lived on sped past. After a few minutes, she'd managed to compose herself a bit and reached forward to put the half-empty packet of tissues on the passenger seat.

'You done?' the driver asked. 'Feel better for that?'

'Much better, and thanks for the tissues,' Emma replied. 'It was my mum's fault, she started it. She knows I hate goodbyes at the best of times.' The driver laughed, a deep rattle courtesy of the half empty packet of cigarettes Emma had seen on the passenger seat. Maybe he was like her dad after all.

'I'm guessing that you're heading away, then?' he asked her. 'I would ask if it's anywhere nice, but I don't think that the planes that go from Brize Norton go anywhere nice, do they?'

Emma laughed. 'Sometimes they do, but I'm heading back to Afghanistan,' she said. In the rear-view mirror, she saw his eyebrows go up in surprise. 'I'm a nurse, working in the hospital out there.'

'Oh, okay,' he replied. 'That makes sense.' He paused before continuing. 'You been back for a break, then?'

'Yep, only a week's R&R, though. Not long enough.'

'Get up to anything interesting?' he asked. Emma thought back over the brief few days she'd had at home. Shopping one day, out with some friends another, but apart

from that, she'd not done much at all. There was one interesting evening at a nightclub where she'd ended up kissing
a particularly cute guy at the end of the night, but other
than a new phone number, there was nothing else in it.
Smiling at the memory, she wondered if he would call her
when she got back from her tour. Her smile faded when
she realised that as she'd only offered up a kiss, he probably
wouldn't.

'Not really,' she replied. 'It was nice, not having to do
anything.'

The taxi driver nodded, before changing the subject. It
was almost as if he'd realised that Emma didn't really want
to talk about home, or Afghanistan, or anything.

'Watford signed a new defender at the weekend,' he
said. 'Some lad called Powell. Got him on a free from
Charlton.' He continued chatting for a few minutes while
Emma half listened, making what she hoped was the right
noises in the right places. The driver, whose name was
Adrian but was known as Ade — he explained the history
to his nickname in some detail — went on to recap the
entire football season for Emma's benefit. Emma couldn't
stand football but was more than happy to listen to him
talking as she watched the miles pass by through the
window of the taxi.

By the time they reached the gates of Brize Norton
over an hour later, Emma knew everything there was to
know about Ade. He'd gone from football and Watford's
promotion to the Premier League through his entire family,
before finishing with an extended one-way conversation
about how he thought the bloke who had the allotment
next to his was poisoning his giant courgettes. They pulled
up outside the doors of the main terminal a few minutes
later, and Ade stopped the taxi.

'There you go, love,' he said, turning round to look at

Emma. 'Safe and sound.' Emma opened her bag to get her purse to pay him. 'Er, I wouldn't worry about that, pet.' She looked up at him, surprised.

'What do you mean?'

'Don't worry about the fare. I'll cover it.'

'No, you won't,' Emma replied, finding her purse and opening it to get the money she'd got out of a cash machine earlier. 'It's over sixty miles. The quote from your firm was £100.' She looked up from her purse at the taxi driver. He was chewing his lip but smiled when he realised that she was looking at him. The wrinkles were back.

'When you get back, use the cash to take your mum out for a decent meal. Or your boyfriend, whoever.'

'Ade, please?' Emma said. 'Let me pay you. That's not fair otherwise.' The taxi driver shook his head.

'Nope, not having it,' Ade replied, his smile broadening 'Now get out of my taxi before I throw you out.' Emma paused, a lump returning to her throat at this stranger's kindness before she opened the door to the taxi.

'Thank you,' she said as she climbed out, dragging her bag behind her. With a wave, Emma walked towards the foyer of Gateway House — the down market RAF version of a Travel Lodge hotel that was used to house military personnel waiting for flights. Her heart sank as she realised how busy it was. All she wanted was a room for a couple of hours so she could freshen up and have some time on her own. Emma walked up to the reception desk and spoke to the bored looking civil servant who was sitting behind it.

'Corporal Emma Wardle, flying to Kandahar later today. I don't suppose there're any rooms spare, are there? I only need it for a couple of hours, just to have a shower and sort myself out.' She watched silently as the man ran his finger down a list in front of him, before looking up. To her surprise, he gave her a broad smile showing off a set of teeth that, if it wasn't for the nicotine staining on them, could be dentures. *Mind you*, she thought, stifling a grin, *they could just be nicotine stained dentures*. He had to be sixty at least, almost certainly holding out for his pension.

'Yep, Room 223,' he said, putting a key on the counter. 'You know the drill, don't you? I remember you from last week.'

'Sure, don't lose the key, don't make a mess.' She smiled back at him. 'Thank you so much. I can't believe how busy it is.' He looked back down at the list for a second before replying.

'I know. The trooper's packed. Lots of people going out.' His smile was starting to waver, and Emma felt a twinge of sadness as she realised that some of the people he was booking in wouldn't be coming back again, and he knew that.

'Okay, no problem. What time's the bus?'

'Wheels are at half two, check in starts at three.'

Emma looked at her watch. It was just gone ten in the morning, so she had plenty of time for a shower before meeting her cousin.

'Thanks again for sorting me out a room,' she said to the civil servant behind the desk. 'I promise to keep it tidy.' He smiled at her briefly, already busy with another new arrival.

Emma found her room on the second floor and dropped her bag on one of the beds. She looked at the threadbare sheet and tattered blanket which were folded up on the end of the bed and picked them up, putting them on the table to make room for her sleeping bag. *Shower*, she thought, *then a power nap*. In that order. She could have showered at her mum's house but hadn't wanted to waste any time that she could be spending with her before leaving.

In the cafeteria a couple of hours later, Emma queued up at the servery to get some lunch, which was sausages and chips, or sausages and chips. She found a spare table and sat down to eat, hoping that the food tasted better than it looked. Emma was about halfway through her lunch when she heard a voice ask her a question.

'Do you mind if I sit here?' She looked up to see a military policeman standing in front of her. She looked around to see if there were any other spare tables around, more to make a point to him than anything else, but in fairness, the cafeteria was pretty busy.

'Er, yeah,' she said. 'Sure.' She carried on eating, eager to finish her meal as soon as she could. Between bites, she looked at the policeman sitting opposite. He was in his mid-twenties, had corporal stripes on his shoulders, and wasn't the worst thing in the world to look at. He looked back at her and waited until she had finished her mouthful.

'Name's James, by the way,' he said, a slight grin playing on his face.

'Hi James,' she replied, deliberately staying poker-faced. 'I'm Emma.'

'Pleased to meet you, Emma,' he said. 'You heading out for the first time, or going back from R&R?'

They chatted for a while as they ate. When James found out that Emma was going back out to Afghanistan, he peppered her with questions about what it was like, whether the food was any good, was it really as hot as everyone said it was, and so on. In a few short minutes, James had managed to give Emma what sounded to her like pretty much his entire life story. He was single, been in the RAF for six years, and was going out on his first operational tour. Although he didn't say anything to Emma, she knew that he was as nervous as anything. Emma didn't really give him anything in return, but instead dodged around his questions.

'So is it true that it's dry out there, then?' James asked Emma when they'd both finished their meals.

'How'd you mean, dry?' she replied. 'It's the middle of the desert, so it doesn't rain much if that's what you mean?'

'Er, no,' he laughed and pointed towards the closed bar in the next room. 'I mean, is it dry?'

'Oh, I see what you mean,' Emma said. 'Yep, completely dry. Not even a two can rule.'

'But surely there must be some booze somewhere? Some illicit still somewhere brewing up sugar and potatoes or something?'

'Er, no. Even if there was, I wouldn't tell you.'

'Why not?' James asked.

'James,' Emma looked at him, not sure if he was trying to be funny or he was just thick. 'You're a copper.'

'Oh, right.' James looked at her with a grin.

'Sorry, James,' she said. 'I'm meeting my cousin, so I'm going to have to run. Nice to meet you.' Emma got to her feet and picked up her tray from the table.

'Maybe we could meet up for a coffee, or something?' James said as Emma was walking away to take her tray back.

Over my dead body, Emma thought, with her back to the policeman and a wry smile on her face.

32

Lizzie sat on a chair in an office on the top floor of RAF Akrotiri's airport terminal. Outside it was a typical summer's day in Cyprus — sunny and hot — although not as hot as it would be back in Afghanistan. She looked out of the large windows, keeping her eyes open for the Hercules transport plane that Adams had hitchhiked a ride on from Lyneham. It was due in at some point within the next few minutes, and Lizzie had spoken to a friend back at the RAF base in Wiltshire who had confirmed that Adams was on the plane.

She brushed a strand of her freshly tinted and cut hair from her eyes and tucked it behind her ear. Lizzie was wearing a summer dress which came down to just above her knees, and while she waited she inspected her tanned legs.

'Your mate's Fat Albert is on finals now, Lizzie,' the flight controller whose office she had borrowed said from the door.

'Thanks, Flight,' Lizzie replied. She turned to the window and looked towards the end of the runway to watch the plane coming in. Just above the horizon, she could see the distinctive shape of the Hercules transport plane silhouetted against the blue sky.

As soon as Lizzie saw the puffs of smoke from the large green plane's wheels as it touched down on the runway, she picked up her bag and went down the stairs into the main terminal building. With a wave to the Corporal sitting behind the terminal desk, she sat near an air conditioning unit to wait.

About ten minutes later, Lizzie saw Adams walking through the door that led to the air side of the terminal, his day sack slung over his shoulder.

'Hey, Adams,' Lizzie said, with a broad grin on her face as she walked across to meet him.

'Lizzie!' Adams replied, putting his bag on the floor and hugging her. 'Thanks for coming to meet me.' Lizzie started to reply when Adams pushed her away from him and interrupted her. 'Oh my God!'

'What?' she asked.

'Look at you. You look very...' Adams was looking at her with his eyebrows raised, '... different.' Lizzie's face fell, and she tried to hide her disappointment.

'Well, thanks very much,' Lizzie said. 'If I had known you were going to be that complimentary, I would have left you here at the airport.'

'But how come you're not in combats?' Adams asked. 'We're supposed to be flying out this afternoon, aren't we?'

'Not anymore,' Lizzie said. 'The plane has been delayed by a few hours. The new departure time is just after midnight, but you know what crab air is like. Could be any time in the next few days.'

'Oh, for fuck's sake,' Adams said, looking at his watch. It was just after two in the afternoon.

'I know, it's an arse,' Lizzie said. 'But it does mean that

you've got some extra time in Cyprus. Just imagine it — a whole ten hours with me!'

'I'd better get some accommodation sorted in case it gets delayed even more,' Adams said. 'I've not got much stuff with me, though,'

'I've already booked you a room in the transit block,' Lizzie said. 'I mean, it's a dormitory, but it's better than trying to sleep in the terminal if the plane doesn't end up going.'

'Are you staying there as well?'

'No, I've managed to get an extra night at my hotel in Limassol just in case,' Lizzie said. 'But I thought what we could do is go back to the transit block so you can get changed, and then head to the strip for the afternoon.'

'Well, that's certainly better than hanging around in Akrotiri,' Adams replied. The strip was a row of shops of varying quality that lined the beach at Limassol. Lizzie's face brightened, and she smiled at him.

'Come on, then,' she said. 'Let's go and book in so we don't have to mess about later, and then we can do one. I've got a car outside.'

A few moments later, having booked in for the flight and received their boarding cards, Lizzie and Adams walked through the glass doors of the terminal building. As they walked into the Cyprus sun, Lizzie felt a wave of heat wash over her and regretted sitting so close to an air conditioning unit while she was waiting in the terminal.

She led Adams towards a small red car parked outside the building and pressed the key fob to open the doors. Adams threw his bag into the back seat while she climbed into the driver's seat and put on her sunglasses.

'So, how was your week?' Adams asked Lizzie as she started the car.

'It was great,' Lizzie replied. 'I've done absolutely bugger all, except lounge around and pamper myself.'

'So you didn't miss Emma too much, then?'

'Not really,' Lizzie said, looking across at Adams. 'Well, maybe a bit. I get why she went home though, what with her mother being unwell and everything.'

'Any news on that?'

'No, nothing.'

Adams leaned around to get his bag from the back seat. As he did so, his hand brushed against Lizzie's bare shoulder. She flinched, but if Adams noticed, he didn't say anything.

'So, how was your week, anyway?' Lizzie asked him. 'What did she say?'

'What did who say?'

'Sophie. Did you ask her?'

Adams took a deep breath before replying, avoiding Lizzie's eyes as he did so. 'I didn't ask her in the end.' Lizzie looked across at him, her mouth open.

'Why ever not?' she asked, shocked. Adams was rummaging in his bag for something, which meant she couldn't see his expression. He pulled his sunglasses from his bag and put them on. When he looked back and she saw his frown, she looked away and back at the road in front of them.

'Lizzie, please,' Adams said. 'I just didn't, that's all there is to it. I don't really want to talk about it.' Lizzie glanced back at Adams, who was now looking out of the passenger window.

'Okay,' Lizzie said, a million questions in her head.

They drove on in silence for a while before reaching the temporary accommodation block, a squat single-storey building painted off-white. Underneath every window was an ancient-looking air conditioning unit, but none of the fans were whirring.

'Here you go,' Lizzie said. 'How long do you want to get your stuff sorted?'

'Give me half an hour or so, I'll have a quick shower and meet you out here.' Lizzie looked at her watch.

'No problem, I'll go and get a cup of tea at the medical centre. One of my friends is working now, and at least he knows how to make a decent cup of tea.' She attempted a smile, but he either didn't notice or ignored her.

Adams opened the passenger door and climbed out of the car without another word. He slung his bag over his shoulder and disappeared through the front door of the accommodation.

'Bloody hell,' Lizzie whispered to herself as she watched the door close behind him. She'd not been expecting that response at all to her question about Sophie. Something had obviously gone wrong if he'd not asked her. But what?

Adams walked into the large accommodation blocks, lined with bunk beds down both sides of the room. He took a deep breath. What a dump. Not just a dump, but a very hot one that smelt of sweat.

It hadn't taken Lizzie long to ask him about Sophie, but he'd hoped for a little bit longer before he had to face that one. He knew he was going to have to tell her what had happened, but wanted to do it on his own terms. When the time was right.

With the exception of an elderly Cypriot cleaner, who was moving water around with a mop that looked as if it was almost as old as she was, the room was empty. Adams chose the bottom bunk in one of the corners of the room and pulled his sleeping bag out of his rucksack to claim the bunk as his, German holidaymaker style. Ignoring the cleaner, Adams stripped down to his boxer shorts and headed for the showers at the far end of the room. As he walked past the cleaner, he smiled at her but received nothing but a stare in return.

'Miserable cow,' he muttered as he walked into the bathroom. *At least the floor was clean in here*, he thought as he stripped off and started one of the showers. He'd forgotten his flip-flops when he had packed his bag for coming back out. While he showered, Adams thought about his week at home. To say that it hadn't worked out as he had planned was an enormous understatement. At one point, he had even wished that he had stayed in Afghanistan instead of going home.

One thing Adams did need to do was to apologise to Lizzie for being so abrupt when she'd asked about his week. He knew that it wasn't her fault that he'd had a crap time, and he also knew he was out of order talking to her the way that he had.

Once he had towelled himself dry, Adams wrapped the towel around his middle before walking back through the dormitory towards his bunk. As he passed the cleaner, he gave her an even broader smile but received the same stony stare in reply. He reached his bunk and unwrapped the towel before hanging it on a hook on the side of the bunk bed. With satisfaction, he heard a disapproving 'tut' from the cleaner behind him. Adams was tempted to scratch one of his buttocks, but he thought that would be childish.

Adams pulled his shorts and T-shirt from the bag and threw them on. He still had ten minutes before Lizzie would be back, so he walked outside to read his book while he waited for her. He sat on a plastic garden chair that was outside the accommodation block, and tilted his head towards the sun, enjoying the sunshine on his face.

Lizzie thought that Adams was asleep when she pulled up in the car outside the accommodation block. He was sprawled in a chair, dressed in a wrinkled blue T-shirt and bright red swimming shorts. She laughed when she saw that he still had his combat boots on. Lizzie got out of the car and walked over to him.

'Hey, sleeping beauty. Wake up,' she said, shaking Adams's shoulder.

'Sorry,' he said, waking with a start. 'I must have nodded off.'

'No problem.' Lizzie pressed a bottle of water in his hand. 'Here's a cold one for you,' she said.

'Cheers,' Adams replied. 'You must be a mind reader.'

'Come on, then,' Lizzie said. 'Limassol is waiting.' Lizzie looked down at Adams's boots. 'And hopefully, there's a shoe shop open somewhere.'

'I know, I can't believe it,' he said. 'I forgot my sandals.'

Lizzie turned and walked back towards the car as Adams got to his feet and followed her.

'I'm sure we can find somewhere that sells sandals,' she called over her shoulder. 'Mind you, I'm not sure what colour would go with bright red and blue.'

Lizzie started the engine, but before she could drive off, she felt Adams's hand on her arm. She looked over at him.

'Lizzie,' he said, squeezing her forearm. 'Mate, I just wanted to say sorry for biting your head off earlier.' He gave her a half-smile. 'It was out of order, and I apologise. Let's just say that my week at home didn't turn out how I wanted it to.'

'Oh, that's okay,' Lizzie said. 'I wasn't trying to be nosey, I just wanted–'

'Lizzie, please,' Adams interrupted. 'I'm sorry, okay? Can we just leave it there? We've got the rest of the tour to talk about it, so can we just enjoy the rest of the day?'

'Okay, that's fine. Apology accepted,' she said with a slight frown. 'But you will have to buy me a couple of drinks to make up for it.'

'Yep, that's a deal,' Adams replied. She glanced across to see him smiling, but it didn't reach his eyes. With a sigh, she put the car into gear.

They left the main gate at RAF Akrotiri and drove past a small row of dilapidated shops just outside the base. Lizzie stopped the car outside one of them and turned to Adams.

'What size feet have you got?'

'Er, size nine,' Adams replied. Lizzie undid her seatbelt and got out of the car.

'Back in a minute,' she shouted back to him.

A couple of minutes later, Lizzie returned to the car with a paper bag. As she got in, she threw the bag in Adams's lap.

'There you go,' she said. 'They should be a bit less conspicuous than combat boots.' Lizzie watched Adams as he opened the bag and pulled out a pair of pink espadrilles.

'Oh, wow. They're lovely.' He turned them over in his hand to look at them. 'And in my size, too.' Lizzie laughed as she drove off.

As they drove across the salt flats towards Limassol, Adams asked Lizzie what she had got up to during her week off.

'Not much, to be honest,' she said. 'I spent a day at a spa, had a massage, got my hair cut. That sort of thing.'

'I did notice the hair,' Adams said. 'Very nice.' Lizzie looked at Adams with a frown.

'You did not,' she said. 'Blokes never notice that sort of thing.'

'I did too,' Adams protested. 'I noticed it the minute I saw you at the terminal. I just didn't say anything.'

'Yeah, right,' she said. They drove on in companionable silence for a few minutes.

'So,' Adams said. 'Did many young waiter's hearts get broken, then?'

'None at all, Adams,' Lizzie replied. 'What sort of girl do you think I am?' She looked at him with a mock-innocent expression.

'Well,' Adams continued with a grin. 'Seeing as you're not walking like a cowboy, I'd say you've had a bit of a dry spell.'

'Paul Adams, that's no way for an officer to talk,' Lizzie said, pressing her lips together to keep herself from laughing. 'Besides, that's a bit personal.'

They drove on for a few more minutes. Lizzie had been back and forth across this road so many times in the last week that she knew it like the back of her hand. It stretched as straight as a Roman road across the salt flats, and apart from the runway was the only link that RAF Akrotiri had with the rest of the world. Lizzie turned to Adams.

'Are you not going to apologise, then?'

'Oh, yes,' he said. 'Sorry.'

'That was so sincere, it was frightening,' Lizzie said with a laugh. She paused before continuing. 'Can you keep a secret?'

'Of course I can, Lizzie,' Adams replied. 'Mate, how long have we known each other?' Lizzie paused again, before deciding to trust him.

'I've not had so much as a bloody sniff all week,' she said with a deadpan face. Adams looked at Lizzie before dissolving into laughter. 'It's not funny,' she said.

'You are such a lady,' Adams said, still laughing. 'Are you sure you don't just frighten them off when they hear you speak in a Norfolk accent?'

'No, seriously,' Lizzie said. 'I mean, when I went to that spa the other day there was some big IT conference on. About a hundred geeks all milling around in the bar where I was having lunch, and not one of them so much as looked at me.'

'I'm sure quite a few of them did, Lizzie,' Adams said. 'You're not made of wood, after all.' Lizzie laughed.

'Yeah, right,' she replied. 'These eyes aren't painted on. I know.'

'Right, my turn to be serious,' Adams said. He waited until Lizzie looked across at him. 'Lizzie, you are a good-looking woman. Trust me on that one.' She looked at him and suddenly wasn't sure what to say.

33

Emma packed up her sleeping bag and toiletries and looked around the room to make sure that it was tidy. She was supposed to be meeting up with Matthew in twenty minutes or so. She was looking forward to catching up with her cousin, as she'd not seen him for ages, but he worked as part of the ground crew at Brize Norton and from what she'd seen earlier, he might have had a busy shift.

A few moments later, Emma walked into the bar on the ground floor of Gateway House and looked around to see if Matthew had arrived yet. She couldn't see him, so went to the vending machine to get a drink while she waited. While she was searching in her purse for some change, she heard a voice behind her.

'Hello, hello, hello,' the voice said. Turning around, she saw her companion from lunchtime.

'Hi, er, James wasn't it?' Emma said, even though she knew full well what his name was.

'Yep, that's me,' he replied. 'And you're Emma.'

'Well done, James,' she said as she collected a can of

Coke from the machine. 'I bet you're a fantastic police-man.' He missed the irony in her voice and laughed slightly too loudly. Emma looked at her watch again. 'Not being funny mate, but I'm waiting for someone.'

'Do you mind if I keep you company until she gets here?'

'He. Until he gets here.'

'Oh, okay,' James said, undeterred. 'Until he gets here, then.'

With a sigh, Emma figured that she might as well make the most of it. With any luck, Matthew would be here soon and could rescue her from James. The policeman seemed harmless enough, just a bit irritating.

'So, James,' she said. 'How long are you going out to Bastion for?'

'Er, not sure. One, maybe two, weeks.' She looked at him with her eyebrows raised.

'One or two bloody weeks?' she said. 'The way you were talking at lunchtime, it sounded like you were going out for a full tour.' He just looked at her and smiled. 'How come you're only going for a bit, then?' James nodded towards a group of men sitting around a table in the corner of the closed bar. He leaned towards her, not noticing as Emma leaned back at the same time.

'I'm escorting that lot over there,' he whispered. Emma looked at them, noticing that although they were all male, they didn't look like they were military. One of them had a beard, another had a small ponytail, and most of them would struggle with the annual fitness test.

'Who are they, then?' she asked James.

'Metropolitan,' he replied, struggling to pronounce the word.

Emma looked up at James, realising that he'd stopped talking. He was staring over her shoulder. She looked around and with relief saw Matthew standing behind her, his huge arms folded across his broad chest.

'Matthew,' Emma squealed before jumping off her stool. She stood on tiptoes and kissed him on the lips. 'You're late, but I'm so glad you're here.' When she saw the look of surprise on his face she kissed him again and made a small 'shhh' sound before turning back to James.

'James, this is Matthew,' she said, noting with satisfaction the policeman's downcast expression. James nodded at the new arrival as Emma turned back to Matthew before continuing. 'And Matthew, this is James.' Matthew fixed James with a hard stare, making no effort to uncross his arms and offer the policeman a handshake. *Thank God*, Emma thought. Her cousin had got the message at last.

'I was just going, in fact,' James said with a disappointed look. 'Nice to meet you, anyway.' With a glance at the Flight Sergeant rank slides on Matthew's uniform, he turned and walked towards the group of policemen in the corner.

'That'll be a pint you owe me, then,' Matthew smiled at Emma. 'But what would you have done if I'd kissed you back, though?' he said. Emma looked at him with a mock frown.

'Well, I'd have kneed you in the bollocks,' she said, 'because, for one, you're married, and for two, you're my cousin.' Matthew laughed and fed some coins into the vending machine.

When Matthew had a can and Emma had a chocolate bar, they made their way over to a spare table near the door of the bar. Emma saw Matthew look over at the group of policemen in the corner again and raise his eyebrows. As they sat down, he clinked his can against Emma's.

'Cheers, anyway,' he said. 'Good to see you, and sorry I'm late.'

'No problem,' Emma replied. 'You got here just in time.' She took a sip of her drink and looked at Matthew. He looked tired, although Emma knew his post heading up the ground crew that prepared the large transport planes was a busy one, so she wasn't surprised. 'Busy shift, then?' she asked him.

'Bloody nightmare,' he replied. 'We'd almost finished loading up the TriStar when that lot turfed up.' Matthew nodded towards the policemen. 'Then we got a phone call from the duty officer down at Air Command, who told us that the Commander in Chief wanted them to be extended "every possible courtesy" to get them on the next plane out to Kandahar.'

'But they're civvy coppers, though?' Emma said. 'One of them's got a bloody ponytail.'

'That chap there is the boss, the one with the flasher jacket on,' Matthew said, causing Emma to spill her drink as she laughed. He reached into his pocket and threw her a handkerchief.

'Thanks,' she said, using it to dab at the table, still laughing.

'He's a nice enough bloke. Wouldn't want to get on the wrong side of him, though.' Emma regarded Matthew, surprised. He was well over six feet tall and built like the proverbial brick shithouse. Matthew's ears alone told the story of a fanatical rugby player, and Emma knew that he didn't scare easily.

'How do you mean?' she asked him.

'I don't know. He's just got a way about him that makes me nervous. Even though I've done nothing wrong. At least, nothing that he'd be interested in.' Matthew sat back in his chair. 'They've got loads of kit as well. We had to bump a load of pax off the plane to make room for it all as their stuff couldn't go in the hold. Too sensitive, apparently.'

'Pax?'

'Sorry, passengers. I keep forgetting you're Army,' Matthew replied with a grin.

'So why are they going to Kandahar anyway?' Emma asked.

'Well, here's the thing.' Matthew leaned towards her and dropped his voice to a conspiratorial whisper. 'I phoned home to let Caroline know I'd be late back, and I told her about the coppers. She then texted me about an hour later. You know her brother's a copper, right?'

'No, I've never met him,' Emma replied. She'd met Matthew's wife a couple of times, but never her brother.

'Anyway, she phoned him to find out who they were.' Matthew looked at her and took a long drink from his can. She raised her eyebrows at him.

'Well, go on,' Emma said.

'You can't say anything. It's all really hush hush.' She laughed at his serious expression.

'Yeah, yeah, of course it is,' she said. 'Come on, spill the beans.'

'All their kit, it's forensic stuff. Like off that Crime Scene Investigators on the telly. That's why it can't go in the hold.'

'Ooh, exciting stuff.' Emma opened her eyes in mock-horror. 'Crime Scene Kandahar.'

'They're not going to Kandahar,' Matthew replied. 'Well, they are, but then they're going on to Bastion.'

Emma looked across at the group of policemen who were getting up to leave.

'So who are they, then?' she whispered. Matthew paused before replying, also in a whisper.

'Major Investigation Team, apparently. Like on that murder squad program that used to be on the telly.'

'Seriously?' Emma said, her eyes wide for real this time. 'Shit!'

'You can't say anything, though,' Matthew said quickly. 'You'll get me an interview without coffee.'

'Whatever.' Emma waved her hand dismissively. 'If they are murder squad, everyone in uniform between here and Bastion will know about it already. You can't keep stuff like that quiet for long.'

'Fair one,' Matthew replied as he finished his drink. 'Just don't drop me in it, that's all. I need to get going, anyway.'

Emma and Matthew got to their feet, and he gave her a bear hug so tight it made her wince.

'You stay safe out there, mate,' he whispered. 'Your mum needs you back in one piece.'

'She's not said a word,' Emma replied. 'But I'm so worried.'

'Yeah, so's Caroline,' Matthew said. 'We'll keep an eye on her, though, don't worry. You concentrate on finishing your time out there.'

'I will, Matthew. Easy tour so far, and I'm over the hump now so will be back before you know it. Easy peasy.' She tried to keep the tremor she could feel in her throat out of her voice, but as she looked at Matthew's expression, she knew that he'd caught her out.

'Yeah, right,' he said. 'Just stay safe.'

34

Adams looked up at the eight-storey 'Pier Beach' hotel that Lizzie had pulled up outside. It was a square, uniform-looking building with a bunch of balconies making the most of the location a couple of hundred yards away from the beach.

'Nice place, Lizzie,' he said.

'Piss off, it was cheap as chips,' she retorted. 'It's got a bed, a shower, and a balcony. And it's right next to the beach.'

'Fair one,' Adams replied. 'It just looks like it was built in the Balkans.'

'I need your boots,' Lizzie said. 'The car's being picked up later this evening, so if you leave them in the car, they'll be gone and there'll be a Cypriot lad with some nice new footwear.' Adams sat on a bench near the car and unlaced his boots. He rolled his socks off his feet and stuffed them into the boots before handing them to Lizzie.

'There you go, mate,' he said. 'You might want to leave them on the balcony, though.' Lizzie wrinkled her nose and took the boots between her thumb and fingers.

'Yeah, thanks for that,' she replied. 'I think I will.'

Lizzie walked into the hotel, clutching the boots, while Adams struggled with the espadrilles that she had bought him. Finally getting them on his feet, he regarded them warily. They fit, but that was about the only positive thing that he could say about them. He relaxed back on the seat, enjoying the view over the sea in front of him. Closing his eyes, he relaxed with the sun on his face. It was a different feeling to the sun in Afghanistan, softer and more welcoming. He let the sounds of the seagulls relax him, and started to look forward to the rest of the day.

'Adams, wake up you lazy sod,' Lizzie's voice broke through his thoughts a few minutes later. 'That's twice today you've fallen asleep on the job.' He opened his eyes and looked through his sunglasses at Lizzie who was bending over in front of him. Her dress had fallen away, giving him an unrestricted view of the contents of her pink, lacy bra.

'Jesus wept,' Adams muttered, closing his eyes.

'What?' Lizzie asked.

'Nothing,' he replied, shaking his head. 'What's the plan, then?'

'Well, I was thinking we could bimble down to the seafront, and maybe grab a drink somewhere?'

'Sounds like a plan to me,' Adams replied, reopening his eyes and stretching. 'I could do with a pint.'

They walked slowly along the promenade, taking in the sights and sounds around them. Adams watched Lizzie as she flicked through some CDs on one of the beachfront stalls before finally picking out a couple to buy. She looked so different in a dress and out of uniform. More relaxed, more human somehow. He wondered what Sophie would think of Limassol, and thought that she probably wouldn't like it that much. Not that it mattered anyway, he thought with a sudden pang. He pushed thoughts of home to the back of his mind as Lizzie walked back over, clutching a thin plastic bag with her CDs in.

'My God, you look a bit serious,' she said. Adams looked at her, and his reflection in her sunglasses, before replying.

'I'm just a bit concerned that you're buying dodgy CDs from a seafront stall.'

'Why? What's wrong with that?'

'How are the artists going to get the royalties?' Lizzie laughed at his reply.

'Oh, piss off!' she said. Grabbing his arm, she pulled him towards her. 'Come on, let's go and have a look at the pier.'

Lizzie and Adams walked along the wooden pier that jutted out into the Mediterranean. When they got to the end, they both turned and looked back towards Limassol.

'Well,' Lizzie said. 'It could be worse.'

'You're right there,' Adams replied. He pointed towards a small bar at the end of the pier. 'How about that place?' He asked her. 'Do you think they do beer?'

'I'm pretty sure they do,' Lizzie said. 'Seeing as it's got a bright green neon sign that says "Beer" in the window, I'd be very surprised if they didn't.'

A few moments later, they were sitting at a table by the window, both with a glass of ice cold beer in front of them. Adams watched a couple of youngsters trying, and failing, to surf. They were persistent, he would give them that. He turned to look at Lizzie, who had her hands on either side of her face and was looking at him with a half-smile.

'Do you know something?' she asked him.

'What?' he replied.

'We've never talked about what happened back at

Sangin, have we?' Adams looked at her as her smile disappeared.

'No, you're right,' he said. 'Do you want to talk about it?' He watched her expression as he asked the question, but couldn't read her face at all. He was crap with women most of the time, and it looked as if today was no exception.

'Not really,' Lizzie said. 'I was just thinking that it was weird how we never talk about it.'

'To be honest, mate,' Adams said, 'I've kind of put it away in a box.' He thought for a second before continuing. 'But that might be because I don't want to talk about it.'

'Did you tell Sophie what had happened?' Adams felt a flicker of anger cross his face as Lizzie mentioned his girlfriend's name, and he made a concerted effort to hide it.

'What? That you nearly got shot in the arse?'

'No,' Lizzie laughed. 'Not that specifically, more the whole thing. What happened to us.' She paused, and by the time she continued, any trace of humour in her voice had gone. 'That you shot someone.'

'I don't think she would have got it,' Adams said. 'I don't think she would have got it at all. But that doesn't matter anymore now. It's all in the past.' He picked up his glass and clinked it off Lizzie's. 'Cheers.'

Lizzie didn't reply but just stared at him with a deadpan look on her face. Adams watched as she crossed her arms over her chest, uncrossed them, then crossed them again before her expression softened.

'What's all in the past?' she asked. 'You slotting someone, or you and Sophie?' Adams's heart sank. *Bollocks*, he thought. He'd been rumbled. 'Spill the beans, Adams, and stop taking me for a fool.' He thought for a while before deciding that now was as good a time as any.

'When I got back to our flat, she wasn't there.' He took

a sip of his beer. 'She was gone.' Adams looked at Lizzie, who was staring at him with her mouth half-open.

'Shit,' she whispered. 'Seriously?'

'No, Lizzie,' Adams replied, leaning back in his chair. 'She was only joking. Sophie burst out of the cupboard in the bedroom a few minutes later wearing nothing but a smile.' He laughed, but it was short-lived. 'I wish. She was well gone by the time I got back. Left a note, though. Not quite a "Dear John" letter, but not far off it.'

'What did it say?'

'Do you really want to know?'

'Would I ask if I didn't? Of course I want to know.'

'It said that she didn't think there was a long-term future between us,' Adams replied, trying to keep any emotion out of his voice. 'That it wasn't me, it was her. That sort of bollocks. She didn't want, er, what we had to be a long-term thing.'

'She dumped you while you were in Afghanistan?'

'Yep.'

'What a bitch.' Adams watched as Lizzie took a large drink from her beer. 'Have you still got the ring?'

'No, flogged it to a dodgy bloke in Yarmouth. Spent the cash on booze and prostitutes. The rest,' he took a sip of his own beer, 'I just wasted.' That comment, at least, raised a laugh from Lizzie.

'In Yarmouth? Bet they're quality.'

'The money went a long way, Lizzie,' Adams said with a broad smile. 'I won't lie to you.'

The two of them sat in silence for a few moments, before Adams continued.

'Lizzie?'

'What?' She looked up at him, and Adams was struck by the expression on her face. She looked even sadder than he felt.

'I didn't really spend the money on prostitutes. It's back in the bank.' At least that raised a smile.

Later that evening, Lizzie took Adams to a restaurant that she'd been to earlier in the week. It had been recommended to her by the concierge at the hotel when she'd asked if there was anywhere local that she could go for some authentic Cypriot food. She wasn't sure exactly what authentic Cypriot food was, but while she was here, she wanted to try some. It wasn't just that — she was still reeling from what Adams had told her earlier

'I came here on Tuesday night,' Lizzie said to Adams as she pushed open the wooden door to the restaurant. As she walked in, the owner of the restaurant rushed up to her and greeted her like an old friend. As he showed them to a table by the glass windows that looked out onto the street, Adams whispered to Lizzie.

'Well, you obviously made quite an impression on him.' Lizzie glared at Adams.

'Piss off, Adams,' she whispered back. 'He's old enough to be my grandad.' The restaurant owner pulled Lizzie's chair back for her so that she could sit down before rushing back to the bar to fetch a jug of water, glasses, and some menus. 'But at least he's got some manners,' Lizzie said.

Lizzie and Adams studied the menus as the restaurant owner lit the candles on the table before disappearing again. Lizzie looked up at Adams in the soft flickering light and smiled when she saw the frown on his face.

'What's the matter, mate?' she said. 'Do you not see anything you like?'

'It's all Greek to me.' Adams put the menu down on the table.

'Very funny,' Lizzie replied. 'Do you want me to ask him if he's got a menu with pictures in for you?'

'What, you can speak Greek?' Adams asked.

'There's a lot about me that you don't know, Adams,' she said. 'Watch and learn, watch and learn.'

Lizzie turned and waved at the owner who was standing behind the bar polishing some glasses. He came bustling over, retrieving his pad and pencil from the pocket in the front of his apron as he did so. When he reached Lizzie, he looked at her expectantly with his pencil poised above the pad. Lizzie pointed at the menu in front of her and shrugged her shoulders. The restaurant owner laughed, and went back to the bar returning a few seconds later with two menus which he exchanged for the ones he had given them earlier. Adams opened his menu and, seeing the pictures of the food next to the text, started laughing.

'Nicely done, Lizzie,' Adams laughed. 'But you really are full of shit sometimes, you know that?'

They both looked at the menus for a few minutes, although Lizzie knew what she was going to have already, which was exactly the same thing that she had had on Tuesday. She figured there was no point chancing it and ending up with something that she didn't like.

'Do you know what you want?' she asked Adams.

'I think I'm going to have the one that looks like a kebab,' he replied, pointing a finger at one of the pictures on the menu.

'Good choice,' Lizzie said. 'It's called "Soulvaki" or something like that, I think.'

'What are you going to have?' Adams asked her. Lizzie pointed at another picture on the menu.

'I think I'm going to have that. I've got no idea what it's called, but I had it the other day and it was divine.' Lizzie waved the owner back across to their table and ordered their food by pointing several times at the menu. Then she turned the menu over and pointed at some drinks on the back.

'What are we drinking?' Adams asked.

'Wine, hopefully,' she replied.

A different member of staff came back a few minutes later and exchanged their menus for napkins and knives and forks. He also brought a large jug of white wine and two glasses which he put down next to them. Lizzie saw Adams looking at the wine with suspicion.

'That looks like a quality vintage,' he said.

'Oh, stop whingeing Adams,' Lizzie replied. 'I had some the other night and it was fine. Maybe not the finest wine I've ever drunk, but it did the job.' Adams picked up the jug and poured a dash of wine into Lizzie's glass.

'Would Madam care to taste it, even though it looks like a urine sample?'

'Why, thank you.' Lizzie took a delicate sip from the glass after swirling it around and sniffing it. 'Mmm, I'm getting autumn leaves with a hint of citrus.' She drained the glass. 'Just fill her up,' Lizzie said as she stretched out her arm with the empty glass. 'Come on, I'm dehydrating while you're farting about trying to be posh.'

By the time the waiter returned with their food, Lizzie and Adams had polished off the first jug of wine. Lizzie pointed at the jug, and the waiter nodded at her as he put their plates in front of them. Lizzie was pleased that the food had turned up as she was starting to feel the buzz from the wine, and she had not eaten since lunchtime. The warm flush the wine had given her was not unpleasant, though. She watched as Adams picked through his food, moving bits and pieces around with a fork. The waiter returned with another jug of wine and filled up both their glasses before putting it on the table between them.

'What's up?' Lizzie asked Adams. He looked up at her and smiled.

'Nothing, nothing at all,' he replied. 'I know I'd said that I would have the one that looks like a kebab, but…'

'What's wrong with it?' she said.

'Well, it is a kebab. The only thing that's missing is the polystyrene box.' Lizzie looked at Adams and they both laughed.

'Just shut up and eat it,' she said. 'This time tomorrow we'll be back in Afghanistan, and this time next week you'll be remembering this meal as the best one you've had in months.' Lizzie watched as the smile slowly dropped from Adams's face.

'This time next week,' he said, 'we could both be dead.'

35

Private Dave Moffat was admiring the colours of the sunset over Sangin and wondering how his beloved Sheffield United would fare in the Premier League next season when the bullet hit him in the face.

It entered just below his left eye, nicking the bone of his cheek which diverted it upwards. Ripping through his optic nerve, it carried on through the soft tissue in his brain before smashing its way through his skull on the crown of his head. When it met the hard Kevlar of the helmet that Private Moffat was wearing, the bullet flatted and ricocheted back through the hole it had just made before finally coming to rest in his brain stem.

The cavitation pressure wave that the bullet produced as it passed through his brain had already caused irreparable damage to Private Moffat's medulla oblongata and motor cortex. Private Moffat would have died from the damage to these two key areas, but the pressure wave finished the job regardless. Even if he had somehow survived the initial trauma of the high velocity round, the resulting cerebral oedema from the tissue damage would have herniated his brain, killing him at some point down the line.

None of these things really mattered to Private Moffat, because although he was still standing, he was dead. His body rocked backward until his knees buckled, and he fell with a thump onto the wooden floor of the lookout tower that he'd been standing on. The half-smoked cigarette that he'd been so careful to hide the glow from rolled onto the boards next to his body. He never heard the echoing gunshot ring out across the village.

A few hundred yards away from Moffat, Lance Corporal Jackson woke with a start, not sure what it was that had disturbed him. He was usually a pretty heavy sleeper, so whatever it was must have been significant. Unzipping his sleeping bag, he pushed aside the mosquito net that covered his camp cot and got to his feet. Around him some of his platoon were also stirring, so something must be going on.

'For fuck's sake,' he said as he looked at his watch. It wasn't even eleven o'clock — so much for an early night. He slid his feet into his boots after giving them a quick shake to check for camel spiders or scorpions. He'd heard the old wives' tale about the soldier who'd put his foot into his boot and been bitten by a camel spider and, while he thought that the story was total bollocks, wasn't going to take any chances.

He padded towards the door of the small room that he and five of his colleagues called home. Jackson pushed the door open, wincing as the hinges complained. When they'd taken over the compound, they'd rehung all the doors so that they opened outwards, not inwards, in an attempt to stop the doors being blown open if they were attacked. But this one had never been the same since they'd done that.

As he looked out of the door into the courtyard, he heard a shout from near one of the watchtowers that stood in each corner of the compound.

'Man Down! Man Down!'

'Bollocks,' he muttered as he broke into a run and started jogging towards the watchtower. After a couple of yards, he turned back and ran into the accommodation block to grab his body armour and weapon. When he ran into the room, the rest of his platoon were still in their cots. 'Wakey wakey, boys!' he shouted, 'Sounds like there's a stand to!'

On hearing this, the soldiers all started fighting their way out of their sleeping bags and mosquito nets. Jackson said to one of them as he picked up his weapon and body armour, 'Can you make sure that the Doc's up and about mate? He might be needed.' The soldier swore as Jackson's Kevlar helmet banged off the metal corner of his cot, but at least Jackson knew he was awake.

Without waiting for a reply, Jackson left the room and resumed his run across the courtyard, trying to slide his arms into his body armour as he did so. Despite the dim light he could see a couple of soldiers near the bottom of one of the watchtowers, so he ran towards it to see what was going on. As he arrived, a soldier looked down from the top of the watchtower.

'It's Moffat, Jacko!' the soldier shouted before turning to look out over the village. 'He's well dead.' Jackson opened his mouth to tell the lad to get back down into the compound when another shot rang out.

The soldier on top of the compound was thrown backward off the top of the watchtower, landing with an explosive gasp on the dirt by Jackson's feet. The thud he made as he hit the earth was closely followed by the echo of the shot ringing out across the village beyond the compound walls.

'Fuck, fuck,' Jackson said, kneeling down next to his colleague. 'Mate, are you okay?' he said, although as soon as he said it he realised it was a stupid thing to say. The soldier at his feet was gasping for breath, each exhalation punctuated with a bloody bubble of saliva. As Jackson watched, the breaths slowed down and stopped within a few seconds. 'Don't go near that fucking ladder!' he shouted at the other soldiers, who were standing like statues, staring at the body on the ground. Jackson rolled the soldier lying in front him away from him and peered at his back. 'Fuck me, that's gone straight through him,' he said as he saw the large exit wound in the middle of his body armour. So much for the Kevlar plate.

Jackson could hear the compound coming to life around him, and soldiers started to stream out of the accommodation blocks and get into their well-drilled positions. He heard footsteps behind him and turned to see Major Fletcher, the CO, arrive.

'What's going on, Jacko?' he barked.

'Gotta be a sniper, sir,' Jackson said. 'Somewhere in the village. Hit this lad up on the watchtower.' Jackson looked again at the soldier lying on the ground, but he couldn't work out who it was in the near darkness.

'Dave Moffat's up there, sir,' one of the remaining soldiers said, finally recovering from the shock of seeing his friend die right in front of him. 'He's hit too, I saw him go down and then heard the shot.'

'Moffat's dead too, sir,' Jackson added.

'Well, he's staying up there for the moment,' Major Fletcher replied. 'I want no one on the towers. No one. Got it?' They all nodded in reply. 'Jacko, I want you to go round and make sure that all the fire teams know that there's a sniper in the village somewhere. I'm going back to the CP to call it in, see if we can get some support or eyes in the sky. I don't want a single head above the parapets until we know exactly what we're dealing with. Okay?'

'Yes, sir,' Jackson replied. 'On my way.'

'You,' the Major nodded at one of the soldiers. 'On me.' The two of them hurried off toward the Command Post.

Grabbing the remaining soldier by the arm, Jackson pulled him over to a small group kneeling by the side of the large reinforced wall that surrounded the FOB. He didn't want to just leave the lad behind with his dead friends, but at the same time didn't trust him to go off on his own.

'Lads,' Jackson said as he reached the group. 'Stay down, okay? There's a sniper in the village somewhere.' He looked up to see where the next group of soldiers had gathered when he heard a faint pop from the direction of the village. The noise triggered something somewhere in the back of his mind. He was trying to place it when a mournful whistling noise sounded, closely followed by an ear-splitting explosion in the middle of the compound. The Taliban had worked out a while ago how to adapt Chinese 107mm rockets and use them as impromptu artillery shells, but they'd never been this accurate before.

Jackson managed to stay on his feet, despite the powerful shock wave that buffeted him and the other soldiers, and out of the corner of his eye, he saw the soldier who'd been standing next to him land on his backside as they were showered with clods of earth. Above his head, he could hear the whine of metal fragments, some of which ended up in the wall they were sheltering behind with a determined thud.

'Mate, you hit?' Jackson shouted above the whining in his head. He saw the young man shake his head from side to side. Jackson wasn't sure if he was nodding 'no', or just trying to clear his head from the blast. Jackson quickly looked at the small group of soldiers who were all trying to get to their feet and into one of the bunkers that they'd built just for this reason when they'd arrived. He looked around at the area where the rocket had hit, but all he could see was a cloud of smoke. 'Bollocks,' he said. 'Where's the CO?'

36

'Bloody hell, Adams,' Lizzie said, leaning back in her chair and looking at him. 'What sort of a thing is that to say?'

'What do you mean?'

'This time next week, we could both be dead. For God's sake. Where did that come from?' She stared at him, incredulous.

'It's true,' he replied. 'Isn't it? We're both lucky to be sitting here now, to be honest. Aren't we?'

'Jesus, I still can't believe you said that.' Lizzie stared at Adams, who was fixated on something in his lap. She'd never seen him look like this before, and if she'd been asked, wouldn't have a clue how to describe him. 'Is it Sophie?'

Adams looked up at her and Lizzie saw an entire range of emotions cross his face. Anger, sadness, fear, and something else she didn't recognise flitted across his features in rapid succession.

'What do you bloody well think?' he snapped. 'Of course it's Sophie. It's not just her, though. It's everything.'

Lizzie was just about to tell him not to take it out on her when she thought better of it. From the look on his face, that wasn't what he wanted to hear. She reached out her hand and took his, squeezing it and smiling at him.

'It'll work out, mate,' she said. 'It always does.'

They both looked up as the restaurant owner cleared his throat theatrically. Lizzie looked around the restaurant and realised that they were the last customers. She glanced at her watch.

'It's late, Adams, we should go.' Adams nodded and finished off the last of his wine.

'Okay, I guess you're right. I'd better head back to Akrotiri. He's just trying to clear the table, though. How about a nightcap at your hotel? One for the ditch?'

'I'm just nipping to the toilet,' Lizzie said. 'I'll get something on the way back.'

As she washed her hands, Lizzie looked at herself in the mirror. She didn't want Adams to go back to the base like this, but at the same time, she couldn't see him being in the mood for a nightclub. *You poor bastard*, she thought, drying her hands.

Adams sat on one of the chairs next to the large windows that looked out over the seafront. They'd walked back to Lizzie's hotel in silence, her arm linked through the crook of his elbow. She'd seemed to realise that he didn't want to talk.

He eased off one of his espadrilles and put his foot onto his thigh so that he could rub at a blister on the back of his heel. While he did so, he looked up to see Lizzie was leaning against the counter, trying to talk to the concierge. She was waving her hands around, obviously trying to make him understand that they wanted something else to drink, but the concierge was just looking at her blankly. He watched Lizzie stand on her tiptoes and start pointing at the bottles behind the counter. The movement brought her calves into sharp definition, and he could see that the dress she was wearing was a lot thinner than he'd realised.

As he watched, he saw Lizzie's dress slide back down to just below her knees as her heels went back to the floor. Although he'd seen her in civilian clothes before, he'd never seen her in a dress. He'd definitely never seen her looking like she looked this evening.

Adams looked back towards the concierge to see if Lizzie had managed to get some wine out of him, and he realised that Lizzie's reflection was looking straight at him in the mirror behind the concierge's desk. Had she seen him staring? He thought for a moment that he might have got away with it, but when he looked at the quizzical expression on her face, he realised that he probably hadn't.

'Bollocks,' he muttered.

Adams watched as the concierge brought out a bottle of wine and a couple of glasses, placing them on the counter in front of Lizzie. She picked them up and walked back towards him, her dress swaying around her hips as she did so. He really was quite distracted by what was going on in his head. Lizzie was a friend, an old friend, and yet tonight he was seeing her in a completely different light. Adams was torn. In one part of his head, an alarm bell was ringing and a voice was telling him that he was in a dangerous situation by being here, with her, alone in a hotel. Another voice was telling him that he should just have a glass of wine and then just fuck off to find a taxi back to the base. A third voice — this one between his legs — was telling him something different altogether. Try as he might to silence it, this third voice was the one that was shouting loudest at that precise moment in time.

'Bloody hell,' Lizzie said as she put the bottle of wine on the table and set out the glasses next to it. 'That was a lot more complicated than it should have been.' She threw her room key down onto the table, and the noise it made as the large wooden fob attached to it hit the glass made Adams jump. 'You a bit jumpy there, Adams?' Lizzie asked him.

'Er, no,' he replied. 'I just wasn't expecting to have a key attached to a log thrown at me.' Adams eyed the key fob. 'You could have put the window through with that.'

'It stops people nicking them, I reckon,' Lizzie said. 'I mean, it's not as if you could walk around with a piece of wood that size in your pocket or handbag, is it?'

'I guess not,' Adams replied. He looked at the large numbers painted on the fob. 'Still, nice of them to put your age on it.' Lizzie looked down at the large numbers four and five that were painted in bright red paint onto the wood and laughed.

'Piss off,' she said. Lizzie opened the bottle of wine and filled up both glasses. Leaning forward, she put a glass in front of Adams.

Adams was acutely aware of her dress falling forwards as she did this. He looked at her face, determined not to let his gaze wander. Was it his imagination, or was Lizzie leaning forward to see what he would do? To see if he would glance downwards? In his peripheral vision, he could see that if he did glance downwards he would be able to see down the front of her dress. Adams concentrated on her eyes, ignoring the flash of pink fabric in the corner of his eye.

Still leaning forward, Lizzie said, 'There you go, one of Cyprus's finest vintages, apparently.' She stayed in the same position for a fraction longer than Adams thought was necessary before sitting back in the chair. Had he passed that test? He'd managed to maintain eye contact with her, but perhaps by doing this, he'd actually failed it.

'Anyway,' Lizzie said, 'I've got a bone to pick with you.' One of the voices in Adams's head pointed out that Lizzie had said wood and bone in fairly short succession. Ignoring it, he picked up his glass and took a sip of wine.

'What's that then?' he said.

'Well, more of a question,' she said, and then paused. Adams noticed the faint smile that was playing around her lips. Adams looked at Lizzie and knew for sure that he had indeed been rumbled. 'Was it my imagination, or were you looking at my legs just now? For quite a long time?'

Adams took another sip of wine, playing for time. His immediate reaction was to deny everything, make out that she was mistaken, but he knew that plan wouldn't work. He decided instead to go on the offensive.

'It's your fault,' he said, 'for wearing that dress. I didn't actually realise that you had legs.'

'Really?' Lizzie regarded him with a smirk. 'I've always had these legs, but you never seem to have noticed them before. So why were you staring at them just now?' Adams sighed as he watched the smile playing across her face.

'Lizzie,' he continued, 'if I told you, you wouldn't like the answer.'

'Try me,' she said, the smile disappearing. Adams raised his hands as if surrendering.

'Okay, but don't slap me,' he said, noticing with relief that the faint smile had reappeared. 'I'll be honest, I was looking at your legs, I'll admit that much.' He paused before continuing. 'But that's only because I think that they are a particularly fine pair of legs.' Adams looked at Lizzie, concerned that he had said the wrong thing. To his relief, she started laughing.

'Oh for God's sake, Adams,' she said. 'You sound like something out of an Emily Brontë book!'

Lizzie leaned forward in her chair and put her arms on the table. To Adams's relief, she wasn't leaning as far forward as she had been earlier, but then she folded her arms in front of her, which he was fairly sure would have an effect on his view were he to look down.

'I don't know whether to be flattered or terrified,' Lizzie said. 'But I'm probably a bit of both, to be honest.' She paused, examining her wine glass for a moment, before continuing. 'Can you keep a secret?'

'You know I can,' Adams replied.

'I don't think that your legs are too shabby either,' she said in a whisper. 'Even when you are wearing pink espadrilles.' They both looked at each other in silence for what to Adams seemed like ages.

'What's changed, Adams?' Lizzie said.

'What do you mean?'

'I've always had these legs, but like I said, you never seem to have noticed them before.'

'To be fair, I don't think I've ever seen you in a dress before,' Adams said. 'So, I've never actually considered the fact that you have legs.' He was trying hard to relieve the tension that seemed to have suddenly descended on the hotel lobby. They sat in silence, neither of them looking at the other, the only sound a lone mosquito whining around the room.

'We've known each other for ages,' Lizzie said, eventually breaking the silence. 'But it's never been like this between us.'

'What do you mean, like this?' Adams replied. Lizzie didn't say anything but just looked at him. Looking toward the ceiling, he let out a deep breath and leaned backward in his chair. 'I don't know,' he said. 'I honestly don't know.'

'Is it what happened at home?' she asked him. He looked at her, wondering where she was going with that question.

'It must be.' He paused, before continuing, 'Although, to be honest, it's more than that. It's this tour, and what it's done to us. I killed someone, Lizzie.' He paused again. 'You were nearly shot right in front of me. So, it's all of that. And it's you.'

'What do you mean, and it's me?' she asked.

'You,' Adams continued, 'in that bloody dress.' He ignored the alarm bell in his head that had suddenly got louder in the last few seconds. Adams reached across the table and took Lizzie's hand in his, running his thumb across the back of her hand. 'Mate, I'm really sorry, but I'm sitting here now looking at you, and I'm just thinking, how beautiful you are. And I can't believe that I've not noticed that before. Not properly.'

'Adams,' Lizzie said in a whisper, her cheeks red in the soft light of the bar. 'We've got to be at Akrotiri in a couple of hours.' Adams took a deep breath before replying, glancing at Lizzie's hotel room key as he did so.

'We could do a lot in a couple of hours.'

———————

37

Jackson ran across the scrappy patch of land in the middle of the compound towards the area where he'd last seen the CO. He couldn't see jack shit through the cloud of smoke that was rising from the crater in the centre of the compound. As he ran around the edges of the crater that had appeared, he heard another 'crump' from beyond the compound walls.

'Shit,' he muttered as he tried to pick up speed across the rough ground. Although he knew the chances of a rocket landing anywhere near the same place was remote given the crude targeting systems that the insurgents used, a rocket was a rocket. Jackson heard the explosion of the incoming rocket beyond the walls of the compound and swore again as he saw another smoke cloud start to rise up. At least that one landed outside the walls.

Jackson broke through the other side of the smoke, and with relief saw the CO standing in the open, staring at a crater in the earth. One entire side of the Major's uniform was covered in earth. Jackson ran across to him, pulling up sharply as he reached the officer.

'Sir,' Jackson panted. 'You okay?' The CO turned to look at him, and Jackson saw that his face was covered in dirt as well as his uniform. The only patches of clear skin were lines where sweat had dripped down his face, washing the mud away. He could also see the fear in the officer's eyes. Grabbing the CO by the arm, he pushed him towards the door of the Ops Room. 'Come on, sir. Let's get inside.'

Once the two men reached the relative safety of the Ops Room, the CO turned to Jackson.

'Fuck me, that was close. Landed right behind me,' the Major blurted the words out like bullets from a machine gun. 'Fucking knocked me right on my arse.'

'Are you hurt, sir?' Jackson said. 'You're limping.'

'Don't think so. Twisted my bloody leg when I went over.' They both jumped as a loud explosion shook the small building. 'Jesus,' the CO barked as dust started to filter down from the ceiling. He strode across to the corner of the room, where a young 2nd Lieutenant was hunched over a radio. 'Have you called it in?'

'I'm trying, sir.' Jackson could hear the tremor in the officer's voice. 'I can't raise them, though.'

'Well, keep trying. We need to get some support up here. Whatever they've got.'

The three men ducked instinctively as another rocket whined overhead. Jackson braced himself for a blast, but there was nothing other than a muffled crump off in the distance. The aiming system for the large 107mm rockets that the insurgents used was often nothing more than a few bits of wood under the shell to aim it in the general direction of where they wanted it to go. Although that made them wildly inaccurate, it also meant that by the time any air support had pinpointed the firing point, the insurgents were long gone. The inaccuracy didn't matter when they got it right, though.

'Sitrep, sitrep,' the CO mumbled under his breath. 'Need to get on top. Understand the situation. Jacko?'

'Sir?'

'What's your understanding?'

'Two dead, sir,' Jackson replied, 'and a whole load of rockets coming in.' The Major stared at him.

'No shit, Sherlock,' he said with a grin that was bordering on manic. 'Right, we need to plan an offensive counter-attack,' he muttered, more to himself than the other two soldiers. 'What have we got?'

'Sir?' Jackson said.

'What?'

'Maybe we should hunker down instead. At least until we get eyes in the sky. They could be trying to draw us out into their sniper arc.'

'Go on,' the Major said. Jackson took a deep breath before continuing. The CO was frowning, but at least he was listening.

'There's a long gun somewhere in the village. They'll know that we've taken casualties, so they could be waiting for a Chinook to come in. They won't know they're grounded.' Another rocket whistled over their heads, followed by an explosion. *Close*, Jackson thought, *but still outside the compound*. 'Or they're hoping that we'll go after them, in which case their sniper will pick us off one by one. Or they'll wait.'

'They could be trying to grind us down,' the young 2nd Lieutenant said. 'Keep us up all bloody night with rockets, and then attack at first light when we're knackered.'

'That's probably more likely, sir,' Jackson said to the young officer.

The CO sat heavily on a canvas chair and ran his

fingers through his hair. Jackson watched him try to decide what to do, before realising that they should probably all be wearing helmets. Not that it would do much good if one of those 107mm rockets came in through the roof of the CP.

'Right,' the Major said loudly, startling them both. 'That's what we'll do. Hunker down. Jacko — get out there and make sure everyone's in cover. Any more casualties and get back here with a sitrep. We'll keep trying to raise Bastion.'

Jackson made his way over to the door, picking up his helmet as he did so. He was fiddling with the strap under his chin when he heard the CO calling his name.

'Sir?' Jackson replied.

'Thanks, Jacko. Just make sure the boys know what to do. Keep their heads down and out of trouble.'

'Got that, sir,' Jackson replied as he stepped back out into the compound.

Adams watched as Lizzie leaned toward him, sitting forward in her chair. Apart from a slight widening of her eyes at his earlier statement, her face was impassive. Her eyes flicked between his, and for a moment Adams was certain that she was about to kiss him. She grabbed the bottle of wine from the table and filled up his glass before pushing her chair back, its legs scraping on the stone floor of the restaurant.

'I thought,' she said, her voice barely above a whisper, 'that you had a bit more respect for me than that.' Picking up her room key from the table, she nodded in the direction of his glass of wine. 'Fill your boots,' she said, her voice back to normal. 'Enjoy. I'll see you in a few hours at the airhead.' Lizzie nodded towards the concierge who was still sitting behind his desk pretending to read a book. 'He'll get you a cab.'

Lizzie walked off towards the staircase. Adams hoped that she would at least look round and say goodnight, but she pushed her way through the door without a second glance. He looked at the full glass of wine in front of him and knowing that there was no chance of him standing up in the next few minutes, took a sip and looked out at the lights of the harbour.

'Well, fuck it anyway,' he said under his breath. 'That went well.'

It took Lizzie a couple of tries to get the key into the keyhole of her hotel room. Whether that was the wine, what had just happened, or a combination of both wasn't obvious to her. She opened the door, and locked it behind her, fighting tears as she did so.

Lizzie put the half-full bottle of wine down on her bedside table and kicked off her sandals. She looked around the room, saw her half-packed suitcase on one of the armchairs, and was reminded as she set her alarm for two hours' time that not long after it went off, she would be going back to Afghanistan. Lizzie thought about Adams and hoped that the concierge had been able to sort him out with a taxi, before thinking again about what would be happening if he was here with her now.

Lizzie slipped off her dress, letting it crumple in a heap before shivering. She rubbed her arms to try to get rid of the goose bumps. It wasn't cold in the slightest, but she still had goose bumps. Lizzie looked across at the sink where her toothbrush and toothpaste were sitting, but decided that she really couldn't be bothered to do her teeth. There was no point if she was only going to be asleep for a couple of hours. She picked up the bottle of wine, and realising that she'd left her glass downstairs, drank directly from it.

'Classy, mate,' she said to herself. 'Really bloody classy.' As she said the words, she realised that she wasn't sure whether she was talking about Adams or herself.

She pulled back the covers to her bed and slid into it. There was a lot of empty space in the bed, plenty of room for two, but it was too late for that now. Lizzie picked up the headphones for her iPod, jamming the earbuds firmly into her ears. She flicked through the music on it, before settling on a Snow Patrol album that she had bought just before going out to Afghanistan. She lay there, listening to the music, thinking about what could have been happening if she'd not walked off. She thought about Adams as she shut her eyes tightly, the fact that he was her boss, the fact that he was a friend. Lizzie knew in her heart that she didn't really care about any of these things. The only thing that she could think about as the tears started rolling onto her pillow was him.

Adams knocked softly for a second time on the bedroom door. He looked at the numbers on the door, certain that he had the right one. After all, they had been painted in large letters on the key fob that Lizzie had thrown on the table earlier. He listened but couldn't hear anything. Lizzie had only gone to her room a few minutes ago, and he didn't think that she would be asleep just yet. Maybe she was ignoring him? He wouldn't be surprised after what he had said, but as he had watched her walk, away he had realised immediately that he had made a big mistake. He just wanted to apologise, that was all.

He thought for a second about trying the doorknob to see if the door was open but instantly dismissed it as a really bad idea. Reluctantly, he turned from the door and walked back down the corridor to the stairs. When he got to the lobby below, he walked across to the concierge's desk. As he arrived, the elderly man behind the desk looked up at him with a surprised expression.

'Taxi?' Adams said. 'Please?' The concierge's expression changed to one of sadness as he looked at Adams. He reached for the telephone and said to Adams with a thick Greek accent.

'Akrotiri?' Adams nodded his head. The concierge dialled a number, and a few seconds later was talking rapidly to someone on the other end of the line. The only word that Adams understood was the name of the base. As he put down the telephone, the concierge held up his hand with his fingers and thumb extended and said something in Greek that Adams assumed was 'five minutes'.

He thanked the concierge and went back to sit in the seat that he had been sitting in earlier by the window of the hotel. Adams looked at the door to the stairs that Lizzie had disappeared through, hoping that she might reappear. He caught the concierge looking at him, the sad expression back on his face, and considered how ironic it was that the old man had picked up on exactly what had happened even though they weren't able to understand a word that the other one could say and were probably separated by over fifty years.

Adams closed his eyes and thought back to when Lizzie was sitting opposite him. He replayed in his head as much as he could remember. How she looked, how she sounded, and the way his heart skipped when she was leaning toward him and he thought she was about to kiss him.

'For fuck's sake,' he said to himself. 'What have you just done?'

He looked out across the seafront, and the twinkling lights of boats moored in the bay reflecting off the water. All in all, his rest and recuperation had been absolutely shit. On the other side of the road, a dilapidated Skoda with a magnetic taxi sign on the driver's door pulled up. With a sigh, Adams stood and walked towards the hotel door, waving at the concierge as he did so. He stepped out into the cool night and walked across the road to the taxi.

38

E mma woke with a start, not sure for a moment where
she was. She blinked a couple of times before
remembering that she was on the TriStar out of Brize,
heading back to Afghanistan. Her heart sank at the
thought, but when she remembered that she would be
seeing Lizzie when the plane got to Cyprus, she brightened
a little bit.

According to her watch, it was just after eight in the
evening, United Kingdom time. Cyprus was two hours
ahead, so it would be gone ten o'clock there. Emma
wondered for a moment what Lizzie was up to. If she had
any sense, Emma thought with a smile, she'd be propping
up a bar somewhere getting a few last-minute drinks in
before the flight.

Emma stretched, easing her neck from side to side to
work out a muscle spasm. She must have gone to sleep in
an awkward position, but at least she had a bank of three
seats to herself. When all the passengers were being
boarded, the loadmaster in charge of the cabin, a miserable looking Warrant Officer who no doubt had seen it all

before, had checked all their boarding cards. Most of the soldiers in the line, including the policeman she'd been talking to earlier, had been sent to the right and down into the main body of the plane. When the Warrant Officer checked Emma's boarding card, he almost cracked a smile and nodded towards the right-hand side where a curtain separated the front of the plane from the rear.

'You're through there,' he'd said in a gruff voice before turning his attention to the soldier behind Emma. She stepped through the curtain and realised that the seats in the front of the plane were spaced much further apart from each other than in the back. There were a few people in flying suits lounging around, and as far as she could see, she was the only non-RAF person in that part of the plane.

'Hey,' a young Senior Aircraftman had said to Emma as she looked around the cabin. 'You must have friends in high places for the Warrant to send you up here.' Behind them, on the other side of the curtain, they could hear the Warrant Officer arguing with someone. The conversation ended with the loadie telling whoever he was arguing with that he didn't care if he was a full Colonel or not, he could sit in his allocated seat or get off the plane. Emma looked at the young man in front of her and they both laughed.

'I don't know about friends in high places,' Emma had said as she took the cup of coffee that was being offered to her. 'But I think maybe I have got friends in the right places.'

The crick in her neck finally appeased, Emma nipped to the toilet. As she came out of the cubicle, she peeped through a small gap in the curtain into the rear of the plane. It was crammed full of soldiers, most of them sleeping, a few of them giving her filthy looks. She giggled and closed the gap in the curtain before returning to her seat.

The next time Emma woke up, it was because the young Senior Aircraftman was shaking her shoulder. She opened her eyes and saw that he was holding a cup of coffee in his hand.

'Here you go, mate,' he said, pushing the cardboard cup in her direction. 'It's not Starbucks, but it's the best we've got.' Emma straightened herself up in the seat and took the coffee.

'You're a star, thank you.'

'No problem,' he replied. 'We're coming in to land in Akrotiri in about twenty minutes. The layover's about ninety minutes, so you can stretch your legs and what have you.'

'Can't I stay on the plane?' Emma asked.

'Not when it's being refuelled you can't, no,' the young man said with a smile. 'We've all got to get off. Even Grumpy over there.' He nodded toward the loadmaster, who was deep in conversation with a man in a flight suit who barely looked old enough to shave, let alone fly a passenger plane. 'So how did you end up here, anyway? In the front?'

'Probably my cousin, Matthew. He works on the ground crew at Brize.'

'Big ugly bloke? Mashed up ears?'

'Yeah, that's him.'

'Don't tell him I said that, mind.'

'I won't, don't worry,' Emma laughed. 'Not as long as you keep bringing me coffee.'

Half an hour later, Emma stepped down the stairs of the TriStar and into the muggy heat of the Cyprus night. Following the directions of the bored-looking ground crew, she made her way into what could only be described as a holding pen for passengers. It was surrounded by chain-link fences and had a couple of Portaloos in the corner. At least they looked reasonably clean, but Emma had no intention whatsoever of finding out if they were or not. Inside the fence, there were already quite a few people milling about. They hadn't got off the plane, Emma realised, so they must be joining the flight.

Emma looked around to see if she could see Lizzie, but all the new passengers were male. As she scoured the faces, she recognised one them — the Flight Lieutenant from the TRT. Adams, she thought his name was, as she walked over to where he was sitting. When she got to within a few feet of him, Emma realised that he was wearing bright pink espadrilles.

'Hi, sir,' Emma said. 'How's tricks?' He looked up at her, dark circles under both eyes.

'Hey, Emma isn't it?'

'Yep, that's me.' Emma smiled at him, pleased that he knew her name. 'How was your R&R?'

'Bit hit and miss, to be honest,' the officer replied with a sigh. 'How about yours?'

'Yeah, it was okay,' she said. They looked at each other for a few seconds before Emma continued. 'Is Lizzie about?'

'She's about somewhere,' he replied. 'Or at least, she should be.' He looked down at his hands as an awkward silence developed. Emma was on the verge of asking him about his footwear when a door in the building behind him opened and Lizzie walked through.

'Talk of the devil,' Emma said, crossing to greet her.

They hugged, but the combat boots Lizzie was carrying made it difficult. 'How you doing, babe?'

'All good, mate,' Lizzie replied, glancing across at Adams. 'Hang on a sec.' Emma watched as she walked over to Adams and dumped the boots at his feet. 'You left these in my room,' Emma heard Lizzie say. He mumbled a response that Emma didn't catch as Lizzie walked back over to join her. 'Come on,' Lizzie said. 'Let's go over here and grab a seat.'

Emma let Lizzie pull her arm and lead her over to an empty bench. The two women sat next to each other, and Emma saw Lizzie glance over at Adams who was trying to pull his espadrilles off his feet.

'Lizzie,' Emma said in a firm voice. 'What's happened?'

'What do you mean?' her friend replied, trying and failing to sound nonchalant.

'Please tell me you've not slept with your boss?'

'No,' Lizzie barked back. 'I haven't.' Emma stared at her, not sure whether to believe her or not.

'Something's happened, though?' Emma pressed. Lizzie said something under her breath that Emma didn't hear. 'Sorry, mate?' Emma asked. 'I didn't catch that.'

'I said, I nearly did,' Lizzie replied. She looked at Emma, tears in the corner of her eyes. 'His girlfriend dumped him while he was away. He was going to ask her to marry him as well, but when he got back, she'd done a runner.'

'Bloody hell, the poor bloke,' Emma said. 'So what happened between the two of you, then?'

'We'd been out, had a few drinks and a meal, and he just asked me if I wanted to go to bed with him.'

'What, he said that?'

'Well, not in so many words, no,' Lizzie said with a sigh

before continuing. 'But that's what he meant. I didn't know whether to slap him or kiss him.' Emma started giggling. 'What's so funny?' Lizzie asked her.

'You could have done both.'

'Oh, shut up.' Lizzie looked at Emma, and Emma could see in the dim light that she was at least smiling. 'If I'd done that, then we would have ended up in bed.' They sat in silence for a few seconds before Emma replied.

'Would that have been such a bad thing, mate?'

'Oh, Emma,' Lizzie said, her voice breaking. She turned around on the seat so that she was facing away from Adams, who was trying to pack his espadrilles into his small rucksack. 'I don't need this. What am I going to do?'

39

L ance Corporal Jackson shook his head from side to side to clear the tiredness. He was crouched down by one of the walls, deliberately not sitting down so that he wouldn't fall asleep. Although he wasn't on sentry duty, he didn't want to waste any time trying to wake up if something happened. Over the last couple of hours, rockets had been flying over their heads at irregular intervals. Only one of them had landed inside the compound, impacting not far from the accommodation, but it hadn't detonated. One for the bomb disposal guys at some point in the future. Sporadic gunfire sounded from the village, but Jackson knew that it was only the insurgents letting them know that they were still there, and doing their best to keep the soldiers awake. The problem was, it was working.

Around him, the other soldiers at the FOB were mostly dozing fitfully, even though they were all wearing helmets and body armour. As Jackson watched, one of them half woke up, grabbing his rifle which was balanced on his lap as he did so, before closing his eyes again. On the other side of the wall, the black sky was slowly lightening as the dawn approached.

Jackson saw a bright light over on the other side of the compound and squinted at the door that had just opened. The CO, Major Fletcher, was standing there staring at Jackson, beckoning him over. *Bloody hell*, Jackson thought as he got to his feet, *he's got good eyesight if he can see me from there in this light.* But standing in an open door with a bright lamp behind him probably wasn't the smartest thing to do with a sniper still out there somewhere. Jackson broke into a run so that he could get the Major back into cover.

'Jacko, get in here,' the CO said as the Lance Corporal approached the door of the Command Post. 'We've got an update.'

Inside the small CP, the young 2nd Lieutenant was standing over the radio. He looked up at Jackson with tired eyes before glancing across at the CO.

'Er, sir, Jacko. I mean Lance Corporal Jackson…' the 2nd Lieutenant stuttered before gathering his wits. 'I'm on with Bastion Ops, they're trying to get something out to us.'

'What? What are they trying to get out here?' the Major snapped back. Jackson glanced at the officer, who looked dead on his feet.

'Don't know sir,' the 2nd Lieutenant replied. 'Whatever they can, I think.'

'Well, we fucking need something. They do know we're getting the shit kicked out of us, don't they?' The 2nd Lieutenant looked up at the CO, and Jackson could see the same terrified look in his eyes that he'd seen earlier.

'Yes sir, they know.'

All three men turned as one and looked towards the door as they heard the loud bark of a machine gun from somewhere within the compound. There were three short bursts of fire, then a pause, then another longer burst of fire. Jackson took two long steps towards the door and flung it open.

'Where are you going?' he heard the Major shout behind him.

'There's a sniper out there somewhere,' he replied. 'And whoever's firing that machine gun had just told him where he is.'

Jackson ran through the door and stood just outside the small building, looking around to see if he could identify where the firing was coming from. Another burst of fire rang out from the back of the compound, so he turned and started jogging towards the area. As he ran, he wondered why the firing was coming from the side of the compound opposite the village. The only positive thing that he could think of was that if the sniper was in the village somewhere, which Jackson was fairly sure he was, then whoever did have their head above the parapet should be out of sight of the sniper. That wouldn't help if another rocket came in, though.

Jackson reached the reinforced wall at the rear of the compound and saw a small group of soldiers gathered by one of the firing positions. He shoved one of them in the shoulder, and when he turned to look at him, Jackson said, 'What's going on, mate?'

'Movement over by the ditch, Jacko.' The soldier gestured with his hand to the area beyond the wall. 'There's fucking Taliban moving around, we can see them.'

'You should be in cover, there's 107s coming in, for fuck's sake,' Jackson said. 'If they're not firing at you, you shouldn't be firing at them.' He saw the soldier look at him with an incredulous expression.

'You fucking serious?'

'No,' Jackson shot back. 'I'm fucking Coco the Clown. That could be a fucking shepherd looking for his goats for all you know. And while your boys are trying to plug him, the real Terry is over that way...' Jackson pointed back towards the village, '...lining up another fucking rocket that's got your name on it.' The two men stared at each other. For a second, Jackson thought that the soldier was going to take a swing at him, which he wouldn't have minded because he knew that this would give him a reason to have a swing back. 'Get your lads under cover,' Jackson said, keeping his voice deliberately low. 'Now.'

As if punctuating what he had just said, Jackson heard the sound of another rocket whistling in over his head. His instincts took over and he started to crouch down, pulling the other soldier with him by grabbing his sleeve. The rocket exploded about a hundred metres away from where they were squatting with an ear-splitting thump. Jackson got back to his feet when the concussion wave had washed over them and looked across to where smoke was starting to mushroom up after the explosion.

'Fuck, direct hit,' he said more to himself than to the other soldier. He turned to the group who were still standing on the fire step and shouted at them. 'Get your fucking arses under cover!'

'Jacko?' He felt a hand tug his arm. 'Can you hear that?'

Jackson stood stock still and angled his head towards the smoke. Faintly at first, then with more volume, he could hear screaming coming from the other side of the compound. Lots of screaming. He started jogging towards the area, and as the screaming grew louder, he broke into a run which soon became a sprint.

As Jackson got to a few metres or so of the smoke that was billowing into the air from the latest explosion, he slowed back down to a jog, distracted by something lying on the dusty ground in front of him. It looked like a discarded toy that a child had thrown from a pram, but as he got closer he could see the bloodstain underneath it. Jackson stopped and leaned over to examine it more closely.

It was only when he saw the watch that he realised what it was that was lying on the sand. A severed arm. He looked at the stringy flesh at both ends and a blackened tattoo that was barely visible. A forearm. No hand, no discernible wrist, and nothing above the elbow. It was just a forearm.

Fighting nausea, he looked up towards the column of smoke in front of him. The sound of a man screaming filled his ears. Jackson had done a tour of Bosnia a few years ago, and one morning he'd been woken up by the sound of pigs having their throats cut in the farm just next to their detachment. The screams that the pigs made were exactly the same as the ones he could hear now, except this time it wasn't pigs screaming. It was a soldier. A British soldier. One of his own.

He walked slowly toward the remains of the bunker that the smoke was billowing from. It looked as if the rocket had hit the flimsy shelter directly. Jackson looked around to see if anyone else was coming to help, but it was just him. He walked past lumps of what looked like roast pork, each of them surrounded by their own stain of blood in the sand. As he got to the remains of the bunker, he could see that the person screaming was the soldier that had been by the watchtower earlier. The one who Jackson had shoved towards the bunker, telling him to take cover. The lad — in reality, only a boy — was sitting against the wall of the bunker trying to get the coils of intestine that were strewn across his lap back into his abdomen. Screaming like a Bosnian pig being slaughtered.

'Jesus fucking Christ,' Jackson muttered as he took in the scene in front of him. Another soldier lay on his back, gasping like a stranded fish, and there were another couple of lads who were flat out unconscious. One of them was missing an arm and for a surreal instant, Jackson wondered if it was his watch that he'd seen just now and whether he should go back and get it.

Jackson flinched as a new noise assaulted his ears, vibrating his eardrums. He crouched instinctively, putting his hands over his ears.

'What the fuck?' he said as he felt the noise in his chest. He looked up into the sky in time to see a metal grey fighter jet pass over the FOB at low level, before it sped over the village beyond them. It looked as if it was flying just above the top of the watchtowers. Jackson had been in the military for years and was quite used to working around aeroplanes, but the jet still scared the shit out of him. A few seconds later, a second jet roared over the village, chasing the first one in the scariest game of 'it' that he'd ever witnessed. The noise was just as deafening, but Jackson was expecting the second one. He watched as both planes banked around and started to line up for another run over the top of the village, but this time from a different direction.

He turned back to the scene of carnage in front of him, at a loss for what to do first. He could smell a mixture of blood, shit, and cordite. It was so strong, he could almost taste the individual components. Jackson walked across to the unconscious soldiers to try to find out whether they were unconscious or dead. Either way, he knew that there wasn't a great deal he could do. Jackson reached out his hand and shook one of the bodies lying on the ground by the shoulder.

'Mate?' he whispered. 'Mate? Can you hear me?'

There was no response from the soldier on the ground. Grabbing the material of his uniform, Jackson rolled the soldier over onto his back. As the body rolled, its head lolled towards Jackson who realised that where there was supposed to be a face, there was just a mass of shredded tissue. The only thing that still identified it as a face was a single lidless eye amongst the torn flesh.

'Oh fuck,' Jackson said, stumbling away from the body. He got a few feet away from it and fell to his knees before he vomited in the sand. As he knelt, retching, the jets completed a second pass over his head. Jackson didn't even hear the noise of the planes, or the machine gun that had opened up somewhere in the distance.

He looked up to see the 2nd Lieutenant from the CP standing next to him, his eyes wide as he took in the scene around them. The officer opened his mouth to say something when there was another 'crump' nearby, and one of the reinforced walls shook as it showered dust over the soldiers sheltering behind it.

'What the fuck?' the officer said.

'Sounded like an RPG to me,' Jackson replied. 'Not a rocket. No whistle, low level trajectory. RPG, for sure.'

'What does that mean?'

Jackson looked at the 2nd Lieutenant, who looked as terrified as Jackson felt. Looking at the young officer's face, Jackson hoped that he was hiding the fear better than his colleague.

'It means they're coming.'

40

B rigadier Foster turned himself over in his camp cot, annoyed that he was awake in the middle of the night. He wasn't sure what had woken him up — there was no tell-tale ache in his bladder that told him it was time for a pee — but since being forced to give up beer when he'd got to Afghanistan, those early morning calls had gradually subsided. He sighed and punched his pillow to try to get more comfortable when he heard a soft knock at his door.

'Oh, for God's sake,' he mumbled, swinging his legs over the edge of his camp cot. One of the few advantages of being a senior officer was that he didn't have to share a tent with anyone else, but had a small sectioned off living area at the rear of his office. Other than that, it was still a bit shit.

Foster was rubbing his eyes when another soft knock sounded on his door. He got to his feet and crossed the few yards to the door. Opening it, he saw one his lieutenants standing with his hand raised ready to knock again.

'Abbot,' Foster said, trying to keep the annoyance out of his voice. 'I'm not your dad. If you need me to wake up, knock properly on the bloody door.' When he saw the look of confusion on the young officer's face, Foster managed a weak smile. 'What's going on?'

'Er, sir, there's a situation developing up at FOB Robinson. They took a couple of KIA last night from a sniper, and have been shelled all night.'

'Last night?' Foster replied, looking at his watch. It was almost five in the morning. 'Why am I only hearing about it now?'

'They've only just called it in, sir.'

'For fuck's sake,' Foster said, more to himself than the Lieutenant. 'How are we supposed to maintain situational awareness if they don't call it in?' The Lieutenant didn't reply but just looked at Foster. 'What else?'

'They're under attack, sir. Sounds like Terry wants his compound back. They're now reporting multiple casualties from rockets, and they're being hit with RPGs and all sorts of stuff.'

'Bloody hell,' Foster replied, suddenly very awake. 'Right, let's get the seniors out of their scratchers and into my office. Brief in twenty minutes. And Abbott?'

'Yes, sir?'

'Have we got any coffee?'

'Yes, sir. Brewing now, and it's the decent stuff before you ask.'

The Commanding Officer's tent in the hospital was almost full, although there were only four people in it. Colonel Nick watched as the Brigadier took off his rimless glasses, polished them with a cleaning cloth, and put them back on his face. *He can clean his glasses all he wants*, Nick thought, *he still looks like shit.* They all did.

They were waiting for the Lieutenant from the Ops Room to come and give them a sitrep. On the other side of the office were Squadron Leader Webb and Major Clarke, deep in conversation about something. All four officers turned as the door opened, and the Lieutenant walked in and stood smartly to attention.

'Brigadier Foster, sir,' he barked. 'Lieutenant Abbott, ready with your sitrep.'

'Stand easy, Abbott,' Foster sighed. 'For God's sake, just relax would you.' The Brigadier walked over to the chair behind the folding table that doubled as his desk and sat down. 'Gentlemen, make yourselves comfortable and let's see what's going on.' He gestured towards the chairs dotted around the office. 'Grab a seat,' he continued, looking at the Lieutenant. 'Including you, Abbott.'

Colonel Nick looked at the senior officer with frustration. He didn't understand why the Brigadier wasn't more concerned about the situation. If he was the CO, Nick would have made the Lieutenant stay at attention while he delivered his update, before dismissing him so that he could plan the next phase. The way things were going, they were going to have a cosy little chat while men out on the ground were probably dying. As Nick watched Foster walk across to a chair, he reflected on the fact that the Brigadier wasn't a doctor — even though he was in charge of the hospital. Stupid decision, in Nick's opinion. Not that anyone ever asked him for it.

'Right then, Abbott,' Foster said when they were all sitting down. 'What's the story? And I don't need a Sandhurst brief. I want to know what we know, and what we don't know. Okay?' He smiled at the junior officer. Nick fought hard to keep quiet. It was turning into Santa's fucking grotto.

The Lieutenant took a deep breath and looked at the notes that he had brought in with him.

'Last night, just before midnight local, FOB Robinson up in Sangin came under attack from a sniper located in the village. Two dead.' He looked around at the officers in the room before continuing. Nick could almost taste the tension in the air. *Two dead*, he thought. *Shit.*

'They've been under sporadic rocket attack for most of the night. First light,' the Lieutenant glanced at his watch, 'around forty minutes ago, they took a direct hit to one of the sangers. But it wasn't a reinforced bunker, just a normal sangar. Two more dead, quite a few casualties. That's just from mIRC chat, not a 9-liner. They're now reporting small arms fire from the village and multiple RPG hits to the exterior walls.'

'Fucking hell,' Nick murmured, exchanging a look with Major Clarke who had gone white as a sheet. 'Sounds like Terry wants his house back.'

'Thank you, Colonel,' Brigadier Foster said, quietly but sharply and without even looking in Nick's direction. 'Not that helpful, really. Abbot, carry on.'

'Reinforcements wise, there's not much in the area,' the Lieutenant continued. 'There's a Special Forces unit in the south who've been monitoring a location where the Taliban have been operating illegal checkpoints, but it's going to take them at least a couple of hours to get there, and it's only a four-man unit scaled for reconnaissance, not kinetic operations.'

'What about air?' Brigadier Foster asked. 'Is there any support from them?' Lieutenant Abbott looked confused for a second and shuffled through his notes until he found the right page.

'There's not a lot that's close by. There were a couple of Tornado GR4s on their way back to Al Udeid after a run. They were turned around for a show of force, but didn't have any ordnance and not much fuel. Rotary wing wise…' he looked for another piece of paper, '…two Apaches left here about ten minutes ago, so they should be on location in about twenty minutes. Ops up at Kandahar are trying to scrape together a Quick Reaction Force and a Chinook, and we've got a Chinook on the ground here.'

'Sorry, Abbott,' Foster asked. 'Did you say we've got a Chinook? As in one?'

'That's correct, sir.'

'Where the fuck's the other one?'

'It's stuck up-country. Some sort of technical problem.'

'Bloody hell,' Foster replied. 'They spend more time getting fixed than they do flying. Timeline?'

'Unknown, sir.'

'So, Colonel,' Foster said, turning to Nick. 'Is the TRT ready to launch?'

'Half of it is, sir,' Nick replied. 'Corporal McDonald and myself. The replacement medics are with the other Chinook.' He saw the Brigadier's forehead crinkle, so decided to pre-empt his question. 'R&R, sir. Although the rest of the regular team is due back at some point this morning.'

'Let me see if I have that right. I've got at least four dead and several wounded from an attack on a FOB that's still ongoing?' The Brigadier pushed his glasses back up his nose. 'And I've got one Chinook, and a two-man TRT.' Nick looked at his hands as the Brigadier stared at each man in the room, none of them having the balls to reply. Eventually, the Lieutenant piped up.

'That's correct, sir.'

'Why is my single Chinook and half a TRT still on the ground, as opposed to positioning in the area?' the

Brigadier asked. Nick kept his gaze down, even though he was sure the question wasn't aimed at him.

'Sir,' the Lieutenant said, much to Nick's relief. 'The OC of the Chinook detachment won't launch into a hot LZ.' The young officer looked across at Nick. 'Not after what happened last time. Apparently, someone back at Air Command wasn't happy that they nearly lost one of their helicopters.'

Nick saw the Brigadier's frown deepen before he replied.

'What exactly does Air Command think that we're doing out here, I wonder?' The Lieutenant started to speak, but the Brigadier cut him off. 'That wasn't a question for you, Abbott.' Foster paused for a second, deep in thought. 'Right, go back to casualties?'

'Well, that's not clear, sir,' Abbott replied. 'There's so much chatter about the contact itself that we've not got much. They have confirmed four dead, at least. The last mIRC message about casualties just said "multiple", but didn't go into any more detail.'

Brigadier Foster looked at the clock on the wall of his office.

'So there's been a contact going on since last night, and they've not even put a 9-liner in?' he asked Abbott.

'That's correct, sir.'

'Jesus, they must be getting the absolute shit kicked out of them.'

'That's correct, sir.'

'Well then, gentlemen?' the Brigadier asked. 'What are our options?' A silence spread across the office. Nick looked at the other three men, all of whom were either deep in thought or at least doing a decent impression of looking as if they were.

'We should launch the Chinook,' he said, adding 'sir'

when the CO looked sharply at him. The Brigadier continued to stare until Nick started to feel uncomfortable.

'Launch the Chinook? That's your plan, is it, Colonel?'

'Er, well, we need to get some medical teams on the ground to retrieve the casualties,' Nick replied. 'We at least need to know what we're dealing with, and we can't do that unless we're on the ground.' He sat back in his chair, satisfied that he'd recovered the situation. The look that the Brigadier was still giving him told Nick that he probably hadn't.

'Colonel, thank you for your input,' the CO said through gritted teeth. 'But we need a bit more of a plan than "launch the Chinook", don't you think?'

Nick looked at both Squadron Leader Webb and Major Clarke, but Webb was examining something under his fingernails, while the Major was currently fixated with one of the light fittings hanging from the ceiling of the tent. *No support from them, then*, Nick thought. *Bloody arseholes, the pair of them.*

An uncomfortable atmosphere filled the room like acrid smoke. Brigadier Foster took off his glasses and polished them again before putting them back on his nose with a determined shove from his index finger to cement them in place.

'Right, gents,' he said. 'We need to run through some options. Clarke?' Major Clarke looked up with a start.

'Sir?'

'I need a bed state of the entire hospital, especially intensive care. We might need to start looking at emptying out what we've got, so fire up the aeromed teams and get them ready to go. I'm fairly sure they've got at least one patient in there. Speak to HQ up at Kandahar, see what the availability's like in the other hospitals in the area. We could potentially use our single bloody helicopter to empty us out before they go to the scene to pick up whatever's up there, but I'd rather get a Hercules in from the other end to clear the beds in one go.' Major Clarke scribbled furiously on a notepad that he'd pulled out of one of the pockets in his trousers.

'Yep, okay, got it, sir,' he said. 'There is a Herc inbound from Kandahar later, though.'

'It'll have the rest of the TRT on it,' Nick added, pleased to be able to contribute something useful.

'Abbott,' Foster said, ignoring Nick. 'Speak to Kandahar, see if they can add some more medics to the inbound Herc and hold it here to empty our back doors.'

'Roger that, sir,' the Lieutenant said, making a note on his pad.

The Brigadier turned to Squadron Leader Webb.

'Andrew, I want to focus in on the staff here. We need the ITU prepped to move their patient or patients, and as many from the wards as we can.' He turned back to Major Clarke. 'Clarke, make sure that if Kandahar can send something they send escorts as well. I don't want to find out all my medics have got onto a bloody plane back to Kandahar.'

'I'll get theatres warmed up as well, sir,' Webb chipped in. 'And let the labs know, just in case we need to do a blood drive for extra supplies.'

'Nice one, Andrew. Thanks,' the CO replied. 'Right, what else do we need to do chaps?' He looked from face to face, stopping when he got to Lieutenant Abbott. 'Abbott? You look like you've got something to say?'

Abbott looked at the Brigadier as if he was surprised to be asked his opinion. Nick thought that it was probably the first time that the young man had been asked what he thought by a senior officer, and was curious as to what he was going to say. He watched as Abbott did a reasonably good impression of a goldfish for a few seconds before replying.

'I was just thinking, sir, Kandahar is spinning up a QRF to reinforce the FOB. When they've been dropped off, that might give us an extra Chinook to play with.'

'Good spot lad,' the Brigadier replied. 'Clarke, speak to them and see if they'll play the game.' Clarke made yet another note in his book as Foster glanced at his watch. 'If there's anything to update me on, though, I want to know straight away. Try to get a casualty estimate if you can. It's 0530 now, so let's meet back in here in thirty minutes for an update.' The Brigadier looked at the other officers in his tent, a grim smile on his face. 'Let's get to it, gentlemen. I think we have the beginnings of a plan.'

41

Adams yawned as he stepped through the door of the TriStar and onto the rickety stairs that led to the ground. He looked at his watch, which he'd not changed since leaving the United Kingdom, and tried to work out what time it was now. Cyprus was two hours ahead of the UK, and Kandahar was ninety minutes ahead of Cyprus. He frowned as he stared at his watch, before giving up on the arithmetic.

'What time is it, mate?' Adams asked the military steward standing at the top of the steps.

'About ten to six local, sir.'

'Jesus,' Adams replied. 'That's harsh.' He looked at his watch again. By his reckoning, he'd had about three hours sleep in the last twenty-four, and most of that was when he was squashed between two burly soldiers in the back of the plane. Lizzie, for some reason, had been allowed through to the front cabin with her friend Emma, but when he'd tried to go the same way he'd been advised in no uncertain terms by a miserable bastard of a Warrant Officer that his seat was in the back.

Adams felt the heat wash over him as he descended the steps onto the cracked tarmac of Kandahar airport. In the distance, the sun was just starting to rise over the top of the snow-covered mountains that looked over the airhead. How it could be so bloody hot here, Adams thought, and still have snow on the mountains was beyond him.

'Head that way, sir,' another steward at the bottom of the steps pointed at a caged area that looked depressingly like the one back in Cyprus. 'We'll come and get you from there for your onward move.'

'Right, cheers,' Adams replied as he trudged over to the compound. God forbid that anyone should wander around Kandahar airbase unescorted. He eyed up a bench inside the wire with no-one on it and picked up his pace before anyone else got there.

Once he'd bagged the bench as his, and his alone, he sat back and watched the rest of the passengers disembark the TriStar. The vast majority were Army, infantry from the looks of them. Adams saw the steps shaking as the soldiers made their way down to the tarmac. They weren't fat — they were just big. Behind them was a group of Ghurkas. Much smaller, but arguably more dangerous, man for man. Pound for pound, the Ghurkas would win hands down and, not for the first time, Adams was very glad that they wore the same flag on their shoulders as he did. Behind them was Corporal Wardle, and behind her was Lizzie.

Adams watched as the two women made their way across to the compound, their progress followed by many sets of eyes, not just his. Lizzie looked so different back in combats, but Adams was struggling with the difference between how she looked now and how she had looked back in the hotel in Cyprus. Before he'd fucked everything up.

When he realised that Lizzie was staring at him, Adams sighed before looking away for a second. When he raised his eyes again, hoping that she had moved on, she was still staring at him. Not only that, but she was walking directly toward him.

Bollocks, Adams thought. He got to his feet and walked over to the Portaloos behind the bench he was sitting on. He took a deep breath before opening the door — there was no way of knowing when they had last been emptied — and stepped inside. The stench inside was something else, so he fished in his pockets for a cigarette.

Ten minutes later, he flicked another butt into the darkness underneath the toilet seat. It disappeared, and a second later, he heard a fizz as it landed in God knew what. Adams wasn't about to shine a light into the ditch below the Portaloo — he'd made that mistake before and it wasn't pretty — but at least by now, Lizzie would have moved on.

Adams opened the door to the Portaloo and took a grateful breath of the fresh air outside. He had just closed his eyes for another lungful of untainted oxygen when he felt a hand grip his arm just above his elbow.

'A word, Adams,' Lizzie said as she pulled him around to the rear of the Portaloos, her fingers digging into the soft flesh above his elbow. When they were out of sight of the rest of the crowd milling around the compound, Adams turned to face her.

'Lizzie, listen,' he said, his hands in front of him in mock-surrender. She didn't reply but shoved him back against the chain-link fence.

'No, you listen,' she barked at him as the fence rattled behind them. 'Do you really not want to talk to me that much that you have to hide in a portable toilet, smoking? How dare you.'

'Um,' Adams replied, not quite sure what to say. 'Um, how dare I what?'

'Oh, Jesus,' Lizzie sighed. 'Don't be a twat all your life, Adams. You know exactly what I'm talking about.' In all the time he'd known Lizzie, Adams had never seen her this angry.

'I'm sorry.'

'What?'

'I said, I'm sorry. Not for what I said — because I meant that — but I'm sorry that what I said upset you.' They stared at each other for a few seconds.

'Adams, what you said didn't just upset me. It hurt me.'

'How come?' He saw her eyebrows go up as she crossed her arms over her chest.

'I can't believe you have to ask that,' Lizzie replied. 'How would you feel if one of your best friends just saw you as an easy lay. A quick shag to relieve the frustration of not getting your end away when you were on R&R?'

'Ouch, Lizzie,' Adams said. 'Bit harsh, that one. But that's not what—'

'How would that make you feel? Just answer the question, would you?'

'If that's really what they thought, then I'd feel like shit.'

'Thank you.'

'But I didn't ask you because I see you that way.'

'So why ask, then?'

'Because you're you.' Adams paused before continuing. 'Fuck, Lizzie. Because I've never been able to ask you before. Don't you get that?' Adams closed his eyes to think about what he was going to say next, but when he opened them again the only thing he could see was Lizzie walking away from him.

Colonel Nick swore under his breath as he jogged down the main corridor toward the CO's tent. It was a minute to six, and in the Army at least, if you weren't early, you were late. Around him, the hospital was slowly coming to life for what could be a very busy day.

'Nice of you to join us, Colonel,' the Brigadier said sharply as Nick entered his tent.

'Sorry, sir,' Nick said, trying to emphasise the fact that he was breathless so had at least been making an effort to get there on time.

'Just sit down. Abbot, what's changed?'

'We've got some casualty information in, sir,' the Lieutenant replied. 'According to the 9-liner we've just had come in, there's two Cat As, four Cat Bs, and at least seven Cat Cs.'

'So, thirteen in total?'

'That's right, sir,' Abbot said before adding in a quiet voice. 'So far.' A silence played around the tent for a few seconds as the occupants considered this.

'What's the state of play with your returning medics?' It took Nick a second or two to realise that the Brigadier's question was directed at him.

'They're inbound, sir,' he replied. 'I've sent Corporal McDonald down to the main runway to get them when the Herc gets in. He's going to brief them that they might be needed straight away.'

'That's not ideal when they've been on one plane or another most of the night.'

'Can't be helped, sir,' Nick said. 'They'll be okay.'

'Clarke?' Foster barked. 'Hospital sitrep?' Nick took a deep breath, relieved he was off the hook and watched as the nurse struggled to read his notes.

'Um, well, Brigadier,' Clarke said. 'If we can use the Hercules that the TRT is coming in on, then we can pretty much empty the hospital.'

'Good, well done Clarke. What's your manning like in the hospital?' Nick grimaced as a broad grin broke across Major Clarke's face. 'Better than the TRT's, sir,' the nurse replied. 'I planned it out to avoid any major shortages.' *Fat little smug twat*, Nick thought. He was just about to say something in his defence when the Lieutenant cut him off.

'Brigadier, if you don't need me anymore?'

'That's fine, Abbott. Cut away. But if anything changes, I'm the first to know. What time is that Herc due in?' The Lieutenant looked at his watch before replying.

'Should be leaving any minute now, sir. There's a bunch of Canadian medics on board with stretchers fitted, as requested. Plus the team from the Met.'

'Okay. Make sure that someone's there to meet the policemen. They've got quite a lot of kit, apparently, so they'll need a bus. And I want to speak to their team leader, or whatever he's called, the minute they get here.'

'Understood, sir,' Abbott replied. 'Will there be anything else?'

'No, off you trot,' Foster said with a nod towards the door.

After the lieutenant left the CO's office to return to the Ops Room, the four remaining officers sat in an uncomfortable silence.

'So, gentlemen,' the Brigadier said. 'How are we going to get fourteen casualties back here with only one medical team? Nick? Have you got any ideas on the best way forward?'

Nick tried desperately to think of something useful to say, without any luck. Just as he thought the Brigadier was going to cut him off, he had a brainwave.

'We could put more medics in the air, sir,' he said, trying not to spit the words out. 'Especially if we do manage to get another Chinook.'

'Go on,' the Brigadier said, his stare just as intense but now less fierce-looking.

'The normal TRT is four people, we could go with three teams of two instead. If we added another couple of medics to the mix.' Colonel Nick looked at Webb and Clarke. He saw Clarke looking back at him, and knew that the nurse knew exactly where he was going. 'The Cat As on one Chinook with one team, and the Cat Bs and Cs on the other helicopter with the other two teams.'

'Sir, with all due respect, you need people in the hospital for when the casualties get here,' Clarke said, with a sideways glance at Nick. 'I'm not sure that Colonel Nick here fully understands what he's suggesting.'

'Colonel, what exactly are you suggesting?' the CO asked Nick. 'Take some medics from the hospital and put them on the TRT?'

'Yes sir,' Nick replied. 'I mean, it wouldn't be a proper TRT anymore. But that's exactly the sort of configuration that we used back in Iraq. They had nurse and medic teams, doctor and nurse teams, all sorts. Didn't they Clarke? You were there then, weren't you?' He saw Major Clarke swallow before replying.

'I was there, yes. And that is the type of teams that were used. But it was completely different.'

'Different how?' Brigadier Foster asked him. 'Casualties are casualties. And this is potentially an extreme situation. We need to be able to adapt.'

'But you can't expect people to work out in the field, and then come straight back and carry on working in the hospital,' Clarke added. 'That just wouldn't work.' The

Brigadier looked at Clarke, and Nick noticed with delight that the nurse was red-faced and sweating.

'Why not?' Foster asked Clarke. 'It's not ideal, I grant you. But I think it would work.'

'But we don't have the kit, sir,' Clarke replied. 'Or the experience.'

'We've got spare TRT rucksacks,' Colonel Nick said, silently thanking Adams for being so anal about having spare kit ready to go. 'And as far as experience goes, we can split the teams up so that there's an experienced member on each one. We're all soldiers, after all.' Nick looked at Clarke. 'Aren't we?'

Brigadier Foster didn't reply to Nick's suggestion at first, but he looked as if he was considering the plan, at least. Nick glanced across at both Clarke, who looked furious, and Webb. Nick could see a small vein pulsing on the side of Clarke's forehead. The idea of him popping a blood vessel, preferably in his head, was quite amusing to Nick, and he struggled to keep a straight face as he looked at Webb. The other doctor was just sitting there, expressionless, with his arms folded across his chest. As Nick looked at him, Webb raised one eyebrow at him, and Nick had to suppress a laugh by turning it into a cough.

'Right then,' the Brigadier finally said after a couple of minutes. 'This is the plan. Or at least, this is the plan now. Clarke — who's your deputy?'

'Er, Sergeant Derbyshire sir, but–'

'He can run with getting the Emergency Room, then. I want you out on one of the teams.'

'Sir, I really don't think that's a good idea,' Major Clarke complained. 'Sergeant Derbyshire still needs a lot of supervision, and–' Brigadier Foster cut the Major off.

'No, he doesn't. At least, that's not what you wrote in his appraisal. I seem to remember you rated him very highly. So I want you on one team. I need the experience out there.'

'Sir, I really don't think that this is-'

'Clarke, shut up and stop whining. The decision's made.' Brigadier turned to Squadron Leader Webb. 'Webb, you know what I'm going to ask you, don't you?'

Webb gave the Brigadier the name of his deputy without complaint. Whether that was because he'd just seen Major Clarke getting chewed out or not, Colonel Nick wasn't sure.

'Nick, how do you want to do this?' Brigadier Foster asked.

'I'll probably keep Corporal McDonald with me. He's the weaker one of the team by some distance. I'd suggest Major Clarke teams up with Sergeant Jarman, and Squadron Leader Webb with Flight Lieutenant Adams.' Colonel Nick nodded to emphasise his decision. 'I'd say that's the best skill mix.'

'Right then, decision made. I'm going to the Ops Room to keep an eye on things as they develop. How long do you think it'll take you to get up and running?' Colonel Nick's eyes flicked to the clock on the wall.

'Give us ten minutes, sir,' he said. 'And we'll be good to go I reckon. The minute the rest of the team get back with Corporal McDonald, we can deploy.'

'Good stuff.' The Brigadier looked at all three of them in turn. 'Let's crack on.'

Nick got to his feet along with the others, and they made their way towards the door. As they reached the corridor, Major Clarke turned to Colonel Nick and glared at him. *Say something, you fat bastard*, the Colonel thought. *Go on, just say something*. Without a word, the nurse turned away and walked down the corridor towards the Emergency Room. Behind him, Colonel Nick heard Webb clear his throat. He'd barely said anything at all during the whole time they'd been with the Brigadier, which was unusual for him.

'Priceless, Nick,' Webb said. 'Absolutely fucking priceless.' Nick grinned at him in return.

'I know,' he replied as the other doctor walked away down the hospital corridor.

42

J ackson ran across the dusty earth of the compound, ignoring the cracks of gunfire he could hear from beyond the walls, and opened the door to the tiny Ops Room. Major Fletcher looked at him as he burst in, and Jackson saw his brow furrow.

'You okay, Jackson?' the Major asked.

'Fine, sir,' he replied. He could tell that the Major wasn't convinced but carried on regardless. 'I thought you might want a sitrep.'

'I do, crack on.'

'Four dead, confirmed, sir,' Jackson said. 'Two by the tower, and another two in a bunker that took a direct hit off one of the rockets.' Major Fletcher's face paled.

'Fuck,' he whispered.

'Casualties wise, I'm not one hundred per cent sure, I'm afraid. Definitely two Cat As, four Cat Bs, and a bunch of Cat C's. I can't remember exactly how many we told Bastion, but I think it was six or seven.' Jackson took a deep breath, realising that he was talking way too fast.

'Everyone's still hunkered down, so no-one's been moved to the regimental aid post.'

'But you've put a 9-liner in for the casualties?'

'Yes, sir. As soon as the medic confirmed the categories, we put one in then.'

'Good job. Probably should have done that sooner.'

'Sir, with all due respect, we have had other things going on.'

'I'm not criticising you, Jackson,' the CO replied. 'I probably should have done that sooner, not you.'

Jackson looked at the Major and his 2nd Lieutenant, both of whom looked knackered and scared. Just like he probably did.

'There's not been any more rockets,' Jackson said. 'We could start moving round inside the compound.' The Major remained silent, deep in thought.

'I'm not sure,' he said after a minute or so. 'There could be more 107s lined up, and I don't want anyone else getting hurt.'

'Thing is, sir,' Jackson replied, 'we're now getting incoming small arms fire, so Terry's out and about in the village.' The Major looked blankly at him.

'So what?'

'Well, they know how bloody inaccurate the rockets are. Getting a direct hit was an absolute fluke.' Jackson paused, waiting to see if the Major would take the bait or if he would have to spell it out for him.

'So, if they're now out and about, they probably know there aren't any more rockets.' Jackson nodded as Major Fletcher realised what he meant. 'Because if there were, then they'd still be hiding.'

'They're not going to risk dropping rockets on their own heads, are they?' the 2nd Lieutenant offered, backing up Jackson's thoughts.

'That's what I reckon, sir,' Jackson said. 'It's a risk, but with casualties on the ground I think it's one worth taking.' Another pause. 'But you're the boss.'

'No, Jacko,' Major Fletcher replied. 'You're right. But I don't want anyone on the walls or in the towers. That sniper's still out there somewhere.'

'That's probably what they're trying to do,' the 2nd Lieutenant said.

'What do you mean?' Major Fletcher asked him.

'Draw us out,' he replied. 'They put some rounds into the walls, we pop up to return fire like we always do. So does the sniper.'

'That's a good point,' the Major said. 'Nice one.' Jackson could see the colour returning to the senior officer's face. He was starting to sound more confident.

'Incoming transmission, sir.' The 2nd Lieutenant put his headphones back on and turned to the radio, scribbling furiously on a pad while Major Fletcher drummed his fingers on the desk.

'That was Ops at Bastion, sir,' the 2nd Lieutenant said, slipping the headphones off his head. 'There's a Hermes UAV on point above us, and two Apaches about five minutes out.'

'Right, this is the plan. Listen in, both of you.' He looked at Jackson, then the 2nd Lieutenant, then back at Jackson.

'Jacko, I want you to grab some hands and move the casualties to the aid post.' The Major's voice was strengthening with every word. 'As far as that bloody sniper goes, if we can get him to take a shot, then the UAV should be able to identify where he is for the Apaches.' Jackson felt himself grinning as the Major gave his orders. 'With the sniper out of the way, we can pop up and say hello to the Taliban. So, go and get a decoy ready.'

'Yes sir,' Jackson said, still grinning. 'On my way.'

He closed the toilet door behind him and, hands shaking, locked it.

'Shit, shit, shit,' he whispered to himself. 'Fucking police.' He took a deep breath, held it, and then blew it out before taking another one. Holding his hands in front of his face, he could see them shaking. He had to get a grip before time ran out. There could only be one reason why the civilian police were on their way out here. For him. They were here for him.

He'd been so careful, he thought as he sat down on the closed lid of the toilet. All the work that he'd done, all the research, all the planning. It would all be for nothing if he was caught now. He just needed one more. That was all, just one more.

Being caught was something that he'd thought about when he was putting the plan together. It was always at the back of his mind, but he never thought for a second that he would actually be caught. He couldn't see how. Adrenaline was invisible, especially in casualties who'd been resuscitated. It was the first drug that the medics reached for when someone arrested. That was what had made his plan so perfect. He'd been over and over it, so many times that he thought he probably knew more about it than a pharmacist. He'd looked into so many different drugs, knew which ones he could potentially use and which ones he definitely couldn't. When he'd seen the box of adrenaline ampoules sitting in the stores waiting for destruction, it was almost as if it was a sign.

What could he do now? Would he actually be caught after all? There was a massive difference between the coppers knowing that there was something going on, that one or two of the casualties were being shepherded on their way, and actually proving it. And even then, they would have to tie it to him somehow. With all the evidence disposed of in incineration bins and by now burnt beyond all recognition, even the most determined copper would have his work cut out for him. It wasn't as if he'd shared his plans with anyone.

He took another deep breath, trying to calm himself down. He could feel his heart thudding in his chest and his legs trembling. Despite the air conditioning in the hospital, he was sweating. Even the palms of his hands were damp. The irony that this physical reaction was caused by adrenaline wasn't lost on him.

One more. He only needed one more. It had to be three of them to make it right.

Lizzie was about twenty feet away from the Portaloos when she started slowing down. Around her, the caged compound was almost full of tired soldiers. The majority of them had just sat on the dusty ground and spread out, making the most of the opportunity to stretch their legs, and the bench that Adams had been sitting on had been taken over by a group of three Ghurkas. They sat in silence, passing a cigarette between them.

She thought back to what Adams had said just now as she stopped walking. If she remembered it correctly, he'd said that he was sorry. *Not for what I said, because I meant that.* He'd apologised for upsetting her, but not for the words that had upset her.

'Oh, Jesus,' Lizzie sighed as she ground to a halt. Emma's comments came back to her. *Would that have been such a bad thing?* Adams had looked so lost, both back in Cyprus and just now round the back of the toilets. Hardly a romantic memory — a conversation behind a row of Portaloos — but she needed to go back to talk to him. Or something.

Lizzie spun on her heel and turned to walk back to where she'd left Adams. He was still leaning against the chain-link fence, staring up at the sky. When she reached him, he looked at her and she saw that his eyes were full of tears. He opened his mouth to say something, but then closed it again. Lizzie walked up and took his hands in hers before pulling him away from the fence and wrapping her arms around him.

They stood in a silent embrace for a moment before he whispered in her ear.

'I'm sorry, Lizzie.'

'Don't be,' she whispered back. 'Let's just get through this tour and see what happens.'

In the distance, Lizzie heard the distinctive cough of a Hercules plane as its engines started.

'Guess that's our bus,' Adams said, extricating himself from Lizzie's arms.

'Great,' Lizzie replied with a grim smile.

The first thing Lizzie saw when she climbed into the squat transport plane was a group of eight Canadian medics scuttling around. They were fitting stretchers to stanchions and turning the front of the plane into a mini-hospital. She'd approached the most senior member of the Canadian team to be told that they were picking up casualties from the hospital at Bastion. No, the Canadian Flight Lieutenant had told her, he didn't know why.

'What do you think's happening?' Lizzie shouted at Adams over the noise of the plane's engines.

'No idea,' he replied, 'but it can't be good.'

At the other end of the plane, an RAF loadmaster was talking to the civilian policemen. Lizzie had seen the look of concern on the group's faces earlier on when the TriStar had started its descent into Kandahar, and the policemen had all been instructed to wear blue body armour and helmets. Lizzie watched as the policeman with the ponytail — if he was actually a policeman — fiddled with the strap underneath his chin to try to get the helmet straight on his head. Their eyes met for a brief few seconds, and she could see that the earlier look of concern had been replaced by another expression — fear.

Lizzie closed her eyes as the Hercules taxied along to the end of the runway. She shifted in the uncomfortable orange webbed seat, but they were made for function, not comfort, so she gave up after a few seconds and resigned herself to the discomfort. At least it was only a short hop from Kandahar down to Bastion.

The noise of the engines dipped briefly before they roared into life, and the large transport plane lurched forward. In the seat next to Lizzie's, Adams was pushed up against her by the acceleration. He shuffled on his seat to move away, but Lizzie put her hand on his arm to keep him where he was. Even though she could barely feel his body heat through their combat clothing, Lizzie was grateful for the contact.

Jackson set off at a fair pace across the dusty earth in the middle of the FOB compound. He reached the Regimental Aid Post, which was nothing more than a small building nestling up against the wall of the compound surrounded by sandbags. The only indication that it was a medical facility was a small red cross that the FOB's medic had nailed to the door of the building. Without knocking, Jackson pushed the door to the building open.

'Doc?' he called out. 'You in here?' A dishevelled figure appeared from the back of the room, half-hidden in darkness. The medic, Corporal Rowley, was sitting in the corner of the room on a small camping stool, repacking his medical bags after treating the casualties by the bunker. He was enclosed in body armour and wearing a helmet that looked about two sizes too big for him. In front of him was a single stretcher, balanced on a couple of trestles made out of wood that had been lying around the compound when they'd arrived.

'Yep, here,' he answered, getting to his feet. 'What's going on? Can we get the casualties moved in here?' He pushed the helmet back on his head and squinted at Jackson.

'Good to go, doc. We're pretty sure that there aren't any more rockets coming in.' He watched as the medic grabbed one of the medical bags from the floor of the RAP. 'There's a fair bit of small arms fire, and there's a sniper out there somewhere, so keep your head down. As long as you don't go for a walk along the top of the walls, though, it should be fine.' Corporal Rowley nodded in agreement, and hurried out of the door, hitting his medical bag on the door jamb as he did so.

Jackson followed the medic out of the RAP, and Jackson saw him break into a run towards the remains of the bunker on the opposite side of the compound where a thin wisp of smoke was still rising. As the sound of a machine gun rattled in the distance, Jackson set off in a different direction. He reached the shadow of the compound wall and followed it around until he got to a bunker. This one still had a roof, and soldiers sheltering in it, so Jackson slapped his hand on the corrugated iron roof. Although the sound was deadened by the sandbags on top of the roof, a head popped out of the opening.

'Jacko,' the soldier said. 'You alright?'

'Mate,' Jackson said, 'you and whoever else is in there,

get your arses over to the bunker by the south wall. The doc's over there, he'll need some help.' The soldier ducked his head back inside the shelter and relayed the message to the other soldiers. With a couple of them swearing as they did so, they started scrambling out of the bunker. 'And we also need to get some bodies over to the tower to get the…' Jackson paused, '…er, bodies, er, out of the sun.'

'Roger that Jacko, on our way.'

Jackson made his way around the walls of the compound, stopping to talk to the groups of soldiers huddled by the walls. At least there were no more casualties. When Jackson was sure that he'd spoken to all of them, he stopped in a shaded spot and unbuttoned the strap on his helmet. Taking it off, he put it on the ground and squatted down as Major Fletcher walked up and stood next to him.

'Are you happy, sir?' he said. The Major took off his helmet and sat on the ground next to Jackson.

'Getting there,' the CO replied. 'I think we're getting there.' He took a stained sweat rag from a pocket and used it to mop his brow. 'Ops at Bastion have confirmed that the UAV is on point,' Major Fletcher pointed his index finger directly upwards, 'and that the Apaches are over the horizon somewhere. So let's get a decoy up on the walls, see if we can't draw out the sneaky bastard with the sniper rifle.'

Jackson's attention was caught by the shadow of an object sailing over the wall that they were sheltering by, and a muffled thud sounded a few feet from them. It sounded like a stone being thrown onto the sand at a beach. Major Fletcher turned in the direction of the sound, and they both watched as the object kicked up a small cloud of dust.

The only thing missing from the grenade that was rolling towards them was the pin.

43

Adams and Lizzie stood next to each other by the door of the TRT tent, watching Ronald go through the equipment with Major Clarke and Squadron Leader Webb at the other end. Ronald had both of them wearing combat vests, and was filling the various pockets with medical equipment. Adams could see that Ronald was being his methodical self, putting the same equipment into the same pockets for both of them. They'd applied the same principle to the combat vests as they did to the medical bags themselves where all the kit was essentially identical and with the same stuff in the same place. Even from this distance, Adams could see that Major Clarke was sweating profusely despite the air conditioning in the TRT tent.

On the way back from the runway, Ronald had filled Adams and Lizzie in on what they knew so far. There'd been a big contact up in FOB Robinson. At least four dead and loads injured. From what Ronald had said, every available asset in the area was heading there now.

'How do you think this is going to pan out, then?'

Adams heard Lizzie ask. He shrugged his shoulders in reply.

'No idea to be honest.'

'I'm not convinced,' Lizzie continued. 'Why do we need more medics on the back? It's crowded enough as it is. The more medics we put on board, the fewer casualties we can carry.'

'From what Ronald was saying, there's a second Chinook with a QRF that'll meet us at the FOB. That's why we've got a couple of extra medics. Apparently, the Brigadier wants three teams of two.'

'How many casualties are there then?'

'No idea,' Adams said. 'Ten or eleven I thought Ronald said. It sounds shite out there though, from what he was saying earlier.'

'Where is the bloody Colonel, anyway?' Lizzie said. Adams looked at her, surprised by the angry tone in her voice. Her face matched her voice.

'Alright princess,' he said. 'Calm down. I don't know where he is.'

'Oh, bugger off, Adams,' Lizzie retorted. 'I'm not in the mood. This has got Colonel Nick's name all over it. What's the betting that the whole thing is his idea?'

Adams privately agreed with Lizzie, although he didn't say anything to her. He wasn't thrilled in the slightest to have extra medics on board, either. They'd spent so long getting themselves together as a team it didn't seem fair to just drop another couple of medics in. It was almost a criticism — as if they wouldn't be able to cope with whatever was thrown at them.

'You're probably right,' Adams said to Lizzie. 'Do you think I should talk to the Brigadier?'

'No bloody point,' she replied. 'You know what he's like. Once he's made up his mind about something, that's it.' She paused. 'I could go in there and flash my tits at him, and it wouldn't make a blind bit of difference.' Adams couldn't help but smile as she said this. 'What are you smiling about?'

'Your language,' Adams replied. 'The more tired you are, the worse it gets. That, and the thought of you running into the Brigadier's office with your fun bags bouncing around.'

Lizzie slapped Adams on the arm. 'Fun bags?' she laughed. 'Sodding fun bags? Oh, you are such a gentleman.' She raised her hand to hit him again, and he dodged away to avoid another slap.

'Come on, let's go and see what Ronald's up to,' Adams said, walking across to the small group on the other side of the tent. He could hear Lizzie following him, and glanced over his shoulder to make sure that he wasn't going to get belted when he wasn't looking.

As he got to Ronald and the others, he could see that while Squadron Leader Webb was quite comfortable with the equipment that he was wearing, Major Clarke was far from it. The Major had a face like a beetroot and had beads of sweat rolling down his face even though he was only wearing the combat vest. Adams knew from experience that once the body armour was on, things got way more uncomfortable. Add a weapon and a helmet — and turn up the temperature a fair bit — and the Major was going to struggle.

Adams looked at Lizzie and could tell from the expression on her face that she was thinking the same thing. If Major Clarke had to go out on a shout, with full kit and in the heat of the day, it could be a problem.

'Are you okay, sir?' he asked Major Clarke. 'You're looking a bit hot there.' Major Clarke looked at him with a pained expression.

'I'd be fine if your mucker here wasn't filling the pockets on this vest up with the world's supply of stuff.' Adams was relieved to see a faint smile on the Major's face.

'Well, hopefully it'll come to nothing,' Adams replied. 'All a bit premature if you ask me. We've not even got a proper idea of casualties.'

'It sounds bad, though, Adams,' Squadron Leader Webb said. Adams looked at him, surprised. Even though they'd worked in the same hospital for the last few weeks, he didn't think that the Squadron Leader had ever spoken to him before beyond a handshake and a 'pleased to meet you' when they'd first been introduced.

Major Clarke fiddled with one of the pockets on his combat vest, pulling a couple of latex gloves out which fell to the floor.

'Bollocks,' he muttered under his breath. They all jumped as Colonel Nick walked into the TRT tent and clapped his hands together.

'Right then, team,' he said. 'Casualty update, five minutes.' He looked at all of them in turn. 'Clarke, Webb, I want both of you in the Ops Room.' As they both started to unclip their combat vests, Colonel Nick turned to Adams. 'You too, I suppose.'

Adams looked at him, unsure of what to say. If the Colonel had been the same rank as him, he probably would have come back with a pithy reply. But he wasn't, so Adams kept silent. Major Clarke and Squadron Leader Webb shrugged their way out of their combat vests, leaving them in a pile on the floor before heading towards the door that opened onto the hospital corridor. Adams took his vest off as well and put it onto a chair before he followed them. As he approached the door, he glanced back and saw Lizzie blow him a kiss before starting to laugh.

Colonel Nick pushed the door to the Ops Room in the hospital with a determined shove, keen to make his mark. As he strode into the room, his determination was slightly deflated by the irritated look that Brigadier Foster gave him from the other side of the room where he was standing next to the radio operator.

'Sorry, sir,' Nick mumbled as he walked across to join him.

'No need for theatrics, Colonel,' the Brigadier replied. Nick just looked at the floor, not knowing what to say. His discomfort was saved by the arrival of Webb and Clarke, closely followed by Adams. 'Gentlemen,' the Brigadier continued, 'thank you for coming. I think it's time for an update.' Brigadier Foster turned with a grim expression to the 2nd Lieutenant standing behind him. 'Is that so?'

'Er, yes sir.' The young officer looked nervously at the new arrivals before shuffling his notes. Colonel Nick watched him take a deep breath before starting his brief. 'Right, this is what we know so far.' He paused before continuing. 'The earlier 9-liner is confirmed. Four dead, two Cat As. One with a major head injury, one with abdominal extrusion. There's also four Cat Bs, and at least seven Cat Cs.'

Colonel Nick's jaw dropped slightly at this news. He knew it was bad, but four dead in a single attack was something that he'd not been expecting. From the looks on the others' faces, they were as surprised as he was.

'Jesus Christ,' Colonel Nick heard Major Clarke whisper. With relief, he saw Brigadier Foster turn his irritation towards the Major.

'Clarke, enough.'

'Sorry, sir,' Clarke said with a lot more conviction than

Colonel Nick had managed. 'It's just, well, I wasn't expecting that many fatalities.'

'No, and I'm sure that the troops at the FOB weren't, either,' the Brigadier replied. 'Right then, let's talk this through. We've got one Chinook here at Bastion, and another one up at Kandahar with a QRF on board.' He ran one hand through his silver hair. 'If they're reporting that many casualties, there's almost certainly more, so I'm going with Colonel Nick's plan to load extra medics on board to give us more flexibility. Our Chinook is winding up now and they've got launch authority. There's at least one UAV over the scene, and two Apaches providing cover. Apparently, the Americans have got some air assets they can offer up as well, so the ground should be fairly secure when you go in.'

Nick looked at Major Clarke's face. He had lost some of his ruddy complexion and was almost starting to look pale. Squadron Leader Webb, by contrast, was just standing there, arms folded, soaking it all up. The more he saw of Webb, Nick thought, the more he liked the guy. As he looked at the pair of them, he noticed Adams studying him carefully. *What the fuck is he looking at?*

'Okay, so launch and then what?' Brigadier Foster said. Nick looked at him before realising that the Brigadier was thinking out loud, and not actually asking them a question. 'Major Incident, blood drive, what else?' he muttered to himself.

'Sir?' Nick said, interrupting the senior officer's train of thought. 'Is the brief concluded?'

'Yes, yes,' the Brigadier replied. 'All done, thank you.' He dismissed the group in the Ops Room by turning his back on them and walking across to a map tacked to the wall of the tent, muttering as he did so.

'Come on then, chaps,' Nick said to the other medics.

'We're launching. Back to the TRT tent to kit up, and then to the pan.'

As they approached the door to the TRT tent, Nick felt a hand grab his upper arm. He turned to see Major Clarke looking at him, wide-eyed.

'Nick, this really isn't a good idea,' the Major said. Colonel Nick wasn't sure, but he thought there was a tremor in the other man's voice. 'Neither I nor the Squadron Leader are pre-hospital care trained. We shouldn't be out in the field.'

'It's Colonel Nick, Clarke. Or sir. Not Nick,' the Colonel hissed, watching with satisfaction as the Major took a half step back. 'Now man the fuck up and get on with it.' Nick opened the door to the TRT tent and held it open for Major Clarke, staring at him as the nurse walked through.

'Colonel?'

'What is it, Adams?' Colonel Nick turned as he heard the voice behind him.

'Just ease up on him a bit,' Adams said. Colonel Nick stared at him.

'What did you say?'

'I think you heard me fine, sir.' Adams replied. 'Just ease up. He's shitting himself. We've been there, we know what it's like outside the wire.' Nick looked at Adams, unblinking. 'He doesn't,' Adams continued.

'Well, he'd better bloody well start then, hadn't he?' Nick replied. 'This isn't the time for fucking about.' Adams didn't reply but just looked at the Colonel impassively. After a few seconds, Adams walked past him and into the TRT tent.

44

Jackson and Major Fletcher both stared at the grenade as it rolled to a halt. They both reacted instantaneously, Major Fletcher back-pedalling away from the small round device, Jackson launching himself towards it. The Lance Corporal scooped his hand down, picked up the grenade, and lobbed it as hard as he could towards the wall it had just sailed over. Jackson then turned and rugby tackled the CO.

They were inches from impacting the ground when the grenade exploded, peppering them both with white-hot shrapnel. Jackson winced as he felt something slice through the back of his thigh, but then he and the Major both had their breath knocked out of them as they hit the floor.

'Jesus wept,' Major Fletcher gasped as they disentangled themselves from each other. 'Bloody hell, that was close.' Jackson didn't reply but turned to examine the back of his leg. There was a six-inch long rip in his trousers, and through the jagged tear, he could see blood. 'My God!' the Major said. 'You're hit. Jacko, are you okay?'

'I'm fine, sir, I think,' Jackson replied, prodding at the

wound. 'It's pretty superficial.' He scrabbled in his trouser pocket for a field dressing.

'Here,' Major Fletcher said. 'Let me help.'

As the CO was bandaging Jackson's thigh, making a right old mess of it in Jackson's opinion, a group of soldiers was getting a decoy ready over by a wall. Just to the side of the main doors of the compound was a firing slit — a hole in the wall to shoot through — and they were preparing one of the oldest tricks in the book. A helmet, on a stick.

Jackson got to his feet gingerly and examined the bandage.

'Cheers, sir,' he said with a grin. 'Although you're not that much of a medic, are you?'

'There's gratitude for you,' the Major laughed. 'Although what you just did was quite remarkable.' He held out his hand for Jackson to shake. 'Thank you, Jacko. I think I owe you a couple of beers.'

'I'll take you up on that, sir,' Jackson replied. 'Soon as we can. I knew those years playing cricket at school wouldn't be wasted. We'd better get into cover.' He nodded at the soldier crouched down under the firing slit, a helmet balanced on top of his rifle. Jackson and Major Fletcher moved to the side of the compound wall as the soldier popped the helmet into view before dropping it back down again. Hopefully, from the outside, it would look like a soldier lifting his head to look out of the firing slit for a second. The soldier waited for a few seconds before repeating the manoeuvre.

The second time he lifted the helmet up, there was a loud metallic zing which threw the helmet back into the compound. It rolled over and over in the soft earth. Clouds of dust from the wall covered the soldier holding the rifle who, to Jackson's surprise, started laughing as a loud boom echoed around the compound.

Less than three seconds after the sniper had taken out the decoy, Jackson, Major Fletcher, and every other soldier in the compound jumped as a missile screamed over their heads, less than fifty feet above the external walls. A couple of seconds after that, there was a large explosion beyond the walls.

'What the fuck was that?' Jackson asked the CO. Major Fletcher looked at him and laughed.

'That, Jacko,' the officer replied, thumping Jackson on the upper arm, 'is the sound of one less sniper.' In the distance behind the compound, they could hear the throbbing of helicopter blades getting louder and louder. 'Now, let's get all firing points manned and show Terry that we're still here.'

Jackson winced as he tried to run across the compound to get the rest of the troops into their firing positions. The wound on his leg might only be a scratch, but it still stung like a bastard. Above him, two angry-looking black Apaches swept over the top of the compound. He looked up, the child in him wanting to wave at the pilots, but they had their minds on other things. As both chain guns on the front of the helicopters opened up in unison, Jackson could hear the cheers of the other troops in the compound. By the time the Apaches had finished, there probably wouldn't be much left for them to shoot at.

'Bastion Ops, this is Sandman 34, requesting permission to lift.' Flight Lieutenant Davies keyed the microphone as Taff completed the pre-flight checks in the co-pilot's seat next to him. While he waited for a reply, Davies looked at the lightening sky through the cockpit glass. One of the only saving graces of this country, he thought, was that every once in a while, you got to see a view like the one he was looking at now. He got the authorisation from Bastion Ops and looked over his shoulder into the back of the Chinook. He could see Kinkers standing by the rear ramp, and the medical teams sitting down the sides with their equipment strewn across the floor.

Davies eased back on the cyclic and felt the twin-rotor blades start to bite into the thin air. As the helicopter started to rise into the air, both pilots heard a warning over the radio about another Hercules transport plane from Kandahar that was coming in on finals.

'Should be at our ten o'clock,' Davies said. 'We can either go up and over when he's on the ground or go round the northern perimeter.'

'Probably not much in it,' Taff replied. 'I'd just go straight up, mate.' Davies adjusted the controls and the Chinook started gaining altitude. 'There he is,' Taff said, pointing out of the cockpit window at a small shape near the horizon.

'I have him, thanks. Up and over will be fine.'

Once they'd reached their cruising altitude, Davies put the helicopter's nose down, and they sped toward their destination.

'What do you think then, Davies?' Taff said after a few minutes. 'Bit of a close shave last time round coming into this FOB.'

'Yeah,' Davies replied. 'But we've got a lot more support this time around. Sandman 55 is on his way from Kandahar with a full QRF on board. The Americans are sending an A10 as well, apparently.'

'The Uglies are going in first, right?' Taff had missed

the detailed mission brief with what he'd called an 'urgent admin issue'. In other words, he'd got the shits something awful, and had to go to the medical centre for what he'd described to Davies as a 'chemical cork'. Taff had taken so much of the stuff that Davies thought he probably wouldn't shit for a week.

'Yep,' Davies said. 'Uglies and Sandman 55 first. Unload the cavalry, then they're lifting, and we'll be going in a few minutes later to collect the first round of casualties. Two of the medics are staying on board with us, the others are getting off and getting back on Sandman 55 for the second pickup.'

'I bet Lizzie and Adams aren't getting off,' Taff said with a smile. 'Not after last time anyway.'

'Probably not,' Davies laughed. 'But at least this time we've got some more horsepower. The LZ is slap bang in front of the FOB, as soon as the QRF and the boys on the ground have pushed back the perimeter, we'll drop in.'

'Probably would have made more sense to have the LZ there in the first place,' Taff said, spreading out an aerial photograph on his lap and studying it intently. Davies watched as he ran his index finger across the picture.

'This is the way we came in last time,' Taff said, pointing his finger at a location on the photograph, 'and this is the general area that the RPG came from.'

'There's not much left there anymore, though,' Davies said. 'I think it got fairly flattened.'

'So if we assume that the area's clear, we could come in from the east, flare-up over the FOB and then put down.' Taff prodded the photograph again to make the point.

'Sounds reasonable to me,' Davies agreed.

They flew at five thousand feet, well beyond the range of any small arms or RPGs. Davies felt calm up here, where it was safe. He checked his instruments in front of him.

'Ten minutes out,' Taff said.

'Roger,' Davies replied and turned round to make sure that Kinkers had got the message in the back. Sure enough, he had both hands up in the air with his fingers outstretched to let the medics know the timings. Davies saw them stirring into life, collecting bags and weapons. As he watched them, one of the new medics, a Major who he didn't recognise, looked up and caught Davies's eye. Davies put a thumb in the air, which the Major returned. Despite the thumbs up, the pilot could tell from the look on the medic's face that he was far from okay.

45

B rigadier Foster sighed as he scrolled through the e-mail in front of him, probably for the tenth time that morning. He looked at his watch. It was still early, and he felt as if he'd been up for hours. Which in reality, he had. He'd only been in bed for about thirty minutes the night before when he was woken by the Duty Officer who apologetically informed him that he had an incoming phone call in fifteen minutes. The Duty Officer was ever so sorry, but at the same time insistent that the Brigadier got up to take it.

Foster had got up and made his way to his office. As he'd walked into the room, the Duty Officer pressed a cup of coffee into his hand. Foster was fairly sure that he'd thanked him, but as he sat in front of his computer now, he made a mental note to say thank you again. It really had been an excellent cup of coffee. The night shift in the Ops Room obviously kept the decent stuff to themselves, as every other time Foster had been in there and been given a coffee, it had been rancid.

'What on earth is going on?' Foster mumbled as he re-

read the e-mail and recalled the conversation he'd had earlier. The person on the other end of the phone was a three-star Lieutenant General back in London, who was having an even worse night's sleep than Foster given the time difference. The General had been quite specific in his instructions to Foster on how 'the people in Town' wanted this particular situation dealt with.

Foster looked up towards the door to his office as he heard a gentle knock.

'Yes?' he said. The door opened, and the Duty Officer from earlier poked his head through the gap.

'Sir,' he said. 'I've got the visitor you've been expecting with me if you're free?'

'Of course, I'm free,' the Brigadier replied. 'Please, come in.' He got to his feet to greet his guest, although he wasn't looking forward to the conversation ahead. The Duty Officer stepped back from the door, and his visitor walked into his office. Foster appraised him, as he always did when he met someone for the first time. Especially when that person was potentially dangerous.

'Brigadier Foster?' the visitor said. 'I'm Detective Inspector Griffiths. I'm hoping that you're expecting me?'

'Yes, I am,' Foster replied. He walked towards the policeman with his hand extended. As they shook hands, Foster continued, 'Pleased to meet you, but I would have preferred slightly different circumstances.'

'A lot of people say that,' Griffiths replied with a cautious smile. 'Or at least, words to that effect.' Foster turned to the Duty Officer, who was hanging around the door like a bad smell.

'Could you rustle up some more of that coffee for us both please?' The young officer nodded and hurried away. 'Please, have a seat.'

Foster watched as the policeman walked towards a

green canvas chair. He looked to be late-thirties with acne-scarred cheeks, dressed casually in cargo pants and a check shirt almost as if he was off for a walk in the country somewhere. Other than looking tired, which was under-standable given the journey that he'd just had, Foster thought that the policeman was fairly nondescript, even down to the man bag that he was carrying like a satchel. Until, that was, the policeman looked at Foster. It was obvious to him that Griffiths was a very serious man, and the glint in his striking blue eyes was quite unnerving.

They both exchanged small talk as they waited for the coffee to arrive. How tiring the flight was, how nice it would be to spend a bit more time in Cyprus, and wasn't it hot. No, Griffiths had not been to Afghanistan before, and no, he'd not considered joining the military. Foster was polite but cautious as he waited for the real discussion to begin. Another knock at the door signalled the arrival of the coffee, and the two men paused as the Duty Officer brought in two mugs and some sachets of sugar.

Foster watched Griffiths take a tentative sip of his coffee, which he took black with no sugar. *Whoopie Goldberg*, Foster thought, before shaking his head slightly.

'Wow, that's good coffee,' Griffiths said, 'I was expecting something like the mud we get in our canteen back home.' Foster smiled.

'Good, glad it's okay.' He looked at the door to make sure that it was closed. 'Shall we get down to business, then?' Foster looked at Griffiths as he put his coffee onto a small table next to him. *There it is again*, Foster thought. *That piercing look*. Opening his satchel, Griffiths took out a small notebook and a pencil. As he opened the notebook with a practised flourish, Foster almost expected him to lick the end of the pencil.

'So, Brigadier...' Griffiths checked his notebook, '...

James Foster. You're the Commanding Officer of the hospital here, is that correct?' Foster nodded, knowing full well that Griffiths knew this already. 'I'm Detective Inspector Malcolm Griffiths from the Serious Crimes Unit. For the record, this is an informal discussion, but I am going to take notes if that's okay with you, sir?'

'Detective, please. Call me Foster, not Brigadier. My first name's James, but I'm known as Foster. It's a military thing, using surnames or nicknames all the time.' Foster laughed, briefly. 'You're a civilian after all. And of course, notes are fine. I'm not interested in any sort of dick waving competition here, that's not my style. Regardless of the instructions from my seniors back home, you've got my full cooperation in this unfortunate matter.' Foster didn't want to go into the details of what those instructions actually were with the policeman. At least not while he had his notebook out. He watched as Griffiths sat back in his chair and seemed to relax. The glint in his eyes had definitely softened.

'That's good to hear, Brigadier.' Griffiths corrected himself, 'Sorry, Foster. And I'm Malcolm.'

'So,' Foster said. 'Malcolm. Where do you want to begin?' Griffiths reached into his bag and brought out a handful of notes.

'Well, as you know, we're out here to investigate a series of suspicious deaths. In your hospital.' Griffiths looked at Foster, the glint starting to return. 'Now at this stage, this isn't a murder inquiry and we don't technically have a suspect.' Foster raised his eyebrows at this statement.

'That's not what I've been led to believe,' he said. 'The e-mail suggested that there was a "murder squad" coming out to arrest one of my medical staff.'

'Something's got lost along the way in that case. We've not been called a murder squad for years, regardless of what the newspapers call us. At the moment, we have suspicious deaths, not murders, and a "person of interest" who we'd like to talk to,' Griffiths explained. 'But to an extent, we're talking semantics based on what terms we're allowed and not allowed to use.' Foster nodded. It wasn't that different in the military.

Griffiths shuffled through his notes. 'Do you want me to talk you through it? I've checked your clearance, and I can discuss all of it with you.' Foster fought a smile as he considered that his clearance was a lot higher than the policeman's would be.

'If you would, Malcolm,' he said. 'That would be appreciated.'

In the back of the Chinook, Adams was going through his well-rehearsed drills for landing on, as around him the other occupants did the same thing. Everyone except Major Clarke and Squadron Leader Webb. Adams made a mental note to buddy-buddy check them extra carefully before they landed.

Adams picked up his medical bag from the floor to make sure that one of the others didn't pick it up by mistake. It shouldn't make any difference when all of the bags were packed the same, but Adams had got a bit super-stitious about having his own bag. Lizzie was exactly the same about hers, and he watched her pick up her bag and check the black tape covering the bullet holes on the sides.

He opened the right-hand pouch on his combat vest to get some chewing gum out. It was the same every time they came in to land — his mouth dried up and no amount of water made any difference. At least having some chewing gum took his mind off it. He rummaged around, feeling in the pouch for the packet amongst the syringes and ampoules that were in there.

'Ouch, for fuck's sake,' he said as something sharp in the pouch ripped through his finger. Pulling his hand out, he could see a deep cut across his middle finger. 'What the fuck was that?' he said, putting his finger in his mouth to suck the blood off it. When he pulled his finger out of his mouth, he examined the cut which wasn't much deeper than a bad paper cut. It still hurt like hell, though. He pulled back the top of the pouch and looked inside it. Among the plastic ampoules in the pouch were a couple of glass ampoules, one of which had shattered. Adams looked across at Ronald, who was responsible for restocking the vests, but he was busy helping Squadron Leader Webb get his rucksack on his back.

Adams reached into the pouch and carefully pulled one of the ampoules out to see what it was. He held it between his finger and thumb, rotating it carefully to read the tiny writing on the side. It was adrenaline, one in a thousand. The last thing that should be mixed in with the saline flushes that should be in that pouch. He'd have to pull Ronald to one side when they got back. Adams reached back into the pouch and grabbed one of the plastic saline ampoules. He twisted the top of the ampoule, but he couldn't get the plastic lid off so he reached with his left hand for the scissors that were tucked behind one of the straps on the front of his combat vest. He frowned as he realised that his scissors weren't where they were supposed to be.

Adams looked at the front of his vest and saw that the scissors were on the wrong side. He must have picked up the wrong vest when they kitted up back at Bastion. Grabbing the scissors anyway, he managed to get the top of the ampoule off even though they definitely weren't his scissors. He squeezed a few drops of the saline onto his cut finger.

Within seconds of the liquid touching the cut, the pain in Adams's finger was excruciating. He instantly knew that whatever the liquid was, it wasn't saline. He stuck his finger back in his mouth and looked at the ampoule. There was a small drop of liquid on the bottom of it, and as he squeezed the ampoule some more leaked out of the base. Adams squinted as he looked at the base of the ampoule and wiped the fluid away. There was a small hole just visible in the base of the ampoule. A saline ampoule with not saline, but something else in it. *Adrenaline. It must be adrenaline*, Adams thought. *But why would anyone put adrenaline into a saline ampoule? That could be fatal.*

It was when the word fatal entered his head that Adams put everything together. The unexpected deaths of soldiers who should have survived. If they'd been injected with neat adrenaline by someone who thought they were using saline, then that would kill them. But who would switch the contents? Whoever was wearing his vest? It was the vest that he'd put on that had the adrenaline in the pocket, so that was a fair assumption.

Adams looked around the inside of the Chinook at the front of the vests that the others were wearing to see who had his scissors, but apart from Lizzie, they all had rucksack straps hiding the front of the combat vests. *Fuck*, Adams thought. *What the fuck am I supposed to do now?*

46

'Okay, we're investigating three deaths.' Foster leaned forward to listen carefully to what Griffiths had to say. 'The first one that came to our attention was actually the most recent. At the post-mortem, the pathologist initially thought that the poor chap had died from his wounds. That's what he'd written in his preliminary report.' Griffiths paused to take another sip of his coffee. 'Then the toxicology reports came back from the laboratory, and one of the observers at the original post-mortem noticed something unusual.'

'Observers?' Foster asked. He wasn't sure he liked the idea of a post-mortem of one of his soldiers being open to observers. 'Why on earth are there observers?'

'Trainee pathologists,' Griffiths replied. 'They don't see many post-mortems like these, so they're used as a training opportunity for the students. It's all tightly controlled, though.' Annoyed that he'd been read so easily, Foster just nodded while Griffiths continued.

'The toxicology screen showed very high levels of adrenaline. Now I'm not a medic, but I wouldn't have thought that this was unusual under the circumstances. That's what the pathologist thought as well.'

'Adrenaline is one of the drugs that's used in resuscitation as well,' Foster added. Griffiths pointed at one of the pages in front of him.

'Precisely,' he said. 'Again, that's what the pathologist highlighted. But this student had been reading about a case in the United States where someone in a hospital was using adrenaline and some other drugs to murder her patients. So the pathologist checked the other soldiers' toxicology screens, and they all showed the same thing. Increased adrenaline levels, much higher than normal.' He handed over a couple of pages of his notes to the Brigadier. Foster reached for his glasses and began reading the dense text.

'When I say normal, I mean in comparison to other violent deaths,' Griffiths continued as Foster frowned at the notes he was reading. 'At first, the pathologist thought he was just seeing something unique to military trauma, but based on what the student had said, he decided to do some digging to see if it was possible to identify what type of adrenaline had been used. Whether it was natural adrenaline from the trauma or pharmaceutical adrenaline.' Griffiths paused before continuing. 'And that's where the Chinese come into it.'

Brigadier Foster took his glasses off and polished them with his bright red handkerchief. He looked at the Detective Inspector sitting opposite him.

'What on earth have the Chinese got to do with any of this?' He saw Griffiths smile at his question.

'Well, they're not directly involved,' Griffiths replied. 'But they've been forging pharmaceuticals for years. The big drug companies got fed up with it quite quickly, not surprisingly. So they started putting markers into their drugs. Then they can quickly identify forgeries. If the markers aren't in the drugs, then they're fake.'

'I knew that the Chinese could forge a lot of things, but hospital-grade drugs? Really?' Foster asked.

'Indistinguishable from the real thing, apparently,' Griffiths replied. 'Almost perfect and a tenth of the price. Hence the markers.' He looked at his notebook, searching the pages for the one he wanted. 'The advantage for us is that it's not just possible to trace the drug, but also the batch. According to the toxicologist report, the adrenaline that was found in all three bodies was from the same shipment.' Griffiths ran his finger down the lines in his notebook. 'Which was delivered first to a warehouse in Farnborough after being bought by the Ministry of Defence, and then shipped out to Kandahar. That's as far as we've got.'

'Have you got a shipment number?' Foster pointed to the policeman's notebook. 'Can I see?' Griffiths handed over the notebook and Foster stood, moving to the desk. He picked up the phone, dialled a number, and looked at the notebook while he waited for a reply.

'It's the CO,' he said when the phone was answered. 'Get me the Quartermaster.' Foster paused for a few seconds, listening to the reply. 'Well get him out of bed, then. I need to speak to him now. In my office,' he snapped, slamming down the phone. Foster walked back and sat down next to Griffiths. 'We should be able to track the shipment if it's come through us. My QM is a lazy bastard at the best of times, but nothing gets past him.'

Davies eased forward on the cyclic to start a slow descent to the FOB. He knew that the UAV was circling above the village, so he wanted to give the area a wide berth. Although it was small, it still would hurt the Chinook if they collided. He carefully spiralled down over what he hoped was a deserted area behind the FOB, and then spun the helicopter around into his final approach.

'Widow 49, this is Sandman 34, inbound in three minutes.' Without waiting for a reply, he glanced over his shoulder to make sure that Kinkers was manning the machine gun on the window. 'We all set, Taff?' Davies asked his co-pilot.

'Roger that,' Taff replied. 'We're green.'

Neither Davies nor Taff realised that the helicopter had been hit until the alarm systems started warbling loudly in their headphones. Without realising, they'd flown almost straight over the top of a technical vehicle with a fifty-calibre machine gun hidden in a wadi about seven hundred metres behind the FOB.

'Fuck, fuck, we're hit!' Taff shouted, pressing the buttons to silence the alarms. Davies pushed the cyclic hard over to the right to abort the landing, before pulling back on the stick to try to gain altitude. He could hear Taff next to him screaming into the radio. 'CONTACT, CONTACT, Sandman 34, incoming fire two clicks east of FOB Rob, turning north.'

In the corner of his eye, Davies could see one of the Apache helicopters speeding towards the area, it's forward-mounted machine gun moving from side to side as the pilot looked for the source of the gunfire.

'Sitrep, Taff,' Davies said through gritted teeth.

'Wait out,' Taff replied, concentrating on the control panel in front of him.

'Anyone hurt in the back?' Davies asked, switching channels.

'Negative,' Kinkers said, 'but we've got fluid pissing

from the ceiling. Not sure if it's hydraulic, I think it probably is. Lots of vibration though, something's not right'

Adams felt the helicopter lurch violently. He looked out of
the window to see that they were only a hundred feet or so
above the ground. Looking across at Kinkers, he saw him
prodding at the control panel near the rear ramp, flicking
switches and looking panicked. *What the fuck is going on?* He
looked across at Lizzie, who was staring at the ceiling of
the helicopter. Adams looked up to see what she was
looking at and could see clear fluid dripping from a seam
in the roof.

As the flow increased, Kinkers jumped across to the
same area and stared at the ceiling, talking frantically into
his microphone. Lizzie caught Adams's eye and just
shrugged her shoulders as if she hadn't got a clue what was
going on. On the other side of the helicopter, Adams could
see Ronald sitting on the canvas bench, the lead for the
radio dangling down from his helmet. *For fuck's sake*, Adams
thought. *You're supposed to be plugged into the intercom.* They had
no other way of finding out what was going on. Adams
reached across to try to slap Ronald's leg and get his attention, but Ronald was a couple of centimetres too far away,
and Adams didn't want to leave his seat.

Adams felt the helicopter wheel around, aborting the
landing. He looked through the side windows behind
Ronald's and Lizzie's heads and could see nothing but
ground through them. The Chinook levelled out, and the
nose tipped down slightly. Adams turned his head to look
out of the window behind him. He could see the ground
zipping past and if Adams's sense of direction was correct,
they were heading away from the FOB. He looked across

at Major Clarke, who was staring back at him, while Squadron Leader Webb was just sitting next to Clarke with his arms crossed and eyes closed as if he didn't have a care in the world. As Adams looked at the pair of them, he realised that they hadn't got a clue what was going on. The whole experience was almost certainly so alien to them that they wouldn't be able to work out what was normal, and what wasn't. And what was going on at the moment was far from normal.

47

'So, let me see if I've got this straight,' Foster said, the sinking feeling in his stomach bordering on nausea. 'Your pathologist found high levels of adrenaline in all three of my soldiers, which was all from the same batch. And that batch might be here?' He watched as Griffiths nodded, and reached out his hand for his notebook back.

'Could I get that back please?' he asked Foster. 'I need to check something else, but that's pretty much it.' Foster handed the notebook back to the policeman.

'But if they were all resuscitated in the same place, then the adrenaline used would be from the same batch anyway, wouldn't it?' Foster asked.

'That's what I wanted to check,' Griffiths replied, leafing through his pages. 'There's something in here about the concentration. It was the wrong one for resuscitation if I remember right.' Foster waited as the policeman looked for the information he needed. This was all looking very grim, he thought, and he wasn't looking forward to his next telephone call back to London. His three-star wanted an update as soon as Foster knew what was going on.

'Here we are,' Griffiths said. 'Found it. The markers were linked to a batch of one in a thousand adrenaline, and the strength used in resuscitation is one in ten thousand.' Griffiths looked at Foster. 'Does that make sense to you?' Foster nodded in response.

'Yes, one in a thousand is much stronger. It's normally diluted down and used in infusions, and even then only in intensive care units,' Foster explained. 'I think only one of the three casualties got as far as intensive care.'

The two men sat in silence, both of them lost in their own thoughts. After a few minutes, the Brigadier broke the silence.

'Would you like some more coffee while we're waiting for the QM? I could certainly do with another cup.'

'Yes please,' Griffiths replied. 'I wouldn't say no.'

As Foster was on the phone to the duty officer to rustle up some more coffee, there was a brisk knock at the door.

'Yes?' he said, one hand over the mouthpiece of the telephone. The door opened and a dishevelled looking Captain walked in and stood to attention.

'You wanted to see me, sir,' the Captain said.

'Yes, QM. Sorry if I woke you up.' Foster looked at his watch, and then at the Captain. He waited to see if the Quartermaster would say anything about the time. When he remained silent, still at attention and staring forwards, Foster sighed. 'Come here and take this.' He held out a piece of paper that he'd copied the shipment number onto. With a brief look at Griffiths, who was either studying his notes hard or at least doing a good impression of being busy, the Captain strode across to Foster and took the piece of paper from him. 'I need you to find this shipment, what it is, and when it got here,' Foster said.

'Yes sir,' he replied, looking at the piece of paper. 'Can I ask why, sir?'

'No, Captain. You may not,' Foster said. 'But please report back directly to me as quickly as you can. That'll be all.' The Captain brought himself back to attention and replied.

'Thank you, sir.'

As the QM left the Brigadier's office, the Duty Officer came in with two more cups of coffee which he put on the table in the office. He collected the empty cups without a word and left. Foster walked back to the chair and sat down next to Griffiths.

'That was quick,' Griffiths said, picking up his cup.

'Yes, it's a rank thing, I think,' Foster replied with a wry smile. He picked up his cup and took a deep breath through his nose. 'Smells fantastic,' he said as he took a sip. 'So, Malcolm, you said that there was a "person of interest" in all this. Can we talk about that while the QM's doing his thing?'

Griffiths put down his cup and reached into his bag, pulling out a manila file that was filled with paper. He handed the file to Foster who put it on his lap and opened the front cover. Attached to the first page with a paperclip was a photograph of a very familiar face.

'Oh,' Foster said. 'Really?'

Davies managed to level the helicopter out at about three hundred feet, torn between going high to avoid any more ground fire and staying low in case they had to make an emergency landing. He decided to stay low until they'd been able to fully assess the damage. Davies looked at the control panels, quickly assessing the readings on the various dials and instruments.

'Okay, not sure what's going on, but the temperatures

and pressures all look good. The cyclic's not responding how I'd like it to, but I'm going to head north and then loop round to the west to head back to Bastion.' He paused for a second, thinking hard. 'If we have to, we can put into FOB Price.'

'That'd be a fucking nightmare, getting back from there,' Taff replied.

'Better than trying to get back from here, Taff,' Davies barked back. He saw Taff look across at him, but didn't have the time to apologise. He'd sort that out later. 'We're straight and level, so I'm not going to put out a Mayday. Everyone happy with that?' He saw Taff nod and heard two quick clicks on the radio from Kinkers in the back.

'PAN-PAN, PAN-PAN, PAN-PAN. Bastion Tower, this is Sandman 34, calling in PAN-PAN.' Davies was using the emergency code for 'we're a bit fucked, but not dead yet'.

'Sandman 34, this is Bastion Tower, go ahead.'

'PAN-PAN, Sandman 34, CH47 with nine souls, forty clicks northeast. We've been hit with something, handling tricky but systems okay. Request Runway 19 and emergency services.' Runway 19 was the closest possible place that they could land and still be within the boundaries of Camp Bastion.

'Sandman 34, this is Bastion Tower. Copied, good luck and see you soon.'

Davies and Taff flew on for a couple of minutes in desperate silence. Taff was concentrating on the control panels, while Davies was just focused on keeping them straight and level. Above their heads, the twin motors were both struggling to maintain the lift required to keep the helicopter airborne. The left-hand engine had been hit in three different locations, and the damage to the gears which powered the rotors was extensive. As the oil leaked from the internal housing, metal started to grind on metal.

Unseen by anyone, a spark flared, followed by another. And another. The final spark ignited the flammable vapour that had built up inside in the engine casing, and with a whoosh, the entire engine burst into flames.

'Fire, port engine!' Taff shouted. Davies flipped the switch on the emergency fire suppression system, and above them the engine compartment filled with halon.

'Okay, shutting down port,' Davies said, starting the process to close the engine down. He'd been through this manoeuvre time and time again in the simulator, but this was the first time he'd had to it for real. 'Confirm fire suppression.'

'Confirmed,' Taff said. 'Port engine powering down,' he continued, keeping a close eye on the myriad of dials and gauges on the control panel in front of him. Neither Davies nor Taff was particularly concerned about losing an engine. The Chinook was designed to be able to fly with only one operating, but again, this was something neither of them had done outside the simulator.

Davies felt the shift in handling as the rear engine powered down. The left-hand rotor continued to rotate, driven by the other engine, but it was completely different in terms of flying the thing. Flying on one engine meant that Davies wouldn't be able to undertake much in the way of manoeuvres, but instead was limited to straight and level flight. In the environment they were operating in, this made them a sitting duck to anyone on the ground. He wouldn't even be able to avoid an RPG if one came at them.

'Davies?' Kinkers's voice came over the radio. 'We're losing a lot of fluid back here. I'm not getting any warning indicators on the hydraulics though.'

'Transmission, it's transmission fluid,' Taff shouted. Davies looked sharply across at the control panel. He could see the transmission fluid gauge needle was to the left of where it should be — and falling fast.

'Fuck, fuck!' Davies shouted, his heart in his mouth. The transmission was the only thing that kept the rotors spinning without hitting each other. If it went completely, and the rotors desynchronised, that would be catastrophic. They would just fall from the sky.

A loud hiss above Adams's head caused all of the medics to look upwards in unison. It broke through the monotonous sound of the engines and rotor blades, and when Adams looked up, he saw puffs of mist being forced through the seams in the roof towards the back of the helicopter. He sensed, rather than felt, a change in the pitch of the engines. Was it his imagination, or had the Chinook suddenly lost speed? Adams looked across at Lizzie, who from the look on her face had felt the same thing. She looked terrified. Kinkers was getting more and more frantic over by the panel at the rear ramp. Adams could see a whole bunch of flashing warning lights, but he had no idea what they meant. The only frame of reference he had was the way that the loadie was almost punching the screen.

Adams scrabbled round to try to find the seatbelt straps that he knew were somewhere behind him. He hadn't got a clue what was going on, but everything in his experience told him that something really fucking bad was happening. Out of the corner of his eye, he could see Lizzie doing exactly the same thing with her hands as she desperately tried to find her seatbelt. Across from Adams, Major Clarke was looking at him with wide eyes, his mouth hanging half-open. Adams didn't have time to do anything to help the Major — he was far too busy trying to untangle the strap that was stuck under his backside and bring it across his lap to meet the other one.

Just as Adams freed the strap under his buttocks and slammed the buckle together, the helicopter violently tipped onto its side. Adams was pressed hard into the back of his seat and across the aisle he could see Lizzie dangling with her arms waving in the air. *At least she managed to get her seatbelt done up*, Adams thought bizarrely as his stomach lurched as if he was on a roller coaster. He was dimly aware of equipment and bodies flying around the cabin as the pressure on his back decreased, and he realised that the helicopter was almost on its side in the air.

Adams closed his eyes. He'd never prayed in his life — but now seemed like a good time to start.

$\mathbf{B}$ rigadier Foster looked at the photograph in the file on his lap. He looked up at Griffiths, surprised. 'Now that is a shock. I never would have thought, well, I'm not really sure what to say.'

'Nothing's confirmed, of course, Foster,' Griffiths said. 'But he is someone that we want to talk to quite urgently.'

'Can I ask how you got to him?'

'Of course, although your personnel people back in Aldershot haven't exactly been particularly helpful.'

'In what way?' Foster asked.

'They won't release a copy of his personnel file unless he's actually been arrested. But we can't arrest him yet as there's not enough evidence. That's why we need the file.' Griffiths paused. 'Bit of a chicken and egg situation, really.' Foster looked at the policeman, thinking that there almost certainly wouldn't be anything of interest to the police in the personnel file, anyway. There was an easy way to find out, though.

'I think that I might be able to help with that,' Foster said, getting up and walking over to his computer. After a couple of clicks of the mouse, the printer on his desk whirred into life. 'I'd appreciate your discretion on this one, Malcolm,' Foster said as copies of pages of a personnel file were spat out onto the desk. 'But it might save you some time.' Foster waited until the printer had finished and searched on his desk for a stapler.

'Thank you, Foster,' Griffiths said. 'I wasn't dropping hints there by the way.'

'Of course you weren't, Malcolm,' Foster replied, knowing full well the game that was being played. 'But as I said, I'm determined to help you with this issue.' By tracking the shipment, and providing an unofficial copy of the personnel file, Foster figured that he was two nil up at the moment, and might need a few favours further down the line depending on how this all panned out. He stapled the pages together and handed them to Griffiths. 'I doubt there'll be much useful in there, to be honest.'

'Thanks,' Griffiths said. Foster returned to his seat and picked up the file that Griffiths had given him.

'So, how did this chap become your person of interest, then?' Foster asked, holding the file in the air. 'I know it'll all be in here, but I'd prefer your take on it.'

'It was his psychiatrist who tipped us off,' Griffiths replied. Foster frowned, regretting handing over the personnel file. It shouldn't have any medical details in it, but there could be something. 'He wasn't a military psychiatrist though, it was a private practice,' Griffiths continued. 'Your man started seeing him after his father died. He didn't want the Army to know that he was seeing one, especially considering the manner of his father's death.' Foster raised his eyebrows, wondering how best to put the obvious question. 'It was suicide,' Griffiths said, pre-empting Foster.

'It's all in the file,' Griffiths continued. 'But he left a

suicide note that basically blamed the Army for ruining his life.' He looked at his notebook, finding the correct page. 'Sad story really, the father leaves the Army under a bit of a cloud. Allegations of bullying by other soldiers, apparently.' Griffiths checked his notes again. 'He comes home after years of being away and starts drinking too much. The mother decides she's had enough and leaves a couple of months later, which just sent him into a spiral of pouring his pension down his throat until one day he just decides he's had enough. Your man's father got pissed one night and decided to connect a hosepipe to his car exhaust and sit in the garage until it's all over.'

'Who found him?' Foster asked. Griffiths looked at the file in Foster's hand.

'Guess?' he replied.

Brigadier Foster looked at the file that Griffiths was waving at him.

'You're going to have to wait for a while before you can speak to him, I'm afraid,' Foster said.

'Why's that? He is here, isn't he?'

'Oh, he's here alright,' Foster replied. 'But at the moment he's in the back of a helicopter heading up to one of the Forward Operating Bases. We've got an ongoing incident.' He saw the policeman frown at the news.

'Damn,' Griffiths said. 'I did think about asking the Military Police here to detain him while we were on our way, but it would have made the timelines tricky for questioning.'

'I wouldn't worry too much,' Foster said. 'There's not many places that he can go, are there?' Griffiths thought for a minute before replying.

'I guess not,' he said.

'Could I just have that personnel file back for a second, Malcolm?' Foster asked. Griffiths passed the sheaf of papers back to him, and Foster looked through them. 'There should be something in here about the father's suicide. That sort of thing gets flagged up pretty quickly, for obvious reasons.' He leafed through the pages until he found the one he wanted — a summary sheet of family relationships. Foster read the page and sighed. 'Nothing. All it says here is "estranged". We missed it.'

Brigadier Foster sat down at his desk and started typing an e-mail to his three-star in London. The phone call would have to wait until he was alone in the office. There were a few things that he wanted to feed back home that he didn't want the policeman to hear. He paused for a second, thinking.

'So, what did the psychiatrist say?' Foster asked the policeman.

'Your chap went to see him just after the father died,' Griffiths replied. 'He was depressed, apparently, and having a really hard time dealing with it. He'd found the body, read the note. It was quite uncompromising in blaming the Army for everything. Even the mother leaving was the Army's fault.'

'Really?' Foster said, his eyebrows raised. 'How could that be our fault?'

'The mother ended up living with someone else. We think that there'd been something going on between them before the father left the Army, but we're not one hundred per cent sure.'

'This other person, I'm guessing that they're one of ours, then?'

'I'm afraid so,' Griffiths checked his notes. 'A Lieutenant Colonel McCarthy.' Foster shook his head, not recognising the name. 'Also in the house were a stack of unpaid bills, financial demands, various threats from bailiffs. The father was only a couple of weeks away from being homeless when he killed himself.'

'Bloody hell.' Foster sighed and rubbed his eyes.

'According to the psychiatrist, your chap was not depressed but had a long history of psychosis which he'd managed without any real problems for years. If your doctors hadn't picked it up, he obviously hid it well.' Griffiths explained. 'But the father's death tipped him over the edge, and at the last session he had with the psychiatrist he was making threats towards the Army. They were all vague threats, but there was enough in them to make the psychiatrist so concerned that he contacted us.'

'Why would he go directly to the police though, and not us?' Foster said. Griffiths nodded towards the police file that Foster was holding.

'I'm afraid he did go to the Army. Twice. He heard nothing back from them and found out that your man had deployed over here, so he came to us. We had both the psychiatrist's report and the pathologist's findings come up at the same weekly briefing. I know the police might be a bit slow sometimes, but in this case, even the slowest copper could put that together.'

Foster resumed typing, thinking hard as he did so. This was going from bad to worse. He paused when he heard a knock at the door and barked out a reply. A second later, it opened and the QM poked his head around the door.

'Sir, I've got the details on that shipment,' the Captain said.

'That was quick,' Foster replied. 'What have you got?' The QM glanced towards Griffiths and then back at Foster as if he wasn't sure whether he should be talking in front of him. 'Please,' Foster said. 'Carry on.'

'Okay sir, thanks. 'That shipment number belongs to a

batch of one in a thousand adrenaline that was shipped here, arriving on the first of May.' Foster looked at Griffiths, who was scribbling in his notebook. The QM continued, 'At some point, probably in Kandahar, the shipment was left out in the sun and went over its temperature limits so was scheduled for destruction. It went into the incinerator on the tenth of May.' Ignoring the jibe at the ground team in Kandahar, although Foster knew that the QM was only covering his back, the Brigadier thanked him for the information.

'There's something else though, sir,' The QM continued. 'A discrepancy if you will.'

'Go on,' Foster said.

'Well according to my records sir, we received thirty boxes in the shipment.' The QM paused. 'But we only destroyed twenty-four boxes.' Foster looked at Griffiths who had stopped writing and was staring at the QM.

'Thank you, QM,' Foster said. 'That's all.'

When the Captain had left, Foster stood with his hands on his hips and looked at the ceiling. Griffiths had returned to writing in his notebook when Foster broke the silence.

'I cannot believe that we can track ampoules of adrenaline halfway around the world, and identify exactly where and when they were destroyed, but can't identify when one of our soldiers is psychotic and in crisis.' Griffiths didn't reply, which Foster was quite grateful for. He knew that there was nothing really the policeman could say. 'Malcolm, I have quite a few things that I need to do. Would you excuse me?' Griffiths looked at the Brigadier, not without sympathy Foster thought.

'Of course, shall we meet later?'

'Yes,' Foster glanced at his watch. 'I'll come and find you in an hour? You should have the isolation ward at your disposal. I'd asked for it to be made available to your team, and for locks to be fitted.'

'Okay, no problem,' Griffiths said as he got to his feet. The two men shook hands before the policeman walked towards the door. He turned when he reached it and looked at Foster.

'Foster, I know this is an awful situation for you,' Griffiths said, 'but thank you.'

The Brigadier said nothing in return. When Griffiths had left and closed the door, Foster sat down behind his desk and put his head in his hands.

49

The first part of the helicopter that hit the ground was the leading edge of the forward rotor blade. The thirty-foot long rotor was spinning round about five times every second when the tip hit the ground, shattering with a deafening snap as the steel and resin were torn apart in the impact. Large shards of the rotor blade flew in every direction, including back towards the main cabin of the helicopter. The next blade smashed into the ground a split second later, followed by the third blade. Fragments of the rotors flew through the air like a swarm, slamming into anything in their way, and in some cases, through. By the time the rear blade hit the ground and came apart in the same way, shrapnel from the first one had already hit the soft skin of the Chinook.

Peppered by the fragments from the blades, the main body of the helicopter crunched into the ground. Davies's last-minute actions had minimised the force behind the fuselage, but the total force of the impact was still immense.

Inside the helicopter, Adams had got absolutely no idea

what was going on. The noise of the impact was deafening, and he barely heard the whistling of the rotor fragments as they passed him by, let alone recognised the sound for what it was. The impact jarred every bone in his body, and his head slammed against the back of the seat, forcing his helmet forward over his eyes. He felt a wet, warm, spray of liquid on his face as the breath was forced from his body, and he gasped like a drowning man suddenly breaking the surface of the ocean.

Despite the wounds in the sides of the helicopter from the blades, the main body of the fuselage had remained intact but buckled from the impact. As the remains of the rotors flew hundreds of yards into the air, the helicopter body warped and flattened before finally coming to rest on the rocky ground. As it settled, thick black plumes of smoke started pouring from the rear engine.

Directly opposite him, Lizzie was restrained by the seatbelt as the main body of the helicopter hit the ground. Her body jackknifed around the seatbelt across her lap, and her legs flew up just as her upper body was forced forwards. With horror, Adams saw her left knee had smashed into her face, and he realised that the warm spray of liquid he had felt a split-second before was her blood.

Immediately to his left, Adams saw a body smash into the canvas webbing of the chairs. He couldn't see who it was, but a loud snap told him that they had at least one broken limb. He pushed his helmet back on his head so that he could see properly, and immediately saw Lizzie dangling from her seat which was now above his head. She was completely limp, blood was streaming from her face and dripping from the end of her shattered nose.

He struggled with his seatbelt, trying to unclip it so that he could stand up. His back hurt like fuck, but he didn't think that he'd done himself any serious damage. Adams finally managed to get his fingertips under the clasp of the belt and he threw the clip open. He gingerly got to his feet and looked up and down the interior of the helicopter. It was carnage. There were bodies and equipment strewn around. He couldn't tell if he was the only one who'd survived or not, but no-one else seemed to be moving.

He turned his attention to Lizzie above him. He needed to get her down so that at least he could check her airway, although he wasn't even sure whether she was breathing or not. Adams braced his feet on the floor of the helicopter, which should have been the wall if it was upright, and tried to push her back into her seat to take the pressure off her seatbelt. She barely moved on the first try, so he readjusted his feet to try to get a better position and pushed as hard as he could with one hand while he fumbled with the belt. With a snap, the seatbelt flew open and took the skin off the back of his hand as it did so. Lizzie's body fell out of the seat and he stumbled under her weight, managing to get a hand under one of her arms and stopping her from crashing to the floor. As he lowered her to the ground as gently as he could, Adams heard the unmistakable sound of a pistol slide being drawn back and released.

'It's over, Adams,' a voice said. 'Just put her down and step away. It's over.'

50

F oster glanced up at the clocks on the wall of his tent. There were three of them — one showing the time in Zulu, one local time, and the last one the time in London. It was the last one that he was most interested in. It was mid-morning back in the United Kingdom, so at least he wouldn't be waking anyone up with the phone call he was about to make.

'MoD Operator?' a tinny voice said on the other end of the phone. The phone network that Foster was using was secret, meaning that while the line was secure, the quality was pretty bad.

'Lieutenant General Bertram, please,' Foster replied.

'Please hold.'

As he waited, Foster tapped his pencil on his desk and wondered how many layers he would need to go through to get to the man himself. It was normally three, perhaps four. The next voice he heard was female.

'This is General Bertram's office. How can I help you?'

'I need to speak to the General, please,' Foster replied.

'Who's calling?'

'Brigadier Foster. I'm the CO at–'

'Please hold,' the woman cut him off, leaving Foster listening to a series of clicks and whirrs on the end of the line.

'Foster?' a gruff voice said a few seconds later. Foster mentally pictured the Lieutenant General, probably leaning out of his office window in Whitehall with a cigarette.

'Sir, good morning.'

'It was. I have a feeling you're about to ruin it.'

'I take it you're up to speed on the situation out here, sir?'

'I've been briefed, yes.' Foster heard a wheeze on the end of the line. He'd been right about the cigarette. 'Have they arrested him yet?'

'Not yet, sir. There's a situation out on the ground that we're dealing with. Four dead, multiple casualties.'

'Bloody hell, Foster. And he's swept up in that?'

'He is, sir. But as soon as he gets back, he'll be arrested.'

'Right. You got a pen?'

'Yes, sir.' The General reeled off a series of numbers, which Foster dutifully wrote down. 'That's my desk line. It's not secure, but call me when it's done and I'll get things going over here. Bloody Red Tops are going to have a field day with this one.'

'We can't do much about the rubbish that the tabloids print, sir,' Foster said. 'Do you need anything else from me at this point?'

'I don't think so, Foster,' the General replied. 'I've got a Min Sub ready to go. I'll get it e-mailed to you to check before I send it out.' A Min Sub was a Ministerial Submission — a formal note from the military to whichever Minister was responsible for the subject it talked about. In this case, the General's note was intended for the Prime Minister himself.

'Okay, sir. Thanks,' Foster said. The next thing the General said would have been funny if the situation hadn't been so serious. Just before he'd put the phone down, General Bertram had effectively killed Brigadier Foster's career dead in the water.

'There goes your OBE, Foster.'

'What the fuck are you doing?' Adams stared at the gun in Major Clarke's hand, forgetting any military etiquette about the use of rank. 'Don't point that at me, for fuck's sake.'

'Shut up, Adams,' Clarke replied with a sneer. 'It doesn't matter, it's all over.'

'What's all over? What are you talking about?'

'This.' Clarke waved the gun around before aiming it back at Adams. 'All of this, all over. We're dead, Adams. Any minute now the fucking Taliban are going to come charging over that hill and kill us all.'

'Rob, come on,' Adams said. 'Put the gun down and stop arseing about. I need to see to Lizzie and the others.' Adams started to kneel next to Lizzie when Clarke shouted at him.

'Don't fucking move, Adams!' Clarke pointed the gun directly at Adams. 'Leave her, she's dead. Look at her — her face is smashed in.' Adams looked down at Lizzie. Her face was covered in blood, and it was impossible for him to tell whether she was breathing or not because of the combat vest that she was wearing. Adams was desperate to at least check her airway, but as he looked back up at Clarke, he could tell from the look in his eyes that he wasn't fucking about. Adams put his hands in front of his chest, palms facing towards Clarke.

'Okay, sir,' Adams said. 'Okay, no problem. It's all cool.' Adams had a million thoughts rushing through his head. *What was going on?* 'Are you hurt?' he asked Clarke.

'Oh, I'm just fucking peachy, Adams,' Clarke laughed as he staggered on his feet, taking a step forward. Adams stepped forward with one arm out as he stumbled, but Clarke jabbed the gun at him. 'Step back,' he growled. 'Leave me alone.'

'What's going on, sir,' Adams said. 'I don't get this.'

'You know, don't you?' Clarke replied.

'Know what?'

'Know about the adrenaline,' Clarke said. 'I saw you looking at the ampoules just before we got hit.' Adams looked at the front of Clarke's combat vest. He could see the handle of his left-handed scissors sticking out from behind one of the straps. If Clarke had his vest on, then he must be wearing Clarke's, Adams figured. Which meant that the adrenaline in the pocket belonged to Clarke. 'I didn't have time to get rid of it before we left, and then you picked up my fucking vest.'

'You swapped saline for adrenaline?' Adams said. 'But why? Why would you do that?' With a growing sense of dread, Adams realised that there was nothing wrong with Clarke other than the fact that he was absolutely fucking bonkers.

'Shh,' Clarke said. 'Do you hear that?' Adams listened and could hear the sound of a vehicle in the distance. 'Here they come, Adams. Terry fucking Taliban's on his way to say hello with an AK47.'

'Rob, for fuck's sake,' Adams said, trying to keep the fear out of his voice. He didn't know which was worse. Clarke waving a pistol at him, or the approaching insurgents. 'We've got weapons, we can defend ourselves until a rescue party gets here. They can't be far away. There were Apaches back at the FOB, they'll be here any minute.'

'Well I can't hear them, can you? And why would I want to be rescued, anyway? Who do you think those coppers back Bastion have come for?'

'You don't know that, Clarke,' Adams said. 'They could be here for anything.'

'No, they're here for me. They've found out somehow.'

'Found out what?'

'Found out that I killed those soldiers.'

Adams's heart was thumping in his chest as he considered his options. He could try to grab the gun from Clarke, but he could see from the whiteness of his knuckles that he had a good grip on it. By the time he managed to get near him, Clarke would have pulled the trigger. Adams tried to calculate the chance of his body armour stopping a bullet, but that was a huge risk. His only option was to try to talk Clarke down from the ledge he was on.

'Why, Clarke?' Adams said, almost in a whisper. 'Why did you kill them?' Clarke didn't reply, but just readjusted his grip on the gun. As Adams watched, he noticed that Clarke's eyes had welled up with tears. A fat drop started rolling its way down his cheek.

'Because,' Clarke said, his voice breaking. 'Because they killed my father.'

'Who did?' Adams almost asked him what the fuck he was talking about, but he thought better of it. 'How did they kill your father?' he said instead.

'The fucking Army,' Clarke replied. 'They drove him to

it, he never had a chance. They destroyed everything he held dear. His career. His family. Everything.'

'Drove him to what?' Adams whispered. He had to keep him talking. Help had to be on the way. Where were the Apaches? If he could get Clarke to put the gun down, then at least they'd have a chance of surviving until reinforcements got here.

'They drove him,' Clarke replied through gritted teeth. 'They drove him to hook himself to the exhaust pipe. It wasn't my dad that did that, it was them. The bullies. The Lieutenant Colonel who stole my Mum from him.' Tears were streaming freely down his face as he spat the words out. 'I found him. I fucking found him. And I promised him that I'd make it right.'

'My God, Clarke,' Adams said. 'I had no idea. I'm so sorry.'

'You're sorry? That's what they all said at the time. Even the coroner was fucking sorry when he signed the death certificate that said suicide. But it wasn't suicide, was it? It was murder.' Clarke straightened his arm, pointing the pistol right at Adams's face. 'And I promised him that I'd make it right.'

Adams and Clarke stared at each other in the back of the helicopter. Adams knew he only had a few seconds at most to do something. The only problem was he didn't have a clue what to do. What he did know was that he didn't want to die like this. They both listened to the noise of a vehicle getting louder every second. There was a screech of brakes, followed by a door slamming a second later. The faint sound of footsteps on the rocky ground filtered through to them.

'So this is it, Adams,' Clarke said. 'This is our corner of a foreign field.' His finger tightened on the trigger, his knuckle white as a sheet. 'Forever England, right?'

51

The firing pin hammered into the rear of the round in the chamber, igniting the primer which in turn ignited the main charge of the round. The propellant in the main body of the round pushed the bullet down the chamber as the grooves in the barrel dug into the bullet to rotate it. If the bullet had further to travel, it would have started to turn in the air, but as it was only travelling a short distance through the back of the helicopter, by the time it hit its target it was still gathering speed and hadn't started rolling. The pointed end of the bullet found its target, punching its way through soft flesh.

It wasn't the first time that a British soldier had shot one of his colleagues, but it was the first time that this had happened in Afghanistan. This time around at least.

The entry point was just above the left nipple. After the bullet tore through the body armour, missing the Kevlar plate across the breastbone that would have stopped it, it hit a rib. This deflected the round further into the thoracic cavity where it tore through the descending aorta. If it had nicked the blood vessel, then survival was a possibility. A slim chance, but still a possibility. But it wasn't a nick. The bullet caught the main blood vessel that brought blood back to the heart full-on, shredding the walls of the aorta. Every pump of the heart that followed just pushed blood into the thoracic cavity instead of the heart. Starved of blood, the heart sped up to try to compensate for the lack of fluid coming back to it.

He gasped once or twice, before sinking to his knees. It didn't hurt. He'd always thought that getting shot would hurt, but he couldn't feel anything at all. He glanced down to look at his chest and the rapidly spreading red stain on the front of his combats. A red bubble grew and popped from the entry wound, and he knew that whatever else the round had done inside his chest, his lungs were badly damaged.

Why doesn't it hurt? As the edges of his vision started to blacken, he felt his body falling backward. Into nothing.

Even if the gunshot wound had occurred with the casualty right next to a fully equipped and staffed operating theatre, the chances of survival were exactly nil. But he didn't know that. He didn't know anything at all.

taff Sergeant Partridge lowered the SA80 rifle, taking
his eye away from the SUSAT sight. The split-second
decision he'd just made would either make his career or see
him spend the rest of it in a military prison in Colchester.
He'd just shot an officer.

Partridge got to his feet, brushing sand from his knee as
he did so. He looked back towards the WMIK that he and
the other members of his patrol had arrived in after
tearing their way across the desert towards the billowing
plumes of smoke of the crash site. As they'd arrived and
stopped the Land Rover about fifty yards from the
wreckage of the helicopter, Partridge had knelt down and
swept the area through his sight to make sure that it was
clear for them to approach. Through the reticle of the rifle
sight, he'd seen Major Clarke in an approximation of a
shooter's stance — his pistol pointing straight out in front
of him at another person with his or her back to Partridge.
The Staff Sergeant had a clear line of sight through the
ruined back of the helicopter, and as he'd watched, Clarke
had said something to the other person. From the look of

the Major's body language and his grip on the pistol, Partridge knew that he was about to shoot.

Pulling the SA80's trigger was instinctive. Partridge hadn't considered his actions, the consequences of them, or what was going on in the back of the Chinook. He'd just pulled the trigger, aiming for the Kevlar plate at the centre of Clarke's body armour. It was an instinctive action — he'd not wanted to kill Clarke but just put him out of action. A high-velocity round from an SA80 would have done that. Partridge knew that it wouldn't penetrate if he got the shot central on the Kevlar plate. But it didn't look as if he had.

As Partridge started running towards the burning wreckage of the Chinook, one of the other members of his patrol called out to him.

'Staff, what the fuck?' Partridge ignored him and continued towards the helicopter. 'You just slotted one of ours.'

Partridge couldn't tell where his round had hit Clarke until he got closer. As he approached the CH47, he could see a bloom of red on the Major's chest and knew that he wasn't as good a shot as perhaps he thought he was. Partridge ran towards the back of the helicopter and jumped up into the fuselage. He glanced down at the unconscious body of the Australian loadie that was lying by the ramp and walked towards the figure standing with his back to him. As he approached, the figure turned around and he recognised Adams.

'Sir, we need to get a shift on,' Partridge said. 'There's smoke pouring out of this thing. We need to get out.' Adams regarded him blankly, the shock obvious on his face. 'Sir,' Partridge continued. 'Fucking sort yourself out. We need to get going.'

Adams looked down at Lizzie, and then across at Clarke. Partridge watched as Clarke gasped several times, his eyes fixed on the ceiling. He didn't look as if he had long left. Partridge had seen that type of breathing before, just before his Nan died in a nursing home.

'Help me,' Partridge heard Adams say as he knelt next to Lizzie, pressing his fingers against her neck. Adams paused for a few seconds. 'She's still alive, we need to get her out.'

The two men each grabbed an arm and unceremoniously dragged Lizzie towards the back of the helicopter. As they did so, Partridge looked around the interior of the fuselage. He heard a groan from one of the crumpled bodies on the floor as they dragged Lizzie's unconscious body across the floor. As they got to the back of the helicopter, Partridge saw two of his patrol standing just outside.

'Oi, you two. Get in there and get the bodies out. There's at least one alive, so find him first. Is the perimeter secure?' Partridge clocked the nod from one of the soldiers. 'Come on, Adams. We'll take her to the WMIK. The others can clear the helicopter.'

Partridge and Adams dragged Lizzie across the rocky earth towards the Land Rover, her feet leaving a pair of tram lines in the ground. As they approached the vehicle, Partridge saw a black speck on the horizon.

'Cavalry's coming, mate,' he said. Adams looked up and squinted.

'Thank fuck for that,' he replied.

They reached the Land Rover and placed Lizzie gently on the ground next to it. Partridge watched as Adams took her helmet off and pushed her blood-stained hair away from her face.

'I need to roll her over, can you give me a hand?' Adams asked. Partridge knelt next to him and together they rolled Lizzie onto her side into the recovery position. 'I need my med kit. It's in there.' Adams nodded towards the wreckage of the Chinook. Black smoke billowed from the crumpled heap of metal. Time was ticking.

'Adams, you stay here. I need to go and help the others,' Partridge finally said. He was torn between the need to get anyone else who was still alive out of the burning wreck, and leaving Adams where he was. The bloke had just been in a helicopter crash, after all.

'No, I'll come back with you. I want my kit, not someone else's,' Adams said, getting to his feet.

As the two men jogged slowly back towards the wreckage, Partridge put a hand on Adams's arm before slowing to a walk.

'Sir, what the fuck was all that about?' Partridge asked. 'Why was the Major about to slot you?' Adams looked at the soldier, and his brow furrowed.

'I'm not sure,' he said. Partridge knew from the look on Adams's face that he was lying, but decided to give the officer a second or two before calling him on it. 'Maybe he'd had a smack to the head when we ploughed in or something,' Adams said, his eyes avoiding Partridge's.

Partridge stopped walking, tightening his grip on Adams's arm to stop him from walking off.

'Bullshit,' Partridge said. 'You're going to have to do a fuck's sight better than that, Adams.'

'What do you mean, bullshit?'

'I mean what I said. You're talking bullshit. You either need to tell the fucking truth, or learn how to lie properly and pretty bloody quickly.' Partridge fixed Adams with a

piercing stare before pointing at the smouldering helicopter. 'There's an officer in there with one of my bullets
in his chest. And that's going to need some explaining. So
have a fucking word with yourself, sir.'

Adams looked at Partridge's back as the soldier walked off
towards the helicopter. What he had just said made perfect
sense. Adams knew that if he couldn't even bluff Partridge,
he had no chance of hiding the truth from the police. He
would just have to tell them everything, instead of hiding
it. It would all come out anyway, but Adams had been
thinking that he might be able to protect Major Clarke
somehow, even though he'd been about to shoot him.

He followed Partridge towards the wreckage, keeping a
short distance behind him. As they got closer, Adams saw
Davies stumbling about near the front of the cockpit, so he
broke into a jog and ran towards the pilot.

'Davies?' Adams asked as he got close to him. He could
see blood on Davies's flying suit, but he didn't look injured.
Just dazed. 'Are you okay?'

Davies looked at Adams, the confusion obvious on his
face.

'Taff's dead, Adams,' he said. 'Taff's fucking dead.'
The pilot pointed towards his chest. 'Rotor blade, big frag-
ment. Got him here.' Adams reached out and grabbed
Davies's uniform.

'Mate, head over there towards the WMIK,' Adams
said. 'I'll meet you there in a minute, I just need to grab
my medical bag and I'll be over.' Davies looked blankly at
the Land Rover. 'Davies,' Adams pushed the pilot gently in
the small of his back. 'Go, I'll see you there.'

Davies stumbled towards the WMIK, looking over his

shoulder at the wreckage of his helicopter. Adams watched him, wondering if he'd ever fly again, or if that would be it for him. He walked towards the cockpit and looked in through the shattered glass. Taff was still sitting in the co-pilot's seat, his head slightly forwards and with a jagged shard of black carbon sticking out of his chest. The remaining glass in the cockpit was covered in blood. It must be Taff's blood all over Davies, Adams realised.

Adams walked around the helicopter to the ramp just as the Apache that he and Partridge had seen in the distance roared overhead. As the noise died down Adams could hear the distinctive 'thud thud' of a Chinook in the sky as well. He breathed a sigh of relief. At least they'd be out of this shithole soon. Adams stepped up onto the ramp just as Partridge and another soldier were helping Colonel Nick off the helicopter. The doctor was cradling his arm and had a trickle of blood running down from one of his ears.

'Colonel, you okay?' Adams stepped closer to Colonel Nick and examined his ear.

'Been better, Adams,' the Colonel replied. Adams could see that the blood was actually coming from a deep cut just above his ear. While the cut would need stitches, this was much better than bleeding from the ear canal itself.

'You've got a nick just above your ear,' Adams said. 'Might need a plaster, but I think you'll live.'

'Thanks, Adams,' Colonel Nick replied with a faint sneer. 'I feel so much better now.' He stepped off the ramp and started walking towards the WMIK which had now been joined by two other vehicles. A small group of soldiers was running towards the helicopter, some of them carrying what Adams knew were body bags.

'No one left, Adams,' Partridge called out over his

shoulder as he walked alongside Colonel Nick. 'No one for you, anyway.'

Adams stepped up onto the ramp and walked into the interior of the Chinook, which was starting to fill up with smoke. Waving his hand in front of his face, he found his medical bag and picked it up, slinging it over his shoulder with a grunt. He stood there for a second, looking around the ruined cabin. Major Clarke was lying on the floor, his sightless eyes staring at the ceiling. Beyond him, Adams could see the crumpled body of another soldier. Must be the anaesthetist, Adams thought as he stepped carefully across towards him. He was still a few feet away when he could see that the doctor was dead. Not just dead, but not in one piece anymore. Fighting down bile, Adams turned and walked back towards the fresh air.

53

B rigadier James Foster rubbed the corners of his eyes with his fingers. He could feel a headache coming on as if he had a bad hangover, despite the early hour and the fact he'd not had any alcohol since leaving the United Kingdom weeks ago. His small personal stash of vodka, disguised as a bottle of water, hadn't lasted the first week. Foster knew that there was some booze in the hospital somewhere as he'd smelt it a couple of times, but as the boss, he couldn't exactly ask anyone who had any.

Foster jumped as someone hammered hard on the door to his office. He dislodged his glasses, which fell on the desk next to the telephone. As he swore to himself, the telephone started ringing.

'Come in,' he shouted as he picked up the phone, holding a hand palm outwards at Lieutenant Abbot who was standing at the door, hopping from foot to foot like a child who needed the toilet. Foster listened for a few seconds before putting the phone back in its cradle.

'I know,' he said to Abbott. 'I'm needed in the Ops

Room.' Foster got to his feet and walked across to the door. 'What's going on?'

'Helicopter down, sir,' Abbott replied. 'One of the TRT helicopters has gone in.' Foster looked blankly at him, trying to absorb the news. As if the day couldn't get any worse.

~

'Okay, sitrep,' Foster barked as he walked into the Ops Room. The busy chatter that he'd heard filling the room before entering fell away.

'Good morning, sir,' the Duty Officer said. Foster appreciated the man trying to be formal, but he could hear the shaking in his voice. 'This is what we know so far. The CH47 with the medics on was coming in to land on the FOB when they came under fire from somewhere. The pilot wheeled away and aborted the landing, but then the helicopter went in a couple of miles away from the FOB.'

'Have we got any assets at the crash site?'

'Yes, sir, we have now. One of the QRF patrols the other Chinook had put down took off sharpish in a WMIK when the TRT helicopter disappeared. They're on the scene now — we're just waiting for an update on casualties from them. There's a couple of Apaches overhead, and an A10 from Kandahar providing overwatch.'

'That was sporty, following a helicopter in a bloody WMIK,' Foster said. 'Probably not the best tactical move, but understandable I suppose.' The Duty Officer paused, and Foster looked at him. 'Carry on,' he said.

'The other Chinook managed to get into the FOB and retrieve the casualties from the earlier incident. And the bodies.'

'Are they coming here?' the Brigadier asked.

'They're going to Kandahar, sir,' the Duty Officer replied. 'Kandahar Ops insisted. The FOB's back under control, at least for the moment. One of the Apaches neutralised a sniper hiding in a school.'

'What with?'

'A hellfire, sir,'

Foster winced at the thought of a hellfire missile hitting a school. Sniper or no sniper, that wasn't going to go down too well back at home. Something that the Duty Officer had just said reminded him of the team of policemen waiting to interview Major Clarke.

'Shit,' Foster whispered to himself, breaking one of his cardinal rules about swearing in front of the troops. He looked around to find the young officer who'd come to get him earlier. Finding the Lieutenant, he beckoned him over.

'Go to the isolation ward,' Foster said when the young man reached him. 'Get Detective Inspector Griffiths, and bring him here.'

'Here, sir? To the Ops Room?'

'Yes, here,' Foster said through clenched teeth. 'Now, please.'

Foster ran his hands through his hair, looking up at the clocks on the wall. He was going to have to get back on the line with his three-star. This wouldn't be something that he wanted the Lieutenant General to wake up hearing on the radio while he ate his sandwiches. He felt a tap on his arm and, looking round, saw a cup of coffee being pressed towards him.

'Thank you.' He managed a smile at the officer who'd brought it to him. He took a sip, managing not to grimace at the taste. Where had the decent coffee gone? He took a few steps across the room towards the radio operator, who was busy scribbling on a pad of paper. Foster waited until he had stopped writing before saying anything, not wanting to disturb him. 'What have you got?' he asked.

'Casualty report from the crash site, sir,' the radio operator said. 'Two Cat Bs, three Cat Cs, and one uninjured. Three KIA. The casualties are inbound, with an ETA of twenty minutes.'

'Okay, thank you. When the Detective gets here, could you have him brought to my office, please? I need to make some calls.'

Foster walked into his office a moment later, leaving the door open behind him. He crossed to his desk and sat down before opening a drawer and pulling out a notebook. As he flicked through the notebook to find the number that he had scribbled down earlier, he saw Detective Inspector Griffiths at the door of his office.

'Come in Malcolm, please. Take a seat.' The detective walked in and sat down opposite Foster, who had found the number that he was looking for in his notebook. 'What a morning.' Foster sighed.

'Well, you don't have to be a detective to tell that something's going on,' Griffiths said with a wry smile.

'Yes, well, it concerns your man Clarke. A helicopter's gone down just outside FOB Robinson.' Foster watched as the smile disappeared from Griffiths's face and was replaced by a frown.

'Oh,' the policeman said as if he wasn't sure what to say. Which, Foster figured, he probably wasn't. 'What's a FOB?' Griffiths asked.

'Sorry, Forward Operating Base. A platoon house near

one of the villages that we're trying to influence.' Foster paused, remembering the hellfire missile and the school. 'Although influence probably isn't a word that I'd use at this precise moment in time.'

'Right, I see.'

'I don't know if Clarke is wounded or dead. There's both casualties and bodies from the crash on their way back here. It was the helicopter with the medical team on board that went down,' Foster said. 'Would you excuse me for a second? I need to make a phone call, and it's probably not going to be pretty. If you go down to the Ops Room and knock on the door, they'll be able to get you a coffee. Tell them I sent you, and that I said to give you the decent stuff. Not the crap they just gave me.'

Griffiths got up from his chair and walked out of the office, closing the door behind him. Realising that this wasn't a conversation he could have on an insecure line, Foster picked up the secret phone with a sigh.

'MoD operator?' a voice the other end of the line said.

'Lieutenant General Bertram please.'

'Please hold.'

Foster listed to the bland on-hold music for what seemed to him like forever before the three-star came on the line. Straight through this time, Foster realised. No staff officers to go through anymore. Things back in Whitehall must be hot.

'What?' the senior officer said. He wasn't known for his manners, like most military personnel at that rank.

'Sir, Brigadier Foster here. CO of Bastion Hospital. I have a situation here that I need to appraise you of.'

Foster spent the next ten minutes bringing his boss back in the United Kingdom up to speed. The three-star had said nothing other than the odd grunt now and again.

When Foster had finished, he paused to see what the outcome was.

'Okay, get me a proper sitrep on the dark side when you have it. I particularly need to know the status of Clarke. Far too late to cover it up now, of course. But there may be things we can do to, er, smooth things over as it were.' The Lieutenant General seemed more bothered about Major Clarke than the downed helicopter and union flag-covered coffins that would be winding their way through British roads in the next few days.

'No problem, sir. I'll get it to you as soon as I can.' Foster was just about to say goodbye when he realised that the General had already hung up the phone. 'You're welcome, sir,' Foster said to the empty line.

He put the handset back on the cradle and looked up at the clock. The casualties would be here in a few minutes. Foster thought that he should probably go to the Emergency Room when they arrived to see who had made it. He'd got no idea how on earth the three-star thought that anything could be smoothed over, with the hospital full of policemen, but he couldn't do anything about that. Maybe Foster wasn't the only one who was going to lose out on a gong from the Queen over this sorry mess?

54

Emma Wardle's heart was pounding in her chest as she watched the medics bustling around in the Emergency Room. There were several faces that she didn't recognise, and several faces that should have been there but weren't. She'd heard various hurried reports of casualties from two separate incidents. There could be as many as ten casualties, but no one seemed to be sure exactly what was going on. She'd overheard a conversation between one of the doctors and an Ops Officer who were talking in the corridor as she'd walked past, and Emma was sure she'd heard them talking about a helicopter crash. They'd both fallen silent as she walked past, and when she asked the Ops Officer what was going on, he'd just replied with a stare. When she arrived in the Emergency Room, she looked around for Major Clarke who should have been in the middle, coordinating the troops, but she couldn't see him anywhere.

'Do you know what's happening?' Emma asked a medical technician who was hurrying past with a tray full of equipment.

'Not sure, mate,' he replied. 'No one's briefed us yet. All anyone really knows is that a major incident's been called.'

Emma was desperate to go to the bathroom, but she didn't want to be seen leaving the Emergency Room. She looked around again for Major Clarke, knowing that he wouldn't mind if she nipped away just for a second, but she still couldn't see him. As she searched for the senior nurse, a hush descended over the room. Brigadier Foster was standing by the entrance, with a man standing behind him. She recognised him as the policeman that her cousin Matthew had pointed out to her at Brize Norton the previous evening.

'Ladies, Gentlemen,' the Brigadier said. Although many of the medics in the room had already seen him and quietened down, there were still a few who were talking. Foster repeated his introduction, more loudly this time, and the room fell silent. Emma moved a couple of paces towards him, anxious to hear what he had to say, just as another Ops Officer entered the room behind the Brigadier and handed him a piece of paper.

'Ladies, Gents, we have a situation,' Foster said, his voice back to a normal volume. He glanced down at the piece of paper and frowned. 'Are you sure?' he asked the Ops Officer next to him, who just nodded in reply. Foster continued, 'We have one Chinook inbound, ETA about six minutes. FOB Robinson came under attack at first light, and they sustained heavy casualties. One of the Chinooks that was sent in to retrieve the casualties came under attack, we think.' Foster turned to the Ops Officer, who nodded again. 'It was brought down not far from the FOB, and there are casualties inbound from that incident. As well as the TRT, Major Clarke and Squadron Leader Webb were also on that helicopter.' There was a collective gasp around the room as the gathered medics realised that two of their own team were involved, and Emma pressed her hand to her chest in shock. 'The other earlier casualties have gone to Kandahar.' Foster paused, and Emma watched as he surveyed the room. 'There are KIA from the helicopter incident, we think three. But we don't know for sure. It's all quite confusing, as you can imagine.'

Emma listened to the Brigadier carry on outlining how little they actually knew about what was going on, but his words barely registered. Her friends were on that helicopter. Lizzie, Adams, and even though Colonel Nick was a cock sometimes she'd never wish him any harm. And Ronald too, as well as Clarke and Webb. She felt tears pricking at her eyes, but tried to blink them back. Above the hospital, Emma heard the familiar sound of helicopters.

'That was never six minutes,' she muttered as she wiped the back of her hand across her eyes. Emma walked towards the rear entrance of the Emergency Room to wait for the ambulances. Walking outside, she wished that she smoked, even if was just for something to take her mind off what was going on.

Emma stood in the morning sun and watched the Chinook wheel round and disappear behind the accommodation tents. A few minutes later, with the rotors of the helicopter still beating, she saw three battlefield ambulances tearing in convoy towards the Emergency Room. The first ambulance pulled up to the doors and swung around, reversing a few feet towards her. The doors flew open and several soldiers jumped down from the back, quickly manhandling a stretcher out of the vehicle. Emma took a few steps backward, knowing that she should really be helping them with the casualties, but she had to see who was in the ambulances.

As the first stretcher was wheeled past her, Emma craned her neck forward to see if she could recognise the casualty. Although he was wrapped up in foil blankets, she thought it was Ronald. She bit the nail of her index finger as the next ambulance was reversed into position, and the same process repeated. It was the Australian loadie on the stretcher, with one of the pilots walking behind him, blood spattered down his flight suit. Still no sign of Lizzie.

The last ambulance was finally manoeuvred into position, and as the back doors were opened Emma noticed a metallic taste in her mouth. Looking at her finger, she realised that she had managed to bite right through the skin by her fingernail, which was now bleeding.

The first person to step down from the ambulance was carrying a large medical bag. He turned around, and Emma recognised Adams. Thank God, he was okay at least. He looked shattered, his face was covered in grime, and he had bloodstains on the front of his uniform. Emma stepped towards the back of the ambulance, trying to see around him into the back. The next person she saw get out was Colonel Nick, his arm in a sling and a large bandage wrapped around his head. A couple of soldiers came back out of the Emergency Room to help with the stretcher that was still inside, pushing past her to get to the ambulance doors.

As the stretcher was pulled out into the sunlight, Emma almost cried as she recognised Lizzie's face, half-covered by a bloodstained oxygen mask. She looked as if she'd been battered half to death, but Emma saw Lizzie blinking rapidly in the sunlight.

'Thank God you're okay, Lizzie,' Emma said, almost in a squeak. Lizzie raised an arm and grabbed the oxygen mask, moving it from her face so that she could speak.

'I might need to borrow a bit of your make up later,

mate,' Lizzie said, her voice hoarse and weak. 'I think I might look a bit rough.' Despite everything, she managed a wry smile at Emma.

Lizzie put the mask back on her face and closed her eyes as the stretcher was wheeled away, closely followed by Colonel Nick on foot. Adams turned to face Emma, running his hand across his head.

'Where's Major Clarke? Squadron Leader Webb?' she asked him. Adams looked at her, and she could feel the tears start to run down her face. He didn't have to say anything at all to let her know that they'd not made it.

Adams reached out a hand and rubbed her upper arm.

'I'm sorry, Emma,' he whispered before he turned to follow the others into the Emergency Room. Emma watched him walk away, the tiredness obvious in his entire body. She sank to her haunches, put her hands across her face, and cried.

And cried.

55

ONE WEEK LATER

A dams reached across Lizzie's stretcher and pulled hard on one of the restraining straps. They were in the back of an ambulance, waiting for a driver to take them to the HLS. From there they'd be put onto a helicopter to Kandahar, and from there onto a TriStar to Brize Norton. Next to them was another ambulance with Colonel Nick and Ronald, who were destined for the same flight.

'Oi, you bugger,' Lizzie laughed. 'I can't breathe.' Adams pulled on the second strap just as hard, pinning her legs to the stretcher. 'You sod, un-tighten them,' she complained, still laughing.

'Don't want you kicking yourself in the face again on the way back to Blighty, do we?' Adams replied. He looked at her, his eyes softening. Her face was still bruised beyond recognition, dark circles under her eyes from her badly broken nose and fractured eye socket. Lizzie's nose had been reset in the operating theatre so at least it was straight, but he knew that she was looking at at least one more operation when they got back home to put some metalwork in her eye socket. The surgeon had also managed to replace the tooth that they'd found embedded in the flesh just above her knee, once they'd worked out that it was hers. If she was lucky, Adams had told her in the hospital as she'd recovered, they could maybe do a spot of liposuction at the same time?

'This time tomorrow, we'll be home, mate,' Adams said. 'Can you believe that?'

'I know,' Lizzie replied. 'Do you think we'll get any grief for coming back early?'

'Er, I wouldn't have thought so. We have been through the mill a bit.'

'Speak for yourself.' Lizzie tried to raise an arm to touch her face, but the strap across her midriff stopped her. 'Come on, loosen these bloody straps.'

Adams picked up his day sack from the floor of the ambulance and reached into it, pulling out a crossword magazine and a pen. He leaned back into the seat and opened the magazine, putting his feet up on the edge of Lizzie's stretcher.

'Oh, come on,' Lizzie said when she noticed Adams with the magazine. She struggled against the straps, but couldn't move her arms at all above the elbows. 'That's my bloody magazine.'

A shadow passed across the sun shining into the back of the ambulance, and Emma Wardle climbed up into the cabin. She grabbed the magazine out of Adams's hands and gave him a playful slap round the head with it before leaning over Lizzie to undo the straps.

'Sir,' she said to Adams as she unbuckled them 'That's bullying, and I might have to report you for it.'

'Yeah, too right. And he was hitting me too, just before you came to rescue me.' Lizzie raised her arms in the air and stretched. 'Thanks, mate. You're my hero.'

Adams looked at the two of them and smiled, knowing when he was outnumbered.

'It's a fair cop,' he said. 'I'll come quietly.' As soon as he said the word 'cop' he saw Lizzie's face darken. He could have chosen his words a bit better, he thought.

'Are they on the same plane?' Adams knew that Lizzie was referring to the policemen who'd been in the hospital all week, questioning people, digging their noses into everything.

'I think so,' Adams replied. 'They're not that bad, though. I got interviewed God knows how many times by the head copper, Griffiths is it?'

'Yep, that's him.' Adams saw Lizzie looking across at Emma, who was grinning. 'Emma, wipe that bloody grin off your face.'

'How's me being interviewed by the police funny, anyway?' he asked.

'Oh, it's not that,' Lizzie replied. 'It's one of the policemen. Emma's got a new friend. With a pony tail and everything.'

'Shut up, Lizzie,' Emma said, blushing. 'You promised you wouldn't say anything. I wish I'd not rescued you now.'

'Don't worry, my lips are sealed,' Adams said. 'I won't say a word.'

'Liar,' Emma replied, looking at her watch. 'We need to get going. I'll go and see where the driver's buggered off to.'

Emma hopped out of the back of the ambulance. Adams and Lizzie sat in silence for a few minutes before Lizzie finally broke the silence.

'Do you think the others are on the same plane as well?'

'Who, Clarke and Webb? And the others?'

'Yep.'

'I don't know Lizzie. But if they are, we won't know about it, will we?'

'Guess not.' She shrugged. 'Even so, it'd be kind of fitting if they came back home with us.'

'I suppose so,' Adams said after a pause.

They both sat in silence, lost in their own thoughts. Adams wasn't sure what to think anymore. They'd all been through so much that all he wanted to do was to go home. He was fairly sure that Lizzie felt the same way.

'What are you most looking forward to when you get home then, Lizzie?'

'Home cooking, I think,' she replied. 'I've been fading away over here, I have.' Lizzie grabbed a non-existent roll of fat around her stomach. 'I wonder what my mum's going to say when she sees the state of me?'

Emma's face reappeared at the open doors at the back of the ambulance.

'Right, you two,' she said. 'I've found the driver.' Adams heard the front door of the vehicle open, and felt the ambulance tilt as someone got in the front. 'You good to go?' Adams and Lizzie both nodded, and Emma shut the doors to the ambulance.

As the ambulance rumbled away from Camp Bastion hospital, Adams grabbed Lizzie's hand.

'I know exactly what she's going to say when she sees you, Lizzie.'

'What?' Lizzie replied.

'Welcome home.'

AUTHOR'S NOTE

Hi again. Nathan Burrows here.

I hope you enjoyed reading *Man Down* as much as I enjoyed writing it. When I finished the book, I was really curious about what would happen next with Adams and Lizzie, so I decided to keep writing for a bit to see what happened.

The result is *Unfinished Business*, a novella (30k words) that looks at the aftermath of the events at the end of *Man Down*. It's a very different type of book—all about characters, not combat—but it does feature some of the people you've just spent some time with.

You can download a copy for free from my website. It's not available anywhere else, and never will be. This exclusive content is just for readers of *Man Down*, so please don't share the link.

https://nathanburrows.com/ub

Enjoy!
Nathan Burrows

.

GLOSSARY

9-Liner — a standard NATO medical evacuation request template.

A10 — The Fairchild Republic A-10 Thunderbolt II is a single-seat, twin turbofan engine, straight wing jet aircraft developed by Fairchild-Republic for the United States Air Force (USAF). It is commonly referred to by the nicknames 'Warthog', 'Hog', 'Flying Gun, or 'Tank Buster'.

Apache — An attack helicopter used extensively by the Army Air Corps in Afghanistan from 2006 onwards.

Cat A / B / C — evacuation priorities used in the NATO standard 9-liner request. Cat A is 'urgent', Cat B is 'urgent surgical', Cat C is 'priority'. There are also two further categories - Cat D ('routine'), and Cat E ('convenience'). See also 9-Liner and Triage.

Chinook — a twin-engined, tandem rotor, heavy-lift helicopter developed by American rotorcraft company Vertol and manufactured by Boeing Vertol (later known as Boeing Rotorcraft Systems). The CH-47 is among the heaviest lifting Western helicopters.

CH47 — see Chinook.

Crabs — a (mostly derogatory) term for members of the Royal Air Force used by other services. The exact origin is unknown, but probably related to 'crabfat' (the grease used on gun breeches by the Royal Navy, which was the same colour blue as an ointment used to treat genital lice and the RAF uniform).

CO — abbreviation for 'Commanding Officer', the officer in command of a military unit. See also OC.

Command Post / CP — see Ops Room.

Dit — a military slang term for a story.

ETA — abbreviation for 'Estimated time of arrival'.

Fat Albert — an affectionate military slang term for the Hercules transport plane. See Hercules / Herc.

Forward Operating Base — Also known as a 'FOB', a Forward Operating base is a secured forward military position that is used to support tactical operations.

GSM — abbreviation for 'Garrison Sergeant Major', the senior warrant officer of a garrison and holds the rank of Warrant Officer (Class 1).

GSW — abbreviation for 'Gun Shot Wound'.

Hercules / Herc — C130 Hercules transport plane. A four-engine turboprop military transport aircraft designed and built originally by Lockheed (now Lockheed Martin). Capable of using unprepared runways for takeoffs and landings, the C-130 was originally designed as a troop, medevac, and cargo transport aircraft.

Hermes — a type of UAV, based on Israeli designs, used by British troops in Afghanistan.

HLS — an abbreviation for 'Helicopter Landing Site'.

KIA — an abbreviation for 'Killed in action'.

Loadie / Loadmaster — an aircrew member on civilian aircraft or military transport aircraft tasked with the safe loading, transport and unloading of aerial cargoes.

LZ — an abbreviation for 'Landing Zone'. See HLS.

mIRC — an internet relay (text based) chat system used widely by the military.

Mucker — British slang term for friend or acquaintance.

Negligent Discharge — a type of accidental discharge of a firearm. A chargeable offence in the British military on the grounds that anyone carrying a weapon is in full control of it at all times.

OBE — Order of the British Empire. A British order of chivalry, rewarding contributions to the arts and sciences, work with charitable and welfare organisations, and public service outside the civil service. Sometimes referred to as standing for 'Other Bugger's Efforts' in the British military.

OC — an abbreviation for 'Officer Commanding' or the commander of a sub-unit or minor unit (smaller than battalion size). See also CO.

Ops Room — a military Operations Room. May be a small room with only one or two personnel, or a much larger facility. Also known as a Command Post, or CP.

Pan — a military term for an area where aircraft park, taxi, or take off.

Pan Pan — The message PAN-PAN is the international standard urgency signal that someone aboard a boat, ship, aircraft, or other vehicle uses to declare that they have a situation that is urgent, but for the time being, does not pose an immediate danger to anyone's life or to the vessel itself.

Quartermaster / QM — in land armies, a relatively senior soldier who supervises stores or barracks and distributes supplies and provisions.

Red Tops — A derogatory terms for the tabloid newspapers in the United Kingdom. It refers to the red banner across the top of several of the newspapers.

RPG — a shoulder-fired anti-tank weapon system that fires rockets equipped with an explosive warhead.

SA80 — standard issue 5.56x45mm rifle for UK military since 1987. A selective fire, gas-operated assault rifle.

Sangar — is a temporary fortified position built of sand-bags or similar materials.

Scratcher — a military slang term for sleeping bag, or more generally, bed.

SUSAT — a 4x telescopic sight often fitted to SA80 rifles. The Sight Unit Small Arms, Trilux, or SUSAT, has tritium-powered illumination utilised at dusk or dawn. See also SA80.

Terry — a military slang term for a member of the Taliban.

Triage — the process of determining the priority of patients' treatments based on the severity of their condition. From the French verb 'triager' - to sort.

UAV — Unmanned Aerial Vehicle. A remotely controlled aircraft without a human pilot on board.

Ugly — A common nickname for the Apache helicopter, based on its appearance. Also a commonly used callsign for them, with the individual helicopter identified with numbers, for example, Ugly 19.

WMIK — Pronounced 'Wimick', a WMIK is a common name for a type of Land Rover Wolf based on the Land Rover Defender. The acronym stands for Weapons Mounted Installation Kit, which adds machine guns to the rear and passenger side.

Zulu Time — a time zone used by the military which indicates Coordinated Universal Time (UTC).

ACKNOWLEDGMENTS

There's a whole bunch of people without whom this book would never have seen the light of day! There's even a few people who may recognise bits of themselves in the book — if you do, well, you know who you are so I'm not going to name you here! There is a story behind this story, but I have taken many liberties and any errors are entirely mine.

I'm not a fan of the term 'self-publishing' — there's a whole team behind me that I couldn't do without. So in no particular order, here they all are.

Cara F., my editor has been fantastic as always (and I promise that one day I will learn how to use commas properly!). My small but perfectly formed team of advisors deserve a special mention — so in strict first name alphabetical order, massive thanks are due to Alistair G., Bob S., Cynthia G., John K., Marianne E., and last but not least, Sue S. Thank you all for your help, support, and most of all, encouragement!

Stuart Bache., my cover designer, deserves a special mention for stopping me from trying to do my own covers and showing me how it should be done!

Finally, this acknowledgement section won't be complete without thanking my much better half without whom none of this would be possible.

Irene — thank you for everything.

Nathan Burrows.

Printed in Great Britain
by Amazon

72368310R00255